HINDSIGHT

A NOVEL

HINDSIGHT

MINDY TARQUINI

Published 2016
Printed in the United States of America
ISBN: 978-1-943006-01-4 (pbk)
ISBN: 978-1-943006-02-1 (e-bk)
Library of Congress Control Number: 2016943979

Cover design © Julie Metz, Ltd./metzdesign.com
Formatting by Kiran Spees

This is a work of fiction. Names, characters, places, and incidents either are the product of the author's imagination or are used fictitiously. Any resemblance to actual persons, living or dead, is entirely coincidental.

A love letter to my parents and grandparents.
And especially to my son, Avi, the brightest star in my constellation.

Amor vincit omnia.

When you come back . . . find me.

I have the gift. I was born with a caul. That means the amniotic sac didn't break when Ma pushed me out. It's rare, but it happens. People think that gives me second sight, the ability to see the future.

People are wrong. The caul didn't cover my face, it covered my butt.

I see my pasts.

I have hindsight.

2

My name is Eugenia Panisporchi. I'm thirty-three years old and my mother irons my underwear. My sister is twenty-seven, my brother, thirty-six. Ma irons their underwear, too. We don't need them ironed. Ma does it because we live at home. We don't live at home because we want to. We have no choice.

We're Italian.

Not in actual Italy. We're Italian in South Philadelphia, in a fifteen-foot wide by thirty-five-foot deep brick-faced row house near the corner of Twelfth and Shunk. A place which resembles Italy as much as textured vegetable protein tastes like steak. We venerate the same martyrs as our *paesani* across the water. We celebrate the same masses. Baptize our babies in white lace. Dispatch our elders in black drape.

And when we marry, we do it big, with festoons of flowers and full-skirted frippery. Like this taffeta Dijon-mustard-colored off-one-shoulder monstrosity fastened with a couple of freaking hook-and-eyes I can't reach.

Because, guess who my brother Joey's intended decided would be *puuuurfet*. Just purfet, purfet, purfet—oh-gosh-golly-gee-she's-just-so-damned-excited-aren't-ya-excited-Eugenia?—to have for her maid of honor.

This is me. Excited. Right down to my panties. Panties Ma keeps well-pressed.

Perfectly.

Ma hands off my bouquet. She squashes against the bureau and squints with me into the mirror to get the full effect of chrysanthe-mums speckled in shades of pumpkin and mulberry against the dress's warm ochre. Colors known to the non-marrying world as orange, purple, and yellow. She slaps a palm to her forehead. "That reminds me. I forgot to toss the three-bean salad."

"That's it." Elbows pretzeled, happy the last two hook-and-eyes wouldn't fasten, I undo the ones I managed. "I'm going as a guest."

Ma spins, powder-blue chiffon sleeves fluttering, surprisingly nimble for a lady who constrains herself with support hose and Spanx. She clamps my arms to my sides. "The wedding party will be uneven." Then she spits over her left shoulder and goes *sotto voce*, taking a moment to sweep her gaze across the space behind me. "You'll invite the *mal'occhio*."

The dreaded *mal'occhio*. Like the Evil Eye waits its chance to break from the wars and earthquakes and plagues and famines to cast its baleful glare on an uneven wedding party. I break Ma's hold and flounce the layers and layers adding to my already ample backside. "I got yer *mal'occhio* right here."

Ma crosses herself, exasperation stiffening every millimeter of her five-foot-two-inch frame. She raises a crooked knuckle to her teeth and bites hard. "I like the dress," she says in the tone she uses to sweet-talk the butcher into giving her free soup bones. "It's got presence."

"Presence?" I bunch my mousy brown tresses, heedless of the time it took to wrangle their unruly weight into submission. "This dress could sign a lease on its own apartment." I point to my sister. Standing by the door. Decked out in tasteful silk of muted green with a sweet-heart neckline and dramatic V-plunge down her back. "Let Angela wear it."

Angela joins us, lifts a taffeta layer, and lets it flop. "If I wanted to dress in drapes, I'd change my name to Scarlet."

Ma flicks a thumb and forefinger against Angela's temple, then straightens my tiara, tweaking the tines deep into my scalp. "You should be honored Carlotta asked you to be maid of honor. Shows she really wants to be part of the family."

"Because she's *stunad.*" I stretch the second vowel into the seventh inning—the *ahhhh* so long, if Ma had a tongue depressor, she could check my tonsils—then flick my hand at Ma's reflection in the mirror. "What normal person would *try* to be a part of this family?"

Dual laser beams of disapproval bore into the gap between those still undone final hook-and-eyes. Ma takes me by the shoulders, puts me in my place, and goes to work.

Angela scoops a pack of cigarettes out of an old cigar box on her side of the dresser. She lights up and flops onto her bed, lustrous black curls flopping with her. "Careful, Eugenia. That *stunad* has cousins. Maybe you'll meet one."

I feel myself blanch clear down to my crinoline underskirt. My last foray into dating a cousin-by-marriage ended *in medias coitus* when a shake of that cousin's head reminded me of a younger brother in one of my past lives. Since that night, close on three years now, I've kept my legs crossed and my prescription for birth control unfilled.

"But this color is perfect." I hold the taffeta against Angela's cheek to show how well its warm Dijon-ochreness complements her flawless complexion. "Look, Ma. All Carlotta's *stunad* cousins will be fighting to get a crack at her."

Ma snatches my hand back. "You get first introductions."

The ten-inch alabaster Blessed Virgin Mary on the dressing table titters.

I'd respond. Tell the Very Blessed Busybody to mind her own business. But Ma and Angela can't hear my personal peanut gallery. Only I can hear Her. And the last thing I need, especially in this dress, is Ma and Angela watching while I holler at a statue.

See, I've been Italian six, no seven, times. My last life, I got to be Greek. But not in actual Greece. I got to be Greek in Northeast Philadelphia, a life almost exactly like the one I'm living now. Except I crossed myself in the opposite direction when I prayed. This time I had put in for a life as exotic, as un-Catholic, as far removed from South Philly as Rand-McNally and Rudyard Kipling convinced me were possible.

Not far enough. The Blessed Mary Quite Contrary got hold of my application. She took a big red marker to the vellum and substituted ITALIAN for INDIAN, PUDGY for PETITE, and PHILLY for PUNJAB, then redacted and rearranged, reassessed and rejected, condemning me with the biggest red word of all scrawled across my signature: UNREPENTANT.

I'll give that Blessed Virgin Malfeasant unrepentant.

I wrench from Ma's grasp and risk waggling a finger in Mary's direction for the titter, then fix Ma with a we-are-soooo-not-having-this-conversation-again glare. "Don't go introducing me to anybody. Most of the single cousins my age are divorced. The rest will be losers. Some will be both."

Ma corrals the finger, no doubt presuming the waggle was meant for her, and wrenches me back into position. "Your brother found somebody."

I wrench again, pleased to feel a recently fastened hook-and-eye give way. "He found her six weeks ago. That makes Joey the *other* kind."

"What kind is that?"

"The kind who gets his girlfriend pregnant."

Ma presses her lips together. She scrunches her eyes and flares her nostrils so wide, I can tell she's two ticks from exploding. Trying to keep the hair on her tongue. Prevent what she really wants to say from exiting. She opens a closed fist, sweeping it in an arc. "Don't say what you don't know."

"But it's okay for us to stand here and think it?" I crack my neck like Joey when he's dodging a foul ball. "Yo, Ma, meet Carlotta. Wier postin' banns on Wenzday, Tursday, and Friday. The weddin' is Satuhday. Four in d'affernoon. See ya there."

I clutch my flounces. "No woman with sufficient time to plan would ever choose this dress."

Ma goes back to fastening. "Carlotta did the best she could. Not easy finding something off the rack on such short notice. Especially in your size."

Angela snorts. Smoke shoots out her nose. She waves her cigarette, tip streaking red above her fingers. "Have you both been into the Sambuca? There's nothing thrown together about this wedding. The reception's at Twelve Caesars. You gotta book it months in advance. And those invitations? Engraved. That takes weeks."

Ma should be protesting Angela's cigarette. Should be complaining how it's near impossible to get the stench off the rose-printed wallpaper, but all Ma does is stammer. "You're sayin' Joey got engaged, set a date, planned a wedding, ordered . . . ordered . . . boutonnieres. And didn't tell us?" Ma's face goes all convoluted and confused. "Why?"

Angela gives my arm an *are-you-stupid?* smack. "Because Eugenia here doesn't like Carlotta."

Nailed. Angela's statement hits like a hammer. Cracking the rotten core of truth.

I don't like Carlotta.

Why should I?

Carlotta's a thief. A manipulator. A *puttana* who'd coldcock a puppy if it suited her purpose, best fitted for purgatory's ninth circle, surrounded by nose pickers, toenail biters, and wizened old men with phlegm-filled hacking coughs. I've kept my distance for four hundred years. I can't keep my distance in this life if she'll be putting presents under the same tree at Christmas.

I can't tell Ma that. She doesn't have hindsight. And I can't stand the weight of Ma's indignant scrutiny on top of the weight of this dress. I point to my backside. "Can I at least get rid of the bow?"

Alabaster Virgin Mary hisses.

Seriously. She's hissing over a bow. All this life, I've been making nice. Doing my best. Avoiding curses and kisses. Controversies and complications. Minding my manners. Keeping my nose clean. And all without a single "atta girl" out of the Queen of Heaven. Not one teeny tiny concession from the Mother of Consolation.

I consider retrieving my own pack of cigarettes from where I hid it beneath my box spring, my own lighter from where I taped it to the underside of the dresser drawer. Lighting up. Smoking the whole thing, the whole pack. Right here, right now. Anything to avoid the creeping sense Carlotta may be the curse I *can't* avoid. "Come on, Angela. Wear the damned dress. I'll give you money."

Angela's gaze takes on a mercenary glint. "How much?"

Ma seizes Angela's cigarette and stubs it out, then pulls a can of Lysol Disinfectant Spray with Antibacterial Action, the Fresh Scent, from the cleaning basket in our bedroom closet. She aerosolizes a germ-killing cloud over the ashtray, the lighter, and the rest of Angela's pack. "Eugenia will wear the dress. The oldest always wears the dress."

Ma's eyes mist over. "The dress is beautiful and you look beautiful in it. I wish your father could be here to tell you." She hugs my shoulder and puts out an arm like she's presenting a tray of *antipasti*. "Angela, tell your sister how beautiful she looks."

Angela pokes at my bodice. "Your boob is sagging."

The hell? That side's got more supports than the Ben Franklin Bridge. Works on the same principle. Suspension.

Ma pushes Angela out the door. "Get the duct tape."

Please, Blessed Mother, not the duct tape.

But duct tape it is, swathed around my rib cage and under my bra band, stretching all the way to my left breast to clamp it in place. Ma refastens the hook-and-eyes, then tap-taps me on the cheek. "Beauty is pain. Pretend it's not there. When you get married, you can pick a dress with as many straps as you want."

I pull her hand off my face and hold it in both of mine, saying with as much conviction as the duct tape permits, "I'm not getting married, Ma. Get it? Never. As in not ever in my entire life."

"Between saying and doing lies the sea." Ma searches my face, eyebrows don't-mess-with-me high. "Is that what this is about? Joey's getting married, so now it's your turn."

Blessed Mary chokeholds my conscience, the impression of Her voice in my head tart and tinkly. "Stir the *stracciatella*, clean up the spatters."

I'm acting on feelings Ma and Angela don't understand. To settle a score only I remember.

It's not fair.

Not to Ma, not to me, not to my *stunad* soon-to-be sister-in-law. I give Ma the answer she wants to hear. "That's what it's about. Except it's not my turn. It's not required. Times change."

Ma pats my hand, then rubs a thumb across my wrist like she used to before the dentist went to fill a cavity. "Times don't change, chipmunk. They just look different. People are born. They grow up. They marry. They die. Be happy. Joey's finally settling down. Life can start for you girls."

Fuck it. Fuck Mary. Fuck the donkey She rode in on.

I won't be Catholic next time around. I won't be Italian. I won't live in a concrete box in a crumbling neighborhood. I want what I want, and what I want is the chance to choose my next life.

And all the people who live it with me.

Rudyard was clear. "It's not so much the demands you make, woman-child, but how you explain them after." And if, as he promised, a brave heart and courteous tongue will carry me through this jungle, then I'll be as pleasant and agreeable a woman-child as required.

Ma stops at the door on her way out. "Eugenia."

"Yeah, Ma?"

"Start liking Carlotta."

3

Four hours later. Four *freaking* hours later, Joey's hitched to Carlotta.

And Ma's hitched to me, hauling my backside to Wedding Reception Table Number Thirteen. There to meet another of Carlotta's cousins. "Don't you worry about those first twelve," Ma whispers, hoarse and hopeful. "I got a lucky feeling about this next one."

Lucky Cousin Number Thirteen stands.

"My daughter teaches at Temple University." Ma puts a hand on the small of my back and pushes me forward. "Chancre."

"Chaucer, Ma."

Cousin Thirteen sweeps what smells like a vodka tonic past a collection of empty chairs, and in the direction of the dance floor. "My tablemates." Which I take to mean they're all out dancing. "I—"

The refrain from *Ce La Luna* crescendos. Its spicy innuendo cuts off the rest of Cousin Thirteen's sentence. Ma deposits my pocketbook under the table skirt, shoves my wine spritzer into my fist, and scurries away.

Six empty chairs.

That makes Cousin Thirteen the odd man.

About Joey's age. Average height. Pleasant face. A little paunchy, but not too bad.

Time to find out why he's dateless. "What did you say?"

"I said, I flunked Chaucer in college." The man holds my chair and waits for me to sit. "Dropped my grade point average zero oh three percent."

Zero. Oh. Three. Percent.

That's one in three hundred.

Or maybe three thousand.

Also hindsight's percentage of incidence among the incarnate population.

A tiny alarm sounds between my ears. "That's not a decimal you run into much."

"Unless you're an actuary. Which I am."

"How come you didn't withdraw? To avoid the flunk."

The man tugs at his bow tie, then runs a hand through a crew cut that starts a little back from where his hairline used to be. "That option wasn't . . . convenient."

A guy precise enough to know the percent a flunk in an elective dropped his grade point average, right down to its exact zero oh three, couldn't find zero oh three minutes to tote his patootie into registration and avoid that apparent disaster. "What do you mean *wasn't convenient*?"

He cocks his ear. "I didn't catch your name when your mother introduced us."

Actuary. Balding. Deaf.

And effective at evading unpleasant topics.

"Eugenia." Truth. "But everybody calls me Jenny." Lie. People *should* call me Jenny. Who names their kid Eugenia and actually calls her that?

It's a man's name. With an *a*. "And you are?"

"Dr. Panisporchi?" The question comes over my left shoulder. Male. Enthusiastic. Young.

Dread, cold and clammy, creeps up my spine. The only people who call me Dr. Panisporchi are my dry cleaner and my—

"Friedrich Palmon. You know, from class."

—students.

Not just any student.

Friedrich Palmon. Bony and tall, he misses handsome by quarter inches. Nose too long. Brows too close. Gaze too distant to be truly without guile.

Friedrich Palmon. An engineering student with a penchant for medieval literature, Old English to Modern English, and all the romance in between.

"I saw the name on the napkins." He fans a collection of mulberry-colored ones around a plate of pastries he places in the middle of our table. He glances at my head. "Nice tiara."

Friedrich Palmon. With whom I have a history other than his fondness for Chaucer. A history of which he should be so ashamed, he should present me those pastries on his knees, penitent prayers falling from his lips.

"What are you doing here?" I ask, my tone stiffer than my frock.

Friedrich sweeps a hand over his black and white wait staff ensemble. "Thanksgiving weekend. The caterer offered bonuses." He tilts a chin at Joey, dancing with Carlotta by the laughing cherubs ice sculpture. "That your cousin?"

Shrimp linguini goes leaden in my stomach. Of all the relationships he could have guessed at, Friedrich dredges up the first Joey and I shared. Four hundred years in the past. "No. He's my brother."

Feedback squeals from the sound system. The music stops. Friedrich turns to Cousin Number Thirteen. "Then this is your lover." The last word echoes into the silence.

Heads turn.

Lover. Who says that? Out loud and in a crowd. And to their *professor.*

The actuary keeps his attention on his drink, an up-twitch playing at the corner of his mouth. He stirs and restirs the lemon wedge. And hums. A musical phrase, low and lovely and achingly familiar.

Unchained Melody.

Not the Righteous Brothers version made so famous by Demi Moore and Patrick Swayze during the potter's wheel scene in the movie *Ghost.* An older version.

Feedback again squeals. Music returns, playing the actuary's tune, and overtakes his soft, Perry Como–reminiscent rendition.

The aunts at the next table scooch their chairs in our direction.

One rubs her index fingers together to insinuate a relationship she is too much of a lady to voice. Another nods.

Heat creeps up my neck. I'm taking too long to respond to my student. "This is . . . this is . . ." Shit. *Who is this?*

The overhead lights flicker, strobing the room with split-second darkness. A blonde in a red spray-on cocktail dress appears at the table. Like she poofed in out of nowhere. She throws her arms around my table companion. "Stanley!"

I check behind her, looking for a wisp of smoke.

"Donna!" The newly named Stanley stands. He returns the embrace, hand traveling down her back. It comes to rest on her butt.

Had I applied to do something virtuous with this life, really virtuous, like missionary to Tajikistan, Blessed Mary might not have nixed my plans. I'd be there right now, teaching the beautiful native children of the region to chant in iambic pentameter.

Instead, I'm here. Constricted by duct tape, tiara digging divots into my scalp, waiting with my student for the deaf actuary to cop his feel.

Stanley draws the blonde toward me. "I'm sorry. Where are my manners? Donna, this is Euglena, Joey's sister. Euglena, this is Donna."

Your sister? Your cousin? Your wife? Your mistress? Your stockbroker? And Euglena is a type of protozoan, you moron.

I glance to Friedrich, wondering if etiquette demands I introduce him, or acknowledge him, or at least make him bring us coffee to go with the pastry.

He's gone.

The dance ends. The music with it.

Donna taps my shoulder. A line of beaded silver discs drooping from each of her ears tinkle. Like little bells. "Wow. You look like you stepped out of an early episode of *Mad Men*. And this color? Perfect for your complexion."

Perfect for another time. Another dress. Another wedding.

The next song begins. Donna nudges Stanley. "Doesn't she look beautiful? You should ask her to dance."

"I'd be honored." The actuary bows. Not a tiny half-embarrassed-I've-had-way-too-much-to-drink kind of bow. This guy goes full Captain Von Trapp in *The Sound of Music*, folding at the waist in a way I'd only expect in countries run by military juntas, or where people get presented to the queen. He offers a hand, eyebrows expectant.

He better not be expecting a curtsy.

Our fingers touch. A jolt shoots from his tips, travels up my arm, across my shoulder, and into the back of my throat, filling my senses like a crush of fresh basil.

A bank of gray rolls in, sweeping across my vision. The floor goes unsteady under my feet.

And the room changes.

Overhead LEDs go incandescent. Centerpieces switch from chrysanthemums to carnations. Colors dull. Sounds dim. Even the tablecloth feels different, switching from the artificial satin of blended polyester to smooth, starched cotton.

I'm in the other life. The other time. The other dress.

With another man. His aftershave smelling of citrus. His hand holding mine oh so tight.

Donna reaches past me, jostling my elbow. The other time slips away.

Colors brighten. Chrysanthemums return.

And . . . I'm back to my here and now. Present time. Present dress.

And present man.

The actuary.

Donna picks a *pasticciotti* from the pastry plate and pops it into her mouth. "Carlotta tells me you teach Chaucer."

This blonde-as-blonde-can-be feather of a girl with the calm green eyes and porcelain skin knows of Chaucer.

She picks a second *pasticciotti*. "What did you do for your dissertation?"

You see, Blessed Mother? This is why I say there is no justice. Somebody who can fuse herself into a dress that small should think a dissertation is what comes after dinner. "I'm sure you wouldn't find it interesting."

"My interests are varied. My specialty is poetry of the Thirty Years' War. I'm an associate professor at Penn."

My spritzer blows out my mouth and nose to spray across Donna's red-splashed bosom.

She has the job I've always wanted.

Blessed Mary, my wise and ever present counselor, my help in perilous times, get off my keychain and kill me now.

Keychain Mary hands me a napkin. "Don't be ridiculous. Step out of your comfort zone. Do as Rudyard suggested. Be courteous." She points to Stanley, scrubbing at the spritzer. "Help Dr. Donna get her boobs out of range."

I pull Stanley's napkin from the fray and replace it with mine. "Odd we've never met."

"I've been in Bavaria doing research."

Something tingly and tauter than the duct tape closes around my chest. "Where in Bavaria?" I ask, my words fading with my air supply.

"Near the site of a small town. Little known and long gone. Filled with tragedy and cowardice and sometimes great heroism, its history long forgotten, but yearning to be told."

The room goes sideways, my knees go weak. I slump to my seat, sliding down the back of the chair.

The wedding photographer pops in with a cheery "Smile!"

The flash explodes. Donna blathers on about that little Bavarian town, which she didn't name, but I could.

Oberholt.

Good thing paramedics arrive to drag me out of the banquet hall, give me oxygen, dislodge the duct tape, and lecture me regarding the importance of diaphragmatic expansion. Otherwise, I'd have used the last of my strength to dump the remains of Stanley's vodka tonic on blondie's other tit.

I know that meddling bitch.

4

But the bitch doesn't know me.

She doesn't have hindsight. She's not one in three hundred. Or maybe three thousand.

She's not even on Facebook.

But she's so fascinated by the Thirty Years' War, she's built her career around it. She wanders Bavaria. Perhaps searches records in an ancient church. Perhaps finds reference to Oberholt. Perhaps a mention of an incident. A horrific incident. Four hundred years in the past. And something tugs at her, like Blessed Mary tugs at me. So Donna digs further.

Unearthing what should best stay buried.

Why?

The question haunts me for the next two days.

The Monday morning after the wedding, while waiting for my class to fill, I mouth a silent and more specific query to Blessed Mary on My Keychain. "Why is Donna intrigued with Oberholt?"

Blessed Mary stops fiddling with Her attached corkscrew. "Even the brightest star travels a fixed course."

I pull my lecture notes from my briefcase and arrange them at right angles to the edges of the podium. In a present too filled with my pasts, it helps me concentrate. "Why are Dr. BrightStar and Friedrich fixing on *my* particular course?"

Keychain Mary lets out a long nasal sigh, like a concertina left to deflate on its own. "Because repentance without resolution makes redemption impossible."

"You shoulda thought a little harder before making that rule, Blessed Mother. 'Cause there's no way to resolve something with somebody who doesn't know there's anything needs resolving."

A shadow falls across my lectern, tall and gangly, the knuckle attached rapping the top to get my attention.

Friedrich Palmon. Once a baker in Oberholt during the Thirty Years' War.

Friedrich. Caught up in a religious conflagration which etched itself onto the zeitgeist of the three and a half centuries to follow.

Friedrich. Who dumped my Oberholt self. Along with his Oberholt Catholicism. So he could hitch himself to one of Oberholt's Lutheran conquerors. The *stunad* Carlotta. Who married my brother, but who, four hundred years ago, was the scraggly-haired, shifty-eyed, mealy-mouthed daughter of Oberholt's new Lutheran brewer.

Friedrich. Who spent the rest of his Oberholt life supplying lager to the Lutheran officers at a discount and sawdust-laden stöllens to the Quartiermeister at a premium.

Friedrich. Who left me, his still-Catholic ex-fiancée, without prospects. Without protection. Without remorse.

Friedrich. Who doesn't know. Doesn't remember. Yet, every class, brings fresh-baked pfeffernüsse, a spicy cookie his Oberholt-baker self once considered his specialty.

Who the hell knows why he brings them. They're made from pepper, fer chrissakes.

And that's the quirk in Friedrich's karmic kink. Of all the Bavarian confections he could offer on the subconscious altar of atonement, he chooses one I can substitute for ipecac in the home medicine cabinet.

Aside from never returning the plastic containers for the pfeffernüsse, I've few outlets for expressing my ire over Friedrich's Oberholt-version's humiliation of me.

So I flunk his ass.

Every quiz, every exam, every paper, every semester.

It doesn't matter he gives A-quality work, never misses class, never shows up late, never leaves early, and always writes legibly.

I still flunk his ass.

And why does the philandering fuck feel compelled to keep taking my courses?

Because Friedrich wants to be punished. Beneath his mismatched, hand-knitted, Mr. Rogers cardigan hides a sinner who's waited four hundred years for a tweed-clad dominatrix to grant him absolution.

Friedrich raps my lectern again. "Dr. Panisporchi?"

"Yes, Mr. Palmon?"

"I have something for you." Friedrich hands me a pint-sized container of today's pfeffernüsse. Behind him, a trickle of students arriving for my thrice-weekly wisdom on Middle English poetry take their seats.

"Eugenia," Keychain Mary whispers, her tone deep and mindful and meant only for me. "Be pleasant. Be agreeable. Be *courteous*."

Fine. Courteous. Gotcha. I toss the Tupperware to a gal in the front row. "Thank you, Mr. Palmon."

Friedrich digs into his backpack, retrieves a notebook, and rips a single sheet from its spirals. "Not the pfeffernüsse. I have *something* for you."

He drops a sketch atop my lecture notes, a drawing of a church's bell tower framed by snowcapped mountains sheltering a bakery below.

Slate-tiled roofs. Street cobbles. Small windowpanes frosting in the cold.

Oberholt. Four hundred years ago on Hallowmas. Every door hinge detailed. Every curbstone correct. Down to the drunken soldier Friedrich sketched upchucking by the church steps.

A special drunken soldier.

A lieutenant in the city militia.

A hollow feeling replaces the spot where I just ate breakfast.

Friedrich didn't sketch everything. He forgot Donna, the meddling Thirty Years' War scholar with the size two hips. She should stand at the edge of the square, foot tapping in time to the music. So should her cousin, the Freiherr, the Lutheran toady who supplanted our beloved *bürgermeister*.

The Freiherr's henchman slinks in from off-frame. A pernicious and pockmarked little vermin who is hell-bent to talk with Fräulein Donna. He wants to dicker with her over a bolt of Catholic linen, debate the merits of a Catholic ivory dresser set, and pocket her cash, off to pick his next victim.

The henchman had a name. Maybe, once, a mother who gave it to him, but nobody in Oberholt called him by name. The further I reach for the moniker we used, the faster it recedes. So I concentrate on the space between fuzzy and focus, waiting to see what froths up.

The sketch comes alive. Dance music floods the deep places of my memory—an oompah band the town fathers hired for every public event, from festivals to hangings. The band's donkey-bray beats fill in all Friedrich left out. Couples bobbing and weaving in the square. Soldiers lounging on the edges. Dice scattering across a wooden tabletop. Bawdy laughter. Nervous replies.

Then, there it is. Shouting in the background, from an alley two streets over from the bakery. A male voice, full and foul. "You're a cheat."

My mouth goes dry. The classroom shrinks to a pinprick. If I laid my hand over the sketch like a tablet computer and dragged the image sideways, I'd find the person behind the words, see the people in the square turning to hear, and the Freiherr's henchman slithering off to see how he can exploit the trouble.

"Stop fighting." I whisper, but my voice booms in my head. *They'll come. Stop.*

The gray rolls in and just like that, I'm standing in that alley in Oberholt, night air cool on my cheek, stench of horse piss sharp in my nostrils. In the place all the shouting happened on the night before everything happened.

Suddenly, I remember the henchman's name.

Der Weasel.

And I remember: this is the night before Der Weasel showed up in my family's print shop looking for my cousin, Josef.

My hands shake. My palms go slick. The paper rattles, then drops to the floor, along with the last of my composure.

The gray rolls out. Color returns. My classroom rushes back with such force I'm surprised no gust of wind ruffles my hair.

Friedrich retreats with a little hop-step, a traditional dance every boy and girl in Oberholt knew. He takes his seat and turns up a placard: "Boo."

A challenge from somebody who could be, maybe, might might might, be one in three hundred.

Or three thousand.

No.

Deep cleansing breath, Eugenia. Center yourself. Podium. Chaucer. Start lecturing.

Now.

My words thunder, pronunciation of the Middle English final *e*'s lending a gravitas sometimes missing in modern translations. "For a man may di-e of imagination, So deep an impression he may tak-e. Go, save our life, and that I thee beseech-e."

I scoop the sketch from the floor, shove it into my briefcase, and click the briefcase closed. "In *The Miller's Tale*, Chaucer recounts the story of Nicholas, a poor astrology scholar with promise and a future, who duped his landlord and slept with his landlord's young wife. Today, let us explore why one so blessed would take advantage of those who offered him only their trust."

Friedrich's features go still. His fixation on Chaucer comes clear.

Friedrich Palmon was more than a baker in Oberholt.

So much more. And much more famous.

Friedrich was also *The Miller's Tale*'s main character—Nicholas, an astrology scholar with *sooooo* much to answer for.

Well boo-boo to you, too.

I'll remember you to Mr. Chaucer when I exit this life. Now bring it on and bring Blessed Mary with you. Tell her to send all the Donnas and dough boys and *stunad* brewer's daughters She's got.

Then tell Her to send Der Weasel.

I can take it.

5

In *The Franklin's Tale*, Chaucer admonishes not to scold or complain. He tells us to learn. To endure. If we don't, we will learn to endure.

Yet everybody, at one time or another, sticks their foot in it. Wrath, sickness, the constellations, too much wine, sorrow, changing moods, or being handed a sketch depicting a life lived four centuries before I had my morning coffee—a sketch accompanied by its own audiovisual effects—any of these circumstances could make a gal speak amiss.

Because I spoke amiss, I threw out a challenge. Because I threw out the challenge, I'm staring at a butt crack I last saw draped over a bratwurst stew.

Four hundred years ago.

Der Weasel's butt crack. Sprawled across my kitchen floor, the torso attached to it wedged under my kitchen sink.

The bluster I'd been using to bolster myself since Friedrich's sketch bursts.

How?

No force on heaven or earth possesses sufficient strength to drag that butt crack back alive from the deepest circle of hell into which it must have been cast.

"Leak." Angela lights a cigarette.

"Like a waterfall," a muffled, yet melodic, voice sings from beneath the sink.

The butt crack slithers out. Whoever owns it hitches up his pants, turns over, looks up.

And smiles.

Oh. My. God.

Dark curly hair. Dark eyes with long, long lashes. Well-defined chin. Strong cheekbones. A Caravaggio released from the canvas.

Is there any fire, on heaven or earth, hot enough, transformative enough to have turned Der Weasel into . . . into . . .

This?

He rests elbows to knees, mouthing words I become aware are directed at me. "The pipes are old. I can do an inspection. It's free. You don't want to wake up in the middle of the night and find toilet water dripping into the living room."

Self-respect reasserts. And smacks me upside the head.

This is no Caravaggio, this is Der Weasel. First a leaky sink, then a toilet. Next thing you know, he's replumbing the entire house and redoing the bathroom, no doubt offering discount prices while he sequesters the silverware.

"Toilet's above the kitchen"—I check the name embroidered over his breast pocket—"Luigi. How much do we owe you?"

"Join me for dinner. I'll call it square."

Me? Der Weasel? Dinner?

"Love to." Angela stubs out her cigarette. "Lemme get my purse."

I grab her elbow. "Are you crazy? You don't even know him."

"Sure I do. He's Carlotta's cousin's cousin."

"What cousin?"

"Stanley's cousin. The actuary."

I drag her to the other end of the kitchen. "You can't go out with him."

Der Weasel stops tucking in his shirt.

Angela wrenches her elbow free. "Why ever the hell not?"

I look Der Weasel down, then up—slim waist, broad shoulders, hint of a dimple in the hollow of his right cheek.

But Angela doesn't know what he was. What he did. Can't understand she can't go out with him the same way she can't go out with a Nazi. "He smells like a sewer."

Angela's jaw drops. Der Weasel finishes tucking in his shirt. He rolls his cuffs down over well-muscled and heavily veined forearms to button them, then pulls a pocketknife from his tool belt. He releases a short blade and goes to work on a nail, his movements quick. Precise. And impossible to ignore.

My heart skips a beat.

"Every utensil in the drawer can't be gold." His accent, low and well-modulated, possesses none of the mushy consonants so typical in South Philly. "Some of us are wood, but we're still of use."

Der Weasel. Handsome. Helpful. And paraphrasing Chaucer.

"I'm . . ." Not sorry. I'll never say those words. Not to Der Weasel.

He wiggles the knife to stop me, then turns to Angela. "I'll shower and change. Pick you up in an hour."

He grabs his ski jacket off the radiator. His left foot hits the linoleum with an uneven slap. The sound beelines for the space between my shoulder blades. The resultant shudder shimmies a waggly path to my knees.

I smell bratwurst beneath the scent of Ma's Pine-Sol. Rosewater and chocolate beneath the tomatoes simmering on the stove. I smell acid. I smell sweat. I smell, I smell—

My stomach somersaults into a half twist.

—fear.

And if I don't do something. This minute. I'm. Dead.

My backbone stops doing the watusi. It snaps into place. "What's wrong with your foot?"

"Broke it falling down the stairs." He shows me, bending it this way, then that. "Didn't set right."

Blessed Mary Atop the Refrigerator is heavy. Mahogany over a lead core. One smack across the temple. Now, while he's tying his shoe. One well-aimed wallop. One well-placed opportunity.

And Mary can set everything right.

I open the fridge, grab a beer, slam the door shut to get Her started, but all Weenie Girl does is tremble. "Stop."

Blessed Mary is loud and clear, but here's what's really neat about having a conscience: I don't have to listen to Her. So I toss my purse up there and down She topples, whizzing past Der Weasel's ear to land squarely on his foot.

"What the—" Angela bends to help him, but he waves her off.

"Steel-toe boots," he explains, rising off his knee. "No harm done."

He knocks the toe kick to demonstrate the resilience of his footwear, then retrieves Refrigerator Mary and swipes a handkerchief over Her.

"She's a hefty one." He places Her gently back on Her perch, his next words confirming whatever course led Der Weasel into our kitchen, the universe did not fix him on it by chance. "Lucky She didn't land on my head."

●●●

"Been dating him for two weeks," Angela tells me after Der Weasel leaves. "Where you been? Met him at Joey and Carlotta's wedding. That blonde girl, Donna, introduced us."

She looks past me. "Luigi did a great job on the sink, Ma. He says our pipes are old."

"No he didn't." I give the tomatoes a stir. "He said our house has mold."

Ma's hand flies to her breast.

"Eugenia needs her ears checked." Angela stacks dishes back into the sink and turns on the faucet. "He said he's fighting a cold."

Oh. "He has herpes. Hope you haven't slept with him."

Ma gasps, index knuckle pressed against her lip. "How do you know?"

"Carlotta's cousin, Stanley, told me. You know, the actuary."

Angela drops into a chair. "Stanley told you his cousin has herpes. He just meets you, orders you a drink, then goes, *Oh, by the way, my cousin has herpes.*"

"Not sure. He mighta said hepatitis."

Angela throws her hands in the air. Ma washes her own, then pulls out the Pine-Sol and slathers a spongeful on the floor where Luigi was working. "You haven't slept with him, have you?"

"Ma."

"Let's call Doctor Frangipane, getcha checked out."

"Ma!"

"Just being cautious, pumpkin." Ma throws away the sponge. She unravels a roll of paper towels and starts in under the sink.

Heh. I take a long glug of beer.

Angela lights another cigarette. She lands the lighter on the table. "Luigi can't have herpes. He just got outta seminary."

Ma's head smacks against the sink bottom. Beer overflows my lower lip. Memory of Der Weasel the last time I saw him overflows with it. Dirty fingers over my mouth, dirty words in my ear. "He's a priest. You're dating a priest."

"Of course not, stupid. Luigi left before he took his vows. He was a plumber before he started seminary."

Ma rubs her head. "Why would Stanley say a priest has herpes?"

Jeez. "Maybe that's why he didn't take the vows, Ma. 'Cause he has herpes."

She goes back to scrubbing.

"He doesn't have herpes, Ma. Eugenia's teasing." Angela makes a chop-chop motion across her throat. "Aren't ya, Eugenia?"

Little slut *has* slept with him. And after only two weeks.

Shit and shit and dammit to Schenectady. I don't care if hellfire has transformed him into Saint Francis Fucking Assisi himself, there is no way I'm being courteous to Der Weasel to get myself out of another lifetime of hindsight.

I gotta break these two up.

●●●

Carlotta shuffles through a display of men's dress shirts. She holds up two. "What do you think for Joey, stripes or solid?"

Keychain Mary gives me a nudge. *Stripes.*

"Solid," I say.

Carlotta's expression goes droopy. "Joey wears the same thing every day. White shirts and black socks. I want him to expand his color palette."

Told ya.

Fine, Blessed Mary. Whatever. "Get the stripes."

Carlotta perks up. She squeezes my elbow. "I'm so glad you called. I always wanted a sister."

Take Angela. I'm happy to get her off my hands.

Carlotta pays for the shirt, leads me out of the store, loops her arm through mine, and heads in the direction of the food court. "Let's stop in that bakery. The Bavarian one next to the Greek place. They have these spicy squares. I forget the name. Pepper moose or something."

"Pfeffernüsse?"

"That's it. Do you like them?"

The question rises, like the one and only pfeffernüsse I ever ate: What are the odds my new sister-in-law, a second generation Italian-American, would harbor a penchant for an obscure Bavarian confection?

"I know, I know. I can barely fasten these." Carlotta tugs at her jeans, her waist thin and willowy beneath her annoyingly upright bosom. "But I can't resist. It's like I was born to them."

Settled into the brewpub next door, wedged between other holiday shoppers, Carlotta prattles. About the honeymoon. Her job. Joey's job. The weather. How close it is to Christmas.

And every color she's painting every room of the house she and Joey bought and into which they moved the day after their honeymoon.

"I guess you two picked it out the day after you got engaged to get into it so fast," I say when she comes up for air.

"Oh, no." Carlotta takes a big gulp of herbal tea. "We looked for months, then we had to fix it so we could make settlement soon as we got back from the honeymoon. My mother's a realtor, y'know, so we saved the commission and she cut us a deal with the closing costs and Dad's had workmen there every day getting the wiring and plumbing straight."

Carlotta shuts up, maybe realizing how it sounds for her and Joey to be house hunting and her parents all involved when none of us even knew Carlotta was alive. She thumps the table. "Darn it. Joey should have introduced us sooner. My mother planned time and again to invite your family for dinner, but Joey always stopped her." She takes my hand. "I'm so glad your condition's improved."

"Condition?"

"Joey told me you don't like to talk about it, but there's no need for any of you to be embarrassed, not in this day and age."

What lamebrained condition had Joey invented for me? I want to ask, but I'm here for one reason. "What's the deal with Luigi?"

The sudden topic change seems to confuse Carlotta. "Oh, don't worry. We didn't tell anybody about your condition. Just our immediate family. And some of the aunts because they helped wrap the sugared almonds for the favors."

"Okay, yeah, that's great. I mean—"

"Plus my oldest cousin, Margaret. She's a psychiatrist and knows about this stuff."

Psychiatrist. Wait 'til I get my hands on you, Joey. Seriously.

"And the wedding planner, of course, seeing as your mom was too upset to give any input. And then there was the—"

"Carlotta." Maybe I say it too sharply. I don't care. This girl's words arrive like the waves of an incoming tide, copious enough to launch a ship on them. She was *never* this talky-talky in Oberholt. "I mean what's the deal with Luigi quitting seminary to become a plumber?"

Of all the questions somebody might have about Luigi, mine should be obvious, but the look on Carlotta's face tells me she doesn't get asked it much. "Ma wants to know. Because he's dating Angela."

Carlotta lays a finger to her cheek and wrinkles her forehead, like Shirley Temple did in her movies when she was pondering a problem. I half expect Carlotta to break into song and tap-dance her answer across the bar. "Luigi's dad was a plumber. Luigi helped in the business before he went into seminary. He died a few months ago. My aunt didn't have the heart to sell his tools. Said they reminded her of him."

I imagine candles illuminating a collection of pipe wrenches and C-clamps arranged on a kitchen counter before a statue of Saint Vincent Ferrer, the patron saint for plumbers. "Ah. Luigi came home to take care of his mother."

Carlotta shakes her head. "Plumbers union has great insurance. My uncle was *DEF*-initely worth more dead than alive."

"Then he didn't like seminary."

Carlotta takes the finger off her cheek. She waggles it at me. "He liked it fine."

"He got kicked out?"

Carlotta stirs another packet of sugar into her tea. "Not at all."

"Broke his vow of chastity?"

"Not as far as I know."

"Then he did drugs."

Carlotta's eyebrows shoot to the stars. "God, no."

"Committed a crime?"

"Of course not."

"Jesus, Carlotta. Did he use bad language?"

Carlotta smacks her spoon to the table. "He didn't do anything wrong. He just left. Said it wasn't his path anymore." She zones out, staring at a spot five inches above my forehead. "Weird. Luigi quit seminary the same week Joey and me started dating."

Now *that's* a coincidence that might be worth exploring.

But the tide rolls in again. "Luigi's a hard worker. Deserves a lotta credit. Built that business from scratch." Carlotta's voice hunches, along with her shoulders. "His good-for-nothing father ran it into the ground. Alcohol. Luigi's a good guy, but lives like a monk. Angela's the best thing that's happened to him in a long time."

Angela. Good for somebody.

"You wanna know about Luigi, ask Stanley. They're really close. Hey!" She smacks my shoulder like she just got a great idea. "Maybe you guys could double-date."

Next time I need to know something from Carlotta, I'm texting.

6

At a little trattoria off Passyunk and South, Stanley waves me to a table by the window. "Hard to believe you'd want to see me again. Figured you thought I was dumb as I acted."

He must mean the Dr. Donna nipple-grab.

The waiter offers the wine list. Stanley hands it over. "Little early in the day for me."

I order the house Chianti, then take a long, silent minute to study the menu.

"Soooo." Stanley squeezes a lemon wedge into his water. "Chaucer must be interesting. I mean more interesting than people think. Like actuarial science."

"I gave an entire lecture in Middle English once. Nobody noticed."

Stanley's whole face participates in the smile. A large, even set of uppers appear beneath lips obviously accustomed to the action. His cheeks puff. They crinkle the corners of his eyes, accentuating a skin pucker on his left temple. "Why'd you study him?"

Because Chaucer's a great choice for somebody with hindsight. He's rarely talked about on purpose, and never by accident. Because everybody mistakes him for Shakespeare. Perfect for avoiding contact with a life providing too much input, too many people I recognize.

But I can't say that. Stanley's not one in three hundred. Or three thousand. "Because I seek respite to think carefully."

Stanley channels his inner Rodin, leaning chin to fist, brow studious, like he's thinking carefully, too. "Are you quoting Chaucer?"

"*A Parliament of Fowls*. Or *foules* in the Middle English."

"Wise man. Did you use that quote in your dissertation?"

The question exiting his lips rather than Dr. Donna's doesn't grate. "You're familiar with Chaucer's summoner and pardoner. From the *Canterbury Tales*."

Stanley's eyes move up and to the right and I imagine him accessing the information from somewhere within his mathematics-laden brain. "Yes. I mean not completely, but I remember that much from my failed class."

The waiter arrives for our orders. We give them. We change them. We give them again, settling on the special because the minutes are ticking away. The exchange rides the edges of a similar scene. Another restaurant. Another menu. Another bout of indecision. A ritual now passed into tradition. A joke between two people who know each other so well, they finish each other's sentences.

And a hand. Reaching to take mine to share it.

I blink. It's only Stanley, reaching to take my menu and hand it to the waiter. "Why are you chuckling?"

I have no answer. Underneath, I'm crying, forlorn and silent, over something lost. Something misplaced. Something raising a deep-seated discomfort. Something that needs a moment, maybe two, to drain into those dark recesses where uncertain emotion lingers.

Stanley catches my eye. "You were saying about the summoner and the pardoner?"

His attitude, interested and intrigued, has the effect of marshmallows in warm cocoa. I let it melt away the grumblies. "The summoner called out people who committed sins. He brought them to the pardoner who decided whether to forgive them or not."

"Kind of like a bailiff and a judge."

Most people think a bailiff is the guy on *Judge Judy* who says *All rise*. "Yes. That was the bailiff's task in Chaucer's day. And Chaucer's bailiff, or rather summoner, was corrupt. People paid him not to be called."

"The pardoner would figure that out. His court'd be kind of empty, right?"

"Exactly, so the bailiff, I mean summoner, had to bring in some people. But Chaucer's pardoner was also corrupt. He'd absolve anybody." I point my fork at Stanley. "For a price."

The waiter delivers our orders. Stanley asks for fresh Parmesan. "Nice scam. But the ruler, the mayor or whoever, would notice the jail was empty."

Freiherr, I almost correct him. *Like in Oberholt.* "He would, and that's why the truly poor or unprotected had no way out."

One of those uncertain emotions ceases its uneasy respite, poking at me. I take a big gulp of Chianti, granting the emotion leave to drown itself in it.

"Sucks for them," I finish, my words hollow to my ears.

Stanley doesn't seem to hear the echo. "What angle'd you take for your dissertation?"

"In the General Prologue to the Tales, the summoner and the pardoner appear last in the list of pilgrims. Chaucer calls them friends, so a presumption they worked together naturally follows."

The waiter brings the cheese. Stanley sets it to the side, the enthusiasm in his eye real. "Sounds like they operated at cross-purposes."

"They did. But what if the summoner called them out, then split the pardoner's fee for doing so?"

"That makes the summoner more a henchman than a partner."

Henchman. Yes. The bailiff was a henchman. He did as the Freiherr directed.

Stanley drums the table edge with his knife and fork. *Ratta-tap-tap. Ratta-tap-tap-tap.* A rhythm familiar and friendly and too fuzzy to place. "That's fine for the pardoner. His business depends on the summoner. No good for the summoner. He'd make out better if he failed to summon, kept the extortion for himself."

Most people don't get this far. "Unless the Freiherr had something on the bailiff, something to compel the bailiff to cut him in on the take."

"Freiherr?" Stanley asks.

"Freiherr?" I ask back.

"You said *freiherr* just now. Instead of pardoner."

And so I did.

"You talk about them like they're real people."

They were. "There's no proof either ever existed. But plenty of people think Chaucer based his characters on acquaintances." *Mr. Chaucer himself told me.* "And that was the thrust of my dissertation. I traveled through England. Visited the villages Chaucer traveled. Even followed his path to Rheims when he squired during the Hundred Years' War."

"So you got it right."

"No." *Because knowledge is nothing without proof.* "There was no 'right' to get. I had to revise the thesis."

I dig into my salad, taking too big a bite, as I always do, then chew, letting balsamic vinegar sear the memory of my humiliation.

Stanley pours olive oil onto a plate. He sprinkles it with rosemary and oregano, nudges the mixture toward me with clean, trimmed fingernails. "It happens. I had to push my master's back a year."

"Where'd you go to school?"

"Villanova."

"My brother went there. Got a scholarship and teaching assistantship. Kinda weird. He never had an interest in academics. Lucky for me or there wouldn't've been enough left from Dad's life insurance to get me through school."

Stanley adjusts his collar, hooking a finger along the inside edge to smooth it around the back of his neck. "Grad school is expensive. You get through the best you can."

When Stanley phoned after my text, he called me Euclidea, which is a system of geometry based on a series of intuitive axioms and a major step up from protozoa. A mathematics geek like Stanley must find such a geometry marvelous in its consistency, and if I were in the least interested, I could take that moniker as a compliment. So why swirl the dregs of my Chianti and let the seconds gather between us?

He crunches his salad. A piece of lettuce sticks to the corner of his mouth. I move to remove it, then pull back, the action too intimate for an acquaintance. The Blessed Buttinski talked me into putting on lipstick and eyeliner for this meal, when I'm really here for one reason. And one reason only. "So, tell me about your cousin, Luigi."

Stanley's expression clamps down. "You're interested in Luigi. Christ, Eunosia, you could have done that in a text."

I tried. You insisted on lunch. Truth. "Ma asked me." Lie. "She wanted to know about him on account he's dating my sister."

Hurt rises in his eye. "Long dark hair?"

"Yeah."

He drains his water glass, dabs his napkin at a drop that catches on the edge of his lip, taking the bit of lettuce with it, and straightens, all business. "Got it. The pretty girl. Luigi likes her a lot. Says she's smart."

Angela thinks Africa is a country in South America.

"He's had a hard time getting hold of her." Stanley pulls out his cell, taps the screen, and scrolls. "Says you keep hanging up on him."

"Old telephone lines. We think a mouse might of eaten through the wiring."

"Maybe Luigi could take a look at them for you. He's pretty handy."

Wow. Mathematics is amazing. Mr. Actuary Man gets it right even when he doesn't know there's a right to get. I lean on my elbow, all vindicated and casual-like and peek around the phone edge because—hey!—maybe Stanley's scrolling because the only items left in this round of Pass the Antipasti are the olive pits, and he may as well show me the real dirt. Like Luigi's divorce decree from his secret first marriage the holy Fathers found out about so kicked him from the program.

Stanley stops at my number . . .

And deletes me with a sharp sideways swipe, stainless-steel watchband flashing.

The uncertain emotion takes on form and substance to race roughshod over the cotton-wadded spot in my heart where my deepest regrets are cushioned.

Stanley's gesture, so martial, so confident, is so familiar it seems normal to hear a traditional Bavarian folksong swell over the Puccini piping through the restaurant.

I know this man, his manner, his bearing. At least, I knew him four hundred years ago.

And I'd never want to hurt him.

"I've been unfair." I reach for my purse. "Please, let me get the tab."

"No." Stanley raps the table, a habit four-hundred years old. Still familiar. No longer friendly. "You wanted to know about Luigi. Ask."

"But I—"

"Ask." All vestige of the affable man from Joey and Carlotta's wedding and a few minutes previous disappears, replaced by a stern certainty I know well. One I've longed for since seeing Friedrich's sketch. And now I've gone and let my hatred for Der Weasel destroy any chance of getting close to it again.

"Okay." The word pushes past a lump forming in my throat. "Seminary. Almost a priest. Then Luigi gives it up to be a plumber."

"That's a statement, not a question."

"Fine." He doesn't have to be mean about it. "Why, then? Why give up the seminary to become a plumber?"

Stanley snares his lemon wedge and sucks on it. Its citrus scent rises so tart, I imagine his teeth sinking into the flesh. "You might do better to ask why Luigi gave up plumbing to enter the seminary."

"Okay. Then why?"

Stanley raises an I-will-make-you-pay-for-thinking-I'm-an-idiot eyebrow.

I all but hand him the credit card. "Why did Luigi leave plumbing to enter the seminary?"

"Sorry, sweetheart." Stanley pats my hand, then raises a palm to air scribble on it so the waiter knows he wants the bill. "You'll have to ask Luigi, yourself."

•••

But I won't. Why torture myself asking questions regarding plumbing and priesthood? It's more torturous to sit at the kitchen table, lay my forehead to its cool, laminate surface, stare at the spot where Stanley patted my hand, and remember a kiss, a caress, being cradled in the crook of an arm, my head nestled against rough gray wool that smelled of metal and leather and the soap he used to polish his boots. A strong man, a man of rough duty, but always tender. To me.

Ma pushes a cup of coffee across the table. "Makes a good living, too, Carlotta tells me."

The aroma rises, tickling my curiosity. "Who?"

"Stanley." Ma goes back to her ironing.

"Forget about him. I doubt he'll be calling."

Ma starches a path along the edges of my navy blue yoga pants, her personal Maginot Line against the forces of wrinkles. "Why not?"

There's no way I'll explain how badly I embarrassed us both. "He's hard of hearing. I have to say everything twice."

"Does he listen each time?" Ma runs a wrist across her sweat-sheened forehead. "Better an egg today than a chicken tomorrow."

Either way works out bad for the chicken.

My heart sinks, weighed by a growing despondency. I think of the oompah music, Stanley's imperious gesture that brooked no argument. He was a military man in Oberholt, a soldier, driven when his job required.

Ma sets the iron upright in its cradle. She pours her own cup of coffee, sits opposite me, and addresses my unspoken remembrance. "You can't know about Stanley until you get to know him."

"He's an actuary. I hate numbers." *And sometimes he executed people. You want me to go out with somebody who executed people?*

"That's just his job." Ma taps a finger to her chest. "What matters is his heart."

"Enough." I toss a pile of Angela's undies on top of Ma's to-do basket, then tote my things upstairs.

"We make plans, Eugenia," Ma hollers after me. "Have dreams. But we can't know what direction life will take us."

Hindsight is a noun meaning *retrospect* and *retrospect*, a noun meaning *contemplation of the past*. No matter how hard I fight the current, the only direction my introspections can possibly travel is backward.

Upstairs, I pull Friedrich's sketch from my briefcase to trace a finger along the figure of the drunken soldier, feeling lonely. All this time, Friedrich knew who I was and didn't say anything. Then he sees Joey and Carlotta dancing at their wedding, sees Stanley sitting at my table, Dr. Donna hanging all over him, and draws his little reunion in pen and ink. Friedrich must have recognized Stanley, must have known how much this drawing would hurt.

I give Alabaster Mary a quarter turn. "I have to get him off my roster."

●●●

The following day, Friedrich Palmon drops a binder on my desk. "My final project."

"It's not due until the end of the week."

"I won't be here at the end of the week."

"But you never miss class."

"First time for everything, doc. Even for people like us." He points to the binder. "Take a look."

I leaf through and read a paragraph here and there. "I didn't realize you had such an interest in the summoner and pardoner, Mr. Palmon."

"I don't. Not for four hundred years, anyway."

I bite the inside of my cheek, pulse pounding a bongo rhythm against my aplomb.

Four hundred years. Friedrich actually said the number out loud and in the open. *Ding ding ding.* Cash in your chips, Keychain Mary. Today's game of Pass the Antipasti defaults to me.

I snap the binder shut. "Plagiarism is an automatic flunk, Mr. Palmon. Even if you change the title. Even if you do a search and replace. Even if you update the course of events by three centuries. I recognize the bones and breath. You found my dissertation online and copied it."

"They're my words. Divergent wisdom often births from the same source." Friedrich takes back the binder. "I added aspects you didn't consider. For example, you never mentioned the monk."

Keychain Mary squeaks from the side pocket of my purse. "He doesn't mean any of Chaucer's ecclesiastical pilgrims, he means the monk who broke Der Weasel's foot in Oberholt."

If Friedrich hears Her, he doesn't let on. He opens the binder, shanghais a Sharpie out of a Blessed Mother beer stein I keep on my desk, and marks a passage in red, like Blessed Mary did on my paperwork. He circles it. "You can't have forgotten *our* monk. He stood up to the Freiherr. Told the tale of the bailiff's extortion. Just like Chaucer's friar did in his tale. You should read it. It's the least you can do. The monk got himself killed for it."

I back away, uncomfortable with Friedrich's conclusions and even more with his proximity, the image rising to fill my mind's eye: The Oberholt monk charging into the new Lutheran tavern to test their brew. He and Josef, my Oberholt cousin, dancing on the tables, arms thrown about each other's shoulders. Back in the early days of the occupation. Back when we believed it all might still blow over. Back when curfews were not yet decreed by the Freiherr.

"A kind man. A pious man. A patient man." Keychain Mary near sprains Her corkscrew, pushing at the clasp on her pocket. "And a lover of life."

Friedrich rattles the binder at me. "Each aspect presented by Chaucer's separate individuals—his monk, his friar, and his priest. The best of them embodied in our monk, Oberholt's monk."

Keychain Mary tumbles onto my desktop. "He tried so hard. Can't you remember? Won't you forgive?"

My lips press together, keeping so much hair on my tongue, breath shoots out my nose in bursts. Neither Friedrich's presence, nor his binder, require I think about any of this. And if I decide to think about it, I'm doing it on *my* schedule, not his.

And that goes for you, too, Blessed Ball-Buster.

Friedrich's face smooths out. He stops his advance and messes with my stapler instead, sending spent ones into a saucer imprinted with an image of Mary as She looks on a Miraculous Medal.

I dig around on my desk until I find the Temple University course catalog. "You need to branch out, Mr. Palmon. Give up on Chaucer and go for a minor in history." I point to an imaginary listing. "Bratwurst And Beer, Bread And Brewer's Yeast: A Bavarian Folderol Of Foibles, Peccadilloes, And Infidelity. In Multiple Acts."

I fling the catalog to the floor. "That's an advanced course. I'd be happy to write you a recommendation."

Friedrich picks up the catalog and lays it on a shelf. "Better a class in perception. Object and event recognition. We can give it a go right now, doc. See what other memories we can jog. We still got time."

Gray fuzz rises beneath his words, bubbles up and out, melts away Friedrich's present-day façade, revealing hair far lighter, shoulders far broader, and a demeanor far more taciturn than the chatty bastard playing with my paper clips.

Friedrich, a baker in Oberholt. In the very muscular flesh. Hobnailed boots, woolen britches, long hose, home-sewn shirt. As real and present as last I saw him outside his shop, right down to the fine dusting of flour on his arms and palm prints on his apron.

"We're not supposed to be talking like this, Mr. Palmon," I say, happy my voice doesn't shake, even happier I don't say it in Bavarian. "I'll overlook it for now."

"You got no idea what's coming down the pike, do ya, Dr. Panisporchi? I'm talking a great big wave of total suckitude." He stands tall, sweeps his arms in a grandiose Hawaiian hula motion to demonstrate how big a wave he means. "The world will start to wobble, its colors will go strange."

I hold out the binder, unable to stop my hand from trembling. "Take this back. I'll pretend I never saw it. Bring me a new project when you take your final."

The Baker blinks out. The Student returns. He quotes Chaucer's

Wife of Bath. "I'm not trying to be your purgatory." He shoves the binder toward me. "Keep it. I'm not taking the final, either."

"You're not coming back next semester?" *That's it? I'm rid of him?* "But I saw your name on the roster."

"Much as I hate to miss a class drawing parallels between the Thirty Years' War and Chaucer's war, plans change. So do rosters."

When Friedrich says Chaucer's war, he means the Hundred Years' War, during which Mr. Chaucer was held hostage for a time, an experience some think inspired *The Knight's Tale*, a story of two young men also held hostage to a war. Friedrich's surname alone, Palmon, a name too obvious to have been assigned by chance, makes it clear which young man Friedrich played, that of Palamon. Meaning Friedrich played a double bill in Chaucer's *Canterbury Tales*. And Chaucer's war was also Friedrich's war.

Despite everything, I reach a sympathetic hand. Friedrich latches onto it.

I pull away.

He holds tight.

"Friedrich," I say in a voice far smaller and more vulnerable than I'd ever want him to hear. "Let me go."

His grip goes lax. His fingers slide away, trailing tiny bits of what-might-have-been along my palm.

He bends and this time he really does grab his book bag, hitching it high on his shoulder, all brash and bravado again. "Tell you what, Dr. Panisporchi, if we run into each other next time around, let's skip the courtly conventions and just get kinky with each other."

7

No original to Chaucer's work exists. What survives are rewrites of what he wrote, copied by hand, page by page, in an era before the printing press, the lexicon so uncertain, Rudyard Kipling wrote a story about a man who successfully passes off a forgery as a supposed unknown manuscript.

As with memories of my lives, it's difficult to know what was left out or how much added later. And like Chaucer's best known story, *The Canterbury Tales*, my lives were unfinished, their possible resolutions only hinted at.

My correlation between the Oberholt monk and Chaucer's characters convinces me our courses repeat. Nailing Friedrich as two separate characters in *The Canterbury Tales* clues me repeats are not my singular hell. Recognizing Friedrich's repeat traces connections in never-ending circles.

Like some kind of crazed cosmic Spirograph.

Two days after my run-in with Friedrich, Joey catches me up on my way to the bus stop. He's got Luigi with him. "What's the deal, you calling Carlotta about my room? I said I'd clear it."

"So clear it. I got new colors all picked out and Ma won't let me touch anything without your permission. Says if I move anything, somebody will die." Like Dad did two hours after Ma rearranged the family portraits on her bedroom wall.

Joey slows his step. Maybe he had the same thought.

We pause to cross ourselves for this hour's funeral procession.

South Broad Street is known for its funeral parlors, their names proudly engraved above their entries—Grasso, Monti, Stolfo, Gangemi, and more—crowding each other, competing for the same parking spaces, the same loading zones, the same dead bodies. Most days, most have a gig, making South Broad Street mostly unmanageable.

"Fine," Joey says after a suitable interval. "I'll clear it. Luigi here can help me. Say hello. He's all the way back from Tajikistan where he went looking for Angela after you told him that's where she went when he called yesterday."

I continue my commute, picking my way around snow mounds and icy patches. I found a gray pubic hair this morning after my bath and am in no mood for one of Joey's moods.

Joey chases after. "We'll get Stanley to help. Then I can invite him for dinner. Carlotta's bugging me to set it up so you two can spend time together." Joey pulls me up short. "That all right with you?"

Luigi hops from one foot to the next, hands drawn into his jacket sleeves. "C'mon, Joey. Leave it go."

"Mind your business," I tell him, I tell Joey, I tell them both.

"That trolley car runs both directions, sister." Joey chops his hand left, then right. "Next time you need something from me, don't talk to my wife. You got my number."

I poke a mittened finger to his chest. "I did call."

"And what did I say?"

"You said you'd clear it. So clear it. And if you don't clear it, I'll call Carlotta again and she can clear it. Then she can find those nudie magazines you got hidden under your mattress."

Luigi taps a palm to Joey's shoulder. "I'll catch you up. Gonna get Angela a pack of Swedish Fish." He ducks into the convenience store on the corner.

Joey grabs my arm. "What else did you find?"

"Pictures from the time Aunt Rose let you use her place in Atlantic City. How'd you get all those photos with that big-haired gal without fogging the lens?"

Joey's face goes crampy, like he's got gas.

I play-punch his arm. "Don't worry. I put them away for safekeeping. Want 'em back? Make me an offer." I sidestep, planning to duck around, but slip on a patch of ice in front of the newsstand. Stone on bone rockets from wrist to neck.

A pile of *National Geographic* follows me down.

The newsstand guy, a pudgy, ham-handed man, darts from behind his counter. I think at first he's going to see if I'm all right, but he goes for the magazines.

Joey pushes past him and hauls me up. "You hurt?" He turns on the newsstand guy. "What the hell you thinking, not clearing your sidewalk like that?"

"I'm a newsstand," the guy growls. "I don't got a sidewalk. This is Olivieri's problem." He points to the florist shop behind his kiosk, then hooks a thumb at Mr. Olivieri, helping his driver load funeral flowers into the back of his shop's delivery van.

Joey clenches a fist. "The five feet around your stand are *your* problem. You expect your customers to wade through snowdrifts to buy your lousy magazines?"

"She's not my customer. She's just clumsy."

I stomp my foot. "Dammit."

Both men turn. I twist my arm and show where the boiled wool of my Geiger jacket got scuffed when I hit the pavement. "This is the only stylish thing I own. It's gonna cost to fix this."

Joey examines the fabric. "Shouldn't cost you anything. Mr. *National Geographic* here should pay for it."

"And who's paying for these magazines?" The newsstand guy tosses them into a barrel he provides for recycling. "They're ruined. I can't sell them."

I pick one out of the barrel and hold it up. Tajikistan is the cover story. "Nothing ruins a *National Geographic*."

The newsstand guy grabs the magazine. He waves it at Joey. "First my money, now my stock. You're a crook, Panisporchi."

The sights and sounds of present-day South Broad Street go gray.

And hindsight hoists out another memory from wherever it was hiding.

A pirate, the newsstand guy should have said. *Preying on your neighbors' misfortune.*

I picture the words shimmering in the breeze, then crashing to the ice-covered sidewalk, clinking like coins dropped to the cobbles.

I'm in Friedrich's sketch again. With life-sized three-dimensional action figures working our way through a scene already performed. The oompah band plays. Afternoon turns to evening. The ice disappears. Buildings close in. And we're in that alley two blocks over from the market square. An alley four centuries and another continent ago, night air cool on my cheek, stench of horse piss strong about us.

The newsstand guy's hair changes to blond. His eyes to the color of blueberries. He's not the newsstand guy anymore. He's Ruprecht Vogt, a big-mouth Oberholt pamphleteer who refused to convert when the Lutherans came.

I drop the *National Geographic.*

"I treated you fairly." Joey, his tone low and tense, utters the same words he did four hundred years ago on Hallowmas, when his name was Josef and he was my cousin.

Shop doors open. Proprietors pop their heads outside—the deli man, the stromboli guy, the gal who runs the manicure place.

"Stop it. Both of you." My protest echoes, past and future, then disperses on Joey's and the newsstand guy's rising tempers.

A female voice, soft, strong, and damned familiar sounds from outside my head. "*Maybe* they act on feelings they don't understand to settle scores they don't remember."

Keychain Mary is still in my satchel, muted with duct tape. I whirl, and spy one of Her sisters, a glass Blessed Virgin Motormouth, hanging from the rearview mirror of Mr. Olivieri's van.

The newsstand guy grabs Joey by the collar. Joey grabs him. Mr. Olivieri shuts the back of his van. He signals his driver to pull out, then strides over, past traffic cones placed to preserve the sanctity of the funeral procession. Past me.

He means to stop Joey and the newsstand guy, means to settle the situation, before it draws attention. But Mr. Olivieri's too late. We've *all* been in this situation before. Der Weasel's already on his way.

Luigi bounds out of the convenience store and blurs past Mr. Olivieri. He works his way between Joey and the newsstand guy, pushing the two apart, but the newsstand guy stumbles and sends Luigi staggering toward the curb.

Get him. My scream rises, clogging the back of my throat. *Kill him, before he kills us.*

The gray fog rolls away. The florist's van moves ahead, the nose nudging toward us as the driver maneuvers around the traffic cones. I lunge for Luigi, intent on sending Der Weasel under the van's wheels.

Back to the afterlife. And out of Angela's.

Blessed Virgin Mary Hanging on the Rearview Mirror catches sunlight. The flash blinds me. I miss my mark, grazing Luigi's elbow. Just like in Oberholt four hundred years ago, it's not enough to throw Der Weasel down, but plenty to unsteady my own footing. *I'm going to bruise my hip again.*

Time stretches, doubling over, like the taffeta ribbon candies Dad used to get for me when I was a little girl.

Brakes crunch. Somebody shrieks.

And I tumble over the florist van's hood, South Broad Street arcing under me.

I see upturned faces. I see the hearse plow into Mr. Olivieri's van. I see the coffin shoot out the back. See it skitter into the newsstand. See oncoming traffic.

I see my guaranteed demise.

Bye Joey. Bye Angela. Bye Ma. Game over, Blessed Mary.

I'm shed of this life. I'm free.

I'm soooo making sure next life I'm a freaking size six.

8

*C*haucer's *Pardoner's Tale* recounts the story of a group of towns-people hell-bent on cheating Death.

They plot. They plan. They go to work.

They are unsuccessful. Because Death always wins.

But not today.

I regain consciousness lying face up in front of the dry cleaners, head throbbing, Luigi's hand on my forehead. I fling it off, blood rush of panic *shooshing* in my ears, push up on my elbows, dig in with one foot, then the other, and scuttle back. Smell of exhaust and the breakfast place's peppers and eggs fades to acid and bratwurst, human sweat and alcohol.

"Take it easy." Luigi scuttles after me. "How do you feel?"

A cop, a paramedic, and the lady from the bridal shop with the blonde-blonde hair and the black-black roots, stop my backward flight.

"You should be dead." The bridal shop lady points to where a flattened orange cone beside a spray of white funerary roses crumple under the remains of Mr. Olivieri's van.

Yes, yes! I should be dead. I'm overdue. The bones from this life should be crumbling in my grave and the breasts from my next sprouting on my pubescent chest.

I check my pulse, strong and steady, then eye up Luigi. Panic turns to ice.

You should be dead, too. "Where's my bag?"

Still attached to my shoulder, its contents scattered in a wave beside. I paw through the notepads and Tic Tacs, nail implements and tampons, pluck my cell from beneath Keychain Mary, dial the department's teaching assistant. "Collect the projects. Hand out the review sheets. And take roll." *Friedrich Palmon won't be there*, I almost add.

He knew I wasn't coming today. That's why he handed in his project early.

I glance at the mess about me, aware I could have landed on my head.

And he's not returning next semester because he thought I'd be dead. That's why he dropped the course.

How did he know? More importantly, why didn't he warn me?

The paramedics insist on taking me to Methodist Hospital. So does Maurizio Bracaconi, a lawyer whose squished-up face and pinched nose make him look like a rodent.

"You're a little premature." He shoves Luigi aside. "She don't need a priest."

He crouches beside me and hands me a card.

Joey seizes it. "We don't need your help, Bracaconi."

Maurizio grabs the card back. He tucks it into my pocketbook and another into my coat. "I saw the whole thing. Got an office next to the funeral parlor. Lucky, huh?"

It seems impolite not to answer, so I nod.

Joey flings out an arm, like he's about to hit the brakes and wants to keep me from flying through the windshield. "Don't listen to him. Carlotta's got a cousin."

Maurizio rests elbow to knees, palms out. "That poser? His mother's Greek."

Like having a Greek mother matters.

He shows Joey where the newsstand guy talks to a cop, arms waving, where the pallbearers stand guard beside the casket, where Mr. Olivieri and his driver gather wreaths and pots. "This ain't Ignacio's, Panisporchi. Gonna take more than some fast-talking and a little fancy footwork to clean this up. Poor dead Mrs. Rossi went out the back of the hearse. Dr. Rossi don't look too happy. You need a specialist on this."

Ignacio. I know that name. "Is Ignacio your bookie?"

Joey stops scooping up my belongings, blood draining from his face. "Bookie?"

I've no idea what well drew my question. But Joey's reaction makes me think he's involved in something he shouldn't be, something that isn't any of my business.

Maurizio sneezes.

"Damned roses." He drags a handkerchief across his nose, then picks up Friedrich's sketch, flapping against the wheel of a nearby Ford Taurus. He makes an appreciative whistle. "You got talent, Dr. Panisporchi."

Joey snatches the sketch from him and takes a long few seconds to study it. He folds it into an inside pocket of his jacket. "So now you're an art critic," he says, his voice flat, his words sapped of ire.

The cops come at him with questions. Maurizio thrusts a card into a policeman's hand and pushes Joey toward Luigi.

"I'll bring him by the station later," Maurizio promises the cops. "Get him out of here," he instructs Luigi, and Maurizio is off to ferret facts from onlookers and snap photos of the scene. He doesn't scamper back until they load me into the ambulance.

"Don't jostle her. She could have a spinal cord injury. Might be paralyzed for life." He heaves my bag in after me, landing it square atop my solar plexus. "Whoa. You should clean that thing out, Dr. Panisporchi. Could give a man a hernia."

Maurizio takes the names and badge numbers of the paramedics before he lets them close the doors.

Hours later, after all the x-rays and needles, Mr. Olivieri stops by the hospital. He brings daisies.

So does the funeral director. He brings his lawyer.

Stanley visits, explaining, "Carlotta asked me to check on you," then wonders, "What are the odds of surviving something like that?"

What are the odds Der Weasel would consider the priesthood? That a mercenary would become an actuary?

The cover of the *National Geographic* that somehow followed me to the hospital is populated by a collection of colorfully dressed, smooth-faced young Tajiki women gathered beside a body of water, eyes soulful, expressions serene. They can't answer my question. I burrow into my purse, dig out Keychain Mary, peel the duct tape off Her mouth, and ask, *What are the freaking odds?*

The Very Blessed Keychain points at Stanley.

He checks his charts and tables, scratches numbers on the back of my hospital menu, pulls up the calculator app on his cell, and punches up a couple more. He finishes my Jell-O, swallowing in slow, silent spoonfuls, puts down the bowl, and says, "Zero oh three percent."

9

According to Carl Jung, synchronicity is the coincidence of events that seem related in a meaningful way. I expect Angela to show up the morning after my accident to bring me home from the hospital.

"Let's go, Eugenia. I got things to do today."

But what are the odds she'd also bring Donna, present-day Thirty Years' War scholar who so diligently supported her cousin the Freiherr's Lutheran policies four hundred years ago in Oberholt?

"I'm driving."

Donna's driven before. Last time she drove me too near the Nile and we got eaten by crocodiles.

"Let's get a cab." Not that I expect crocodiles in South Philly. Not in the middle of the day.

"Don't be ridiculous." Donna bends to tie my sneaker for me. "How do you feel?"

"Doc gave me painkillers." I rattle the bottle, then toss it into my purse so Keychain Mary will have something other than Her corkscrew to keep Her warm. My cell *tra-la-las*.

"Dr. Panisporchi? Maurizio Bracaconi here." A dry cough punctuates his words. "I say we go after the funeral director, also. A preemptive strike for placing those traffic cones."

"Just get me enough to cover the scar," I tell him, pointing to the bandage above my eye so Angela and Donna will know what I mean. *And a little for butt lipo would be nice.*

"Sure. Yeah. I can do that for you. But best leave your options open at this stage."

Donna gathers my things, checking the closet and drawers. Silver ear dangles tinkle as she moves, like tiny bells. "I'll bet Mr. Olivieri would pay for laser for the scar if you asked," she says after I hang up. "See if he'll cover the cost of a consult. I know a good plastic surgeon."

I knew that nose couldn't be her own.

Angela points to the night table. "Look at those flowers. Wow. Stanley must really like you."

"Flowers?" I follow her finger. A spray of roses in a squat bas-ketweave vase stand beside the remains of my breakfast tray. Maybe I got more to worry about with that head knock than the possibility of a scar. "I didn't notice these. They're not mine."

Angela checks the tag. "You sure? They got your name on 'em."

Donna caresses a bloom. "White and red. To make a garland for your head."

From *The Knight's Tale*, an observation made by Palamon, the first of the star-crossed cousins, upon seeing Emily, object of their feuding desire, for the first time, gathering flowers. No way this bouquet came from Stanley. They came from—

Angela holds up the card. "Who's Frederick Palmer?"

"Friedrich," I correct before I think better of it. Palmon.

Angela raises a brow. "And who is *Free-Der-Itch*?"

ICK, not ITCH, you dimwit. I snatch the card from her and dump the flowers. "He's the son of the lady I shared the room with last night, dork. These must be meant for her."

Angela snatches the card back and reads. "'Glad to hear you're still alive.'" Her voice rises at the end of the statement, turning it into a question. "'Let's talk?'"

"They're not close."

Angela makes a big show of dragging the flowers out of the trash. "How about you and me take these out to the nurse's station and find out where *Free-Der-Itch*'s mom is so we can get these back to her."

I shove the flowers back in, grab my pocketbook, and plop myself into the required wheelchair. "Too late. She died. Let's go."

Angela shrugs into her coat. "Fine. But Stanley's name is easier to pronounce."

"Where's Luigi?"

"Emergency call. Sewer backup at the homeless shelter in St. Mary's. Luigi does their work for free."

Donna takes the back of the wheelchair. "Luigi organized contractors from the diocese. They take care of all their maintenance."

The whole way down the hall and into the elevator I try to picture Der Weasel cleaning out Catholic sewers before he dragged the actual Catholics before the Freiherr. The whole way down the elevator and into the lobby to wait for the car, I try to work out his angle. Cause a guy like Der Weasel *always* has an angle. "Does the diocese give Luigi referrals?"

The hospital parking valet pulls up in a vintage sports car the color of Donna's cocktail wear. "That's a Miata."

"Yeah." Angela hands the valet a tip. "Isn't it great?"

"Where am I supposed to sit?"

"In the passenger seat." Angela opens the door. She waits.

"Then where're you going to sit?" A Miata has no backseat.

"Where do you think, stupid?"

My backside alone could fill this car, but Angela piles us in, damned near collapsing my lung to pull the seatbelt tight. Donna maneuvers the manual transmission into reverse, then into drive, whipping around the car ahead. She hairpins the turn onto Wolf Street and weaves us home, dodging ice mounds and trash piles. All the while, Angela babbles about how well the Miata handles until Donna pulls into a space directly in front of our house.

A dug out, empty parking space.

A miracle.

The porcelain Blessed Virgin Mary on Our Windowsill gives me a wink.

Donna opens the tiny compartment that passes for the Miata's trunk and removes a bakery box. Angela pulls my bag of belongings from beneath my feet. "Ma's not home. Mr. Olivieri took her to get groceries. Amazing he's even talking to us with the way Joey hollered at him."

"Joey hollered at Mr. Olivieri?"

"Hollered at everybody. Mr. Olivieri. The newsstand guy. The funeral director. Even snapped at me and Ma when we hollered at him for getting into a fight in the first place. About the only people he didn't holler at were poor dead Mrs. Rossi and Luigi."

Joey. Making nice with Der Weasel.

Impossible.

Donna tucks the bakery box under her arm. "If you *think* about it, Joey's actions make sense."

I mean to ask Donna what she means, why *I* should have to think about *anything*, but she zips up the front stoop to let me into the vestibule, then through the inner door and into the living room. "Hello, Stanley."

He's there, right beside Blessed Virgin Mary on the Windowsill, not quite at attention, but not quite at ease, either. "Your mother said it would be all right if I waited. If you're not up for a visit, I can go."

Sweatshirt and yoga pants are not my best look. "Uh . . ."

"Don't be ridiculous, Stanley." Angela shoves past me, near knocking me over. "Eugenia's feeling fine. Aren't you Eugenia?"

My hair has been left to its own devices for a full twenty-four hours. "Well, I . . ."

"See what I mean? Here, Stanley, sit. Smells like Ma already got the coffee going." Angela near knocks me over again, grabs the bakery box from Donna, and heads for the kitchen.

"Cannoli." Donna points to the kitchen door, swinging on its pins. "Plain and chocolate chip."

Angela bustles back through the door in an impossibly short time, coffee arranged on a tray, cannoli arranged on a plate. She grabs her scarf. "Have a nice visit. Gotta go. Meeting Luigi."

Donna pulls on her gloves. "Me, too. Papers. End of semester."

Before I have time to hang up my coat, they're gone.

Soooooo . . .

Stanley perches on the edge of the plastic slipcover. "Last night, after I stopped by the hospital, I got to thinking we got off to a bad start."

Sudden tears sting the inside of my nose. Gray rolls in and hindsight rolls me back. Four hundred years. Conjured by the shadow of Stanley's Oberholt self.

I clutch at the jamb, now framing the entrance to my family's print shop, which I'd just opened to a certain Lutheran soldier. A soldier who also happened to be the Freiherr's cousin. A soldier who steadied a very drunk and very surly Josef under his arm. "I could put him in irons, but the jail is overflowing and doing so would get you and me off to a bad start."

To see him again. Hale. Healthy. His whole life in front of him . . .

I grope for a place on the couch.

The gray rolls out. Ma's living room returns. Along with the scent of coffee.

I pour him a cup, throat taut, expectations stretched on tenterhooks. And go in for the windup. "Start?"

Stanley cinches the bat. He hits it dead-on. "I'd like to try again, go out on a real date with you."

But the ball grounds in the infield. I fumble it, my time to answer Stanley too long. He holds at first base. "I shouldn't have stopped by like this. It's obvious you're tired. Think about it. I really dropped by to give you this."

He reaches into his jacket pocket and withdraws a parcel wrapped in brown paper and twine. He hands it to me and waits while I unwrap it—a book, an antique—pocket-sized, bound in finely grained leather, binding hand-sewn, parchment hand-cut, printing engraved. In my Oberholt life, a commission like this would have put food on our table for months.

Stanley grows taller, his shoulders broader. His jawline goes more square and the smile lines at the corners of his eyes soften.

Hope rises, a balloon on a breeze—

It's him. It's him. It's really him. My Lutheran soldier. Returned.

—punctured by Truth's thorny tyranny.

Stanley was him. Once. He's not him, now.

I return my attention to the book and examine the spine, pushing back nostalgia for a life I'd mostly wanted to escape.

"*Totable Quotes and Pithy Proverbs.*" I flip to the frontispiece. "'Words are, of course, the most powerful drug used by mankind.'"

That's Rudyard. "'Edited by T. N. Mann.'"

The dedication is handwritten, in a neat, precise script. "'For D.— Man's wisdom is an Angel's folly, but it will do for a while.'"

Stanley's hands, strong and capable and uncallused, cover mine. He closes the book. "I picked it up in a secondhand shop."

Propriety tells me it's too much, I shouldn't accept it, but for once, my brain puts the brakes on my mouth. "Thank you. It's beautiful."

"It seemed right for you." Stanley laughs, the sound relaxed and rich. "Easy for me to say now I know you like it. You know what people say about hindsight."

10

People say hindsight is twenty-twenty.

Everybody. Google, Bing, Yahoo, as well as the half dozen smaller search engines I check.

Just like they've been saying since search engines were invented. Just like every encyclopedia and dictionary I checked before search engines.

I check *Totable Quotes and Pithy Proverbs*. There it is, page 32.

Wikipedia gives it a bias, defines hindsight as an inclination to see events that have already occurred as predictable, quantifiable, a well of experience upon which I should be able to draw, keeping my sex protected, my dairy pasteurized, and my deodorant aluminum-free. Yet, mere days after Angela and Donna drive me home from the hospital, I reach for my Vicodin and take Ma's digitalis instead, with the result I spend Christmas Eve in the cardiac unit, watching Stanley eat his way through a GladWare-enclosed sampling of each and every one of Ma's seven holiday fishes.

Ten days later, just after New Year's, I catch an early bus and arrive home to find neighbors gathered in groups. Ma, Angela, and Carlotta waiting on our stoop.

And Joey.

Hollering into his cell, "Panisporchi. P-A-N-I-S-P-O-R-C-H-I. Whaddya mean, first name? How many Panisporchis you got on your list?"

He looks up and sees me. Color rushes across his cheeks. "Why the *hell* didn't you answer your cell?"

Um. Dead battery?

Ma and Angela jabber about how some nutcase with an assault rifle opened fire on my usual bus. Ma twists her rosary. "We thought you were dead."

Joey draws me away from her. He hugs me close. So close the collar of his ski jacket scratches at my cheek, the movement familiar.

And . . . threatening.

"What happens to you affects me." He digs fingers into my shoulder. "Remember that. Be careful."

He lets me go, puts an arm around Carlotta, and kisses her, completely and fully and like he's not so sure he'll ever see her again. He takes her hand, waves goodbye to Ma, and heads home.

Two days later, a car runs a red light and misses me. The next, a rabid pit bull is caught two minutes before I walk by. A day after, a piano being lifted to a second-story window swings clear of its cable and crashes to the sidewalk in front of me.

I. Should. Be. Dead.

The kind of dead that gets you a closed casket because even the best mortician can't do anything about flat.

"It's never that simple," Stanley says the following Saturday evening while we eat dinner at Joey and Carlotta's house. "Actuarial science can only account for the big movements, the macro possibilities. It can't quantify individual choice, what we call free will. Nothing can."

Joey thanks Carlotta for the coffee, but waves off the cannoli, sliding it onto Carlotta's plate to join hers. She digs in, any concern for calories lost in the volume of her newly adapted Boho layers.

He returns his attention to Stanley, his resemblance to my cousin in Oberholt obvious in the tilt of his chin. "You saying Eugenia's got control over what's been happening?"

"Not control, but she can minimize her risk. Read the label. Avoid ice patches." Stanley winks at me. "Watch where she steps when she backs away from a fight."

Joey leans forward, gaze flicking left, then right, like he's watching where *he* steps. "Give me an example."

Stanley mirrors his motion, except he leans backward and gazes to the ceiling. "Say you do something bad. I dunno. You . . . betray somebody for compensation. I can be pretty sure you'll do it again."

"There may have been extenuating circumstances." Joey's jaw goes tight, and his voice accountant cool.

"My point is, once you exhibit a behavior, you're likely to repeat it. At each juncture, however, despite the macro possibility, you might do something different. The choice remains yours."

A tiny itch, just a niggle, pricks at me. I should step in, turn a conversation that feels uncomfortably close, to other matters, but Joey full-steams ahead.

"And what if I didn't betray anybody? What if it was a mistake and I was falsely accused?" He turns to me, fist clenched around his cup. "Statistics based on an incorrect premise is only numbers."

Something deep down wants to answer Joey's accusation, for accusation is how it feels. I even part my lips, thinking my response is required. Stanley squeezes my hand and makes the same sideways swipe I noted in the *trattoria*, curtailing the impulse in a way that feels pungent and present, as if we are both back when it happened at first. Then together when it happened again. And will be when it happens in the future.

I squeeze his hand back, heart buoyant, because the possibility feels hopeful and I don't remember when last I felt that way.

"The formulas account for a certain amount of uncertainty." Stanley reaches for the sugar, his tone too sour for a conversation about mathematics. "But you are correct at the fundamental level. Without facts, hindsight is little more than conjecture."

●●●

Later, in the kitchen, Carlotta wipes down the granite countertop. "So, you like Stanley."

I finish loading the dishwasher. "You got a china setting on this thing?"

Carlotta reaches a freshly done French tip to the machine's keypad, then pulls creamer from the stainless steel refrigerator and sweetener from a Euro-style cabinet. She nudges both across the butcher block table. "Sit. Have coffee. I'll get the pots. You must still be achy from your accident."

Achy. I'll say. My hip feels attached to my leg with barbed wire. But no way I sit until Carlotta does. "I'm good. I'll dry."

Carlotta dons a pair of yellow gloves. "Did you and Stanley do anything special for New Year's Eve?"

"He brought takeout and rented us a movie. Said he doesn't like crowds."

"Because he doesn't hear so well." Carlotta takes her time scrubbing the first pot. She takes even longer rinsing it. She points to her temple, to the spot where Stanley's skin puckers. "It's only the one ear. He hurt himself in grad school. Spent a little time in the hospital."

Long enough to delay his Master's, or so I might infer.

"Wrong place, wrong time kind of thing. All Stanley says is he ducked left when he should've ducked right. Cops didn't do much about it." Carlotta brushes a wisp off her forehead. "Your mother wants me to get you to invite him for dinner."

Whoa. Sucker-punch out of the corner.

Carlotta doesn't mean dinner like we just ate, she means *Dinner*. *The* dinner. The required Dinner with the Panisporchis meant to signal everybody Stanley and I are serious. "My mother also wants Frank Sinatra to do a comeback tour."

Carlotta cocks her head. "He's dead."

Yes, Carlotta. I was employing a rhetorical strategy called sarcasm. Stating the impossible to illustrate the impossibility of a different situation. Ergo, no way I'm inviting Stanley for dinner at our house and if I were, no way I'd cozy up to you to talk about it. "Which means it won't happen."

"Listen, Eugenia. Alls I'm sayin' is things don't start working out, your mother's gonna send you for the Overlooks."

The Overlooks. What you gotta do when you don't know what gots to be done. "That's ridiculous."

"She thinks somebody cursed you. Keeps asking if you got along with everybody at the wedding." Carlotta cocks her head the other way. "I don't get it. Stanley's a nice guy."

"Yep, real nice." I hold up the tray of K-cups. "Let's see if the guys want more coffee."

"No."

"Wine, then."

"No."

"All right. Beer." I go for the refrigerator.

Carlotta gets there first. She squares off and plants her hands to her hips so hard, I half expect them to disconnect from her torso. "Why don't you like me?"

"I like you fine."

"But all through dinner. Every time I talked about something. You changed the subject."

"I didn't want to talk about Tajikistan."

"I mean *every* time."

"Or the weather."

"We had such a nice day at the mall. Now when I call, it always goes to voice mail."

Gotta love those filtering apps.

Carlotta takes her hands off her hips and holds them out to me, palms up. If she draped a dishrag over her head, she'd be Blessed Mary on Ma's Living Room Windowsill. With twice the humility. "Have I offended you in some way?"

Every hackle I ever had raises its pointy little head, popping like cold oil on a hot pan.

Of course you haven't offended me, Carlotta. Not in any way. It's not like you stole my fiancé, setting myself and my cousin, who is now my brother and your husband, on a path that spiraled into disaster.

Not recently.

So let me sit in your brand-new Ikea kitchen and compliment your brand-new loose-waisted threads, no doubt purchased to make room for that brand-new baby making you expand like Styrofoam in a spray can. How silly of me to hold animosity over actions you can't remember. Let's drink coffee. Something flavored and rich and made one cup at a time in your Keurig. I'll try not to feel jealous as shit because, despite our past, you've managed to avoid hindsight and are free to paint every room in your house any color you want because you don't worry hindsight is genetic. Something you might pass to that baby. Or contagious. A karmic virus that can spread misery to those around you simply by letting yourself get too close.

"It's your condition, isn't it?" Carlotta suddenly goes soft, a gentle smile accentuating her abnormally attractive dimples. She places a sympathetic hand on my shoulder, gives it a squeeze. "Joey told me your medication sometimes messes with your mood."

••

When Stanley picked me up tonight, he called me Euphonia, a kind of bird with a melodious song. Over dinner, I was Eulogia, a blessing in the Greek Orthodox church. Now, as he drives me home, I'm Euphemisma. Mispronunciations I'm pretty sure he means in a playful way. Because I lied about how everybody calls me Jenny.

He winds a hand around mine. "What was all that yelling with Carlotta tonight?"

"I saw a cockroach."

"And the banging?"

"Caught it."

"Oh."

I thump the dashboard. "Okay. It's about my dad. He got hit by a bus while walking me and Joey to church. It happened a week before Joey's birthday. Which is today."

"Oh jeez." Stanley lets go of my hand and smacks his forehead. "And there I was going on about your recent near misses and minimizing risk."

"See, every year Ma makes us commemorate Dad's death in some way. Usually we go to mass, but this year Dad's dead twenty-five years." My voice squeezes past a stockpile of resentment. "An entire quarter century. Quite an accomplishment. Ma planned something special."

"Eustacia—"

"We had to go to the cemetery. We brought a picnic lunch."

"In this weather, wow, I'll bet—"

"We brought toothbrushes and Lysol to scrub his headstone. She had us planting crocuses."

"That must've been—"

"We had to bring that Blessed Virgin Mary statue from our backyard. The one surrounded by all the flowerpots."

"The big stone thing?"

"It's tall as me, fer chrissakes. Ma made Joey wrestle Her into his mustang. He had to use a dolly."

"His mustang. How? I mean Her head . . ."

"Through the moon roof."

"Moon roof."

"To the cemetery. And back."

Stanley's mouth works, pulling this way, then that. He tugs at its corners, smoothing down a smile that won't stay secret.

He doesn't know. Doesn't understand. Can't possibly fathom the pressure, the stress, of having every action recorded, every thought judged, every attitude condemned.

He's not one in three hundred.

Or three thousand.

Blessed Mary hounds me. Life to life. My personal albatross. Arbiter of my behavior.

She hangs out on my keychain. Decorates my bookmarks. Provides the cover art for my credit card. She even influenced Ma to appliqué Herself across the tops of my favorite-est pair of fuzzy slippers.

It's not enough. Nothing's ever enough.

Blessed Mary makes damned sure I know it. She set up Her biggest embodiment where I can't fail to see Her every time I take out the trash. I'm talking the mother of all Blessed Mothers. A behemoth unbowed by snow or rain or sleet or gloom of night. So brawny, so beefy, so forbidding, even birds fear flapping past, lest they acciden-tally shit on Her cement awesomeness.

Blessed Bad-Ass Backyard Mary.

My ever-present, four-foot-ten-inch-tall reminder of my fall from grace.

And *that's* the Mary Ma insisted we bring. "Ma wanted a family portrait. She brought Dad's picture with her, duct-taped it to Blessed Mary's fingers. We had to stand in a group around the headstone, Mary in the middle, and try to look natural while my cousin snapped photos."

"And Carlotta brought it up tonight. She wanted to talk about it. That's why you got upset with her."

"She uploaded the photo to Facebook." I pull out my smartphone, punch up my account, and show Stanley the evidence, thrusting the phone in front of the steering wheel so he has to look. "She didn't just post it. She *tagged* me."

Laughter cannonballs from Stanley's chest. He drapes over the steering wheel and shakes so hard the car does a little shimmy all the way to our stoop.

I push open the car door and charge up the steps.

Stanley charges after me. "I'm so sorry. That was inexcusable."

I search through my bag for Keychain Mary so I can get into the house. She's there. I know She's there. I hear Her rattling at the bottom.

"Eugenia. Listen. Please."

I stop searching.

He said my name. My actual name.

Something fluttery breezes across my cheek, bringing with it the scent of leather and citrus, and other words—their consonants abrupt, the vowels cut short, but the voice sweet. *Please. Listen to me.*

A horn taps.

Our street is narrow, a single lane with cars parked on either side and somebody's pulled up behind Stanley.

Stanley waves at the guy to let him know he'll be right there, then goes for my hand. "I think you're overreacting."

I shake him off and go back to searching for the keys.

"I'm not trying to insult you. Let me explain."

The horn taps again.

"You see, I—"

And the horn taps a third time. The driver lowers the passenger side window. "Yo. Romeo. Let's go."

Stanley whips around. "Back it up, Shakespeare. We're having a conversation here."

Not Philadelphia Stanley. Oberholt Stanley.

Confident, commanding. And unaccustomed to being ignored.

I guess Shakespeare thinks so too. He rolls up his window and reverses his car, Stanley keeping an eye on him until Shakespeare disappears down a side street. "I almost ended up in anthropology. Wanted to find out why people act the way they do, how culture and circumstance define them—"

Anthropology. In some big archeological complex like what I read about in the *National Geographic*, the one in the middle of Tajikistan. Me and him, the stars and all that space . . .

"—but I get a pretty good feel for how people behave through statistics."

He takes my hand. My breath takes a hitch. He runs a finger along my cheek, expression serious. "Carlotta sees today's events as a loving gesture. You see it as an embarrassment. Maybe it's a glass half-full, half-empty kind of thing, but take from a situation what you want. Go for the good and good will come to you. But if you want bad . . ."

The vision crumbles. Stanley can't know what I want. I take my hand back.

He jams his in his pockets, like his Oberholt version used to when he got annoyed. "There's another part to my theory. About how you react to whatever you take. That's also in your control and makes whatever results from those decisions your choice."

Exasperation, sharp-edged and swift, takes the express bus up my spine and straight out the top of my head. I shake my phone in his face, angling it so Stanley can see what I'm doing.

I pull up Facebook.

And unfriend Carlotta.

‖

"Bless me Father for I have sinned." It has been four hundred years since my last confession.

Anthropology. I envision Stanley penning his great contribution to the field, *Coming of Age in South Philadelphia: Saints and Sambuca, Pasta and Prayers.*

"I'm not patient enough with people, Father." And I have a real issue with my sister's boyfriend. He's a killer. A cad. Who once made his living dragging people like my cousin before the Freiherr, so he and the Freiherr could split their fines. "I sometimes don't, um, you know, give people the benefit of the doubt. I presume the worst instead of the best."

"Only God may judge a person." Father DiLullo's voice is soft and sonorous and soothing behind his thin mesh. Mesh there to provide anonymity. Anonymity meant to loosen our tongues, bare our souls, strip our defenses.

He knows we know he knows who each and every one of us is. When he gives his homily on Sundays, we pretend not to think about all the secrets and sins poured into his ear the night before, pretend he's not wondering how people so ordinary can harbor so much iniquity.

He assigns me a full rosary for penance.

Hail Mary. Hail Mary. Hail Mary.

On the windowsill. On the dressing table. Even scary Mary in the backyard. As it was in the beginning, is now, and ever shall be.

Words meant to comfort, to assure, except they don't. My now is never what I want.

And what is that?

I glance to Mary Over the Baptismal Font, uncertain how to answer.

Then how do you know you don't already have it?

I stop worrying at the little beads mid-Hail and give Mary's question time to settle, thinking about Stanley, wondering what a life with him would be like.

We'd have a house. Nothing fancy. Just a place all our own.

And children. Energetic little bundles. Sticky fingers marking *my* walls, footsteps racing across *my* kitchen, hammering up *my* steps. Stanley coming home at the end of his day, key in the lock, arms opened wide, to gather us close.

Hand over my belly, I imagine it taut with new life, spirits lifting.

The vision dissipates. It disappears into the hopeless place which houses my heart, forgotten amid floorboards marred by past mistakes, hallways littered in lost opportunities. A place of silence. Of desperation. Of despair.

My cell buzzes. I click it over. It buzzes again.

Dammit. "What?" It's rude. I don't care.

"Dr. Panisporchi? Maurizio Bracaconi here. I just heard from Dr. Rossi's lawyer. The casket that got knocked from the hearse. He's suing."

Butt lipo or not, this guy's more irritating than a boil under my bra band. "Can we talk about this later? Tomorrow maybe. Or the day after. I'm in church."

"In church." His tone takes on an edge.

My stomach lurches. I can almost see a disbelieving knuckle rub along the hollow of his cheek. Familiar and . . . fleeting. "Yes, Mr. Bracaconi. Church."

"Good. Great. Been meaning to go myself. Tellya what. Do us both a favor while you're there. Pray for a miracle."

"Miracle?"

"You don't understand, Dr. Panisporchi. Dr. Rossi is suing you."

Joey drags me past our portico and onto the stoop. He pulls the door shut behind, cutting off its persistent squeak and rattles a manila envelope in my face. "You can't be sued. You're the pedestrian."

Mental note: have Maurizio mail everything to my work.

"You shoulda thought about that before going to the mat over a couple of *National Geographics*." I point to the door, on the other side of which, the family's already imbibing multiple fingers of Aunt Gracie's Special Blend. "Happy fucking birthday. I have to help Ma serve."

Joey pulls the complaint from the packet. He flips the pages, gaze flicking back and forth. "Jaywalking. Failure to obey traffic cones. Pain and suffering. What is this shit?"

I grab the packet back. "Whatever this shit is, it's my shit."

"Give it a few weeks, it'll be everybody's shit." He digs out his cell phone. "We're calling Constantine."

Carlotta's cousin. The one with the Greek mother. I grab Joey's cell away. "Maurizio's getting it out of my suit against the funeral director."

"You flipped over the florist's van. How can you sue the funeral director?"

"The back of the hearse wasn't locked."

Joey grabs the cell back. "You're getting a real lawyer. This is the newsstand guy's fault. Bracaconi should be going after him."

Memory of my failed attempt to send Luigi under the van's wheel rises along with Ma's mashed olives on toast. "Maurizio tells me the newsstand guy's not insured."

"He's plenty insured. He's also a fruitcake. Bracaconi doesn't want trouble going after a mental deficient. He cares too much about his cut."

Honest to Godiva, if I weren't here, standing on the sidewalk, one foot on our stoop's bottom step and looking straight at Joey to see his mouth move, I'd have gotten whiplash.

Because Joey's last sentence doesn't exit Joey. It exits behind me.

Way behind me. Four centuries behind me. And in my cousin Josef's much deeper and Bavarian-inflected voice.

Joey dials and puts the phone to his ear. "You're paying contingency, right? Trust me, before this is finished the numbers will rival the national debt." He checks the faceplate. "No signal." And puts out a hand. "Give me your cell."

Idiot. I push past him, and into the house, Joey close on my heels—

—to find gray rolling in and Dr. Donna transformed to her fräulein self, cousin to the Freiherr from Oberholt, panniers bobbing, Bavarian bodice straining against its laces, and ear dangles jingling. Beside her stands her brother, a smiling young man uniformed in tailored serge.

Stanley. In Oberholt. I mean the Lutheran Stanley who was a lieutenant in the city militia. Starched and stalwart and so very, very sincere.

He heads to the kitchen. I put a hand to my chest, certain my heart will follow.

Fräulein Donna spots us. She holds out one of Friedrich's plastic containers. "Pfeffernüsse?"

Joey waves it off, looking perfectly natural in lederhosen. "Can I borrow your cell?"

"Sorry. Dead battery. There's the kitchen phone." Donna points, like we wouldn't know the way to our own kitchen.

I'm halfway there already, following the scent of citrus and boot polish that always accompanied my Lutheran soldier, but the gray rolls out by the time I swing through the door, taking my memories, and Joey's lederhosen, with it.

Stanley checks his cell, drawing it from a pocket where I know he once kept his flask. He shows it to Joey. "No bars."

Joey goes for the wall phone, a sunflower yellow corded antique Ma Bell original with a rotary dial and a handset heavy enough to be used as a weapon. He toggles the cradle, like they do in old movies when they're trying to get a connection, and holds out the handset, so Stanley and I can hear the *shush* of a dead line. Joey hangs up and runs the gamut.

Cousins. Uncles. In-laws. Aunts.

Finally throwing his hands in the air. "Jesus, Mary, and Joseph. How pure of heart and humble of spirit do you have to be to get a signal around here?"

Luigi gives Joey his cell. "It's already ringing. I got Constantine on speed-dial."

Joey checks the faceplate. He puts the cell to his ear.

No. Way.

I squint, looking for a patch of gray, but the light around Luigi is clear and colorful enough to grow unicorns. I turn my attention back to Joey. "It's Saturday night. Nobody's going to be in the off—"

"Constantine? This is Joe Panisporchi—"

Ma interrupts. "Did you find the photo albums?"

Angela points to a box sitting by the entrance, one filled with Joey's crap I mean to hand him before he goes home tonight. "Sorry, Ma. Me and Eugenia turned the closet inside out. Found all kinds of stuff. But not the photo albums."

She kicks at the box. A cardboard corner splits. A baseball, scuff-marked and scroungy, rolls clear.

Donna scoops it up and examines it. "Tug McGraw? Is this signature real?" She hands Joey the ball.

". . . over the hearse." Joey listens. "Yeah, I'll hold." He taps the mute button, and flips the ball back into the box. "Yep."

Luigi grabs it back out. He looses a low whistle. "May, 1980. You're shitting me."

Angela looks over his shoulder. "1980?"

"The year the Phillies won the World Series, babe. Old Tug here saved the day, knocked out Willie Wilson in the final inning of the final game. This ball is from early in that season." Luigi swipes at it with a reverent sleeve. He turns to Joey. "How'd you get it?"

"My father got it. Ball Day or some such." Joey taps a button again. "Yeah, Constantine. I'm here. Sorry." He listens again. "Okay. Sounds great. See you then." Joey gives back Luigi's phone. He reaches for the ball, but Stanley takes it.

"You should get this appraised. Probably worth a bundle, except for this." Stanley indicates a shallow slash through the ballplayer's last name. "How'd that happen?"

Joey clams up tighter than a congressman under indictment. He shoots Luigi a look straight out of left field.

"Long story." Joey reclaims the ball. "Where's the *scalloppine*? I'm starved."

●●●

At the cheese and salad course, Joey drops his gnocchi. "You're seeing Constantine on Thursday morning."

"*You're* seeing Constantine."

"We both are."

Carlotta's mother looks pleased, like our number came out. "Tell him we say hello. We never see him, poor boy works so hard."

"But he's the best." Carlotta's father half closes his eyes and dips his head, an Italian gesture meaning everything from "Don't worry, I'll take care of it" to "Is this table all right or do you want the one by the window?"

Joey whips a notepad and pen from his pocket. He scribbles something, then stuffs the paper into my purse. "Address and phone number. We're seeing him at eight o'clock. I'll pick you up."

"Constantine's office is near mine." Stanley puts down his fork. "I can duck out, give you a lift to work when you're finished."

Ma looks happy. She stands. "That's settled. Anybody for cake?"

In a minute. "I already got a lawyer."

The ladies pause at half-mast, their intent to clear dinner and distribute dessert forestalled by my declaration.

Joey gets them moving again. "Constantine's a better lawyer. Besides, he's family."

Carlotta takes Joey's plate. Angela takes Luigi's. Carlotta's mother gets Carlotta's father's.

Stanley's remains unclaimed.

Presumably left for me.

The clatter of dishes quiets. All wait, staring at Stanley's solitary plate until Stanley carries it to the sink himself. "I'll be here at seven-thirty on Thursday. If Eugenia wants to see Constantine, I'll take her. If she doesn't, I'll take her to breakfast instead."

Stanley suddenly shines. Every inch Chaucer's Very Gentle Perfect Knight.

Oberholt Schmeberholt. The present ain't looking so bad. The future, unknown. A tongue can be courteous and still taste desire. And a heart armored against a dead past is no less brave for taking the chance to beat.

Maybe, soon as I get Stanley alone, I'll go full metal modern and invite him to run a recon under my flak jacket.

Except my will disappears into a sudden fog that used to be Ma's kitchen and all I see is the cake, bright with candles, Carlotta puts in front of Joey.

Her cake.

Not the Italian Rum Ma ordered special. The cake she stipulated should be baked with an extra generous portion of Bacardi Light and an extra grating of fresh lemon zest under the top layer of cream. The cake occupying its own shelf in the fridge, prettily arranged on Nonna's special cut-crystal stand she brought all the way from Italy. Ma's cake. A centerpiece of true maternal love since Ma can't even eat the thing. She made a promise to God long ago and won't touch alcohol. Not *that* cake but this, this—

"Red Velvet." Carlotta turns it so garish green writing declaring *Happy Birthday, Joey!* faces him. "I got it at Costco."

Angela lights a cigarette. She nudges me. "This should be interesting."

I argued with Joey over Constantine. Forcing Ma to stay at the table and ensure I didn't blow a chance to get a ride with Stanley. Which let Carlotta get to the refrigerator first.

Carlotta's gained the cake supremacy.

And it's my fault.

Angela blows a plume of smoke to the heavens. The tendrils descend to cover me in feather clumps of accusation.

I clap a hand over my mouth.

South Philly row home ceilings are tall, their stairs steep, their hallways narrow.

Donna follows me into the bathroom. She puts a cool cloth on the back of my neck, makes soothing sounds until the worst is over, then helps me to my bed. "A head knock can haunt you for a long time after." She tucks the quilt around me. "Learn from this. Hindsight is always twenty-twenty."

12

In Chaucer's *Knight's Tale*, Emily, desired by a duo of imprisoned cousins, discovers her brother-in-law plans to let the cousins duel for her. Emily doesn't want to marry. Especially not a crazy she has no idea what he even looks like. So she runs to her Blessed Mary, the goddess Diana, begging to become the ancient Grecian version of a nun.

Diana didn't listen.

And neither does Ma, boiling water in the kitchen, the morning after Joey's party. "You're not pregnant, are you?"

Tajikistan looks better every day. *Maybe a cloister.*

Ma plops a poached egg in front of me. She plops a cup of tea beside. "'Cause if you are, there's plenty of time to get the banns posted and the church scheduled before Lent."

A cloister in a remote mountain village accessible only by yak.

Ma gives my shoulder a squeeze. "Maybe you should see Dr. Frangipane. Get yourself checked out."

And only in summer.

Angela pulls a cigarette from her pack. "They got home tests for that now, Ma."

"I'm not pregnant." Yet, my hand goes to my belly. A little flutter. A rush of activity. A dress, a tux. Tiny lace hats. Knit booties.

And a name. Something pretty. Luminous. Like fireflies.

Ma pushes the Blessed Mother Coffee Creamer she uses to hold the Splenda packets toward me. "Well maybe take the test. Just to be sure."

Angela laughs in a cloud of smoke. Ma smacks her on the shoulder, then flicks the cigarette into the sink. She dumps a spent bucket of cleaner after. Pine steam rises. Incense in this tiny house that is our cathedral, Ma's denunciation of its dirt, her supplication.

"Pine-Sol's no good against bad juju, Ma." Angela reaches behind Refrigerator Mary and shows us a bottle. "Aunt Gracie's Special Blend works better."

Ma crosses herself. "Where'd you get that?"

"In the closet. Behind a collection of Joey's jockstraps."

"Put it back. No wonder you can't find the photo albums."

"Ma. Aunt Gracie's Special Blend's got nothing to do with the photo albums."

Ma snatches the bottle. "Fine. I'll do it."

Angela snatches it back and heads into the living room. The door swings hard behind.

Ma puts a hand to my forehead. Her palm feels smooth and cool and smells like Christmas. "No fever. So what's this about? And why are you cutting up the *National Geographics*?"

They're for my next-life scrapbook. A private old-timey Pinterest where I paste pictures of my heart's desires.

"I don't understand." Ma shakes her head. "You're young . . ."

Ma hasn't yet noticed the brand-new wrinkle forming at the corner of my left eye.

"You're pretty . . ."

Probably because she needs her prescription checked.

"You hole up in that college all day long."

"Ma." I slap the table. "That's my job. I get paid by the class and I gotta be there for everything that goes with that class, like office hours and staff meetings, or I'll be looking for a new one. Not a lot of demand out there for readers of Chaucer."

"Well, it'd be enough to drive anybody nuts. Maybe you should go on a cruise."

First I'm pregnant, now, I should go on a cruise. The *National Geographic* at my elbow followed me to the hospital, then home in

Donna's Miata. The young women on the cover look peaceful. And happy. Their glowing complexions hint at lives lived with purpose. Lives given due respect. Lives they take the time to savor. To relish. Now.

Something to think about in a life punctuated by all the breathless people around me charging into the future.

For what?

That thought bears me down.

Sleep. Wake. Dress. Work.

Ma hands me a napkin. "Eat."

Poached eggs smell. Metallic. A little chalky. And the taste. The white firm, then yielding. And the yolk. Ooooh, the yolk. Creamy, rich.

The air lightens. I draw in a bucketful, then take a long, slow sip of tea, allowing the steam to waft, just like the Pine-Sol, conjuring images of quiet Sundays and good books and all the time necessary to enjoy both.

Ma fills the sink. A glob of liquid amber shimmers in sunlight angling through the newly washed window before the soap clears the squeeze tip to undulate into the water. Suds ascend in a happy froth.

We don't have a dishwasher. Ma says they don't get the dishes clean enough. Ma shops for groceries every day, too. She likes things fresh. Watching the breakfast plates line up in formation on the drainer, the cold, hard needle of reality deflates my content.

Ma doesn't wash dishes by hand and go to the market every day to savor the moments. She does it to fill them.

I tell Stanley about it later when he arrives to commiserate with cappuccino and biscotti.

"Her husband's dead and children grown." I give the biscotti a dunk. "Most of her friends have moved to the suburbs. Her days must be getting kinda long. Y'know, lonely."

"She never wanted to remarry?"

The question stops me mid-dunk. "To somebody else?"

Stanley smiles, his eyes going crinkly in a way I lately look forward to. "My mother was the same way when my father died. Old-school

Italian. Made her commitment, stuck to it. Don't see a lot of that these days."

My back stiffens. With a male voice behind it, the notion seems presumptuous, condescending.

How come it's okay for me to think it, but not him? "Is she still like that?"

Stanley bobs his head this way, then that, the way men do when they're not sure how to put something. "She passed. Two weeks after I got my master's. I have a brother, but he moved to Florida years ago. We talk on the phone sometimes."

My cell *tra-las*. Maurizio Bracaconi.

I turn him off. The ringtone seems disrespectful to Stanley's dead mother. My biscotti dissolves, dropping in a clump to my napkin. Stanley hands me a fresh one from the holder on the table and dips a fresh biscotti into his own coffee. He offers it to me. Almond scent rises between us.

Unchained Melody plays, the newer version the Righteous Brothers made so popular back in the sixties. Not in my head. Pouring out of the radio Ma keeps on the radiator. Stanley stands, hand extended. "Shall we?"

We shall. Properly. Right palm in his left, the other on his shoulder, our bodies an elbow length apart, working our way through what used to be called a Supper Club Two-Step, surprised he even knows it in an age when dancing is little more than gyrating in place at cattle-car closeness, and even more surprised I remember it at all.

Stanley glissandos me around the kitchen table and past the counters. Surprise turns to delight.

He moves us from point to point in Ma's tiny kitchen, our progress effortless. I wish I were wearing a skirt, instead of a big shirt over a pair of loose-fitting capri-length sweats. Maybe a little pink number in—*omigod, am I truly thinking this?*—taffeta.

"Wait for me. I'll be coming back. Wait for me." He's crooned those words to me before, in a time and place that won't come clear, so low and sweet I hunger for the memory, certain he's still mine.

Stanley doesn't know. All he's trying to do is keep me from running ahead of him as he takes a turn at the refrigerator. "Why can't we be like other couples?"

I miss a step.

Stanley adjusts his own. "This is us. Dip, weave, circle, turn, evade." He gives me a twirl, then whirls me in, his arm encircling my waist.

So close I could feel his heart beat, if I stopped angling backward. So close, I could read his thoughts, if I'd only let him read mine. So close I could kiss him. So close we could touch.

My body twined around his. His body moving inside mine.

Shut my eyes. Shut out the world. And let the sensations . . . go.

Stanley whirls me back out. "But without that overheated, all-pumped-up, maybe-just-maybe-we'll-have-sex-later feeling."

He turns my palm. "A good strong lifeline. Solid heart line." He taps along it. "But its course wavers. Like it's looking for direction."

I think how much I don't want my course to be fixed. "And you're that direction."

"I don't know." Stanley looks a little sad. "You have to find it."

13

Of all the deaf, Italian, palm-reading actuaries, the one who finds me is a philosopher.

The morning after Stanley's visit, Blessed Mary on My Dressing Table reminds me philosophers have channeled Heaven to the masses.

And to take a scarf because it's cold.

She should set Stanley up with a late-night call-in show on Internet radio. *Actuarial Actualization*. Meanwhile, when I get to work, to shut Joey up, I tell Maurizio I don't want my lawsuit to turn into a federal case, to settle for any reasonable amount, to get this over with.

I turn off my phone, tired of ignoring Joey's calls. And throw up.

Right into the trash can in my office.

I spit a rinse of flat Diet Sprite after the mess, lay my cheek to the desktop, wrap my arms around my head, and beg the Blessed Virgin Beer Stein *cum* Pencil Holder to make the room stop rocking.

"You all right?" Friedrich Palmon asks from the doorway.

I should have reported Friedrich for plagiarism. No. I should have flagged him from my courses after the first flunk. Should've gone for the doctorate in archeology. Should've put in those papers for missions work. Should've refused his proposal in Oberholt. Should've minded my business from the start.

Should've thought. Should've planned. Should've . . . cared. "You're supposed to check in with the secretary, Mr. Palmon."

"She's on break."

"You still have to check in." I point to the doorway. "Get out and wait for her to get back."

"C'mon, doc. Be nice. It'll settle your stomach." Friedrich balls up pages from *The Temple News* and shoots them, one by one, into the trash can. He takes an atlas from the middle shelf of my bookcase. He uses it to top the can. "To seal the smell. It'll soak in." Which I take to mean the newspaper and the vomit. "Easier for housekeeping. They get paid crap, you know."

"You said you weren't coming back to my classes."

"Didn't expect to, but look . . . you survived." He pulls a book from his pack. "I brought this for you."

A collection of writings by John Donne, a Renaissance poet.

Friedrich opens the collection on the desk, flipping to a well-marked page.

"'No man is an island, entire of itself.'" Friedrich recites the whole passage, arm extended, an actor on stage, voice rich and respectful and wrapping the room. He steps away, reciting the last from memory. "'Any man's death diminishes me, because I am involved in mankind. And therefore never send to know for whom the bell tolls. It tolls for thee.'"

He lets the words settle. "You didn't read my project from last semester, did you?"

The power of his recitation recedes. "There's no need to read it. I mostly wrote it."

"You only provided the foundation. Using the literature of Chaucer's war to point up similarities to ours."

Friedrich again chooses a marker from the Blessed Beer Stein. He draws a flowchart with the Hundred Years' War marked at the starting point and the Thirty Years' War placed to the middle. Which war he means to reference with the word "ours," obvious.

"Entire towns were held hostage in our conflict, not just individuals, like Mr. Chaucer." Smaller circles indicate individuals under the Hundred Years' War. Bigger squares represent towns, like Oberholt, caught up in the Thirty Years' War. "Making our war a war without rules, without conscience."

And without limits.

I stop hiding my head in my arms. Did he actually *think* about this?

Friedrich marks a blocky *X* further along the continuum, extending lines off its ends to make a swastika. "I compared the Thirty Years' War to the rise of the Third Reich. Total war to total war. The roots of the second seeded in the aftermath of the first, except under the Nazis an entire race was held hostage. Makes you wonder about the eventual progression, huh?" He crumples the page and shoves it into a pocket.

It's all I can do not to pull it right back out.

He understands.

The past authors the future, each iteration deeper and more developed than the last, circles upon circles, like a, like a . . .

Crazy cosmic Spirograph.

The Spirograph freezes, fixes on a moment. This moment.

Friedrich and I. No longer a couple of timeworn travelers, squeezed dry by four centuries of rebuke, but what we pretend to be, playing out roles assigned in a life which exists by itself without one before and one to come.

Like the other ninety-nine oh zero seven percent who wander this mortal coil without a clue.

The moment thaws.

I point to the swastika. "We're not talking about an entire race. We're talking you. And me. Not quite an island, but not quite an archipelago, either."

Friedrich's gaze sweeps the space behind me, then side to side, finally settling on the door, very much like Ma did before Joey's wedding when she worried the *mal'occhio* might find us. He goes *sotto voce*, too. "We can't change the circumstances that landed us here, doc. We *can* change what we choose to do with the information."

The room takes a breath.

A flash of understanding, the smallest glimmer, gains a foothold in some forgotten cranny of my soul, but before I can examine it, Blessed Mary Beer Stein takes a breath, too, so I grab a pen out of

Her and snatch the breath away before She takes the chance to talk. "If you need guidance, Mr. Palmon, I suggest student services. They have a list of therapists willing to give you all the time you need at discounted rates."

Friedrich kicks at the trash can. "Stuff like this is going to happen worse, doc, like a freight train, like—"

"Yes, Mr. Palmon, like great big waves." I mimic the big hula wavy movements he made at me before winter break. "If you're done with the metaphors, I have work to do."

Friedrich points to the bandage above my eye. "Somebody gave you a reprieve. I don't know what you did to deserve it, so be wise. Grace is bestowed without cost, but cannot be wasted without consequence. There's you. There's me. There's others. Zero oh three percent. Multiplied by seven billion. Enough for an archipelago. Enough for a freaking nation. And guess what? I intend to find them."

He leaves the Donne opened on my desk. The passage marked is another famous one.

DEATH, BE NOT PROUD.
THOUGH SOME HAVE CALLED YOU MIGHTY AND DREADFUL, YOU ARE NOT SO. FOR THOSE WHOM YOU THINK YOU OVER-THROW DIE NOT, POOR DEATH.
NOR CAN *YOU* KILL *ME*.

14

I'm not worried Death will kill me. I'm worried it won't.

Next day's class devolves into a shifting phantasmagoria of past and present. The gal in the front row converts to a Sandra Dee look-alike in bobby sox and poodle skirt. I saw her lounging in the Saturday matinee three . . . no, two lifetimes ago. The pimply faced student behind her puts on a wool tunic to herd goats. The gal beside him goes Grandma Moses, complete with little white cap and spinning wheel, and I'll swear that little urchin scratching fleas in the back row beat me up for a piece of bread during a mercifully short life in a London workhouse.

Hindsight Nation salutes you, Friedrich.

Zero oh three percent multiplied by seven billion strong.

One in three hundred.

Or maybe three thousand.

Or maybe just you and me.

Because maybe Somebody. Somewhere. Forgot to figure out where to put the freaking decimal point.

A waft from the pfeffernüsse sitting on my podium makes me text an emergency plea to the department assistant. I dash for the faculty lounge to lose the oatmeal I had for breakfast, then push out the door and into Dr. Virgule Futz, assistant chair of the Psychology Department, member-at-large on the tenure committee, and round-the-clock dick.

"Are you leaving? I need to speak with you." He intertwines his fingers, peering at me over the tips.

A reminiscent gesture. A dachshund nipping at the heels of my awareness.

Futz taps his index fingers once, twice. The dachshund transforms to a Doberman. "I'll walk you out."

Gray rolls in. Futz's face slips and slides. His eyebrows go higher, his nose wider. His hair lengthens, curling in greasy clumps over his ears. His briefcase becomes a wooden box, tucked under an arm. His ski jacket embroiders in a pattern of pinecones and his fleece cap grows a peak and a round brim. It also grows a feather, tilted at a jaunty angle.

I suppress a giggle along with my nausea. It ends in a gulp.

He's another one. From Oberholt. And he's not even related to Carlotta.

Futz strides me out of the building and babbles about archetypes and allegory. As he talks, cement pathways transform to cobblestones. Broad Street transforms to a town square lined with open-air stalls festooned with wreaths fashioned from dried stalks. Car exhaust gives way to the smell of onion and sweat. Smoke from long-handled pipes vies with the aroma of beer. It's not North Broad Street anymore, but Oberholt's market square on Hallowmas. In every corner, townspeople, extras from *The Sound of Music*, gather to mark a poor harvest capping a hungry summer.

Futz purses his lips, an effeminate gesture I find petulant and, on him, threatening. "No cabs. Let me give you a ride."

With the *Anschluss* taking place around me, the offer sounds more ominous than gracious, an order rather than a kindness. Whoever Futz was in Oberholt was somebody I didn't like any more than the man he is today. Futz was bad. He was bad bad bad.

He was a Lutheran.

The memory wells, depositing what my gut has left to give over Bavarian Futz's leather boots. Triumph wells with it.

Whoever he was, Futz has deserved to be puked on for a very long time.

I point out my bus and cross the street, calling behind me, "So sorry. Talk to you later."

The bus rumbles its way south, the world rotating between Kodak color and battleship gray. At every stop, somebody I once knew gets on. Another I once knew gets off.

Me and that teenager in a school uniform giggled over boys two lifetimes ago. The shifty fellow with spiked hair pushed me into a puddle ten lifetimes ago. That lady in a knitted poncho taught me to spin in a place where there were many sheep.

The bus finally gets to my stop. I fly from it, my purse knocking a pile of fashion magazines from the newsstand in my haste. In a replay of the episode that got me creamed by Mr. Olivieri's van, the newsstand guy retrieves them, dropping them on the narrow counter. I straighten and restraighten them, needing time to convince the sidewalk to stop shaking, the people walking past to stop shifting.

The newsstand guy stops me. "You didn't really think your baker boy was going to marry you, did you?"

Does he mean Friedrich? How can he? "What do you know about the baker boy?"

His eyes narrow. "As much as I know about an accountant. And his lawyer."

He looks like he's going to say more, then looks past me. He crosses himself, blond hair overlaying his gray as Ruprecht Vogt's younger, stronger features bubble to the surface.

I leave the newsstand guy there, caught between two worlds, and push on home, scarf clinging to my condensing breath. Keychain Mary shakes so badly, She drops when I try to fit Her key into the lock. A shadow falls on my efforts, a hand drops over mine, and a familiar voice asks, "You all right? You look like you seen a ghost."

15

hand Joey his tea, white with cream, thick with sugar, the way he likes it. "Since when do you fix hinges? Front door's been squeaking forever."

Joey checks the level, gives the screwdriver another twist. "Left it go. Thought you or Angela might appreciate the early warning. In case Ma interrupts you with your boyfriends."

"I don't have a boyfriend."

"What's Stanley? Your Pekinese?" Joey flips his screwdriver over his head and catches it in his other hand. "Where's Ma?"

"Atlantic City. With the senior citizens."

Joey grunts. He hates gambling. Calls the casinos a checkroom for chumps. "I chased you from Broad Street. That sonovabitch from the newsstand give you trouble?"

I remember how the newsstand guy blanched, how he looked behind me, suddenly got quiet. "Said he knew plenty about an accountant and his lawyer. You know anything about that?"

"I know you shouldn't be talking to him. Where were you this morning?"

Our appointment. And Stanley would have been here, waiting.

I head to the kitchen, checking my text messages as I go. Stanley sent twenty-three.

Joey follows. "I get it. You're a big girl. Can handle things yourself. What you don't get is Maurizio's trouble. By the time he's done, the only person he won't slap with a suit will be the cop that took our statements."

"Stop talking like I'm trying to screw people. My intentions are good."

"Yeah? Well you know where good intentions lead."

To Hell. *Totable Quotes and Pithy Proverbs.* Page 153.

I toss my purse atop of the fridge so Keychain Mary can get a little quality time with her Refrigerator Sister, then drag the big green trash bag out of its receptacle and tie off the top.

Joey takes the bag from me. "If it's the money, I'll take care of Constantine's fees until your settlement clears. Reimburse me out of that."

In our Oberholt life, when Joey was Josef, he promised to take care of things, too. Promised to keep us fed, keep his business away from the shop, keep Der Weasel away from us. "What do you care? Nobody's suing you."

Joey drops the screwdriver into his toolbox. "Give it time."

And just like that, he shifts. No preliminary graying over. No warning sense of unreality.

Just Joey, suddenly Josef, my cousin from Oberholt. Blond. Belligerent. And freckled. Taller by five inches. Broader by two. With longer nose, wider-set eyes.

And heavier burdens.

Reaching a finger to trace the area above my brow, still tender and swollen though the doc removed the stitches a week ago. He finishes his thought. "Give me time to find a solution. Make things right. Get too greedy, you might end up with nothing."

My stomach hops along my innards, tossing my tea into the kitchen sink. Present-day Joey snaps back. He holds my forehead, then sits me at the table. "You'd tell if you were pregnant, wouldn't you?"

I lay my head in my arms. "You been talking to Ma."

"Maybe I should be talking to your Pekinese."

"Maybe you should mind your own business." I get up and get my purse off the fridge and dig through. I toss him the baseball. "Found this in the trash."

"Thought you wanted me to get rid of my stuff."

"Dad gave that to you. It's special. You used to carry it everywhere."

Joey turns the ball over in his hand, expression unreadable.

I want him to explain why he ditched it, jealous he has grief from only one life to remember. Once. Just once. Can't he say something more?

Something significant. Something true. Something we can both take to heart.

Joey shoves the ball into a pocket. He hefts the trash bag. "I used to carry condoms, too. You pull any of those outta here?"

I give up. The living room sofa calls me, tells me to flop on the afghan, wrap it tight around me because it smells powdery like Aunt Theresa and feels cozy like Ma.

Joey pops his head in. "I gotta go. Want me to call Angela to keep an eye on you?"

Angela's about as comforting as a Brillo pad on an open wound.

No worries, Joey. I got my Vicodin and the Special Blend Angela put back in the coat closet, like Ma directed. "I'm fine."

Stanley phones a quarter-bottle later, his voice staticky. "Joey told me you were sick. No wonder you missed our meeting. I'll come over, keep you company. We could play Scrabble."

Sure. But we're ditching Scrabble for dancing, unchained. Whirling and twirling to the melody. Swaying and sighing. Until that all-pumped-up maybe-we'll-have-sex feeling takes over and we don't wait until later. We don't even wait until the song ends.

I imagine Ma walking in on us. Splayed across the plastic slipcovers in the living room. Caught totally by surprise because the front door doesn't squeak anymore.

"I'm really not feeling well," I tell Stanley through the static. "Can we talk tomorrow?"

I click off. Maurizio calls, his introduction brief, his line clear as Ma's chicken broth. "Since Mr. Olivieri shoveled his van's parking space, I'm claiming he should have also shoveled the area around the newsstand."

"What's that got to do with it?"

"He has to keep his sidewalk shoveled. Taking on the parking space so his van has access gives him a *de facto* responsibility to also shovel the area around the newsstand."

"Mr. Olivieri plays bingo with my mother. I cross myself for the funeral director's processions every day. Take the settlement."

"Aw, gee, Dr. Panisporchi." Maurizio sounds like I claimed the last cookie. "I was holding off Dr. Rossi by telling his attorney you don't got a pot to piss in. You take the settlement, suddenly, you got a pot."

"But you're getting Dr. Rossi's pot out of the funeral director."

"And as long as your pot's in his hands, you're fine. But the second it's a done deal, you lose your bargaining position."

Maurizio's statement sinks into the morass, his wheeze scraping metal across stone. "The funeral director mentioned something about including a credit for advance planning. Thing like that could come in handy."

Not soon enough.

I click off, go for the remote, go surfing, let the television's glow gloss over the legal complexities. And tune to a talk show.

"My husband cheated on me five lifetimes ago. He cheated on me three lifetimes ago and he's cheating on me again." An African American lady wearing a T-shirt stretched tight over big boobs pokes a man I presume to be the cheating husband in the chest.

The lady next to her nods. "That's what my man did to me."

Red-haired, freckled, and missing teeth, her accent tells me she's from some southern mountain region. Ozarks, perhaps. Or Appalachia. Her man, a tiny guy with stringy hair, fidgets.

"Ran off with the gal next door six times already," Ozark Lady says. "Figured he'd go off with the gal next door this time around, too. But her man got a gun."

A mouse of a girl too young to leave her trailer park without her mommy *clickety-clicks* her Jamberrys against her mic. "Same with my Horace. Swears he ain't never cheated on me, but he's lying. Only time he didn't cheat was when he was my brother."

Horace, a big man with a beard, overflows his chair, gaze glassy.

"Your husband is your brother?" The talk show host's concerned expression dwarfs his oversized lenses.

"Not now." Trailer Park Mouse takes it up a squeak. "Before. Only been my brother once. Other times we been together, usually married. Don't know why."

"You realize how this sounds to the audience."

"Might sound funny to some people, but when you got the gift, you know." The big-breasted woman flops into her seat, an extra bosom bounce lending emphasis to her words.

The host glides into the audience. He turns. "You ladies keep talking about a gift."

"Sure do," Ozark Lady drawls. "Only zero oh three percent got it." She counts on her fingers. "That's like…one in three million."

Three hundred. Or three thousand.

The bottle of Special Blend thumps to the carpet.

The talk show host talks some more. So do Trailer Park Mouse, Ozark Lady, and Miss Breasts. The audience jeers.

Ozark Lady smacks her husband on the arm. Her husband stretches, smacking Horace in the eye. Horace flings his arms up to defend, smacking his wife, Trailer Park Mouse, on the temple. Trailer Park Mouse squeals over the hubbub. "He HIT me. Y'all are witnesses."

I drop to my hands and knees and sop Special Blend off the carpet with Aunt Theresa's afghan.

There are others. At least these three. A shining example of Hindsight Nation.

And Friedrich wants to contact *them*?

Hell no. Oh holy. Hell.

No.

I throw up, for what I know will be the last time. Over the Special Blend bottle. Over the carpet. Over Aunt Theresa's afghan.

Angela walks in, waving a hand before her nose. "Christ, Eugenia! What happened?"

"Yesterday is back. The present won't stop wobbling. And I can't see the future."

Blessed Mary *shushes* me from the windowsill. She spreads her hands in supplication and begs, in Her own sweet way. "Shut. The fuck. Up."

I stop trying to get Aunt Gracie's Special Blend off the TV controller. "Don't light a cigarette, Angela, you'll blow up the carpet."

16

The next morning, Dr. Frangipane puts my moment of drunken clarity in perspective. "Fever, nausea, headache, body ache. You have the flu."

He gives me sample packs of an antiviral, a shot to settle the nausea.

And a fresh prescription for the Vicodin because of the hamstring I reinjured with all the puking.

Thank God.

●●●

Angela waves her diamond in front of Ma's manicotti. Ma flings a pepper to the plate. *"Non è possibile."*

Angela lights up, takes a puff, shoots smoke to the ceiling. "Why not?"

Water boils on the stove. Macaroni rolls beneath the foam. Beside it, tomato gravy simmers. Ma flings another pepper. *"Non è pos—"*

"Eh!" Angela closes her thumb against her other fingers and waggles it, front to back. "We no speak *Italiano*. You know why? Because you and me and every *cumari* we know was born five blocks from here. At the Methodist."

Angela means the hospital. Not the church.

Ma's face stills. She adjusts the exhaust fan to let out the steam. "You can't get married. It's not your turn. Give Luigi back the ring. Don't accept it from him until Eugenia has one of her own."

"Are you nuts?" Angela waves her cigarette, smoke trailing after like those taffeta candy ribbons from Wanamaker's, each loop collapsing on the next. "Joey will have grandchildren by then."

Ma crosses herself and spits over her left shoulder. Paganism and Christianity share equal, if contradictory, space in the Italian psyche. "Do you want to invite the *mal'occhio*?"

"This isn't Calabria, Ma. Nonna came all the way across the ocean so we wouldn't have to follow all your ancient superstitions."

Ma angles her palm at Angela, fingers closed and rigid. "You keep this ring. You g'head with your wedding plans, and it'll be the same like the others. Luigi'll break it off before your bridesmaids pick out their dresses."

Angela stubs out her cigarette, grinding it into the ashtray. "You can't stop me, Ma. I'm of age."

I wait, but the ceiling doesn't cave in. Ma gives the gravy another stir, lifting a spoon and letting it trickle to test the consistency. Angela lights up again.

In an Italian war of silence there can be no winners, only casualties. Ma tosses a little more oregano into the pot. "Whatsa matter, Eugenia? You don't like Stanley? Or you don't want your sister to be happy?"

●●●

The next morning, Windowsill Mary shakes her head. "You're going about this all wrong."

I walk out the door to go to work.

She shouts after me. "Forget your sister. Forget Stanley. Don't YOU want to be happy?"

My online dictionary defines *happy* as characterized by good fortune. It derives from the Middle English word, *hap*, meaning *luck*, and is marked by pleasure, satisfaction, joy, and—this one stops me— being especially well-adapted.

To *adapt* means to make suitable to requirements, to adjust to different conditions, which would make happiness an inherent quality for a person with hindsight. We're in a constant state of adjustment.

Today's balding actuary was yesterday's Lutheran oppressor. The mild-mannered psychology prof was once a feather-capped front man for the Freiherr. And the shakedown artist who attacked me four hundred years ago?

He's a nice ex-seminary student turned plumber who wants to marry my sister.

Hell, given those adjustments, people with hindsight should be more than happy, they should be downright giddy.

"Then why so glum?" a voice asks from the doorway to my office.

In a sea of faults, Friedrich's ability to respond to my thoughts is fast becoming the worst of them. "My office hours ended two hours ago, Mr. Palmon."

"Yet here you are. And looking a damned sight better than last I saw you."

I get up and look down the hallway. The secretary is there, keyboarding away. "How do you keep getting past her?"

Friedrich pulls back his sleeves, a magician showing the audience he's got nothing to hide. "People see what they want. You saw that talk show yesterday."

He must mean the one with Ozark Lady, Trailer Park Mouse, and Miss Breasts.

"Two days ago." The words are out before I realize Friedrich tricked me into an honest answer.

"They're batshit," I add.

"They're like us."

"Then we're batshit."

"I've been through the DSM-V, Dr. Panisporchi. I haven't found anything like hindsight listed."

DSM-V stands for *Diagnostic and Statistical Manual of Mental Disorders*, version five. It's the listing of recognized mental illnesses. An acquaintance of mine studies neuroscience. She told me.

I click open my briefcase and take out today's lecture. Maybe the DSM-V is where my answers lie. Maybe she'll lend me her copy.

Friedrich snaps his fingers under my nose. "You'd rather be crazy than have hindsight?"

I smack my briefcase shut. "Stop that. Stop . . . reading me."

"It's not magic. Watch." He puts his hand under my desk lamp. "See?"

I squint. "See what?"

"The colors. You know, like an aura." He wiggles his fingers. "They don't transmit words. They transmit feelings, emotions. After a while, you get pretty good at putting it together. Takes a little practice. Sunlight works best. Come outside. I'll show you."

"No."

Something changes in Friedrich's demeanor, the tiniest lessening of the blustering confidence he exudes whenever he walks in here. I wonder if that means my secretary could see him now. Who knows? By the time I sort through my mail, Friedrich is gone.

He reappears for class, where I give my lecture to the room's back wall. It doesn't turn gray. It doesn't shift. It doesn't mock my inadequacies, question my visual acuity, nor gossip how lately I'm mostly hungover and hopeless. The back wall is cinderblock, painted Navajo white.

And safe.

"Chaucer assigned personalities to his characters, granting each a voice unique and compelling," I drone. "In doing so, he elevated them above their estates while deepening the allegory and making each so familiar, people found it easy to find corollaries in their own lives."

"Could you illustrate using the summoner and the pardoner as examples?"

Nobody ever asks questions. Today, Friedrich Palmon does.

The class stops Snapchatting, their ennui broken by this landmark event.

"The beauty of a great work, Mr. Palmon, is application may be made on a broad or a personal basis. The summoner and the pardoner roles were to seek out and forgive. But power without oversight corrupts. An easy present-day example would be any protection scheme that extorts money from businesses or individuals with what is essentially a promise not to attack."

"So, history repeats. The powerful prey on the powerless and the powerless pay up to avoid annihilation."

Something like that.

"What if the powerless chose annihilation? Without prey, the powerful have no power."

"Annihilation is permanent, Mr. Palmon."

"Yet failure to opt out of the game keeps the players in motion."

He's right. But he's wrong. And he's trying to herd me along a course I may not want to go. "One could always choose an alternate route, Mr. Palmon. Stand up to your pursuers."

"How you gonna do that, Dr. Panisporchi? Can't stand up to your pursuers until you pick them out. Can't pick 'em out unless you get in the game." Friedrich leans so far forward in his seat, he all but topples into the student ahead of him. "And you can't get into the game if you refuse to admit it's already in play."

••

After class, Friedrich drops his backpack on my lectern. "Dr. Panisporchi?"

"Yes?"

"I took Chaucer hoping to enlist your help, to understand my own wherefores why I have this thing."

The gray descends. Friedrich's hair darkens and waves. His stature shortens. His book bag becomes an astrolabe, his Levis a set of hose. His burgundy and puce cardigan lengthens to a rough tunic that ends above his knee. His skin goes pasty, his eyebrows pale, and his expression takes on an earnest and mischievous quality, every inch the Nicholas I've always imagined of *The Miller's Tale*, the man who cuckolded his landlord's wife. "It's unfair of me to show up here, semester after semester. Time I moved on. I won't be back next semester. I mean it this time."

Gray fades. And with it, Nicholas. Friedrich becomes his present-day self—a twenty-one-year-old college student who wears his stud in the wrong ear.

And soon he won't be my problem anymore.

Relief, cool and clean and welcome as cash, replaces misgiving with magnanimity. I want to say something encouraging, but not too encouraging, something to let him know there's no hard feelings. And no reason to ever see each other again. "Hindsight is always twenty-twenty."

May whatever celestial force that pulled those words from my mouth spend ten thousand lifetimes stuck in an elevator with Barry Manilow Muzak.

Friedrich snags the last pfeffernüsse. "That'd be a great name for a website."

17

Hindsight is Twenty-Twenty *would* be a great name for a website. But it's easier to make a Facebook page.

If hindsight is real, if it's more than a future listing in the DSM-VI, there must be more butt-caul people out there besides Friedrich and Miss Breasts and Ozark Lady and Trailer Park Mouse. People with questions. People with answers. Most important, people who don't know me.

I set up the account using Friedrich's name from Oberholt and skip filling out his info. For interests, Facebook suggests microbreweries and baking. I skip those and Facebook suggests astrology. I skip that, too. Using Mr. Chaucer for the profile pic feels too close to home, so I use a photo of Rudyard's—not his favorite.

I don't look for Friedrich's friends. He doesn't have any. Can't say where he grew up. He never has. Can't input where he lives. Google maps has no listing for the State of Denial.

Things get weird when it gets to schools. Facebook suggests Temple University. When it gets to what books Friedrich reads, Facebook suggests *The Jungle Book*.

Relationships? That's complicated.

My first and only status is public:

Do you have the gift of hindsight?
you are not alone.

With a link to the actual page: Hindsight is 20/20.

I favorite the page, then enter its URL in the search engines and use Friedrich's name from *The Miller's Tale* to drop the link on a few forums that discuss reincarnation and a few others that discuss theosophy. I arrange for e-mail notifications.

Then I wait.

The next morning, I have three "Likes" on the Facebook page. The day after, I have ten more "Likes" and the e-mail account contains an ad for an eighteen-hour bra for my butt that claims it will lift and separate. On the third day, somebody "Unlikes" me and somebody else wants to help me increase my penis size.

On day four, Mr. Ugawe Ngbabwe, a banker in Nigeria with ties to the entertainment industry, sends a message offering to fund my Facebook page with twenty million dollars if I will only give him my bank account number so he can deposit the money. I also discover it's more about reach and less about likes. I go back to the forums and reseed the links.

The original post reaches twenty people on day five, forty more on day six, and nobody on day seven. On day eight, I add a cover photo. On day nine, I add a description:

PEOPLE WHO REMEMBER THEIR PAST LIVES HAVE HINDSIGHT.

On day ten, three e-mails that aren't advertisements for sex toys wait in the inbox, one from a man who claims he was President Lincoln. "I get terrible headaches where the bullet entered." I presume he doesn't mean Ford's Theater.

The second claims she was Anne Boleyn. "I got a scar on my neck, I can't wear choker chains, and I won't chop wood."

The third is the actress, Joan Crawford. Not *was* Joan Crawford, *is* Joan Crawford. She signs it Elsie Nickermayer, "out of deference for my relatives."

I go back to the forums, make polite conversation and replant the links. The Facebook page's "Like" count grows. Its reach passes all understanding, and so do its e-mails. Each is from somebody claiming to be somebody in a past life. Nobody mails to say he was nobody, not a ditch digger, a shop clerk, an electrician. I get two Kings of England—both George the Third—six Ghandis, four Popes, and enough Cleopatras to field a soccer team.

One person insists he was a member of the French resistance. "The Nazis are on to me." He signs himself, Casablanca.

I update the page's status again:

PEOPLE WHO REMEMBER THE TIME BETWEEN LIVES HAVE HINDSIGHT.

The reach exceeds my grasp. The page's "Like" count soars. Its inbox overflows with tales of floating on clouds, frolicking in flower fields, and walking paths paved in pearls.

Casablanca returns. "Nazis trap people with lesser known details. Unless you want to attract a lot of nutcases, ask something specific, like whether the Jell-O shots are any good at the Dead Poets Society."

Rudyard. Shakespeare. Chaucer.

I tap my touch pad. Maybe it's a good guess.

A newcomer, called Rupee, admires me. "You got balls." Later Rupee mails to say, "But you're breaking the rules. Have you cleared this Facebook page with the guys on the Assignments Committee?"

Assignments Committee.

Maybe it's Rudyard, getting me back for using that profile pic, using the Indian monetary unit to clue me. The e-mail's IP address is no help, its origin listed as "undetermined."

I teach my classes, give my lectures, quiz my students. Friedrich Palmon stays away. Carlotta's sweaters get bulkier. Ma gives in and invites Luigi to The Dinner. I hide a quadruple dose of Ex-Lax among the chocolate shavings in his piece of cake. He spends the next two days in the john. Ma makes Angela stop wearing her ring.

Maurizio Bracaconi calls me with updates, with new ideas, with new angles.

I stop trying to understand what he's doing. Mr. Olivieri stops sending bouquets. Joey stops bugging me about seeing Constantine. I apply foundation to the scar, pay my deductible for my hospital stay, and wonder what mutant gene entices somebody to become a lawyer.

Joan Crawford takes a liking to me. She tells me I'm the only person who understands her pain. "The wire coat hanger story was a lie."

Casablanca takes a disliking to me, asking what game I'm playing. "If you're a Nazi, say so. You'll never find me. This isn't my real e-mail address."

Rupee remains neutral, questioning why I won't answer him. "You got balls," he notes again. "I'll give you that."

Stanley invites me to the movies, to the orchestra, to the theater. We go out for Chinese, for Thai, for French. He makes observations, makes conversation, tells me anecdotes. Whatever he's drinking, he never has more than one. Whatever I'm wearing, he tells me I look nice. He holds me close, holds my hands, and sometimes my boobs. Ma always leaves biscotti or pizzelles waiting on the kitchen table, the espresso ready to brew. Stanley always leaves just after midnight. And when he kisses me goodnight, those kisses are deep and long and sweet and increasingly insistent.

"Because life weaves itself into a whole," he says one evening over veal scaloppini and garlic prawns. "Joey and Carlotta decide to get married, Luigi decides not to be a priest. He meets your sister at the wedding and I meet you. Like stars moving in their courses, we were meant to arrive at precisely that moment."

Stanley invites me to his place. Halfway there, I ask him to take me home, my course still too uncertain and unwilling to let it be part of anybody else's. He does so, tight-lipped, hands clenching the steering wheel. On Valentine's Day he lowers the boom. "You gotta pick your times for things."

"You're breaking up with me? For real."

"We're good together. We really are. But it's like you're waiting for me to do something. Or say something. Or be something. You stare at me. I mean beyond normal staring when you like somebody. It's like you want to peel me—and I don't mean undress—to get at what's inside. But this is me." He sweeps his hand head to toe. "And it doesn't seem to be enough."

I want to tell him I mean it. The words rise, but they won't come out. I want to draw him close, but my arms won't move. I want to decide who I was is not who I am, what I want is standing before me. But I can't see it. And maybe I never will. So he leaves, front door swinging closed after him on hinges now silent. I stare at the door awhile, then go upstairs, lock myself in the bathroom, bury my face in a towel.

And wail.

The next day, I hold an icepack over red-rimmed eyes and send the e-mails from deceased rock stars, heads of states, and several Mother Theresas to the recycle bin, thanking goodness in the world of "Hindsight is 20/20" I am hindsightseeker@gmail.com, mysterious and anonymous. Blessedly anonymous.

Except for this:

Dear Dr. Panisporchi:
I'm sorry I didn't show up for our wedding day and sorrier I treated you so shabbily at Hallowmas. I should have spoken to you before I married the brewer's daughter and should have apologized for my behavior at the outset. By any measure, our days of grace are over. We need to talk.
Sincerely,
Friedrich Palmon, once a baker from Oberholt

18

Four hundred years. Four hundred fucking years I've been waiting for that apology and the fucker waits until he fucking finally gets out of my life to make it.

Friedrich shows up to Monday's class, pfeffernüsse in hand. Students swarm forward, hands outstretched. One flips me an envelope attached to the GladWare, my name, written in black engraver's ink, clear on its face. It's hefty, twenty-five-pound weight, as is the cardstock within on which Friedrich's penned:

> HINDSIGHT—perception of the significance and nature of events after they have occurred.

A coughing fit sends Friedrich out of class five minutes before it concludes. He gives me a two-fingered wave as he goes.

This is a fluke. A one-time thing. Because he had extra pfeffernüsse. He won't be back.

He promised.

On Wednesday, Friedrich returns, scratching a nasty-looking rash on the back of his hand. He drops the cookies, gives me a wan smile, blows his nose. And leaves.

I use a tissue to tip the container into the trash, and a tweezer to open this gem taped to its bottom:

KARMA—the effects of a person's actions that determine his destiny in his next incarnation.

Thursday morning, I find this slipped under my office door:

DESTINY—a predetermined course of events considered as something beyond human power or control.

I'm ready for Friday, snatching the container before Friedrich can leave it. The other students, poised to make their thrice-weekly pounce, pause. I rip off the envelope and toss them the box.

FATE—a final result or consequence; an outcome.

Friedrich shows up in my office a few hours later. I fling the envelopes at his feet. "You said you weren't coming back."

"You set up a Facebook page." Friedrich stoops to gather the envelopes, his voice low and taut as the socks around Ma's cankles. "You used my name."

"A name you haven't used for four hundred years. I didn't mean anything by it."

Friedrich stops gathering. "How about Nicholas? You left that name on a bunch of forums." He straightens to point an accusing finger at my laptop. "With links to the Facebook page."

I clamp a hand over the Blessed Beer Stein to shut Her up before She gets started. "Nobody's going to associate that name with the Nicholas of *The Miller's Tale*. People think he's a fictional character. There have to be a million Nicholases in the world."

"As of Sunday morning, four million, nine hundred forty-two thousand and three. Two hundred twenty-two million, seven hundred and sixty-two since that name's first usage."

"Wow. Google's amazing."

"The Assignments Committee is even more amazing. Out of all those Nicholases, living and dead, they tracked me down and asked what I was doing. They think you're me and now I'm fucked." He flings the envelopes onto my desk. "What were you thinking?"

I'm thinking you're crazier than Ozark Lady, Trailer Park Mouse, Miss Breasts, and Joan Crawford put together. I'm thinking there should be a listing in the DSM-V just for you. I'm thinking I've had enough, been more than patient.

And could use a drink. "Fucked in what way?"

Friedrich coughs. He pulls an inhaler from his pocket, shakes it, and takes a puff. He waves his hand rash in front of my face, pulls back his sleeve, shows me how it's traveling up his arm, cups his fingers, pumps his fist in a masturbatory gesture, and says on his exhalation, "You don't want to know where else I got it."

I should have stopped this when Friedrich handed me that project last semester. No, I should have stopped the day I first recognized Friedrich for who he was. I should've played stupid when he gave me that sketch the first class after Joey's wedding. Should've investigated missionary opportunities in Tajikistan. And feigned a calling. "I'll take down the Facebook page and delete the posts from the forums. You change your cell number and the Messengers in Black won't be able to find you. Deal?"

"This is a big joke to you, isn't it, Dr. Panisporchi?"

Oh yeah. It's a scream. "What do you want from me?"

He drops a chartreuse-colored notice on my desk:

HINDSIGHT: The Unspoken Burden
Support group meets every Monday at 7:30 p.m.
Library Lounge C

"Student Services said I can do this so long as a faculty member signs off." He points to the spot on the application. "You don't have to do anything. Just go."

"Why should I go?"

Friedrich thumps my desk. "Look at me. Listen to my chest. How much time do you think this leaves me?"

My hand strays to my desk phone, aware how empty the department is at this time of day, how foolish I was to allow Friedrich to continue taking my classes. "I believe you have me mixed up with somebody else, Mr. Palmon."

Friedrich yanks his sketchpad from his backpack and grabs a pencil from the Blessed Beer Stein. He draws, large, bold strokes, his expression intent.

I should stand like I'm going to pull something out of my cabinet, then bolt, get past him while he's occupied. But curiosity's killed me more than once, so I wait, intrigued at the delicate way his wrist flicks across the paper.

Friedrich shows me the page. "Have I got you mixed up with her?"

She's young, blonde. Delicate shoulders, high forehead, prominent chin. Myself in Oberholt. I reach to trace the intricate lace collar. Was I ever this young? This pretty?

Friedrich flips to a new page, fingers whitening around the pencil. The graphite breaks, the snap resounding off my stunned silence. He slaps the pad to my desk.

This young lady's short and slight, with square, capable hands, bearing a basket of flowers and dressed in a sleeveless surcoat over homespun gown with a beaded *coif* on the crown of her head, like they did in Chaucer's day.

My mouth goes dry. My hand trembles. My insides quiver.

I grip the edge of my desk. "The bonds that unite us exist only in our minds. That's Proust." *Totable Quotes and Pithy Proverbs,* page 78.

"I'm not an idiot. And you're wrong." Friedrich returns the pencil to the Blessed Beer Stein with such force, She shudders. "Who we are defines those bonds. What baggage we carry determines their manifestation."

Most of the time, Friedrich sounds like how he looks, an unhip twenty-one-year-old college student dressed in bad color combinations. In unguarded moments he sounds like what he is, an old soul, somebody who has taken a spin on the wheel too many times. I study the desperation in his eyes, the determination, then think of Casablanca. "You're not worried this would attract a bunch of nutcases?"

Friedrich's breathing smooths. So does his voice. "We'll weed out the dross. Temple has twenty-five thousand full-time students and eight thousand part-timers. If half of those with hindsight show, that's forty-nine students. If only a tenth show up, it's a start."

I take his word on the math. "For what?"

"To meet others. Figure out the reason for our hindsight and find a way to get rid of it. Isn't that what you want?"

What I want is to be left alone.

"Maybe hindsight isn't what you think, Mr. Palmon. Maybe it's already in the DSM-V. In bits and pieces, partial descriptions. This person hears voices. That person's delusional. The crazy on the corner insists she's seven different people. Maybe it's an atypical presentation of something unusual." I toss his envelopes into my briefcase.

And Slam. It. Shut. "Maybe something that only affects zero oh three percent."

Friedrich grabs his backpack and stuffs the flyer into its depths. He backs toward the door, moving in jerky steps. "If that's what you think, Dr. Panisporchi, why did you make the Facebook page?"

19

Friedrich's question dogs me. As does Friedrich. He leaves voice mail after voice mail. "I know this seems weird. I flipped when I realized its enormity."

Beep.

"We could have coffee. Talk. No pressure."

Beep.

"All I want to do is talk. Even on the phone would be good."

Beep.

"It's not like you run into somebody with hindsight every day."

Beep.

"Doesn't any of this make you wonder?"

And creepiest of all, a message that has my eyebrows lifting to the ceiling and my anxiety scrambling right after: "I know you're there. You're always there on Tuesdays."

Beep.

Beep.

Beep.

One morning, I find this calligraphy love note under my office door: "To forget one's purpose is the commonest form of stupidity."

Very funny. *Friedrich* Nietzsche. *Totable Quotes and Pithy Proverbs,* page 52.

Next morning, I'm greeted by a padded UPS envelope propped beside my desk lamp. It's from Friedrich.

I shake it beside my ear.

No *tic-tic-tic*. Not a bomb, then.

Too bad.

Keychain Mary pipes up. "Your mother would feel bad. Wouldn't you miss her?"

My shaking slows, contemplating life without Ma. Without Angela. Even without Joey.

Blessed Beer Stein Mary rattles her cup. She points me to a letter opener with Her embossed on the handhold, hiding among the pens. I grab the Her end of it and jam the pointy end under the heavy-duty staples Friedrich used to seal the envelope, flipping them off one by one. "Only you, Blessed Mother—Own. Lee. *You*—could put me in the path of a letter bomb and still make it *my* fault if it blows me up."

I flip Mary Micromanager back into Her beer stein. Rip the zip tab on the envelope. Check the contents. A book, buckram cover worn along the edges, binding stitches beginning to give.

Gunga Din and Collected Poems by Rudyard Kipling.

Another note tumbles to the floor, landing face up, a quote from Rudyard: "All the people like us are We, And everyone else is They."

Friedrich shows up in my office an hour later. "I thought you liked Kipling. You sure as hell spent enough time with him."

My stomach sinks, siphoning most of my saliva with it. "You know Rudyard."

"Almost as well as I knew Mr. Chaucer."

That reference seems out of place. Memory of my time with the dead poets goes mushy. Maybe I dreamed it. Or only dreamed I dreamed it. I sag into my chair. Drowning under a shower, a cascade. Loss. Panic. Piercing me clear to my roots.

Friedrich grabs the back of my neck. He shoves my head between my knees. "Deep breaths."

Rustle, thump, zip, rustle, zip, thump follow. A hand appears under my nose. The artist's callus gracing its middle finger swells in bas relief. Dry skin ridges shadowed in ink stains take on the significance of a Georgia O'Keeffe landscape. Two little pink capsules rest in the palm. "Dramamine. It helps."

The carpet beneath my feet sways. "I'm not taking your drugs."

"You think yours work better?" More rustling and zipping follow. Something rattles.

I look up.

Friedrich holds my Vicodin.

I glance to my purse, undisturbed on the top of my bookcase. "Where did you get that?"

Friedrich shows me the label.

Not my prescription. His. Not Vicodin. Valium.

"I dealt stuff like this in my previous life. I know the signs." He points to his eyes, showing me the overdilation of the pupils. He reaches to mine, whisking a fingertip along the lower lid. "Yours are pinpoint. Betcha nobody has picked up on it yet. Be careful and nobody will. You'll get used to all this soon enough and you won't need the meds so much."

I pull off my readers, a recent necessity that only partially clears up the fuzzies, and rub my eyes with a thumb and forefinger, hoping he'll take it as a sign of exhaustion, possibly distraction, certainly not addiction. "Used to what?"

"The heaving and rolling, the graying down. That weird feeling the world around you is evaporating. Couple more weeks, maybe a month, it'll seem normal."

A whisper of paper follows. That damned chartreuse-colored flyer advertising the support group. "This would help, also. Better than the Dramamine. Much better than the mood adjusters."

I snatch the flyer and wave it at him. "This is ridiculous."

"Who the hell else are we going to talk to, if not to each other?"

"I don't want to talk to anybody. I'm doing fine on my own."

Friedrich eyes my desk, my computer, the pile of papers waiting to be graded. He runs a finger along the titles on the top of my bookcase. "You got a nice set up, doncha, doc? Nice job. People respect you. You have a family. Somebody special."

He splays a hand across the bizarre yellow and purple horizontal stripe of his homemade pullover, holds his other like he's leading a partner, and performs a two-step. "Does he mambo?"

I point to my office door. "Get out."

"I get it. None of my business. Neither is your Facebook page. Except I'm all over it."

"You leave voice mails. Send packages. Follow me around campus. Bake . . . bake . . . pfeffernüsse. How am I supposed to interpret this?" I pick up the Kipling quote from the floor and slide it back inside the copy of *Gunga Din*, then slide the book back into its envelope. "Take this. And stop taking my classes. Now. Don't call me or e-mail me or follow me. Or I'll have to report you."

Friedrich takes the package and smacks it against one of his palms. Once. Twice. Three times. "Fine. We'll do it your way."

I loose the breath I hadn't realized I'd been holding. It exits with a mighty *whoosh*.

He drops the package back onto my desk. "Report me. Bring me up on charges. Make your case. Tell them about the pfeffernüsse. Let them listen to the voice mails. Explain how I take all your classes. Then we'll show administration all my exams, my quizzes, my papers and you can explain why you flunk me semester after semester."

My underarms grow clammy.

Friedrich picks up the flyer again. "Or you can stop playing the victim. Help me with this. Before our souls disintegrate and fall through the cracks in the universe."

Playing. Victim.

Rage claws at the back of my throat. Bitter as burdock and bellowing for release.

Down the hall, somebody's computer lets them know they've got mail. A phone rings, once, twice. The third ring cuts off, followed by a brisk, "Hello?"

Outside my office door, normal life continues. I can stand here and let the same two-bit hustler who robbed me of my dignity in Oberholt usher me down his private rabbit hole, or I can . . .

"We're done, Mr. Palmon. I'm not doing your support group and I'm not talking to you about this anymore. You want to complain to administration about your grades, go ahead. They're going to think it strange you waited so long."

Every vein in Friedrich's neck springs into go-mode. "You think I'm it, Dr. Panisporchi? I'm only the beginning. Run. Hide. Your sins will find you. Around a corner. Over a coffee cup. In your dreams. They'll crisscross in unexpected ways. Converge when least convenient. Dim your colors. Blur all you think important to gray. Death will look good to you. You'll long for it. Indulge in behavior to bring it on faster. But it's a false promise. There is no end for people like us."

I imagine this support group he's talking about. Imagine sitting there with Miss Breasts, Ozark Lady, and Trailer Park Mouse. Missing teeth. Acne scars. Poorly fitted bras.

Is this rashy, asthmatic man-boy dressed in mismatched regalia including *me* with *them*?

"Listen up, Friedrich." I flick my left hand. "There is you." I flick the other. "There is me." I fling my arms wide. "And this is why you and me will *never* equal an us."

Friedrich throws *his* hands in the air. "You're in purgatory and don't know it. Don't you understand? What sins you don't expiate, Hell will require you relive. Over. And over. And over."

20

Friedrich storms out of my office and skips class. Next day, a note addressed to Friedrich's Oberholt version arrives in the Hindsight is 20/20 box.

> *If you filed your paperwork, it's been misplaced. Please resubmit with full explanation.*
> *Sincerely,*
> *Mr. Anders Dripzin*
> *Assignments Committee*

Five e-mails later Casablanca lets me know: *Someday the proletariat will rise against the bourgeoisie. When they do, I'm telling the Assignments Committee about your Facebook page. Vive la revolution!*

Rupee warns that the Assignments Committee isn't going to like me putting up a Facebook page without a permit. *They'll visit. Talk to you because you're talking about them. Then they will revoke your angelic privilege.*

Doubt, just a nit, works at me, coupled with curiosity—what in hell is an angelic privilege?

Fuck it. Let them come. I'll put on a fresh pot.

••

Donna checks to make sure Ma's percolator is still warm before helping herself to the last cup. I decline the last cookie. Donna helps herself to that also. "Midway along life's journey, I found myself in a forest dark, my straightforward pathway lost."

Dante. His *Inferno*. *Canto Primo*. The opening.

"I had questions of my own." Donna rests her chin on her palm. "I started the Facebook page to attract like-minded individuals. Got a bunch of, um, interesting characters, instead." Hand wave. Head shake. Earring tinkle. "One guy kept sending me links to his YouTube videos. He dabbled in Play-Doh Goethe animations, of all things. Long-winded affairs mostly involving lectures on dioptrical colors."

I'm not sure where to go in a conversation that features the words *Play-Doh* and *Goethe* in the same sentence. "What kind of colors?"

"Dioptrical. Those caused by refraction." Donna pulls a notepad and a red marker from her purse. She draws a triangle. "White light enters the prism. The prism forces the light waves to bend. The light separates into a rainbow." She draws a red line to mark the light entering the triangle, then fans seven equally spaced lines on the other side to indicate the bending and separation. "Goethe was fascinated by dioptrics. Play-Doh Man felt his animations were a nod to Goethe's artsy side and expanded on his work by adding his own psychological slant."

So far, I'm with her.

"We interpret color based on individual perception." Donna points to the first line fanning from the triangle. "My red may not be your red." She switches to the line in the middle. "Your green isn't my green."

She redraws the triangle, again draws the light entering the prism, this time changing the angles as they exit, thus changing the separation between the colors. "Play-Doh Man took the idea a step further. He decided *we* control how light bends through the prism, thus controlling the refractions, and thereby our perceptions, to put what slant we want on things." Donna puts down the pen and dribbles a little more cream into her mix. "'He was vague on the mechanics. Kept quoting Faust. 'All theory is gray.'"

Faust made a deal with the devil. "What does your Thirty Years' War research have to do with Play-Doh?"

"It doesn't. Not directly. I was exploring another avenue with the Facebook page, regarding how history perceives moments of unrecorded time, those events we must infer because we see what results from them." Donna draws another triangle, this one bowed on the sides. "Those events have their effect. Like increased air pressure would have on a three-dimensional construct of this triangle."

She points to the bowing. "Any light entering *this* triangle would have its very own slant."

My headache returns, *thump-thumpity-thumping* behind my forehead. "What's the name of your Facebook page?"

"I shut it down. It served its purpose, but I worried what happened to the people who commented there. I never responded to their messages, but they seemed to draw comfort from the connection."

Casablanca. Rupee. Even my friend, Joan Crawford.

My cell thuds the theme from *Jaws*.

South Philly row homes were built to last, with concrete firewalls between the houses. It's hard for me to get two reception bars inside the house. I can manage three bars on the front stoop. When Blessed Mary in the Backyard isn't feeling bitchy, She'll grant me four. Every time Maurizio calls, I get five.

Whatever anybody offered, take it, take your percentage, and stop calling me. "Hello?"

"Good news. The funeral director's agreed to the advance planning package, plus adjustments for cost of living."

"Cost of living?"

"Longer you live, more it costs to die. Don't worry, my contingency is based on present value. But I'm upping what you'll need for pain and suffering. Just in case."

"You mean so I can pay Dr. Rossi?"

"No. What he'll have to pay you. We're going to countersue." Maurizio sneezes. "Dr. Rossi's overplaying this grief thing. It's not like his wife wasn't already dead."

21

When Friedrich mentioned purgatory, he must have meant staff meetings.

Today's moderator, an administration toady from the Economics Department, points to charts and graphs, referencing handouts drooping from our tired fingers.

Virgule Futz, sitting beside me, doesn't even pretend to be listening. Music spills from earbuds, a country-western mix I hate more than staff meetings. Futz lowers the volume. "How about we make our escapes?"

The ventilation system clatters to life. It blows a fresh blast of overheated air across the tedium. Futz bends over like he's tying his shoe, grabs his briefcase, grabs mine, and slips gracefully out of the row.

I have to follow.

•••

A half hour later, Dr. Futz sips his half-skinny mocha frappe and flicks cinnamon flecks from his clothing. Sun yellow shirt. Sky blue chinos.

He must get fashion advice from Friedrich.

And speak of the devil.

"Can I get you folks anything else?" Friedrich appears at my elbow, all Campus Co-op efficiency, another student earning college bucks.

Nobody watching would guess two days ago he threatened me with Hell! Purgatory! Blackmail! I'd lay a fiver this is his first day on the job and another ten he paid another server for the privilege of eavesdropping on my conversation.

Maybe Friedrich follows me all the time. Maybe he hacks my e-mail. Maybe he's cloned my phone. Maybe my Google Calendar updates to his iPad. He's an engineering major, who knows what he can manage.

Futz waves Friedrich away.

Friedrich doesn't leave. He regroups at the condiment bar. Refills coffee stirrers. Rearranges catsup packets. Is that earbud for hands-free operation of his cell or does it amplify every word Futz and I say?

The world shrinks until I'm a specimen pinned to a board, the toys and technology I find so wondrous laid bare for what they are, windows onto my soul. My throat closes, pushing down a desire to retreat to my last incarnation, perhaps the incarnation before, to a time when Friedrich's ability to intrude on my life would have been limited by the reach of the telephone cord.

Futz taps his coffee stirrer to the table. He's been talking and now he's stopped. The tapping indicates he expects a reply. I haven't the foggiest what he just said.

He peers over his coffee. "This student really needs the help. It's not the same as a publishing credit for you, but the committee considers that kind of thing."

The entire half hour of blather washes back. I help a grad student define psychological profiles on Chaucerian archetypes and—poof!—the Tenure Fairy gets me a real professorship with full benefits and a place on the track. Like I don't give enough unpaid hours to this job. "Thanks for the coffee, Virgule. I'll think about it. My schedule is pretty full." I gather my satchel and briefcase, then dig for my TransPass.

He lands the coffee stirrer with the force of a gavel. "Of course. Take a few days. I know it's an imposition."

Terror, splintered and sharp, shrapnels through my insides.

What the fuck? "I didn't say it was an imposition."

Futz's shirt muddies to deep brown, its cotton to wool. Coffee smell takes on beer's yeasty tang and hamburger grease mellows to pipe smoke. The campus food court darkens. Floor tiles lengthen to wood planks. Sharp modern edges mute to hand-hewn imprecision. Futz's voice cuts through the episode, his well-modulated Main Line accent tinged with German, an imperfect echo of a similar speech from four centuries earlier: "You're the best person for the job. Seems we could help each other. It's the kind of thing you may wish you'd done, in hindsight."

● ● ●

Two hours later, I let Stanley bend me over the table. One hand, then the other, cover mine. His breath tickles my ear. "Like this. Slow and easy. Relax your fingers. Don't worry about the tip, the chalk keeps it from sliding."

Stanley and I are at a bar near the waterfront. He's teaching me to play pool. Two weeks since our breakup and I miss his voice. I miss his touch. I miss his company.

I also miss my shot. "I'm no good at hitting balls with sticks. Joey tried to teach me to play golf. I couldn't get past the water traps."

"How come he never taught you pool?"

"Joey doesn't play pool."

Stanley puts the cue ball back on the table. He studies the setup, gaze flicking left, then right. "Oh."

"Joey plays baseball."

"Pitcher?"

"Shortstop. Nothing gets by him."

Stanley hefts his cue. "I'll bet it doesn't."

What's this about? "Where'd you learn to play? You're good."

"In college."

That would be Villanova. Joey's alma mater.

I wait, presuming Stanley will elaborate.

He chalks his stick. He taps its butt end to the table leg. He watches the excess dust eddy away from the tip. He places the cue on the table.

And gains even more distance from the conversation by taking time to wipe his hands on a chamois. "Ready to try again?"

For a second, I think Stanley's asking if he and I can try again. The possibility blossoms. Cappuccinos on a Sunday morning. Crosswords and croissants.

But in the second after that, he picks up my cue and hands it to me and I know he's only talking pool. With a capital P. That rhymes with E. Which stands for *Eugenia, get a freaking grip on your expectations.*

The shaded LED downlights suddenly seem harsh. The cork floor, so pleasant to play on, suddenly feels hard. The techno mix piping through the sound system suddenly sounds hackneyed. I arc my neck, hoping I look like I'm admiring the punched tin ceiling, but really to release the tension gathering at the base of my skull. "I've never been to a pool hall. I thought it'd be grimier. Like in that movie with Paul Newman."

"*The Hustler.*"

"That's the one."

Stanley points to well-scrubbed tables filling the restaurant side of the joint. "This hall's upscale. The beer caps are European."

That makes me laugh.

Stanley again bends me over the table. "Give me another shot."

Maybe he's not talking about pool.

He draws back my arm, positions the cue, chest resting on my shoulder blade, abdomen grazing my hip. It feels good. It feels safe. It feels warm.

So, of course, I'm gonna have to spoil it. "You texted me to meet you 'cause you said we had to talk." I straighten. "So talk."

Stanley leans against the table, cue resting in the hollow of his shoulder. "Your Aunt Rose invited me down the shore."

Is that *this* weekend? I go through a mental calendar in my head. Omigod. And Stanley's invited.

"Yeah. I know it's strange." Stanley puts out his hands, palms *whad-dya-want-me-to-do?* up. "I think maybe because I'm Luigi's best man."

Luigi. Dammit. It's always Luigi. "Oh. Don't worry about Aunt Rose. I'm sure she understood when you said you couldn't go."

Stanley goes real quiet.

"You did tell her you couldn't go, right?"

Stanley puts his beer to his cheek. Frosty condensation trickles down the bottle's side. "I meant to. Just . . . she was so sweet on the phone."

Shit. Shit. *Shittedy-shit-shit-shit.* "It's gonna be weird."

"Then we need to figure a way to make it not weird because between your sister and brother and my cousins, even if we're not dating, we're gonna be seeing each other." Stanley puts down the beer and picks up his cue. "I took tomorrow afternoon off. I'm hoping you'll drive down with me. Can you swing it?"

Like outta the park. With me attached to the ball. This is a mess. It's a mess mess mess.

Stanley got an invite because I didn't tell Ma we stopped dating. I go for my phone. I'll call now. Explain.

And pull my hand back.

She'll call Aunt Rose.

Aunt Rose will call Stanley. Rescind the invitation.

Maybe now. While I'm standing here. Guzzling beer and imagining me and Stanley in the car for that hour-and-a-half drive to Aunt Rose's place, the scene somehow familiar, and thrilling. The kind of thrill that starts in my solar plexus and travels a direct route to my groin.

And why shouldn't it? It's been a couple of weeks. We've both had time to think things through. Maybe Stanley's thinking the ride would be a great time to clear the air, get started on a better footing.

Then I wouldn't have to tell Ma. Anything.

"Okay." I pick up my cue, too. "I can swing it."

"Good. Then I'll pick you up first."

"First?"

"Donna's going too."

22

Uncle Lou and Aunt Rose bought their shore house in 1960 when places down in Atlantic City were modest and cheap. The house sits on stilts, has a tiny living room, a tinier kitchen, four bedrooms, and a bath. A dinosaur decorated with blue crabs, boats, and ropes, the house is a pimple marring the sophisticated veneer created by the new beach houses with their state-of-the-art kitchens, elevators, and ultramodern furniture. And, because of a quirk in the geography of its particular one-eighth-acre lot, it's also the only house in their locale to survive Superstorm Sandy unscathed.

Aunt Rose and Uncle Lou have no children. There's no telling what will happen to that house once they pass. So every year, at the beginning of March, despite clouded skies and a biting wind, the family packs up the towels and sheets, sweatshirts and blue jeans, lasagnas and cookies to celebrate Aunt Rose and Uncle Lou's anniversary, eager to find a place in their will.

Except me. I avoid Atlantic City. I had nineteen happy years here two lifetimes ago. What if people I knew from then are still alive and I ran into one? They wouldn't know me, of course, but I'd know them.

That might hurt. A lot.

Most years, midterm exams provide the excuse to skip this weekend. My sophomore year of college, I scheduled my wisdom teeth removal to coincide and three years ago, I thanked Mary for blessing me with a timely root canal. This year, the date snuck up on me. Stanley's offer of a comfortable ride and the thought of him spending an entire weekend with my family without me there to monitor the interactions have me traveling the Atlantic City Expressway before I can come up with a reason why we should both stay home.

The family eats its first meal at Aunt Rose and Uncle Lou's by candlelight. Nothing can be used in this house that did not exist in 1960. Carlotta's blow-dryer fizzles the fuses two hours after we arrive. Lucky for us, Uncle Nic's an electrician. Not so lucky for him. He spends hours cursing from the house's underbelly about ancient wiring and inadequate subpanels. Stanley and I lend a hand, passing flaskfuls of Aunt Gracie's Special Blend to keep him warm.

Stanley gives me a peck on the cheek before turning in for the night. He and the rest of the young men have to sleep in Uncle Nic's camper that he parks in the driveway. Bedrooms are reserved for young ladies, old ladies, old men, and Aunt Rose and Uncle Lou. Kids get bedrolls in the living room. One year, one of the married couples took a room at the motel down the street. They joined us for meals and outings. Aunt Rose and Uncle Lou never invited them back.

Donna scoops up a handful of cookies before we head upstairs. She pokes me in the ribs. "Think about faith and hope. One has to do with things not seen, the other with things not at hand. Saint Thomas Aquinas."

Totable Quotes and Pithy Proverbs, page 67.

"All I'm saying is Stanley's waters run still and deep." Donna's earrings *du jour*, brushed nickel spirals hanging from pearl buttons, sparkle. "And for some, passion engulfs as an avalanche, without warning."

"I'll be sure to wear my snowshoes." *How'd she get an invite?*

I pull Angela aside to ask. She looks to where Donna chats up Carlotta. "Whatever your issue with her, get over it. She's your sister-in-law, for God's sake."

What? Wait. "I didn't mean Carlotta, I meant . . ."

Angela huffs off.

. . . Donna.

●●●

Carlotta and Angela share a lower bunk. Donna chooses an upper. She goes out before the newly restored lights do. The others follow.

Not me.

Caffeine and Vicodin fight for victory, the one pulling me down, the other revving me up. Waves pound. Wind whistles. Moon shines.

I get up to pull the shade. None hides behind billowing fringe curtains. I push on the sash. The window won't shut. I mean to crawl back into my bunk, pull the covers over my head.

I can't.

Because gray blows in and transforms the bunk to a maple dresser, Blessed Mary atop. The tiny night table beside transforms to a spindle-legged chair, silk nightie crumpled across. The other bunks disappear, replaced by a full-sized bed, what we used to call a double, dressed prettily in crisp white sheets, tossed back on the one side like vanilla icing unevenly spatulated across a cake.

Someone grunts, then grumbles. The lacy white counterpane moves, revealing a long, slim, masculine shape beneath, the owner's face obscured by the pillow bunched around his ears. He settles, counterpane rising and falling with his breaths.

I know this room. I know this man.

And I want him back.

A breeze flips the edges of a calendar resting on the night table, a pocketbook-sized freebie of the type once passed out by pharmacies, spiral-bound by a thin metal coil twisted and flattened from use. The flipping pages show the month-at-a-glance, the year clearly visible, 1964, the pages otherwise blank but for red Xs marked in a row of days two pages back, then three pages back, then four pages back.

I've shown the man the calendar. He's assured me he's happy, with words and promises and caresses in places young ladies of the time never spoke about.

The breeze blows harder, flipping the calendar off the nightstand. It cools my cheek and raises the pores around my nipples. My lover's scent still clings to them, sex and cologne, salt and citrus. I reach again, hoping desire is enough to make the vision substantial, enough to let me spend another moment enveloped by his body, his breath in my hair, his pulse between my thighs.

A foghorn out to sea scatters the gray. I return, crumpled beside my bunk, knee throbbing where I must have hit it on the way down, and moonlight in my eyes.

We should have grown old together, enjoyed children and grand-children. Too much drink. A bad set of brakes. That life yanked away in a crush of sea salt and marsh.

I looked for him, waiting with the dead poets. First, presuming he'd be right behind. Second, presuming he'd been held up in process-ing. Third, wondering if he'd gotten there first.

I asked. Nobody could tell me. It's not allowed. We're each respon-sible for our own decisions.

Friedrich's words chase me down, take me by the shoulders, shake hard. Is he right? Must all sins be confessed? All failings relived? I lost my Lutheran soldier. I look to the space by the window, where moments ago I saw the bed. I lost him.

And now. Stanley.

I grab the quilt, wrap my misery deep within, and make myself a nest on the floor, as close to the door and as far from that thought and Cousin Lydia as I can manage. She had adenoids as a kid. The doc who fixed them didn't do such a good job and ever since, Lydia honks when she sleeps.

23

The wind drops off at dawn. Waves quiet with it. My favorite time on the beach. Even when I can't enjoy it in solitude.

Stanley casts his line into the surf, bundled in a cable knit sweater and sucking a stogie. He thanks me for the coffee, poured from an ancient thermos I found in Aunt Rose's cupboard. The thermos boasts an actual glass liner, a hard plastic outside, now a mesh of yellowing crackles, and is embossed with an image of the Blessed Mother. Very like the one I use for work. I got mine on Etsy. This thermos looks like a midway prize from some long-forgotten church fair.

Joey sways with his fishing rod, eyes squinted, sucking his own stogie. All the guys do. Put them in sailor suits, shave their heads, shove a can of spinach into their hands, they'd be a collection of Popeyes.

Joey upends his beer. He pours a last trickle into his mouth. "Hope you brought enough for everybody, not just your boyfriend."

I pass out extra cups and a box of doughnuts, hope Stanley doesn't correct Joey on the status of our relationship. "You boys spend the night on the beach?"

Renzi lifts his cup to me. "The man who sleeps catches no fish. What are you doing up?"

He's Aunt Theresa's son, and younger than the others. He doesn't look comfortable with a cigar. Just as well. Cancer's killed him four times I know of. A student at Villanova, he followed in Joey's footsteps but without the scholarship. Uncle Paul did well for himself and provided well for his family after he died. "Angela kicked me in the head when she went to the bathroom. Safer to be awake."

They don't have to know the rest of it. How I dreamed of Friedrich Palmon, in his present-day self, whirling me round and round at Hallowmas while Der Weasel catcalled from the sidelines, "You got no idea what's really going on, do ya, Dr. Panisporchi?"

I look down the line. "Anybody catching anything?"

"Fishing's not about catching, it's about Aunt Gracie's Special Blend." Joey kicks at an empty bottle. "She sold it after the war, to help make ends meet. Ma ever tell you?"

I presume Joey means World War II.

"Family secret." Ralphie burps. He's Aunt Theresa's older son, also a student at Villanova and more comfortable with vice.

Joey smacks him on the back. "What're the cops gonna do if they find out? She's ninety-five years old." He turns to me. "Aunt Gracie used to pick juniper berries in the park to flavor it. Bought the moonshine from a guy on Porter Street. Tough old coot."

Joey flexes a bicep. He blows air into his cheeks and pulls his neck into his shoulders to show the supplier's bulk, that he wasn't somebody to mess with. "Neighborhood cops didn't care, so long as they got their cut. His son took over after he died. Looks just like his old man. It's widow work. Ma started making it after dad died. I used to deliver her orders."

Memory, mixed-up and momentary, flashes on herb-filled cotton bags, smelling of juniper and orange, on steam, thick enough to touch. And bottles, like the ones Aunt Gracie uses, lined up on the kitchen table. "But Ma doesn't drink."

"She needed the money. Tough times then. I went to work. Paper route. Odd jobs. Did neighborhood deliveries for Mr. Olivieri, mostly for tips. Wasn't much, but kept us in groceries."

More memories. Ma counting out change. Joey, as a boy, counting with her.

He holds out his cup. "You got more?"

Should I wait for a *please*? It won't come. The surf scent rises, marshy, a little rotten, laced with cigars and the odor of oil from a trawler puttering across the horizon.

Stanley reels in his line. "Time we got some sleep."

"No sleeping in that camper." Joey spits over a shoulder. "Smells like anchovies and old boots. I'm hoping the ladies will take pity on us. Let us sack out on their beds after they get themselves dolled up for the day."

Stanley whips around, expression tougher than trigonometry and as hard to interpret. "You stink of beer. Ask the uncles. They won't care."

Joey cuffs Stanley on the shoulder. "You're the one who shoulda gone to be a priest. They'd've loved you. They're into redemption." He drains his cup and casts it aside.

I pick it up for him, shamed. I won't pick up Stanley's dish at dinner, but I'll grope in the sand for Joey's trash. A habit four hundred years out of date.

I toss the cup back to the sand. Joey's not my guardian anymore.

Again, memory flashes on the counting. Ma holding up a finger to explain to Joey. "Only one. Do you understand? You'll share."

Embarrassment over my petty attitude with the cup rises. Only one what?

Luigi reels in his line. "Stanley's right. Better we don't look like we didn't sleep. The aunts will give us trouble."

"Angela you mean." Joey secures his hook to the rod. "Wouldn't have taken you for the type to let a woman push you around."

Luigi keeps reeling. "Depends on the woman."

"One's pretty much the same as the other. Just we don't tell 'em. They like to think they're special. Right, Eugenia? That's what you think about Carlotta. That she's nothing special. Not worthy of your time or attention."

Stanley stops reeling. "That's enough. You're drunk."

I want to come back with a jibe, pass off Joey's words as an old family joke, but the fun's gone out of the fellows, dissolved under Joey's acid comments.

Stanley dismantles his fishing rod. He whispers something to Joey. Joey mutters back. Stanley murmurs something else, his annoyance obvious in the staccato syllables. Joey shoves Aunt Gracie's Special Blend into Stanley's hand.

Dawn grays down. The world goes fuzzy. Aunt Gracie's Special Blend transforms to a bottle of wine. The whoosh of surf becomes the hum of a crowded room. Cigar and salt smell switch to cigarette smoke and sweat. Bottle clinks change to the tinkle of ice in whiskey tumblers.

Joey sharpens. His jacket and hoodie convert to an army uniform, circa 1964.

I'm excited. I'm proud. I'm tipsy. My high heels wobble and the lace bodice of my scrumptious pink taffeta dinner dress scratches across the tops of my breasts. A man beside me whispers something suggestive in my ear. I turn to answer. To give him another kiss.

The gray rolls out. The beach returns.

And I kiss Joey on his cheek.

He puts a hand to the spot, expression bemused, my action obviously unexpected.

But the thought of the kiss, meant for a lover, though it landed in a place appropriate for a brother, gets under my skin. And makes it crawl.

Stanley takes hold of my elbow. "Let's go. I'll walk you back."

24

A vision of Trailer Park Mouse whose husband was her brother haunts me in the following hours, as does the vision in the young ladies' room, the man beneath the counterpane.

And Joey. In uniform. Circa 1964.

On a bench on the boardwalk with Donna and Angela and Carlotta, I babble about the gin pushing, impatient for Vicodin's fuzzy bubble to descend.

Carlotta shoves her hands into her jacket, blue and bulky enough to hide twins. "One of my great-great-aunts pushed gin. She supplied a speakeasy near Broad and Porter."

"Ritner."

Carlotta turns. "What?"

"Ritner." I watch the clouds, so low and foreboding. "The speakeasy was at Broad and Ritner. They tore it down to build the hospital. It was called The Rathskellar. German for Rat Cellar, a basement tavern. Old-fashioned name for it. Went legit once prohibition ended."

Donna holds mittened hands over her nose. "How do you know?"

"My uncle told me." *But not in this life.*

Angela pulls out a fresh pack. She taps it on her forearm. "Wonder if the gin pushing has anything to do with why Ma doesn't drink. Whaddya think, Eugenia? Personal penance, maybe?" She cups a hand, flicks the lighter to the cigarette's tip. "Where'd she set up the still? Next to Backyard Mary?"

That image expands. Ma filling flowerpots with kindling. Striking a match. Adjusting a damper on a makeshift rocket stove. Warming the mash until it sends alcohol steam condensing through the tubing. Draining it, drop by drop, into a mason jar. Offering it to Mary, a priest at communion. "Should I add a little anise?"

A scene both familiar and foreign. Something I've done, if not exactly that way.

I take the cigarette from Angela, take a drag. "No still. She got the base from some guy on Porter Street. Son to the guy who supplied Aunt Gracie. Joey says he looks like his old man."

Donna plucks the cigarette from my fingers and flicks it into the sand. "How would Joey know?"

I don't know which confuses me more, Donna's presumption with the cigarette, or why I wish so badly I could have gotten a few more puffs in before she took it. "Joey picked up Ma's orders."

"No. How would Joey know what the old man looked like if the son supplied your mother?"

The wind dies and the sea calms with the question, Donna's tinkly ear dangles sounding alarm bells in the stillness.

Joey couldn't have known. The old man was dead by the time Ma needed his wares. Joey never would have met him.

The wind picks up again, blowing colder than it did. The anxious creature gnawing at my insides all but burrows a hole through my stomach. My head buzzes. So does my cell. I answer, grateful for the diversion, even after I see who it is. "What is it, Maurizio?"

"What kind of flowers do you like?"

"Um . . . pansies, peonies, orchids. Why?"

"Funeral director's trying to chisel you down with the advance planning package. Wants to give you daisies. You got any idea the difference in cost? Don't worry, I'll take care of him. Orchids, you want, orchids, you get."

"Look, Maurizio, none of this is really important. Put down a number and get people to agree. This is taking too long, and—"

Donna studies me, her expression disapproving. "Prolonged argument benefits no one."

Sun Tzu. *Totable Quotes.* Page 233.

"Dr. Panisporchi?" Maurizio's voice crackles out of my cell, reminding me what I was doing before Donna stuck her nose in my business.

"Roses." I say the next words slowly, so little Miss Meddler doesn't miss a syllable. "Tell the funeral director I want roses. Lots of them."

"You sure? They're horribly allergic."

"I won't care." I hang up. Mary likes roses. That's why they call it a rosary. Then, because it seems related. "Aunt Rose pushed gin, too."

To help save the money to buy her little seashore house and fix it up, because she and Uncle Lou were young and in love and hardworking as he was, he didn't make enough, in the beginning, to afford it.

It's true. I know this.

How I know, I don't know.

●●●

Later that afternoon, over Joey's protests, the guys take us to play pool at an upscale place Stanley knows. It's Luigi's idea. "We used to play all the time."

Joey refuses the cue Stanley tries to hand him, instead opting for a seat at the bar.

Carlotta plops herself on the stool beside and orders a club soda. "Don't you want to learn how to play, honey?"

"He plays," I tell Carlotta.

Joey shoots Stanley a look.

Ha! "He's pretty good, too, I hear."

Ralphie racks the balls. "More than good. He's a legend. Got a picture of him hanging over the sticks at Ignacio's."

One of those dark recesses goes to work, rooting for where I've heard that name before. "Your bookie?"

Renzi laughs. "Campus hangout. Joey's all early Johnny Depp in the picture. White T-shirt. Leather jacket. Too cool to smile. The whole cannoli."

Ralphie dangles a shredded napkin over Joey's forehead to illustrate what he looked like with the longer tousled locks of fifteen years previous. "And he needed a shave."

He points to a squiggle under Joey's eye, at what remains from stitches received a decade or more ago. "No beauty mark, though. What happened? Somebody bite you?"

Joey shoves him. "Yeah. For asking too many questions."

I roll the eight ball across the table to Luigi. "So. You went to Villanova, too? Never mind. Of course you did. You all did. You should have gotten together. Applied for group rates."

Stanley clears his throat. "Anybody for beer?"

●●●

I wear an orangey-pinkish kind of flowing yet fitted thing with a sweetheart neckline for dinner, purchased at Donna's insistence, which, I have to admit, minimizes my hips and makes my boobs look perky. A coordinating evening bag, also purchased at Donna's behest, dangles from my shoulder, which rises reflexively against it, uncomfortable without my big, brown satchel's comfortable weight.

Donna runs a finger along the bag's delicate chain. "Now isn't this nicer? People grow attached to their burdens."

"More than their burdens attach to them. George Bernard Shaw." Page 10.

At dinner, Donna parks herself beside the breadsticks. She takes an extra roll when I refuse the basket and sends the waitress running for more cream for her coffee.

Maybe she takes those capsules that make the fat slide through. Maybe that's how she stays so skinny.

Stanley whispers an apology. "I didn't mean to not mention I knew Joey. It never occurred to me to mention it. Then when it was obvious he hadn't mentioned it, it didn't seem right to mention it without first talking to him about it. We played a little pool, is all. In grad school. It's not like we were friends. I didn't even know his last name until the wedding."

Stanley puts a hand on my knee. He slides it up my thigh. "I'm sorry. Joey's not important. You're important."

My heart soars. It's okay. We'll talk. We'll work it out. We'll get back together. Then, maybe before he drops me home, we'll swing by his loft and—

"What are you waiting for, Stanley?" Uncle Lou waves his wine in our direction, a nice red, matched perfectly to the *bracciole* with porcini mushrooms. "Smart. Pretty. A college teacher. Gal like her comes along once in a lifetime. But she won't hang around forever."

That did not happen. Mary on My Keychain, please tell me that did not just happen.

Ma and Angela and Joey and Carlotta and Luigi stare us down, along with the aunts and uncles and cousins, young and old. One of the kids pipes up. "What's Uncle Lou talking about?"

His older brother punches his arm. "They want Stanley to marry Eugenia before she's too old to have babies, doofus."

Stanley pulls me away from the table. He grabs my hat, grabs my coat, and takes off, dragging me down the boardwalk. I stumble. He pauses. Only long enough for me to slip out of my heels and pick them up, leaving only my nylons between the cold wood of the boards and my feet.

"Stanley. Please. Stop."

He does, by a bench, but he doesn't sit. He paces, back and forth. Hands jammed in pockets, then out of his pockets and running through his crew cut.

My Lutheran soldier made the same kinds of movements, although the only time I saw him do so, he was angry over Josef.

Finally, Stanley waggles a finger at me. "You didn't tell them we broke up."

25

No, Stanley. Sorry. I didn't tell anybody about our breakup. Back home, I slouch beside one of Ma's cupid lamps, guilty and grumpy. I mean . . . neither did he.

Angela brushes a dollop of red along a nail edge. She repositions on the plastic slipcover, folds a fat-free calf under a fat-free thigh. "Of course he didn't tell anybody, dum-dum. He was hoping it'd blow over and he wouldn't have to."

My cell buzzes again. Maurizio.

I click it over. Add orchids. Add calla lilies. Add protected tulips from Holland that have to be flown in. Add anything the hell you want, then add a pot of African violets for your contingency. Just leave me alone.

I grab my jacket and head into the night, stopping on my way past the newsstand, now shuttered, to note the strip of sidewalk where my lawsuit troubles began, unable to believe I let Maurizio bully anybody about flowers. A row of figures lined up on the sidewalk near one of the padlocks draws me closer.

Jesus, Mary, and Joseph. In red, blue, and yellow. Rough, but recognizable, pinched together in a folksy way.

The fragrance of coffee wafts over my left shoulder. "Make them myself."

I whip around, keychain clenched, Blessed Corkscrew poking between index and middle finger, ready to rake Her across the face of whoever is stupid enough to sneak up on me in the dark.

The newsstand guy. Cup in hand.

I relax.

He rubs his mouth, revealing a missing canine, fresh and raw, then holds up a paper bag, uses it to indicate the sandwich shop across the street, their lights dark, the sign in their doorway declaring them Closed. "I'm always their last customer."

I point to the figurines. "What are they for?"

"Protection. Like yours." He points to Mary on My Keychain. "But, I don't talk to mine."

"Leave her alone. She's not bothering you." That voice, friendly and familiar, comes over my right shoulder.

"Mr. Olivieri." Embarrassment gathers under my collar. "He's just talking. I was getting out my house keys."

"How's your mother?" He's a small man, completely bald on top. He doesn't smile much, but his eyes are always dancing.

"She's fine."

"Would you like me to walk you home?"

"I'm good. It's just a couple blocks."

Mr. Olivieri continues on, moving in the strong, even steps I remember from his Oberholt version. He was bigger in that life, a farmer with broad hands and short fingers who always had dirt under his nails and took a lot of pride in his parsnips.

I hope he made it out okay.

The newsstand guy tips his cup to his lips. "A man can't always choose his fights."

Josef's line. Squeezed out through clenched teeth while he and Ruprecht Vogt argued in the alley that Hallowmas.

"A coward gets them chosen for him." The pain-in-the-ass pamphleteer's reply leaps from my lips.

I slap a hand across my mouth, turn my back on Ruprecht's modern-day version, chest tight, gaze clamped on the street corner.

gotta go gotta go gotta go

He's coming.

I back a step, then two, meaning to run, to get out of here, to get

Ruprecht Vogt out, too. *Don't do it.* I tell him in my head. *It'll be your fault. It'll all be your fault.* "Give them to me. Don't put them up."

I turn, half expecting to see the pamphlets, those goddamned pamphlets, in the newsstand guy's hand.

"Give you what?" He pours his coffee onto the sidewalk. Opens the bag, shows me his sandwich. "I got nothing." He turns out his pockets. Flaps the inside of his coat. "Nothing."

The newsstand guy tucks the sandwich bag under his arm. He turns on his heel. He heads down the block.

•••

Next day, over lunch at the little deli around the corner, I lay it out for Maurizio. "This has to end. The hospital bills, laser surgery for the scar, reimbursement for my Geiger jacket. That's enough."

Maurizio eyes up his sandwich, sprouts on rye. He lifts the top slice to peek beneath. "Mayonnaise. You gotta watch like a hawk." He scrapes at it, blobbing it on the side of his plate. "Here's the thing. You got to cover my contingency. You don't ask for more than laser surgery and hospital bills, you still got to cover my percentage. That's why we ask for pain and suffering."

"But you're adding negligence."

"To cover my contingency on the pain and suffering."

"Let's pull Mr. Olivieri out of the loop."

"It was his van."

"Which he was operating at the funeral director's behest."

Maurizio stares at my forehead. "Something like what happened to you can have long-reaching consequences. Trauma can cause cancer." He taps a well-gnawed fingernail to his forehead. "You might have something growing there right now and not know it."

"But that's ridicul—"

"I've seen cases you wouldn't believe. Maybe you'll get headaches. You know, the blinding kind. Maybe it'll hit you at the wrong moment. Like when you're crossing a street. You grab your head." Maurizio puts down his sandwich and demonstrates, face contorted with enough pain and suffering to cover a thousand contingencies. "You don't see the bus. POW! Hasta la vista, baby."

My world pans down, tightening on a single *noir* character splayed across a pineapple smoothie, well-honed *jurisprudence* wedged firmly up his ass. "For all adventures that may still betide, perchance from horse may tumble one or two, and break his neck. See what insurance, then, it is for all, that I within your fellowship did fall."

My descent into Yoda-speak appears to flummox the unflappable Mr. Bracaconi. "Dr. Panisporchi?"

"*The Pardoner's Tale.* From Chaucer. It's the pardoner's litany of reasons to pay him for a pardon because, at any moment, in any of myriad ways, Death may come for you."

"Death comes for everybody."

"Yeah, but if it comes without a pardon, you die unabsolved and go to purgatory."

Maurizio's face freezes, his expression caught between confused and congenial. "Some kind of wise guy, this pardoner. Good scam."

Stanley's observation, repeated from our first disastrous lunch together and without the warmth of Stanley's voice behind it, sounds menacing.

Maurizio sneezes and sneezes again. I dig for a tissue and hand it over, happy for the distraction. A Post-It, covered in Joey's neat accountant's script, comes clear with the Kleenex. Maurizio picks it up. "Constantine DiPiero? Your sister-in-law's cousin?"

I keep the casual in my voice. "Yeah. Joey's using him. Says you might need his number."

Maurizio flicks a thumb to the Post-It. Back. Forth. Back. Forth. He lays it on the table. "It's my job to look out for you, Dr. Panisporchi. Make sure we cover the bases. Even laser surgery won't make the scar go away. Believe me, I know." He points out a faint line running in the hollow of his left cheek.

"Fishing accident." He adjusts his tie clip. Diamond. "I know this looks terribly personal to you. It's not. Most cases like this are handled behind the scenes. The parties involved never hear about it. But Dr.

Rossi . . . he swung a baseball bat into the works. And that threw everybody."

"Then give Dr. Rossi a place to vent his grief. Go after the newsstand guy." The words come out in a rush. My next don't give the impression I'd prefer either, taking on a whiny high school tinge. "He's the one who started it all."

"He's not insured. I told you that."

"He must have something or he couldn't keep his license, the city wouldn't lease the sidewalk space to him. Joey says so."

"Only the minimum. He delivers pizzas in his off hours to make ends meet. And he's crazy. Talks to himself. How am I supposed to make a case with a nut job like that?"

"He grabbed Joey. That counts for something. He set me off balance." I swing my hands back to illustrate. "If I'm scarred for life, it's the newsstand guy's fault."

"Whoa, there, Dr. Panisporchi. You're talking assault and battery. Nobody's levying criminal charges here. It's all civil stuff. And that's where we want to keep it. Get the law involved, no telling what the newsstand guy would do. Crazy guy like that. Lots of people grabbing people, sending them into snowdrifts. Confusing if you're in the midst of it. Different if you stand apart, watch it like a movie."

Like from the window of your office next to the funeral parlor.

"All we know for sure is you did a backflip over Mr. Olivieri's van. And that information is bankable."

And that's your real interest in this mess. I think about how I went for Luigi, how that movement tipped me into Mr. Olivieri's van and this case into my favor.

"This is my job." Maurizio drapes his napkin over his lap. "I spent a lot of years at Villanova learning to do it."

I take a bite of sandwich, hoping I look noncommittally agreeable. "Joey went to Villanova. So did Luigi."

Maurizio smiles. On him, it doesn't set well. He takes a fork and knife to his tomato, slicing quickly.

There's that saying about how your enemy won't share your salt. I nudge the shaker in Maurizio's direction and point to his tomato.

Maurizio nudges it back. "Are you nuts? That stuff will kill you."

••

That evening, Friedrich calls my cell. "A signature, doc. One stupid signature and we can start the support group. Don't tell me you're not curious."

Casablanca. Rupee. Joan. "I blocked you. How'd you get around it?"

"C'mon, doc. We're both cutting it close. Malfunctioning traffic light. Ball left on a stair tread. Uncovered manhole. Bad shrimp. Tick. Tock. Tick. Tock."

Boom. "I think we're making it all up."

"I see. You were fine so long as you had hindsight by yourself, but now I got it with you, we're both crazy." He tsk-tsks me. "You know what they say about denial."

Yeah. It's full of crocodiles.

Friedrich doesn't need to talk to me by cell. He can read my mind. I hang up and open my laptop.

Google gives me ten thousand, five hundred hits for *Rathskeller*, mostly modern. Add Broad and Ritner to the search and the results drop to seven, none meaningful.

Four hundred and eighty-four hits for Oberholt. All surnames.

Do I mean *Berthold*? Google inquires.

I check Google Germany.

Do I *meinten Sie Oberholz*?

No. And I don't *meinten* Oberdorf, Oberstdorf, or Oberostendorf.

I *meinten* Oberholt. But Google contains no notation, no footnote, no history, no offhand remark to indicate Oberholt ever existed.

Then how did Donna find out about it?

Blessed Mary on the Windowsill's question lands like a fresh dog turd. Stinking and steaming and impossible to ignore.

I check the Facebook page's e-mail.

Casablanca lets me know his regrets are his own and he hates the page's cover photo. "Oh, and I've moved. So there's no way you'll ever find me."

Joan Crawford wonders if her children would think it weird if she sent them Easter baskets. "Nothing fancy. Free-trade chocolate bunnies and free-range eggs."

Rupee sounds lonely. "I've run into others. But they're shits."

An e-mail from Friedrich dings in before I log out.

Arriving from a blocked address.

The faster water flows under the bridge, the harder to reclaim what gets swept away. My karmic load is full. I need to make things right. Please understand how important this is.

Phone. E-mail. Class. Even when I'm getting a cup of coffee. Last week, I saw him skulking in the back of my bus, odd-colored, hand-knitted hoodie pulled low over his eyes.

Frustration takes the fast track out my fingertips, sends them flying across the keyboard. "Wanna make it right? Invent a time machine, go back to the point you thought it'd be a good idea to take my class and . . . DON'T."

I hit send, pull a notebook and pen out of my purse, and start drawing. Circles to represent characters. Lines to connect lives.

Like Friedrich did in my office.

FRIEDRICH: Chaucerian star-crossed cousin pining over Emily. Astrology-loving Nicholas boinking the landlord's wife. Two-timing Bavarian-bread-baking-fuck.

How many others? What lives? Who? Where? When?

Why.

Next circle.

LUIGI: Der Weasel.

I flash on a car. On a lift. Butt crack visible from where I wait, near the big overhead door. Knocking against metal. Grease. Gasoline. A . . . mechanic. Working on brakes. He cheated me.

Us.

The other person in that pronoun. The man under the counterpane.

My heart cracks. Fury steams out the fissures.

Really, Der Weasel? Brakes?

I hate him.

STANLEY: Lutheran Soldier. Actuary.

And again that fluttery feeling, the strains of *Unchained Melody* swelling to fill the room. A taffeta dress. A man crooning in my ear. "Darling." Low. Pleasant. And a little off-key.

My pen hovers over a circle, wanting to write the name, whatever that name might be, fighting the horrible feeling I want to write the name under Stanley because I don't want to write it under Joey.

DONNA: She's easy. Nile, Bavarian Meddler, Thirty Years' War Scholar.

CARLOTTA: Brewer's Daughter. Fiancé Stealer. Sister-in-law.

FUTZ: . . . Asshole.

Disparate pilgrims. A far-flung constellation. Spiraling a single point of reference.

Oberholt.

And maybe there are more.

The sky darkens. The wind picks up. The living room window rattles.

Blessed Mary, My Arbiter of Right and Wrong, waves me over from Her windowsill. "Even the stars return to the place where they had been."

And out of mind, pass all things done by mankind.

Keychain Mary jabs me in the kneecap. "No man is an island."

That island is my student. I could get myself fired.

A sudden gust slams the kitchen door open. Backyard Mary. Adamant. Authentic. And authoritative as hell. "Why cry for mercy, if you will not pray for peace?"

Thunder crashes, reverberating like sheet metal smacked with a hammer and ping-ponging off the bones of my skull.

I fall to my knees.

Whimper. Then weep.

Then clamp hands to ears, wanting to wail my answer to the heavens, to finally admit the truth:

I don't give a fuck for whom the bell tolls. I only care when it tolls for me.

26

In Oberholt, I ran barefoot, toes squishing in the dirt, hair streaming, unclasped, behind. Papa kept me with him in his print shop. He had no son to teach. Then my cousin, Josef, newly orphaned and five years older than I, arrived, come to live as apprentice to my father. The chill wind of propriety swept through my world. My roaming days were over.

Mama added hems to ensure my dresses covered my ankles and made me put on shoes. I joined her in the small room behind the shop, hair properly pinned, and spent my days learning to crochet lace as beautiful as hers.

V-stitch. V-stitch. V-stitch. Purl.

Row after row. Hour after hour. Until eyes squinted and fingers cramped and the hook pricked, drawing blood.

My first bout of hindsight descended. Painful. Poignant. Spooky as shit.

I saw myself in a garden, surrounded by blooms. Free to wander within, yet chained by convention.

I cast off my crochet and charged into Papa's shop. I stood behind Josef. Papa gave instruction, constant instruction and only to Josef, never to me. The best way to sew the pages. How to tell the glue was the right consistency. The most efficient way to engrave the sheets.

I traced the letters Papa's press produced, crisp and mysterious and offering a freedom grown faint. "Papa. Teach me to read."

But the church bells rang. For hours. There was shouting, then screams. Clashes and clangs. Metal on bone. Pikes on rock. Boots and hooves and vomit and piss.

And blood. Gallons and gallons, sluicing between the cobbles in the town square.

Papa and Mama were dead.

Oberholt, by order of the Freiherr, was Lutheran.

In those days, Blessed Mary lived on Mama's nightstand. Carved in wood, She was not somber and monotone like Present Day Refrigerator Mary, but dressed in blue with blonde waves framed by a white kerchief and golden halo. Josef made me hide Her under a floorboard. He made me wrap Mama's rosary around Mary's shoulders and ordered me not to speak of Her again.

But sometimes, when Josef was gone, I took Her out. Sometimes I kicked the shoes from my feet, pulled the pins from my hair, looped Her rosary around my fingers, circled it above my head. And danced.

Corner to corner. Counter to door. Scooping straw with my toes and making promises. "Someday. Soon. The moment things settle. You and me will run away and You'll get Your chance to run with toes squishing in the dirt."

And that's what I did, the morning after Hallowmas. Face bruised. Eye swollen. Stench of acid thick about me. Defiant. Dejected. Stupid.

"Where is Josef?" Der Weasel's voice, grating and gruff, sent my heart out of my chest and my wits flying.

I opened numbed fingers and dropped the rosary into the pocket of my apron. Then I turned. "Josef is at church."

Der Weasel scratched a dirty fingernail beside fresh stitches along the hollow of his cheek. "And where is the press?"

"I don't know. We only repair bindings now."

"So Josef claims. Claims he doesn't know anything about the Papist nonsense somebody tacked to the church doorways last night, either. Or the whereabouts of the monk."

Why Der Weasel wanted the monk was obvious from the way he kept flexing his foot. And if he wanted to know about the Papist nonsense, he should have chased down its author, Ruprecht Vogt, the pamphleteer.

I rubbed at the fresh bruise on my hip. Der Weasel leered at the movement, then took my chin in his fist, turning my head to examine the even newer bruise under my eye. "Tell me what I need to know and I'll make sure Josef never hurts you again."

I wanted to fling off his hand. I didn't dare. "I did it myself." I pointed to the ladder leading to Josef's loft. "I tripped on the rungs."

His fist tightened on my chin. He didn't believe me. But I didn't matter.

He let me go. "What is that smell?"

At first I thought Der Weasel meant the sulfuric acid, the vapors wafting from a bottle Josef had purposely left unsecured a few hours before, but Der Weasel pushed it aside. He opened the shutters, then crouched by the hearth. He pulled an iron kettle from a pile of embers, and lifted the lid. "Bratwurst?"

Nobody had bratwurst anymore. Except the Freiherr.

"Herbed rabbit." I edged toward the door. "Josef laid a few snares."

Der Weasel stepped between me and my escape. He pulled a knife from under his shirt and went to work cleaning his fingernails just as he would four centuries and another lifetime later in my family's kitchen. "Only thing I've been snaring lately is rats."

He moved around the room, examining jars, uncovering boxes. He smelled one. "Cinnamon." He checked another. "And chocolate."

"It's old. I'm saving it for something special."

He ignored me, prying lids off barrels and shoving baskets around. He found Blessed Mary, hiding behind a pile of buckram. He held her up. "Is there more?"

I thought of the rosary in my apron pocket, the bulge hidden in its folds. "No."

I should have told Der Weasel the truth. Should have left the rosary with Mary, left both beneath the floorboards. Should've done as Josef ordered. Told him while I could. Should've believed. Should've trusted. Should have cared.

But here's the bitch about memory. It allows us to return to a moment. And leaves us helpless to change it.

In that moment, everything changed. Der Weasel dropped Blessed Mary on the counter and backed me to the buckram. He laid a hand along either side of my skirt, pressed his body to mine, strong and sinewy and stinking of sweat. "Where are the pamphlets?"

I didn't have them. Didn't know. Couldn't hand them over if I wanted. "We only bind now."

He slid a finger along my cheek, a hand down my arm. "The baker's a fool. So is that soldier. They're boys. Not men. They have no idea what they're doing." He ran a hand down my apron front.

And found the rosary.

Der Weasel's face contorted. He whipped out his knife, pressed the edge to the tip of my nose. "Bitch. I asked you."

"I—I meant to tell you. I forgot. It's been there for days." I didn't think. Didn't worry. Didn't listen.

He caught my hair, bent me sideways, shoved my skirts over my hips.

"Please," I whispered. "Don't."

Wooden Mary wouldn't watch. She kept Her head bowed, Her hands folded. Der Weasel held the blade to my waist, hand moving under my blouse, his tongue along my ear.

I felt him grope for his trousers. Felt him struggle to undo the buttons. I head-butted him, grabbed the bottle of acid, and flung the contents into his eyes.

Sometimes the shortest moments last longest.

Engraver's tools scattered. Bottles and buckram shifted. Wooden Mary fell, knocking a vial of rose oil to the floor. It shattered. The scent ascended, strong enough to cover the reek of acid. Of sweat. Of sin.

Der Weasel convulsed. He fell to the floor in a fit of allergic sneezing. He clawed at his eyes. And screamed.

I had to shut him up. People would hear. People would come. So I grabbed the Blessed Mother, cinching Her like a modern-day batter at the plate, cranked back as far as my arms would go.

And swung away. Landing Blessed Mary against the side of Der Weasel's head with all the force my work-hardened muscles could muster. Hard enough I felt the recoil in my shoulders. Hard enough a bit of wood from Mary's cheek nicked away with the blow.

But Der Weasel kept on screaming. So I hit him again.

Then a third time.

Just to be sure.

He landed in the evening stew, butt crack exposed, bleeding into the bratwurst. I wrestled him to the root cellar, opened the hatch, and rolled him in. He came to rest beside the printing press.

In my present-day cement backyard, on the morning after my evening with Google, I explain everything to Backyard Mary.

"I had to hide him. Times were tumultuous, people were testy." I kneel before Her, brushing away the dirt and dead leaves gathering between Her pots, then fling the brush to the cement. "Little turd didn't even know how to read."

Blessed Mary doesn't care. Doesn't listen. It's my fault. Everything's always my fault.

Almost four centuries after I washed Der Weasel's brains off Wooden Mary's halo, and a week after Dad died, Joey clipped Her Blessed Backyard Twin with a baseball. He took a tip off one of Mary's fingers and chipped a divot from Her cheek. Just like the one Der Weasel's skull had claimed. He shoved me on the shoulder and dared me to tell.

The injury mesmerized me. It trailed down Mary's cheek, a shrapnel tear. Awakening memories dead almost four years, and memories dead for a decade, and memories dead a half century.

Just as hindsight had that first time in Oberholt.

I tried to make it up to Mary, putting makeup on Her Backyard Version to cover Joey's sin, lipstick and eye shadow, a little blush to bring out the roses in Her cheek. I filled Mary's tear with Silly Putty and smoothed it over with a fine dusting of dime-store face powder in Sun-Kissed Beige. My act transformed that corner of the yard to a shrine just like Thomas Becket's in Canterbury, and like one of

Chaucer's pilgrims, I made regular visits to keep Blessed Mary looking perky.

But Mary whispered to Ma how it was time to spring-plant Her pots, then forced the sun from behind the clouds so my handiwork shone bright against the yard's gray concrete.

Ma called the priest, certain our yard was possessed. Father DiLullo, very young, very eager, very new to our parish, flung holy water at the daffodils, intoning, "*In nomine Patris, et Filii, et Spiritus Sancti. Amen.*"

A thunderstorm sent my hard work swirling into the storm drain. Once the skies cleared, I made Backyard Mary up again, genuflecting so I could add watercolor to deepen Her robe's weathered blue. Ma called Father DiLullo again, wondering if we witnessed a miracle.

Father DiLullo looked hard at Mary. He ran a thumb over Mary's robe, another across Her cheek, took a finger and lifted my chin, the way Dad used to when he wanted to explain something. "Mary doesn't need makeup any more than you."

Ma clenched a finger between her teeth to understand heaven had no hand in Blessed Mary's makeover. She made me scrub Her with dish soap, then do another kind of pilgrimage, a super-special one we call a *novena*, which means *nine* in Latin and lasts nine days—kind of like a rosary on steroids. Father DiLullo tells the story every year when he makes his annual visitation. Blessed Mary loves it.

I know because I hear Her giggling.

Fine, Mary. Have Your laugh. I'm done kneeling. And I'm done cleaning the debris around Your pots. When this life ends, I'll be ready, waving a writ of wrongful assignment in one hand, and some properly filled out pretense at piety for my next life in the other.

My days of making offerings before manmade constructs are over. I have been entombed. And like Dante on his path through hell, I long to see the stars.

27

*E*yes closed, I scrawl my name across the application, jerking through in one continuous motion. The resulting signature is choppy and pointy and nothing like mine.

Hindsight's always twenty-twenty.

Friedrich folds the application and stuffs it into his backpack. "We're in business, doc. I'll post notices. We'll have our first meeting tonight." He hesitates. "About Thursday. In the food court . . . I mean with Dr. Futz. Listen, how you conduct yourself is your business. I just think—"

"Shut up. Stop thinking. And *never* follow me again."

"Okay. Okay. Can I list your Facebook page on the flyer?"

●●●

A young woman knocks on the entrance to Library Lounge C. She points to the chartreuse poster tacked to the door: HINDSIGHT SUPPORT GROUP. "Is this the Hindsight Support Group?"

Friedrich springs to his feet. He moves toward the newcomer, hand extended, then stops, eyebrows standing out dark and surprised against a paling forehead. "I'm . . . Friedrich."

I wait, but he doesn't introduce me, so I extend mine. "And I'm Dr. Panisporchi. The faculty sponsor."

"Ali." The girl dipsy-doodles around our outstretched hands, pushes a damp clump of medium brown locks out of one eye, and thrusts her chin at the rain-drenched windows. "Does this room have shades? I don't want anybody to find me."

"We're five floors up." Friedrich pries the lid off a plastic container and brings it to her. "Who's looking for you?"

"Everybody." Ali examines the pfeffernüsse, picks one and shoves it into the pocket of her windbreaker. "Are we it? I thought there'd be a lecture. Like AA."

"Have you ever met anybody else with hindsight?"

Ali sweeps the acoustic-tiled ceiling, then peers into the corners. She backs her way to the door, stops at the entrance, bobs past the jamb, and searchlights her gaze on a neck scrawnier than a Slim Jim. Up the hallway. Then down. Finally she shakes her head. "Kinda strange, huh? You'd think I'd run into one every five minutes. Zero oh three percent. That's like one in thirty."

"Three hundred," I say.

Friedrich taps a finger to his teeth. "Three thousand."

"Oh." Ali flops into the seat, her voice tinier than her cup size. "They didn't tell me where to put the decimal point."

She wraps a Keds-clad foot around a metal chair leg. "I found a Facebook page. Seems legit. I write the owner. He never writes back. Maybe he's looking for info. Maybe he's following me now. Nazis do that kind of thing, y'know."

Well, fuck me standing up. Could this be the cantankerous Casablanca?

My mental image of a wiry, muscled fellow in a beret, Gauliose dangling from a contemptuous lip, fades into the scenery along with Ali. "There are no more Nazis. They can't hurt you now."

Ali pushes hair out of her other eye and gathers it behind, fingers flicking one over the other to work it into a messy braid. "You're new at this, aren't you?"

She stands. "Will you meet next week?"

••

A few minutes later, Friedrich gathers napkins. "It went well, don't you think?"

All twenty-seven words of it. "This is a bad idea. We have no way to tell what will walk through that door. We're gonna attract a lot of weirdos."

"Ali's not weird."

"Ali's been to AA. I don't want to be the reason she goes back."

He messes with the thermos. Tightening the top. Untightening it. Tighten. Untighten. Tighten. "Why should you be the reason she goes back?"

I grab the thermos. Mid-tighten. "Are you kidding? Since you stirred up this crap, *I* need AA."

"Don't blame your proclivities on hindsight."

"I'm not. I'm blaming you." I stuff the thermos into a pocket of his book bag, and stuff the pfeffernüsse beside.

Friedrich holds out his hand. For an insane moment, I think he means for me to take it. For another insane moment, I consider it, even take a step nearer, but Friedrich points to Blessed Mary on My Keychain, peeking out of the front pocket of my purse. "I'll finish cleaning up. Let me have the key. I'll bring it by your office tomorrow."

A dropdown menu of all the rules and regulations I'd be breaking lands front and center in my mind's eye. A mental image of me setting my alarm for an early morning meeting drops in front of it.

What's he gonna do? Steal the folding chairs? I work the key off my chain and hand it over. "You know her."

Friedrich yanks a bottle of water from his pack. He unscrews the cap. And sips. "You mean Ali?"

"Mother Theresa. Who the hell do you think I mean?" I snag the chartreuse notice off the door and wave it at him. "This is your idea. We're doing this because of you. If you know this girl, tell me."

Friedrich drinks again, water glugging with each bob of his Adam's apple. He recaps the bottle, tosses it into the waste container, wipes the back of his hand across his mouth. And looks to the doorway.

I pull out my copy of the paperwork I signed for him and wad it tight. "See this? This is what I'm sending Administration when they ask for a progress report." I toss the wad into my briefcase and bang the briefcase closed. I take hold of the handle. "Have a nice life, Mr. Palmon. And have a nice next life. And the life after that. Because that's how long I expect you to keep your distance before you contact me again."

Friedrich beats me to the door and blocks my way, arms outstretched, fingers clutching the jamb. "I don't know her. I swear. Seen her around campus is all."

"So you don't recognize her?"

"Do you?"

I drop my briefcase, grab Friedrich by his shoulders, aware how very fucked I am if any of this is captured on campus security cameras.

And shake. "Who. Is. She?"

"She's the brewer's daughter."

"What brewer's daughter?"

"Shit, Dr. Panisporchi, how many brewer's daughters do you know?"

Ali's lank hair. The quiet demeanor. Her sudden slyness. That self-assured quality she knew more than me. That *I* was the idiot who needed to be taught.

A mental series of white note cards hop to the forefront and drop into place, one after the other:

DUMBFOUND
TO MAKE SPEECHLESS WITH AMAZEMENT. ASTONISH.
SYNONYM:
click
NONPLUS
TO RENDER UTTERLY PERPLEXED. SYNONYM:
click
DISCONCERT
TO THROW INTO DISORDER OR CONFUSION; DISARRANGE.

Heartbeat. Heartbeat. Heartbeat.

PRESUME

TO ACT OR PROCEED WITH UNWARRANTABLE OR IMPERTI-
NENT BOLDNESS.

Deep breath. "But—"

I try again. "You see—"

And a third time, digging nails into palms to get a little traction. "What I mean is, if Ali's the brewer's daughter from Oberholt then . . . then . . ."

Then . . . damn.

Double damn.

Omigod . . . *Damn.*

I dig into my purse. Pull out my cell phone. Click the touchpad. Log into Facebook.

And refriend Carlotta.

28

All the way down Broad Street, Blessed Mary on My Keychain yammers like a Tourette's patient off her meds. "You didn't have to be so hard on him."

"I've been treating my sister-in-law like she's got impetigo."

"That's your fault, not his."

All the effort to get me to agree to this group, the long-winded entreaties. "And our first meeting, our very first meeting, the brewer's daughter shows. And Friedrich makes like he doesn't know her."

"He didn't plan this. Give the grunts on the Assignments Committee a little credit. Of all the people who visited your Facebook page, who finds your meeting? What are the odds?"

My cell phone dings.

It's Stanley.

●●

The next evening, at the pool hall, Stanley chalks up my cue. "I just think it's better if we're clear on expectations." He explains some more. Something about probabilities and angles of incidence.

And I might have had a clue what he was trying to say. But for my knuckles whitening around my cell phone. "Joey. Shut up for a second and listen. I wasn't talking to the newsstand guy the other night. I was looking for my house keys. The newsstand guy happened to be standing there."

"Mr. Olivieri says you do it every day."

"That's nuts."

"You calling him a liar?"

"I'm saying I don't do it."

"Mr. Olivieri thinks you're spying on him."

That statement nixes my nettle. Surprise, pure and profound, takes its place. "Why would I spy on Mr. Olivieri?"

"You tell me. Bracaconi's your lawyer, not mine. Next time the newsstand guy talks to you, keep moving. Pretend you don't hear him. Then Mr. Olivieri won't worry you're trying to hurt him. Got it?"

Joey hangs up. Stanley fishes the lemon wedge out of his drink and chomps on it. "What's Bracaconi doing now?"

Maybe it's a male thing, but calling him Bracaconi seems too familiar for somebody Stanley's never met. I always refer to him as Maurizio.

"He subpoenaed Joey for a deposition." Saying it, I realize how awful that sounds.

"Maybe you should see Constantine. He's very competent. And fair."

"I'm not being fair?"

"You get annoyed with me." Stanley's voice plummets into the next octave. Gravelly. Guttural. German. "Yet Josef should not talk to you that way."

I sweep the hall, searching for any telltale gray. "He talks." Nothing. Not a wisp. "Doesn't mean I listen."

"Don't make the same mistake. Adjust your cue, so next time, it goes right."

"What's that supposed to mean?" I straighten.

My head connects with Stanley's nose. Stanley's hand flies to cover it.

"Omigod! I'm so sorry." I swing around looking for ice, something cold, anything. And close on my beer. I thrust it at him...

And again connect with his nose.

Stanley takes a step back, his face all purple and pinched. He turns away, shoulders shaking, so I can't tell if he's laughing or crying. He fishes a piece of ice out of his drink, clamps it over a nose patch going redder than Rudolph's and points to a spot on the ball. "All I was trying to say was if you hit the ball here and it doesn't go where you want, try hitting it here."

He moves his finger left.

"Or here." He moves his finger right. "Don't keep hitting in the same place, or you'll end up exactly where you did before." He puts down the ice. "Am I bleeding?"

I check. "No. You're fine." And rerack the balls. "Do you believe in karma?"

"Like I criticize your pool shot, you pop me in the kisser, kinda karma?"

"Like mistakes from a past life can bite you in the next kind of karma." I position for the break.

I guess Stanley's gonna live because he bends to help, his breath warming on the back of my neck. "You presume there is a past life. Father DiLullo would disapprove."

"You think we start fresh. One chance. That's it. You never wondered how past life events figure into present life events?"

I straighten again, but Stanley's ready. He sidesteps, forearm raised to guard his face. "What's this about?"

"How can we grasp all we're supposed to in *one* life?" I wave my cue. "Our lives are so short, its lessons so long to learn."

Stanley corrals the cue before it hits anything vital, then goes silent in that particular way he has, mouth pulled to the side, gaze flitting from point to point except I get the impression he's lining up his words instead of his next shot. "If we have lived other lives, perhaps our inability to recall them is a kind of grace. One we can draw upon as needed. To fill the cracks, wash away the dark places."

"Like a well?" I lean in closer. "One along a path that guides us to a blissful place."

He puts a hand on the back of my head, tilts it upward. "Are we talking in Chaucer now?"

I nod. "Where green and lusty May endures and all adventures are good. Where we can cast off all sorrow and be happy."

Stanley kisses me. Long and slow and like he's been waiting a really long time to do so. And I kiss him back, uncertain whether I float or sink. He whispers in my ear. "Whether we live a single life, or a thousand, can't I spend this one with you?"

Joy, buoyant and blissful, bubbles up and out from every dark corner. It bursts through the barriers, barrels headlong along every extremity, crowding my suddenly hair-filled tongue with words I cannot voice, emotions I cannot define. And feelings once believed dead and gone and buried and . . .

Hoo boy.

Stanley takes my hand. "I'm the one who broke us up. I get it. But if you're willing, I'd like to give us another chance."

Of course. Why not? That's all anybody wants.

One more chance. To make the right move. Say the right thing.

Leave the print shop before things get messy. Put down the bottle before it's too late. Tell somebody what they need to know. What will make the difference.

Today. Tomorrow. Forever.

So say it, Eugenia. Tell him. You're taking too long to answer. This moment may not return.

But I don't tell him. I let go his hand.

This life is a way station for me. And those sharing the platform shouldn't be taken lightly. Stanley's planning for the future, yet those same statistics on which he relies pretty much guarantee I won't be there to share it.

The hope lighting Stanley's eye fades. "I shouldn't have sprung this on you. Let's go back to what we were doing." He releases me, picks up his drink, rattles the ice.

The sound echoes another, of dice tossed on the cobbles.

And here comes the gray. Because lately it's always there. Fucking up everything.

Stanley flickers, replaced by his Lutheran self, who smacks his knee with a disgusted snort. "All the rolls go against me. Guess I wasted my luck on that filthy Greek today."

Not Greek like Carlotta's cousin. He means Oberholt's Greek. Josef's Greek.

The mercenary Josef traded goods with to keep us in food.

"For luck." A callused finger taps my ear. Sleeve of his dark gray boiled wool overcoat scratches my cheek. Lutheran Stanley tosses another coin into the pot, flicks a wrist to signal the other players he's finished.

Something flashes in the lamplight. Not my Stanley's modern watchband. A row of brass buttons at his cuff, an officer's buttons. I look up. Stanley's rich hazel eyes are lightened to green. His hair to Billy Idol white. His shoulders are squared, his attitude martial, and his face a geometry of angles honed by short rations and hardened by service.

"Greeks are good for something." The deep-voiced other Stanley leans closer so I can hear him. "Caught one outside the perimeter. A profiteer. Too bad for him. Good for me."

The tang from my Stanley's lemon wedge converts to something related, but sweeter. He lowers his lids. Directs my gaze downward. Opens a fist.

Candied orange peel! A rare and exotic treat.

The gray rolls out.

The orange peel remains.

Stanley, my present-day Stanley, drops a piece into my palm, pops another into his mouth. "Found it on South Street. Shop called Trojan Trinkets. Condoms and candy. Can you believe it? They were almost out. Had to tackle a cripple to get this. It's good as the stuff they sold at Wanamaker's."

I drop the candy. Jesus. This man killed people. And laughed about it after. "I have to go."

"Because of what I said?" Stanley dismantles his cue. "Forget about that. Forget it all. Let's go for supper."

Oberholt Stanley flickers in. "You want to go now? But the music's starting again."

Both Stanleys peer at me. Both put out a hand. "You're shaking."

Shaking. Shivering. And sick. "Have you ever looked at somebody and been sure, absolutely certain, you met them before? Like they're the same person but can't be. Themselves. But also this other . . . thing. And at the same time."

"Like on different planes. Alternate universes." Present-day Stanley runs a hand through his hair. Oberholt Stanley fades. "There's a word for it. Something German. I don't remember what it is."

••

DOPPELGÄNGER: A GHOSTLY DOUBLE OF A LIVING PERSON, ESPECIALLY ONE THAT HAUNTS ITS FLESHLY COUNTERPART.

I click the next link.

DOUBLE WALKER: A SHADOW-SELF THAT ACCOMPANIES EVERY HUMAN.

Shot of gin. Another Vicodin.

A PROJECTION OF A PERSON, SOMETIMES FALSE OR UNFOCUSED. ALTERNATE TERMS: ASTRAL TWIN. BODY DOUBLE. ALTER EGO. DEAD RINGER. CHANGELING.

And most logical. Most reasonable. The one I'm gonna go with:

DELUSIONAL MISIDENTIFICATION SYNDROME—A BELIEF THE IDENTITY OF A PERSON, OBJECT, OR PLACE HAS SOMEHOW CHANGED OR BEEN ALTERED.

29

Friedrich skips class on Monday.

Maybe he's dead.

I head to Library Lounge C and write CANCELED across the notice for the support group.

Friedrich snatches my Sharpie. "What're you doing?"

"Where the hell you been? I left messages."

He pulls at his collar and points me to a run of red, scaly skin along his shoulder. "Turns out I'm allergic to penicillin. What'd you want?"

"I'll need an action plan from you. Concrete delineation of how this group proceeds. Goals and procedures. By Wednesday. Or this group is over."

"You got it." Friedrich clears his throat. "About Ali. We have to be careful with her. I don't think she remembers us."

"How can she not remember?"

"Do you remember who you were in every one of your lives?"

"More or less." Sometimes.

"No skips. No fuzzies." He dovetails his fingers, like he's holding an opened book, then zips his thumb across imaginary pages. "All your lives cataloged like an encyclopedia."

"Okay, okay. No. I don't."

"Well neither do I. Until something jolts a particular life to the fore-front. And we don't know what it's like for her."

"I don't give a rat's ass what it's like for her."

Friedrich makes calming motions. "I know you don't like her. I get it. I understand. But Ali won't. She has no frame of reference for any feelings you have toward her. So we've got to be careful. If we don't, we could—"

Whatever Friedrich means to say is interrupted by *la jeune* French resistance paranoid herself, skittering into the room. "Sorry, I'm late. Had to take a different route tonight. Throw them off my trail." She points to the chartreuse poster, my Sharpied proclamation running corner to corner. "Are we canceled?"

Friedrich shakes his head.

"Good." She smacks rain from her windbreaker, finds a chair, and sits, clutching its edges. "Any of those cookies you had last time?"

"Absolutely." Friedrich places a pfeffernüsse precisely in the middle of a paper plate. He opens the thermos and pours tea. Wraps a napkin around the cup. "Cream and sugar?"

Oh, please. I grab the pfeffernüsse off the plate and toss it into Ali's lap. I'd toss the tea after if Friedrich weren't holding it out of reach.

"Hello." A new voice, warmhearted and whimsical and nuanced as fine wine, interrupts our fun. The speaker elongates her greeting, each syllable a shining invitation. To notice. Take the moment. Respond in kind.

And all this after only one word.

Imagine the effect when she utters two.

I turn. We all do. And discover the voice belongs to a dark-haired, middle-aged woman dressed entirely in Goth gear save for white leather high tops. Metal rings hang from her collar, buttoned fringe from her skirt. Safety pins, bejeweled and beshimmered, substitute as fasteners.

She enters, dragging a green storage tub on wheels. She shrugs off her raincoat, shakes out a black umbrella, hands us each cards, and graces us with an entire sentence. "A customer sent me. I'm Kyra."

My card reads *Buttons, Bangles, and Bongs.*

A head shop. With sewing notions.

Another knocks at the entrance. A woman. No. A man. In a brown velvet pencil skirt. "Who's selling the shoes?"

"Me. That would be me. Me. Me." Kyra waves her hand with the same fervor Ma displays when she makes bingo.

The guy in the doorway must be the customer.

I point to the sign. "Are you sure you have the right place?"

The guy follows my finger. "The ass-caul people, right?"

"Not everybody." Kyra sashays her index finger left. And right. And left. Her words keeping cadence like it's a metronome. "My mother delivered me by caesarian."

Ali taps her temple, gives me a meaningful nod.

Gotcha, Beer Breath. You think Kyra is crazy.

Friedrich whips over to the guy in the pencil skirt, hand extended. "Welcome. I'm Friedrich."

The newcomer leaves the hand hanging. "Tony."

Ali takes a long, noisy sip off her tea. "Tony with a *y* or an *i*?"

"Bless your heart. With a *y*, of course. How kind of you to ask."

Friedrich steps in front of Tony and Kyra, blocking Ali from their view. "How 'bout you ladies—" He tries again. "How 'bout you two finish your shoe business after?"

Tony flicks a finger under Friedrich's chin. "No worries, Snookums. I'll answer to either gender. But underneath it all, I'm a woman. Always have been. I even sit down to pee."

Ali waves an arm, leans to, then fro, doing the dab to get a glimpse around Friedrich. "You can come back as a different gender?"

Tony fingers his graduated cultured pearls. "Apparently." He takes a look at Kyra's storage container. "Can I get a peek?"

"Oh yes." Ali hops to her feet. "I want to see."

"I don't want to delay the meeting." Kyra pushes the storage tub to a corner. "Besides, these are for Tony's personal collection. I'm getting too old for heels and Tony likes vintage wear. But talk to him. He's a representative for Foot Fetish." She eyes up the hole in the toe of Ali's sneaker. "Perhaps he can help you."

Tony pulls a packet of brochures from his Gucci carryall. He presses one into my palm, another into Ali's, a third into Friedrich's. "We sell everything from dressy to casual, private school to shazam.

For men. For women. And for everybody in between." He shows off his classic stack-heeled pumps. "These are from our Work-a-Day line." And peers at my canvas boaters. "We specialize in odd sizes."

Sheesh. "Pfeffernüsse?"

"No, thank you, darling. I'm on a diet. Sweet pea here can have mine." He straightens his cashmere twinset, then waves away Ali's protest. "Don't worry. You'll have plenty of time to puke it during the break."

Friedrich tears his attention from Tony's gams. "All righty, then. Let's get this meeting started. Ali, would you like to share?"

Ali flops into a chair and crosses her arms. "I shared last week. I have to share again?"

Tony points to the sign. "It says support group."

"Yeah, well. I like to keep to myself. In case anybody's looking for me."

Oh fer chrissakes. "What'd you do? Rob a bank, hide the goods, and come back to find it in this life?"

Ali kicks at a spot in the carpet.

Tony holds up a long, thin, and perfectly manicured finger. "You can do that? My goodness. The possibilities. Where do you hide the stuff? You bury it, and thirty years later, it could be a condo project. Put it in a safe deposit box, you still have to hide the key, and maybe the bank's been turned into condos, too. Same with bus terminals. And airports. It's like the entire world's been turned into condos. I hardly recognized the place this time around." He ends his declaration with a hand flourish, an actor waiting for his next line.

I give it to him. "Condos are a lot easier to keep up."

Tony gives me a gap-toothed grin. He chooses his seat and sits, perfume rising. Light. Pleasant. Pretty, yet masculine. Exactly right for *him*. He runs his gaze over Kyra, lingering at her high tops. "What could you share? You don't have hindsight."

She twirls a finger through the magenta streak in her Bettie Page–style bob. "You have hindsight so you can learn from what has gone before. My mitzvah is to help troubled souls make that connection."

"Really?" Tony mimics Kyra's action, twirling a finger into his carefully gelled layers. "Your own soul must be untroubled."

"Everybody progresses at their own pace." Kyra pats my hand like Ma does when she tells me she made the manicotti with part-skim ricotta, instead of the full-fat kind. "Of course, some don't progress at all."

Tony leans toward me. "I have no dwelling in that place. I went. Where I thought it should be, but there's nothing. Not so much as a hearthstone. Those who died there, are elsewhere, remembered nowhere except here." He taps his chest. "And this life?" He shrugs.

I search Tony's face, uncertain if he means Oberholt and looking for the person he may have been. All I see is the shoe aficionado, boasting a pair of ruby ear bobs which complement his deep brown eyes in a way that would make the heaviest heart take flight.

Ali pipes up. "What's he mean about *this* life?"

"He's paraphrasing Chaucer." Friedrich flips a chair around and straddles it, draping his arms over the chair back. "*The Parliament of Foules*. The pilgrim asks if all who have died there have dwelling in another place because our present world's brief space is but another kind of death."

Kyra sighs. "I always loved Chaucer. You know, lots of people mistake him for Shakespeare."

"Chaucer's a troll." Ali stands. "Are we done? 'Cause if we are, we should hold hands like they do at AA and say the serenity prayer."

"Not so fast, sweet pea." Tony looks to me. "We shouldn't disperse without a word from our sponsor."

He has *got* to be kidding. My role as sponsor means this crew can use the room. I'm a neutral observer. My purse vibrates against my calf. Keychain Mary bends out Her corkscrew and stabs me in the leg. "Engage. It won't kill you."

Kyra gives me an encouraging thumbs-up.

I rub at my calf. At semester's end, this support group will end. Once that happens, what're the odds I'll ever see any of them again? "People with hindsight remember people from past lives, right? Ever wonder about the ones you don't get a chance with?"

"Like who?" Friedrich sits up straighter, his tone respectful.

"Like . . . my father. We only ever get a few years. Enough for introductions, get a sense of what he likes. And doesn't. But not enough to really know the man."

The topic seems to strike a chord with Tony. "Like you get off your trolley just in time to watch him catch his."

"Exactly."

"How old were you when he died?"

"This time, I was only nine years old. He was kind. But worked so hard. I barely saw him. I wish . . . I wish I could get the chance to meet him as an adult."

Kyra gives my hand a squeeze. "See? That wasn't so hard now, was it?" She looks around, eyes wide with expectation. "Anybody else?"

Friedrich stands. "I hate having hindsight." He sits. He stands again. "Having it this time isn't so bad. I'm grateful for that."

Tony nods. "Yes, not so bad. I'm grateful for that, too." He turns to Ali. "Are you grateful for anything, sweet pea?"

"Yes." She doesn't elaborate, instead putting her hands out to either side.

We stand with her and gather in a circle. We say the serenity prayer. Like we're supposed to.

Kyra pulls out a perforated metal ball. She opens it, flicks a disposable lighter at whatever's inside, then closes it back up. She arcs it before her, just like the priest during mass. Sandalwood scent wafts across the room. Smoke billows.

Friedrich moves toward her, pulls out his inhaler. "Better put that out. You don't want to set off the—"

A shower of water from the sprinkler system douses his words. The alarm wails.

30

Two days after the incense burner malfunction, Friedrich knocks a snappy rhythm on the entrance to my office. He waggles his cell. "You rang?"

I hold up a pile of forms. "I have to fill these out because of the sprinkler incident. And we can't use Library Lounge C until the carpet dries."

"So we'll use Library Lounge D. Is that all?"

"How sure are you about all this? I mean really sure." I hand him everything I found on Delusional Misidentification Syndrome. About four paragraphs worth.

Friedrich shrugs his backpack off his shoulder, drops into the chair opposite my desk, and reads, eyes flicking, expression going somber. "This is the kind of doubletalk Futz would use to explain it."

The psych head. The guy whose student I'm helping with the archetypes. "I got it off Google."

Friedrich puts down the page. "You don't think Tony was the char lady who cleaned the church."

The image comes clear, the resemblance, if nothing else, in how well Tony fills out a sweater. "But what could a charwoman do to deserve hindsight?"

"I dunno. What'd you do?"

The question, so bald, so unvarnished, drops into my lap. It lays there. Quivering.

My head starts to throb. I push a palm to my temple.

Friedrich hefts his backpack onto his lap. "Hurts to really think about it, doesn't it? Then to admit it. Out loud." He pulls out a sketchbook. "When it gets to be too much, I make a drawing. It helps me sort myself out. Stops the headaches."

He flips from sketch to sketch to sketch. Some are snatches of Oberholt. A couple, reminiscent of Chaucerian woodcuts, depict Friedrich as Nicholas, nose in a scroll.

I point to that sketch. "Were you Mr. Chaucer's assistant?"

"More like his scribe. I wrote half his treatise on the astrolabe."

"What about the landlord's wife?"

"The landlord was actually a stable hand. And she was . . . trouble." Friedrich keeps flipping. Soldiers tromping through what looks like jungle. Squalid living in ramshackle environments. A couple rowboating on the river. A mess of barbwire. Skeletal prisoners in horizontal stripes.

I point to that sketch, too. "Is that a concentration camp?"

Friedrich shoves up a sleeve and points to a birthmark on his forearm, obscured by this week's rash. "It's still there. Three lifetimes later. What're the odds?"

He touches the paper describing Delusional Misidentification Syndrome, then wraps shaking hands around my own. "Soon as I think I have a handle on this, I find some weird-ass explanation like that. It's like getting stuck in a hall of mirrors. You chase down one path, then another. Think if you can find a single point of reference, an immutable constant, maybe you can find your own way out."

Like My Very Blessed Mary. My immutable constant. Ever present. Ever vigilant. Ever . . . ready.

I shrug off Friedrich's touch, reaching for something, anything, less intimate and close on a modern translation of Chaucer. The spine cracks, opening to a single, well-worn point of reference.

"And we are pilgrims, passing to and fro, Death is the end of every worldly sore."

•••

Death's not the end of anything. Blessed Mary may be my point of reference, but she's not showing the way out.

Donna hangs over the front seat of Stanley's Camry. She thrusts her cell in my face. "Because everything we need to know is on our phones."

I shove her cell back and pull out mine. Pull up Google Maps one more time. Speak into it. "Mortuary."

Stanley pilots through an intersection, then ups the speed on the windshield wipers. "Your Uncle Nic looked great at your aunt and uncle's place. Too bad. He seemed like a nice guy."

Yeah, he was a nice guy. Cemeteries are full of nice guys.

Google Maps continues to spin. Because South Jersey is a maze. Located across the Delaware River from Philadelphia, South Jersey's acres of forest and farmland are laced together by a mesh of poorly marked roads.

Stanley pulls over. "We're going in circles. We've been here before."

"But you don't have to again." Donna taps her faceplate. She leans over the seat again and shows us. "See. You'll get there if you make things right before the next life."

●●●

Make things right before the next life. That's what Donna said. I'm not nuts.

"Nuts. Of all things," everybody whispers at the funeral home.

Uncle Nic never had a problem with nuts before he ate a bad one.

"The doctors said sometimes it happens."

Obviously, because there's Uncle Nic, in his best suit, lying stiff and eye-shadowed.

"Just goes to show," everybody clucks, "you never know."

Aunt Celia chose the Tuscany Room. Fake arches shelter fake roses twined up white trellises tacked to walls painted to look like chipped frescoes in an old world courtyard. The flowers dance gently in a breeze descending from ceiling vents.

"We hoped to go once he retired," Aunt Celia murmurs.

My cell phone vibrates. "Hello?"

"It's Virgule Futz. Have you got a minute?" There's background shuffling, like papers being moved about. "I wanted to run some of my student's preliminary notes past you."

"I'm at a funeral, Virgule." I back into a corner, grateful Stanley's locked in conversation with Joey and cup my hand around the mouthpiece. "Can we talk about this Monday?"

I click off and find Angela standing in front of me, hands on hips. "Who's Virgil?"

••

Rain downpours as we leave church. It stops when we reach the cemetery, forcing us to track across the grass in black pumps, sinking in with every step, pulling up a clod of turf with every advance.

Except Donna. She wore flats.

Stanley and I stand in the back beside the pile of Astroturf-covered dirt, comforted by the scent from pinelands and sea. The priest drones. Our Father. Hail Mary. Glory Be. Raising memories of other funerals. Other graves. Backward to less modern times when the words were *Pater Noster, Ave Maria, Gloria Patri.*

Relatives disburse to wander across the plots. "Look! It's Nunzi." Or "Maria's over here. Anybody remember where Carmine is?"

Like a reunion. Minus Aunt Gracie's Special Blend. Plus the plastic-coated mass cards.

My cell vibrates again. "I'm at a funeral, Maurizio."

"Got your e-mail about the settlements. Don't know where your brother's getting his figures, but Mr. Olivieri says his insurance premiums are fine. He's eager to settle. So is the funeral director. And Dr. Rossi will consider taking his share from the pot."

Dr. Rossi will? The newsstand guy's missing tooth lands front and center in my mind's eye. Does Maurizio have mob connections that Dr. Rossi's done such a flip-flop? Does Joey?

"You can't imagine what a guy like that will do once he gets going." Joey. Over my shoulder. Like I conjured him.

"Excuse me." I put away my cell. "Do you know the meaning of private?"

"Aunt Rose wants you. Says she's got somebody she wants you to meet."

There's nobody here I don't already know.

Joey looks down a row of graves.

Shit.

We find Aunt Rose and Uncle Lou a half-section over. She puts an arm around my waist and walks me past headstones sporting final dates from the forties, fifties, and sixties. She checks a couple and moves on. "Emmy was a cousin. From the other side of our family. Been wanting to introduce you to her for ages. You're so like her, isn't she, Lou?"

"Like twins. Hard to believe you aren't blood relatives." Uncle Lou stoops to check another inscription. "She died when she was very young. Car accident. Her husband blamed it on the brakes, but he was drunk. Who knows what happened?"

"He was nice." Aunt Rose rises on tiptoe, stage-whispering into my ear. "College graduate. Very smart. Like your young man."

She checks another inscription and moves on. Another. And keeps going. "I always tell your mother how much you remind me of her. I keep meaning to dig out a photo. She was younger than me, but we were friends." She giggles, the sound girlish and goofy. "Emmy used to help me make gin. I never told your mother. She wanted to remember Emmy through you and I worried she wouldn't if she knew."

Aunt Rose keeps talking but her words mute behind a buzzing in my ear. Emmy's a nickname, but not for Eugenia. What in hell is Aunt Rose talking about?

She stops walking. "Here it is."

Joey bends with Uncle Lou to examine the inscription, stepping on the grave to do so.

I shiver.

"Emiliana Eugenia," Joey reads, his voice flat. "Beloved wife. Beloved daughter. Born 1945, died 1964. Taken too soon."

A wellspring of longing, of regret, breaks free of the recess into which I'd had it chained. A life too short. A love long-missed. Touch on my hand. Lips over mine. Citrus and slow-dancing. Salt pine and marsh.

The gal who so reminds Aunt Rose of me . . . is me.

31

I didn't know I could come back as somebody related to myself.
I google Emmy's husband and find nothing. Americanized versions
of his name turn up references, but all are too young. Son or nephew
perhaps? Ancestry.com is no help. He was born too late to be counted
in the 1940 census, marriage records for 1964 are not yet publicly available, and nobody's put him on a public tree. I consider hiring an inves-
tigator, even pull out my cell and speak into the mic. "OK, Google."

Then I do the math.

If Emmy's husband were still alive, he'd be . . . ten, twenty, thirty,
forty, fifty, sixty, seventy-one, two . . . seventy-eight years old about.

What would I do with him?

Beyond be relieved he's still alive and can't possibly be my brother.

I unblock Friedrich's e-mail from the account attached to the
Facebook page, unblock his number on my cell. I log into the atten-
dance sheets for the semester, change his absences to presents. Why
not? He held my hand, acted like he gave a shit, so why the hell not?

Rupee e-mails: *Make what presumptions you will. What wrong I
may have done you, I beg you to forgive.*

Anders Dripzin worries: *The Committee is concerned with your current tactics. Please reconsider.*

Casablanca gets cozy: *If you're with the Vichy, admit it. As far as I
can tell, none of the others were ever Mossad.*

I forward Casablanca's to Friedrich: *Vichy? The Nazi puppet government in France?*

Friedrich e-mails back: *I doubt she means the water.*

Rupee returns: *They'll send somebody. Don't try to bullshit your way past them. They've been doing this a long time.*

Chaucer remains, but his poetry mocks me. FOR TYME LOST MAY NOUGHT RECOVERED BE.

Virgule Futz drags me for coffee again. I bring the freaking file with the freaking archetypes for his freaking student. He points out the parts that need fleshing out, hands it back, then spends the balance of the hour discussing how we can never be certain what roadblocks the universe will toss our way, the notion coincidence is not random, and how he came *this* close to a department head position at the Kinsey Institute for Sexual Studies.

My work e-mail account chimes.

••

An hour later, Friedrich rattles the chair beside him, then arches a brow to the wall clock. He hands me a pfeffernüsse.

I show him the e-mail. "Administration wants to know what we were doing here last week, why people are lighting incense."

"I'll handle it."

"You said you'd handle things in Oberholt. We saw how well that worked out."

Kyra pokes me and returns her attention to Ned, a member of the ladder company that responded when the sprinklers blew last week. Dressed in lumberjack shirt and jeans, he's broad and muscular, with a nose wide and flat, a beard stubbled and red. And stinks of alcohol. He annotates everything he says with big arm gestures.

Ali, all waiflike and dark shadows under her eyes, flutters fingers at me from across the circle. She makes open and shut motions with her hands to let me know Ned talks a lot and rolls her eyes like we're besties just waiting for the boring stuff to be over so we can hit the mall for a little retail therapy.

I point Friedrich to a new bruise on the back of her hand, purple and bumpy and stretched across skin even thinner than last week. "Your sweetie should stick to scotch and lay off the injectables."

"She's not my sweetie." He hunches, voice mature and monotone, all but erupting with restraint. "She's another pilgrim. With an eating disorder." He looks past me, his expression going confused.

I follow his gaze to a skinny-shouldered young man settling in behind Tony. He has light brown hair, light eyes, and freckles across the bridge of a nose that looks like it's once been broken. "Oh, look. Genghis Khan."

Friedrich's head swivels like it's on a pivot. "You knew Genghis Khan?"

Kyra pokes me again, then pokes Friedrich. "Shhhh." Loud enough to make Tony look in our direction.

Ned doesn't miss a beat.

"I didn't know anybody else had hindsight." He spreads his arms. "Zero oh three percent. What's that? One in thirty thousand? What are the odds?"

"Oh for chrissakes, Einstein." Tony taps a white-gloved fingertip to his pocketbook. "We run into as many as the universe decides."

The skinny-shouldered guy flips open a notebook. He pulls out a pencil. He starts writing.

Tony looks great tonight in a sixties-style green shirtwaist tucked into a flared skirt and paired with a crocheted shrug. A chunky necklace and oversized earrings give it just the right touch of retro without sending it over the top. If Tony dyed his hair blonde, and did a little lipo under his chin, he'd look like a masculine Michelle Pfeiffer who'd been working out to bulk up.

He casts a thoughtful and dramatic glance to the window, where rain slides down in sheets. "'I've been wondering. Does anybody think we notice others more the more experience we have?"

Friedrich scratches under his shirt. "I think it dawns on each of us in our own time. Sooner for some, later for others."

Tony crosses one leg over the other. "Like puberty?"

"More like athlete's foot."

The skinny-shouldered guy snorts. He flips to a new page.

Ali pulls her sleeves down over her fists, first the one, then the other. "My therapist says I block everything out."

Ned looks up from his copy of *Paramilitary Weekly*. "Once I was getting it on with the *primo* mama of Edison High, I mean between her legs and working hard and bam! Turned out, she really *was* my mother." He takes a pull on his water bottle, his voice going slumpy and slurry. "I don' date anymore. I put that enershy into my work. Help people an' if sumpin happenz ta me, nooo sweat."

Tony rolls soulful eyes at him. "The altruistic have no need for hindsight, Flame Master. You figured to up the karmic ante."

"You know it. Next time I'm putting in for open spaces and blue skies. Maybe Montana."

"What part of 'man proposes, God disposes' do you not understand, Cowboy?"

Ned runs a knuckle along Tony's thigh. "Y'man enough ta tell me?"

Tony grabs Ned's crotch. "You man enough to take it?"

Ned springs from his chair. Red, a darker hue than his beard, rushes along his cheeks. He sways, balling a fist.

Friedrich's up and out of his seat so fast it's like his backside is super-charged. "Knock it off."

Lightning flashes. Thunder rumbles.

Ned's bluster collapses. He falls back into his seat, head in hands. "Don't take no notice what I say. I'm drunk."

The skinny-shouldered guy erases something, swishy noises loud.

Ned looks at him. "Watcha writin' there, cuz?

The guy flips his notepad closed. He displays what looks like an ID, freckles bright under the fluorescents. "Who runs this group?"

Tony hooks a thumb at me.

Dismay dashes up my craw. "You're from administration." I'll blame everything on Friedrich. Tell them he lied.

Ali tucks a nervous lock behind her ear. "I don't want to come back. Not ever. Think you could arrange that?"

Ned burps. "He's not from administration. He's a reporter."

My fight-or-flight response flares. "Like from the *Temple News*?"

Ali flips a defiant swatch out of her eye. "I don't care. Report all you want. Ali's not my real name."

The reporter pockets the notepad along with his pencil. "No. Of course not."

She tugs on my sleeve. "Can we do the serenity prayer now?"

Tony eyes up my sneakers. "Can you stay a little, Doc? We totally have to talk about your shoes."

•••

Table to window. Window to table. "He wants a picture, Friedrich. A freaking group picture."

Friedrich stops doodling on the whiteboard. "What do you want me to do? Tackle him?"

"Call the paper. Tell them the group's closed."

"The paper? But, he isn't—"

"Never mind. We won't tell him anything. We'll just shut it down. Close up shop. Tell everybody to stay the freak home."

"Calm down. You're talking crazy." Friedrich pulls a silver flask from his pocket. He tosses it at me.

Mmmmm. Good Kentucky Bourbon. I take a great big gulp. The alarm bells dampen. "What if he prints any of this?"

Friedrich erases his doodling. "There's nothing to print. A cross-dresser propositioned a fireman who wants to be a cowboy. I don't need to read that in the college rag. I can go to South Street and see it for myself." He snaps the cap on his marker. "Forget about him. How many pairs did Tony sell you?"

"Only half as many as he sold you." I take another swig, push down the desire to giggle.

Friedrich pulls a bundle of paper from his backpack. "Progress report. You have to sign it. I have to submit one every week to get the credit."

I scan the top page. "Humanities?"

"What else?" Friedrich rests a shoulder against the whiteboard. "It's not like we started a photography club."

We didn't start anything. "But you need releases from the attendees."

Friedrich hands me another page, points out the rounded script at the bottom, girlish and curlicued, the letter *i* dotted with a heart.

"How'd you get that signature?"

"How do you think I got it?"

"And Ali said, 'fine.' She flips over that reporter, but is okay with administration knowing her troubles with hindsight, her fear of Nazis, and her substance abuse problem? You're going to get me fired."

Friedrich smiles. His features stop crowding each other for attention. They settle into normal proportions and Friedrich's almost handsome becomes for-real handsome. "I'm filing the paperwork. That's all administration cares about."

"What about the others?"

"Ned and Kyra already signed. I'll get Tony next week."

"You like Tony, huh? You were so gallant with him tonight." I tap the flask to Friedrich's chest. "It's all those shoes. Gets you hot under the collar." I page through the progress report. "I don't see anything about that here."

Friedrich takes the flask back, fingers closing on mine before he pulls it away, then makes a grab for the report, but I hold it out of reach. He reaches further, bourbon-rich breath hot on my forehead, chest close to mine. A pulse beats at his throat and sets my nipples tingling.

Whoa.

Friedrich snatches the report. He straightens. He backs away. "Whatever happened in Oberholt, know I didn't do it to hurt you. It was a crazy time. A crazy place. I'm not making excuses. Just stating facts."

The nipple tingle goes flatter than a Diet Pepsi at a Fourth of July picnic.

Friedrich picks up his backpack. And goes.

32

Ma croons into the phone. "A week from Sunday is perfect, Stanley. About one o'clock?"

I follow the cord hand over hand from its origin in the kitchen to where it stretches into the living room, growing tauter as Ma moves. She beats me to the closet, closing the door. I pull on the handle, prevented from pounding, demanding she come out, because the sound will carry over the line. "You don't have to bring anything, just yourself. Oh, there's Eugenia now. She'll be so happy you called."

I heave the door especially hard. The inward pressure releases, landing me on my ass. Ma extends the handset. "It's Stanley."

●●●

Chop. Chop. Chop. Onions. Garlic. Butter. A *soffrito's* essential ingredients. "A week from Sunday is perfect, Stanley. It's wonderful. It's amazing. Christ. We're not even dating." I wave my knife at Joey. "Hand me the marjoram. The red one."

He chooses a canister. Green.

"No. The red one. Never mind," I grab it myself. And go on chopping. "Ma's inviting absolute-a-freaking everybody in the family. I'm surprised she hasn't hired a hall. What am I gonna do, Joey? What the fuck am I gonna do?"

Joey ties off the kitchen trash bag. "Will you shut up and listen?"

And the gray rolls in. No warning. No preliminaries. Just Joey, tightening a plastic tie now turned to leather on a green plastic garbage bag converted to an old grain sack. "Freiherr's cousin or no, if I catch that soldier anywhere near here again, I'll kill him."

My gut goes tight, my fingers numb. I drop the knife. It lands on a floor that's no longer linoleum, but brushed dirt covered in straw. I turn, but Ma's outdated cooktop is gone, replaced by one out of date for four centuries—an iron pot hanging over a low fire.

Joey opens a burlap-wrapped packet sitting beside an onion and a couple of parsnips.

"Where did you get bratwurst?" His voice deepens with every word. "Don't tell me you got it from the baker. His damned loaves are half sawdust."

"Don't be ridiculous." There's nothing in that package but cubed pork for the *soffrito*.

I move to retrieve it, but the room bends outward, taking my equilibrium with it. Joey's white hoodie dissolves into a shirt that hangs loosely from a set of powerful shoulders, his jeans into britches. Outside the window, wagon wheels bump over cobbles. The odor of horse sweat and night soil wafts across the sill. Spring sunshine fades to pre-dawn dull. The air grows colder, the breeze sharp, and the edges of Joey's good-natured countenance blur, swamped by Josef's bleak visage.

"That soldier gave this to you." The doppelgänger waggles the bratwurst at me. "Payment for services rendered."

"My business is my own."

Josef hauls back, lands an open palm to my cheek. Tears spring, filling the places my humiliation leaves barren. "Nothing is your own. Not this shop, nor your life. When you marry, both will go to your husband. Until then, they are left in my trust."

Josef dunks a rag in the bucket on the counter. He hands it to me, indicates I should hold it to my face. "Stop crying. Never cry. I don't care what the baker did to you. I will find a place for you. A family to take the baby. It seems hard, feels harsh. But you can't take up with that soldier. Fräulein Donna is working on a match for you with him. Mark my words. It will never happen. Be polite to her, but adamant I decide these matters."

He draws the shutters closed against the strengthening day and wraps a set of fine porcelain bowls, deposited with him by a Catholic tanner as security against better times.

"I thought you were saving those."

"I can't afford it. Not since the monk left."

The monk was Josef's go between, the layer of insulation that kept Josef one step removed from the authorities. Since he'd gone, Josef had to make all his deals himself. And he didn't like to discuss them. I try anyway; the tanner had always treated me kindly. "You promised to hold the bowls until the tanner's return. They belonged to his grandmother."

"You can't eat my promises." Josef smacks the table. "The tanner's gone too long. He won't return."

Josef considers a set of earbobs, an enameled snuffbox, a finely tooled harness. "Not the silver set, Herr Braun made a payment last week. The shaving kit?" He holds it up, examines the mother-of-pearl handle, the delicate engraving. "I haven't seen the cooper in weeks, have you?"

I shake my head, bite back the questions. Why are you taking so much? Where's everything else? *What's wrong?*

I empty the packet of meat into the pot, give it a stir, toss an onion after. And debate telling Josef the truth of the bratwurst's origin, wonder if my actions have anything to do with his activity. I press the cloth tighter against my cheek, worrying at the price I'd pay for that admission.

Josef swings the pot away from the flame. He lids it. "You can't cook that. People will smell. Do you want to bring the Freiherr's guard down on us?"

"I want to eat. I'm hungry."

He holds up Wooden Mary, turning Her over and over, then runs my mother's rosary across his fingers. He tosses both into his rucksack.

"No." I throw myself at his feet. "Please."

Josef goes back to his sorting. I beg and weep. Josef finally retrieves

Mary and the rosary and places them on the table. "Hide them. If the house gets searched, these alone would hang us both."

"It's Ruprecht Vogt, isn't it?" Last night at Hallowmas. All that yelling. That pamphleteer threatening. The parsnip farmer coming to see what was wrong. Der Weasel slinking in. I trace the cut under Josef's eye, not long-healed and faded like Joey's, but brand-new, still raw. "You should have given him the pamphlets."

Josef shoves my hand away. "You are a stupid, stupid girl. Don't mention that name in this house again."

He goes back to sorting. I go back to chopping, soothed by the rhythmic cadence. How long can I make this food last? Will the Freiherr be forthcoming with more as he promised? "When will you return?"

"When I can. If Der Weasel shows, tell him I'm at church. Keep him out of the house." Josef points to the bratwurst, then to the fire. "Bank that. Use the embers to cook. And by all you hold holy, do nothing to draw attention."

He removes the stopper from a bottle under his work counter. The stench of Josef's engraving chemicals fills the space. "To cover the smell." He hoists the grain sack and points to the bratwurst. "I wish I dared trade it, but the Greek will want more. He'll think I'm holding out."

Mean-spirited elation covers my resentment. I remember how my soldier bragged the night before, the candied orange peel. Josef's going to waste a lot of time today. The Greek is dead.

"You should have warned me."

Gray rolls out. Ma's kitchen returns. Brown and orange cotton chintz again hang at the window. Worn laminate again covers the table. Onion and garlic again sizzles on the stovetop. "Warned you?"

"About Stanley." Joey reaches past me to lower the flame on the burner. "I thought you liked him, wanted to be with him. You should have let me know, made yourself clear to him."

All I could have done, but hadn't. All I wanted to do, but didn't. The words unsaid, opportunities mishandled, the regrets piling, one atop the other until their weight drops me into a chair, Joey's voice strong in my ears.

"You think you'll have plenty of chances, but you won't. Make your decisions. But take responsibility for them. Otherwise, you'll have to live with the consequences. Over and over."

33

Over and over. Like in a fractured fairy tale. One that ends with the evil stepmother getting the prince and Cinderella dying from black lung.

The next day, Stanley rings me three times. His first messages sound self-assured, his last, less so. All ask me to return his call. Friedrich skips class, but Snapchats three times. Variations of "Hey, doc. Need to talk."

On my way home from the bus stop, the newsstand guy waves me over. I sneak a peek at the florist's, but if Mr. Olivieri is watching, I can't tell from where I'm standing.

I could do like Joey says. Keep on walking. Pretend I don't hear.

But this isn't Oberholt. And Joey doesn't get to tell me what to do.

The newsstand guy grins, the gap in his tooth making him look like a jack-o'-lantern. "You and your brother think you're so special. All those fancy degrees, your fancy careers. But you can't make a deal with the devil and not get fried. Ask Rupert. He'll tell ya. I went to Villanova, too."

I wait a heartbeat. "Do you play pool?"

Tires screech. The stench of exhaust follows.

It's Joey, his car parked at a crazy angle. He gets out and barks over its roof, "Goddammit, Vogt! I told you to leave her alone."

Vogt. Vogt? The newsstand guy has a name? And it's *Vogt*?

Joey flicks his car door shut, comes around to the passenger side, jerks me away, takes my briefcase, tosses it into his backseat, tosses my purse after. And shoves me into the front. "Not a word. Do you hear me? Not a word 'til we're out of here."

"*Not a word,*" echoes behind him, the tone abrupt, an order from Josef, one my cousin doesn't question I'll obey.

And along comes the gray. Like a piece of smoked glass. Dropped over the scene by the Great Stagehands in the Sky.

The sound of traffic gives way to an oompah band, but muffled, a street or two over from where we stand. A back alley of Oberholt. Stucco walls. Shuttered windows. Shivering under my shawl. Above, an autumn moon shines. And beneath, night soil runs through a trench under our feet. I wait, all but holding my nose, willing back the South Broad Street spring with its late afternoon cloud cover, willing Joey to shake off his four-century-old twin, to return to our present time and peel off in a burn of rubber. Instead, Joey's modern-day self dissolves along with the newsstand guy's counter until he's in the newly named Vogt's face.

Joey speaks to him, his voice too low to be heard, the tone heated and harsh.

Vogt's greasy gray hair lengthens. It blends to blond. The rawness of the newly present gap in his present-day teeth fades, taking on the look of an old injury.

"There's a time for secrecy and a time to speak." Vogt's voice is certain and strong. "She should know what happened."

I hear the words in both times, Oberholt and today.

Joey walks away, leaving the past behind. He slips behind the steering wheel, closes his door, takes time to position his rearview mirror, looks over his left shoulder for traffic, backs up, and executes a textbook reentry into the stream. He makes the turn onto Porter Street. "Well?"

"He said he went to Villanova. Said he knew you, said you could explain why he didn't finish." Not entirely true, but true enough. "Said something about making a deal with a devil."

"Is that what he calls it?" Joey inches along, finally pulling into a space a half-block short of our turnoff. "He was one of my students during my teaching assistantship. Introduction to accounting. A freshman. He flunked."

Gray hair. Lines deep at the corners of his eyes. Age spots speckling the back of his hands. "He's got at least ten years on you. Maybe more."

"Alcohol does that. The guy's pickled most of the time." Joey's inflection carries a hint of threat, a knowledge he shouldn't have. He puts his car back in gear, signals his exit from the parking space.

I reach over and turn off his key. "He hates you because you flunked him."

"The prof flunked him. I just graded the papers. Few years later, he sets up on South Broad, I do a little accounting for him at discount. And a year after that, somebody slips while he makes change and sues him."

"Like me."

"There wasn't any ice, just a grease spot. Oil leaking from his space heater onto a piece of cardboard lying on the sidewalk outside his stand. Lucky the whole thing didn't go up in flames. The newsstand guy was a sole proprietor. He lost a bundle. So he turns around and sues me, claimed I should have advised him to incorporate. To protect his personal assets. Dummy me hires Bracaconi. Bracaconi tells me he'll settle it fast and quiet. Then Bracaconi finds out the space heater wasn't to code. And was off to the casinos. Ended up suing the poor bastard with the busted head for slipping in the first place." Joey turns on his ignition. "I damned near lost my license."

Mary on My Keychain gives me a tug. Ma counting. Joey counting with her. Only one what? Again the tears well, not in anger, frustration. "His name is Vogt."

"Yeah. Francis Vogt. You didn't know?"

"How should I know? All anybody ever calls him is the newsstand guy."

"And that's all he'll ever be." Joey taps Mary Hanging from His Rearview Mirror. "He had a tough break. Maybe two. I kinda feel sorry for him. What are the chances of this repeating? You slipping in front of his newsstand, Bracaconi getting involved, and Vogt thinking I'm responsible. I mean, seriously. What're the odds?"

Zero oh three percent.

I watch Blessed Mary swing, the sway hypnotic. Back. Forth. Back. Forth. Back. For—"He mentioned a Rupert."

"His middle name. He liked to be called Rupee in college. Wanted to go to India. Had a thing for Rudyard Kipling." Joey puts his car into gear. "He should have studied poetry."

Mary's swing picks up speed. She goes off-rhythm. A metronome without its counterweight.

The newsstand guy is Rupee. The one who visits my hindsight Facebook page and thinks he's e-mailing a baker from Oberholt.

And he's one in three hundred. Or three thousand.

34

Kipling wrote of the common man, characterizing him in a way that made him sympathetic, understandable, even noble. A triumph in a world as class-conscious as the England of his time. And reminiscent of Chaucer's penchant to do the same.

I take another lap around the block to calm my nerves and wonder what either would have made of the newsstand guy. I imagine the two collaborating. Getting the accent right. The word cadence correct. Elevating the bit player to a hero in his own tale.

But I have to stop dreaming, have to return to my everyday world, have to figure some way to live in it. Until I leave.

I climb our stoop, put my key in the lock, open the door.

"Whadderya, nuts? Don'defend'er. She's a bitch. An agin' hag. Duz she think she'll do better'n Stanley? What's the Church say about it?"

Angela. Giving a demonstration of the South Philly accent and cadence.

"We can't force the woman to the altar if she doesn't want to go there."

Gosh. Golly. Gee, Luigi. Ya think?

"Then talk to Stanley. You wanna get married, or not?"

A car horn sounds in the street, startling my door hold. The hinge squeaks. So much for Joey's repairs. I head into the kitchen.

Angela grunts something I think she means for me to take as a hello.

Luigi waves from the stove. "How ya doing, Eugenia?"

I drop my pocketbook to the table. The movement shakes a collection of glass ramekins filled with colored water littering its top. Red and yellow, green and purple dance a rainbow with the vibration, reminding me of those dioptrical colors Donna talked about. The ones that so interested Goethe. I point to eggs, half-dyed with patterns outlined in wax, lined up in cartons on the counter. "Easter's over."

Luigi takes a deep breath and blows into the end of one until his face goes bright red. Egg snot blows out the other. "They're for Pascha. Orthodox Easter. We're going to Constantine's."

The lawyer. The one with the Greek mother.

He retrieves a couple of Yuengling Black and Tans from the fridge, plunks one down beside Angela and hands me the other. "Stanley isn't going. He and Constantine don't get along. An old argument. Long past time they got over it."

Yet Stanley spoke so highly of Constantine. "What's with the tea bags?"

Luigi holds a box so I can see the label. "Chamomile. It's a natural dye. Same with this." He pours water into a ramekin. Cinnamon scent competes with the vinegar. The pot simmering on the stove boils over. He snares the lid with an oven mitt. "Onion skins. I do this every year for my aunt. She took care of me when my father would get—" He pauses. "When my mother needed a break."

The wonder of it all washes over me.

Der Weasel, the Freiherr's head-cracking chimp, now available in a holistic edition who makes organic dyes to please his aunt for a religious observance.

This ain't your papa's Oldsmobile.

I pop the top on my beer. Yeasty alcohol rises to battle the onions and vinegar, chamomile and cinnamon. The odors dissolve to stronger versions. The onion becomes more savory, the vinegar, more acid.

The memory reaches across the centuries. Der Weasel's muscled forearm across my mouth, voice hoarse in my ear, my skirts raised. And his insistent pushing, probing where he had no permission.

Angela drops her eggshell into a ramekin. She lights a cigarette. "Ma won't give me and Luigi her blessing without it at least looking like you and Stanley are making progress."

"He's coming to Dinner. How much more progress you need?"

"Ma canceled it. Says you don't want Stanley there. Told Stanley she scheduled a special memorial mass for Uncle Nic. Said she felt strange having a celebration after."

Relief.

The sudden temerity of Stanley's messages.

Embarrassment.

"So Stanley called you here." Angela blows a stream of smoke to the ceiling. "Said he couldn't get through on your phone. He said he understands. It's all fine. And maybe he'll catch you on the flip side."

Disappointment.

"Nobody's asking you to marry him." Luigi lifts a new egg to his mouth. "But would it kill you to make the guy a little manicotti?"

I smack my beer to the table. "You don't need me making anybody manicotti. You wanna marry Angela. Knock her up. Father DiLullo will make sure Ma gives her blessing."

Luigi and Angela exchange glances. Angela plays with an egg. Rolling it from one end to the other.

No. Really? "It's a sin to smoke if you're pregnant."

Luigi over-sputters, blowing his egg to the floor. He slips the cigarette from Angela's fingers and throws it into the sink. He tosses her beer after.

Angela hops up. She retrieves the beer. "What're you doing? I'm not pregnant."

Luigi pulls the beer out of her hand. "Then why's Eugenia sayin' you are." His accent, so educated, so refined, retreats to goombah-speak.

"Eugenia says a lotta things. I mean how could I be pregnant? We've never . . ."

Luigi lowers his head. He blushes. "No. You're right. Not that way. Not much." He grabs a paper towel, goes to work mopping up the egg. He looks at me. "It's that damned *mal'occhio*. My father invoked his own when I was in seminary. Told me to leave. Get a man's job. Take over his business. I didn't. He told me I was good for nothing. That nothing good would come from my decisions. Don't you see, Eugenia? We can't get married without your mother's blessing. Not with my father's *maledizione* hanging over my head."

"Especially not since Uncle Nic died." Angela waves a hand, looking hopeless. "We get married and somebody else dies, Ma will never forgive us."

•••

A few hours later, Angela flops into the chair opposite the sofa. She crosses her feet on the coffee table, kicking aside printouts from my session with Google. Of 8,390,000 references for the word *reincarnation*, 166,700 couple with *delusion*. "You treat Luigi like fungus."

I hold up a real estate flyer. "I'm not getting married so you and Luigi can buy a house."

Angela snatches it. She runs a finger over the window boxes in the photo. "Luigi's been saving his money. Me too."

My laptop dings, delivering another missive from the mysterious Anders Dripzin: *Failure to comply with committee requirements will result in termination of your agreement.*

Angela lights a cigarette. "That guy, Virgil, called again. Something about a group."

The jerk probably wants me to guest lecture on those damned archetypes. I'm stuck on Emily, whose story is told in *The Knight's Tale*: Emily, object of desire of the brawling cousins. Emily, objectified, little more than a prize. Emily, forever shadowed by the two idiots who put her in that unenviable position. "His name is Virgule, not Virgil. Virgule Futz. He called before?"

"Guess Ma didn't tell you. Lot for her to keep track of. That guy from the hospital called, too. The red and white roses. Sounded kind of young."

Panisporchi's an unusual name. We're the only ones listed.

She smacks her head. "Oh, and I forgot Tony." She lowers her voice in imitation of Tony's baritone. "He said your voice mailbox was full. You two-timing Stanley with him?"

"I'm buying shoes from him." I dig a brochure out of my purse.

Angela reads, "'Hard to fit? Find your Sole Mate with Foot Fetish.' Cute." She flips through, making approving noises. "So you're two-timing with Virgil, then. Or maybe Free-der-ITCH."

"I'm not two-timing Stanley with anybody. I'm not even two-timing Stanley with Stanley. We're broken up. Remember?"

She smacks my laptop shut. "Then why won't you let Ma have The Dinner?"

"Because nobody cares what *I* want."

Angela tosses the Foot Fetish flyer on top of my keyboard and jams the real estate one into the pocket of her jeans. "Your little boyfriend left a message."

The nipple tingle returns along with an image of Friedrich and me stretched across the chairs of Library Lounge C, so powerful and present, my lips part and it's all I can do not to let my legs follow.

Angela eyes me. "He wants you to meet him for coffee. Said it can't wait."

35

Friedrich lets the coffee shop's ancient screen door smack against the equally ancient jamb.

"Wow." He runs a finger along the table's rippled stainless steel edge, then traces what's left of the interlocking triangles patterned in the worn Formica. "You find this place on MGM's back lot?"

I found it eight blocks from my house, on the other side of Broad Street. Folks over here belong to a different parish. They play bingo at a different church hall and buy their pastrami from a different deli. A different funeral parlor buries them and a different bridal shop stuffs their boobies into Dijon mustard–colored, warm ochre bridesmaid dresses.

But when the *mal'occhio* finds them, they must use the same Overlooks Lady to get rid of it. Because she's playing solitaire in the back, roots of her red-orange hair thinner and grayer than I remember. She goes to the same senior citizen's center Ma does. They sometimes sit together on the bus to Atlantic City.

I'm completely screwed.

"*Espresso, per favore,*" I tell the lady at the counter, then lean in to mutter at Friedrich. "Call me at home again, you get to change genders. Just like Tony."

Friedrich shoves a paper across the table. "Administration denied my application to continue the support group."

I shove the paper back. "I told them you forged my signature."

"You did not. They'd have expelled me."

I wait for the lady to leave the espresso. "Take the group off campus. A church basement or something. I don't want to be associated with it. Things are getting messy."

"Messy is good. Messy is the only way to progress."

"Progress without me. Forget my job, I'm not doing anything that gives anybody on the Assignments Committee any reason to mess with my paperwork next life around."

Friedrich runs a thoughtful finger along the rim of his cup. "This is because I didn't fuck you the other night, isn't it?"

The room goes silent. The Overlooks Lady makes a big deal of turning over her next card so I won't guess she's eavesdropping.

The ace of spades.

Friedrich whisks away the crema marking his upper lip. "I almost went there. Just . . . I dunno. It would've been too weird to have sex in the same room my wife just vacated. And . . . well, there was Tony."

Heads turn.

"Let's go." I pull Friedrich's cup from his mouth and clatter it into the saucer. Grab a biscotti from the glass jar sitting atop the display case. Toss a ten dollar bill on the counter. Take Friedrich by his backpack. And propel him out the door.

I hang on to him until we reach the corner, then give him a shake. "So. You've screwed everybody at that meeting."

He opens his mouth, but I shove the biscotti into it. "Shut up. Everything you're saying is stupid."

I sidestep a scaffold and drag him across the street. The steady sound of nail guns punctuates my pique for another quarter block before Friedrich spits out the biscotti and pulls me up short. "I wasn't trying to insult you. Not in the coffee shop and not the other night. I don't know how it is for you, but for me, sex in this life stinks. I want it. I need it. But every time I go for it, it goes flat. Because I get turned on by the person somebody used to be. Never for who they are. It feels fake."

Memory of the nipple tingle intrudes, stronger than the actual feeling at the time. And something comes clear. Friedrich's bizarre ensembles, the mismatched colors, the general ill-fittedness . . .

This is how Friedrich hides. I use Chaucer, he uses poor fashion choices. He doesn't want to be attractive to a potential partner, doesn't want to deal with his pasts any more than I want to deal with mine.

Friedrich nods. "You think I want to jump Ali, but you're mistaking kindness for interest. You carry a jealousy that no longer has reason to exist. That's because in this life, we don't get to be who we are until we resolve who we were." He spreads his hands in an arc between us. "Think of all the things you've done you're not proud of. All the times you wish you'd done better. This is it. Right here. Right now. This is your chance to make them right."

Here. Now. Standing next to a double row of illegally parked cars two blocks off Passyunk. Now's my chance to make things right.

My life sucks.

"What fantasy do you live in, Friedrich? You lie. You cheat. You fake paperwork. You forge people's signatures. This life's already a bust."

"Okay. All right. Maybe there's a pattern with me. But there's a pattern with you, too. Fate didn't throw us together by happenstance."

"You picked my classes out of the lineup when you first registered at Temple. You didn't have to take Chaucer to fulfill your English requirement. But you recognized me from my photo in the course catalog. You thought you might use that connection to your advantage. If that's your idea of Fate, then Fate is a bitch."

"Fate's not a bitch, Dr. Panisporchi. But, sometimes she's an asshole. So am I. There's plenty I messed up with on my own, but sometimes I was just in the wrong place at the wrong time and I can't keep being blamed for the circumstances I couldn't control."

The sound of nail guns fades, its steady rhythm replaced by that of heavy boots on cobbles. In a back room of my memory, a door unlocks, swinging open on rusty hinges to reveal Oberholt's bell ringer, a big man with broad shoulders, red-blonde hair, square jaw, who lived at the church, his mild harelip curled in a permanent sneer. A man in the wrong place. At the wrong time. Blamed for the thing that happened, that made everything happen.

The bell ringer makes his way across the square, waving his arms in grand circles and shouting to any who could hear, "Hurry. They're coming."

The gray rolls in, but this time it's welcome, casting everything into comfortable shadow. A shadow I can observe and not engage. "The bell ringer was Ned."

"Yes." Friedrich all but collapses against the scaffold, voice relieved, expression weary.

My Lutheran soldier had gone to see to the press. It had to be moved. And Josef wasn't there to help. He went looking for the Greek, the man he'd never find because the Greek was dead.

The headache begins. I rub my eyes, blinking hard. "Go away."

"Oh my god, Dr. Panisporchi. We're never going to get anywhere if you won't even allow yourself to remember."

"I don't want to remember. Don't want to know. Why does any of it matter? We were nobodies. Baker, bookbinder, bell ringer, brewer's daughter . . . girl."

"That's what we need to figure out. At those meetings." Friedrich pulls the application out of his pack again. "Just sign it. Please."

The paper flaps between us, its edges frayed and dog-eared, begging me to acquiesce. I shift my satchel and reach, thinking I'll stuff the application into a side pocket, consider it better when I don't have Friedrich yapping in my ear, but the look of relief on his face reminds me too much of Ruprecht Vogt's smug assertion. Mr. Fucking Loud-Mouth Pamphleteer. "You didn't really think your baker boy was going to marry you, did you?"

"Sorry, Casanova." I crumple the paper and cast it to the breeze. "But I'll give you an A for the effort."

Friedrich sweeps an arm to indicate me and him and the street beyond. "You really don't get it, do ya, Dr. Panisporchi? None of this is real. It's a stage, a maze the Assignments Committee wants to see how well we negotiate."

"Why?"

"To see how well we do. Help us get to the next level." He looks at me in wonder. "Did you honestly think you could make a deal with the devil and not get fried?"

My life stretches behind, a string of dots leading backward from Stanley to Donna to Luigi to Carlotta to Joey to Maurizio and the newsstand guy. Joey's scholarship that garnered me enough funds to complete my doctorate so I could get my teaching position at Temple.

So Friedrich could take my class.

The memory door widens. It sucks me in, the mirrors beyond reflecting this decision and that, laid out like the type in a printing press, course fixed. I cast about for a new path, desperate to shift it. "I made no deal."

Disbelief travels a direct route from my proclamation to Friedrich's expression. "Everybody makes a deal, doc. Just some of us aren't willing to admit it."

He turns and hurries up the street, beating a zigzag path through the line-up at the light. Brakes squeal. Drivers hurl invective.

I shout after him. "The support group is over. Do you hear me? Finished. Done. Come within a hundred yards of Library Lounge C, I'll . . . I'll . . ."

Friedrich cups his hands around his mouth like a megaphone, his words clear over the car tops. "You'll what, Dr. Panisporchi? Flunk me?"

36

Nicholas, the poor astrology scholar who rented a room from a well-heeled carpenter in Chaucer's *Miller's Tale,* is a sly and crafty creature who convinces his landlord the world is coming to an end as part of an elaborate ruse to get his landlord's wife into bed. The landlord constructs three barrels which he suspends from the rafters and into which they each climb so they will be safe from the coming catastrophic flood. Once the landlord is ensconced in his barrel, Nicholas leaves his own and sneaks into the wife's, who is a willing participant in his chicanery.

Nicholas provides endless fascination for readers of the *Tales* for his limitless hubris, boundless imagination, and willingness to do pretty much anything to achieve his goal. Readers *love* Nicholas' antics.

Because readers don't have to deal with them.

I rush into the meeting and past the latest version of Friedrich's sign:

Hindsight Support Group
No Open Flames or Smoke
No Photography

I rattle a packet in Friedrich's face, copies of five semesters of his work, each stellar example marked with a big black *F.* "So now it's blackmail."

"Blackmail's such an ugly term."

"How's breaking and entering for ya?" I point to the door. "How'd you get in?"

"You gave me a key."

"And you gave it ba—" *Shit.* "You made a copy. Doesn't matter. You don't have paperwork. I won't sign."

"You already did. In triplicate. And look what I found on Google." Friedrich hands me a paper.

From Lifehacker. FIFTEEN RULES EVERYBODY WHO RUNS A SUPPORT GROUP NEEDS TO KNOW.

"First rule: Pick a topic. Why do we have hindsight? That's a good one." Friedrich points to rule number seven. "And hey. Look. Since I'm facilitator, I can choose to call on people."

Friedrich folds the list and stuffs it into the side pocket of my purse. "You're first."

Every piece of every bit of me returns from wherever it's been railroaded, choo-choos up my gullet, and steams out my mouth. "I don't want to be first, Friedrich. I don't want to be here at all. What gives you the right to do this? To risk my job, my . . . my life, my, my—"

I look past Friedrich's shoulder to the door. "Fuck."

Friedrich looks to the door, too. And blanches.

It's Futz. He strides over.

"Virgule," I murmur, my career crumbling. "What brings you here?"

"Curiosity. Saw the poster."

"It's Friedrich Palmon's project." I turn to introduce them, but Friedrich's melted away.

Futz's gaze settles on Tony, standing with Ali who examines a pair of red medium-heeled pumps. "The closed toe is all business. But the color and cutouts show you know how to have fun."

I find Friedrich across the room, standing with the *Temple News* guy. I catch his eye and point meaningfully at my watch. He returns a sullen glare. I yank a chair into the circle. "Let's get started. Tonight's topic is why we have hindsight."

"Oh, good." Tony arches a waxed brow. "I want our newcomer to share first."

"No." Ali points an accusing finger. "He's a Nazi."

Futz tents his hands, taps the index fingers together, looks mildly surprised. "Are you speaking to me?"

Friedrich crosses the room, grabs my arm, shoves me out the door. He makes me go with him all the way down the hall and into the stairwell. He faces off. "You invited him."

"I don't even want this meeting to happen. Why would I—"

"Then make him leave. He's the Freiherr."

A fleeting image pecks an uncomfortable divot in my disbelief. Well-tailored wool jacket embroidered with branches and pinecones. Hawk-like nose. Feathered cap. "You're wrong. One of the Freiherr's flunkies, maybe, but not actually . . . him."

"Are you blind?" Friedrich tents his fingers in imitation of Futz, then thumps the wall. "He killed people."

"He didn't kill anybody. Somebody you think he was killed people."

"They're still dead."

"It's been four hundred years. Of course they're dead."

So how come you can't be so generous with Luigi?

Blessed Mary Mind-fuck really knows when to pick Her moments. "Fine, Friedrich. I get it. You don't want a psychologist here. You're afraid there's a perfectly rational explanation for all this."

Friedrich twists a knuckle through my belt loop. He pulls at it, closing the space between us. "Futz is your responsibility. You're the one who wants him to stay." His breath, spicy like the pfeffernüsse, warms on my ear. "Make note. You can be certain others are."

Why? How? I want to ask, but my inhalation to do so is too large, too intimate against the hard muscle of his chest. The question catches in my throat, collapses to a breathy mush.

Friedrich unhooks me and retreats into the hallway, my heart tripping a fluttery pattern, my panties moist.

The door catches with a gun-cock . . . click.

The door clanks open again. Kyra pulls me into the hallway. She drags me back, shoves me into the meeting. "Hurry up. Ned's hollering."

Ned slams his water bottle to the carpet, his tone damning, his color high. "You're making excuses."

Futz turns his palms up. "Even if I'd heard of this place, this . . ." He looks to the *Temple News* guy.

"Oberholt," the *Temple News* guy offers.

"Thank you." Futz returns his attention to Ned. "Even if I knew of this place. Even if all you say is true and I'm this dreaded . . ."

"Freiherr," the *Temple News* guy offers again.

"There's nothing I can do. I don't remember."

Ned makes one of his big-armed movements. "You sent your goons after me."

"Members of the militia," the *Temple News* guy corrects. "Acting on orders from the duke."

"Yo. Walter Cronkite. Enough." Ned turns back to Futz. "So you deny it."

"To deny would mean I had some notion of what you're talking about."

"He's not a Freiherr." Ali's voice trembles. "He's a Nazi."

The *Temple News* guy again consults his notebook. "He's a Lutheran."

Futz rubs at the bridge of his nose. "My parents raised me Methodist."

Tony claps his hands two times in quick succession, like the nuns did when they wanted our attention. "We're boring the good doctor. Since he doesn't know what we're talking about, let's discuss something he does. Let's discuss the doctrine of synchronicity."

"Acausal parallelism. Or, laymen's terms, meaningful coincidence." Futz goes into lecture-mode. "Jung first coined the term. A way of granting meaning to the meaningless. Like assigning pictures to star patterns, thinking their position affects our destiny. Adherents believe unrelated incidences are part of a cohesive whole, a grand dynamic, a notion sometimes summed up by the adage once is happenstance, twice is coincidence, and three times is enemy action."

The *Temple News* guy looks up, pencil poised. "Did Jung say that also?"

"No. Auric Goldfinger. From James Bond."

Ali kicks at the carpet. "What's synchronicity got to do with James Bond?"

Tony shakes his head. "Don't you find anything weird about this group, sweet pea?"

"Sure I do. It's always storming. And nobody here has any idea how to run a support group. We're supposed to have a lecture. We're supposed to share. And we're supposed to say the serenity prayer." Ali pulls a pfeffernüsse from her pocket, holding it so we can see the nibbles around the edges, the bits of hair and the lozenge wrapper stuck to its top side. "And we're always eating these cookies."

"Because the baker wants us to remember." Tony makes a clucking sound. "This is all a setup. Not for us. For him. He's trying to tip the balance in his favor."

"What did he do?"

"Who would know better than you, sweet pea?"

Friedrich hops to his feet. "This is a safe place to discuss our situation. We won't get anywhere by bullying one another."

Tony runs a finger along a pectoral muscle well-developed enough to call a breast, the gesture angry, meant to convey a moment Tony and Friedrich have shared.

Indignation, searing and seething and acid with acrimony, cauterizes my cut-off switch. "You *did* sleep with him, um . . . with her . . . with . . ."

The *Temple News* guy flips back through his notebook. "Eleven times. Fourteen if encounters other than strict intercourse are included."

Eleven. Fourteen. My mind numbs around the numbers, grateful for the descending haze, grateful the Vicodin is finally working its magic. "Omigod. Friedrich. You can't even be faithful when you're being unfaithful."

Friedrich rubs at his chest. Sweat breaks on his forehead. He points to the reporter's pad. "Do you keep everything in there?"

"Wouldn't be much of a reporter if I didn't." An obliging flash of lightning emphasizes his statement.

Kyra sprinkles something at Futz's feet. "Salt. To keep evil at bay."

Ali pulls her sleeves down over her wrists. "I don't believe in evil spirits."

Tony grabs Ali's arm and pushes a sleeve back up to reveal what looks like a scabbed-over cigarette burn. "Because you make your own, sweet pea."

Kyra stands in the middle of the circle, a clump of fluff in her hand. "Chicken feathers. To carry away contentious words." She tosses the feathers into the air. They catch the air currents, and float, landing on carpet, table, chairs. And shoulders.

Friedrich makes a strangled sound. "Kyra. Not chicken. I'm allergic." His words exit in a wheeze. He sucks at his inhaler, struggles from his seat, then slides to the floor, the tendons on his neck too prominent.

Ned's on it. He whips out his cell, hits a single key, gives the 911 operator succinct details. And pats Friedrich's pockets. "Do you have an EpiPen?"

Friedrich kicks at his backpack. Ned upends it. Notebooks. Pencils. Papers. And a shower of prescription bottles.

Ned reads the labels. "Darvon. Oxycontin. Tylenol3. Prozac. Welbutrin. Xanax. Ambien. Where's the Epi, bro?"

Ali picks a bottle from the fray. "Can I have the Prozac?"

The *Temple News* guy moves into the corner, hands sequestered under opposite armpits, his expression unreadable.

"Better make it snappy," Ned tells the dispatcher. "His lips are blue."

This may be it for Friedrich. Another few minutes and he may be debating his best moves for his next life.

More thunder rumbles. It takes on the cadence of boots on cobble. In the distance, a siren wails. And . . . church bells. Tolling the nine o'clock hour.

Oberholt descends, in all its panicked, primal, final moments. People shoving, scraping, scrabbling.

For life.

Help Friedrich, Blessed Mother. Pray for him. For me. In times of sorrow. Of joy. In desperation I call out to Thee. Certain in my uncertainty. Whatever course Friedrich might have fixed us on, I do not want to stumble along it alone.

Ned digs back into the empty backpack, feeling along the lining. He upends it again, and out tumbles the long-sought EpiPen. He retrieves it and slams it into Friedrich's thigh.

Swollen seconds pass. Friedrich's breathing eases. His posture relaxes.

Ali glances at the clock. "We should do the serenity prayer now. Going to be hard to form a circle once the paramedics show."

37

utz is a word meaning *fool* or *idler*. *Virgule* is a punctuation mark also known as the oblique-diagonal, or separatrix, related to the Latin *virgula* meaning *little rod* or the more vulgar *little penis*.

Conclusion? Virgule Futz is a time-wasting dick.

And the dick's wasting time in my office, elbows resting on my desktop. He hands me a report. Numbers. Graphs. On every page, the salient term repeats—False Memory Syndrome. "Cops see it time and again. People feed off each other. The subject sees a car accident, but presumes the ambulance. Let it be known a dark sedan fled the scene, everybody will claim they saw it."

Or the florist van pulling in front of a pedestrian. Or the newsstand guy who shoves an ex-Weasel and overbalances the Chaucer professor into a backflip. "Yes, well, that's very interesting, Virgule, but I'm pretty busy at the moment, and—"

"Not that False Memory is anything official in the DSM-V. Pretty controversial still. And it's not an illness, more like a coping mechanism. Your group is unique because all claim memory of past lives in the same place. That's my premise. That the memories are contagious."

Like lice.

"Like a fungus. A primary plant sends out spores and where fertile ground is found, in this case a roomful of suggestible personalities, the memory is picked up and elaborated on. That fireman remembered me as the Freiherr, and the one in the dress . . ." Futz *snap-snap-snaps* his fingers. "What's his name?"

"Tony?"

"Yes. Tony. He could suddenly confirm it." Futz runs a hand through his salt-and-pepper stubble. "The fact the group focused on me, a stranger in a position of relative authority, confirms my theories regarding what I like to call Conjoined Reverse Scapegoat Syndrome. Allow the delusion to persist and the logical next step is devolvement into self-induced schizophrenia." He checks his watch. "It's pretty damned fascinating."

Quite.

He indicates the report. "I hope to submit it in early fall. If you ran the group through then, it'd be a big help. I understand the participants have already signed permissions. I'll put your name on it as contributor, of course."

My department's interested in work on literature, not lunatics. "Last night was the last meeting. It's too risky." I point to the pile of forms I have to fill out because of Friedrich's episode, open my laptop, and head over to Google, hoping I'm conjuring the appropriate symptoms of Polite Interest, But I Have to Get Back to Work Now Syndrome. I add *false memory* to my search for *reincarnation* coupled with *delusion*. The hit number shrinks to 11,300.

"Too bad. The physical similarities among the participants alone would warrant a grant."

I mentally group Ned, Tony, Ali, Kyra, and Friedrich in an imaginary police lineup. "Similarities?"

"I asked a few questions when you and Mr. Palmon left the session. The men reported they were colorblind. As am I."

Friedrich's sweaters. All those bizarre combinations. And Futz. Mismatched socks, over-orange polo, green-tinged slacks. "But you don't claim to have hindsight."

"No. The complexity of the construct is intriguing, but the concept is laughable." Futz retrieves his report. "How are you doing on those archetypes?"

●●●

A half hour later, I get Dr. Frangipane on the phone. "Google's got it right here. 'MACULAR DEGENERATION—a loss of color perception afflicting the over-fifty population which causes them to lose the ability to differentiate pastels and eventually tones all hues to gray.'"

"It's probably eyestrain." Dr. Frangipane sounds all soothing and I-soooo-got-actual-sick-people-I-gotta-see. "I can refer you to somebody, but it's rare as hell in people your age. Something on the order of zero oh three percent of reported cases."

An hour after I hang up with Dr. Frangipane, Friedrich stops by. He tells me I'm being stupid on purpose. "You're making yourself nuts trying to convince yourself you're nuts."

"Did you resubmit that paperwork? The library director e-mailed. She doesn't understand why we're still meeting."

"Bureaucracy. I'll do it again." Friedrich flicks a finger under my chin. "Futz isn't going to recommend you for a permanent position. Not now, not when one's available, not ever."

I glance to the corners, run a surreptitious hand under the rim of my desk. I imagine feeling under the drawer bottoms, shining a flashlight on the undersides of shelves, unscrewing the hand piece on my telephone, maybe even dismantling the desk lamp. "Do you have this place bugged?"

"Seriously?"

"One more incident over this group and I'm going to get canned."

"The support group won't get you axed. Futz will beat us to it."

"Then why's he so keen to continue through the summer?"

"To keep an eye on us, get his info for his stupid paper. You're a threat. You know who he was. We all do. He's created a happy little world that makes us all crazy. The crazier we are, the saner he looks. He won't be satisfied until this group is closed down, the door barred, and hindsight has a listing in the DSM-VI."

"Well, see? Futz and I *do* have something in common."

"What will it take to convince you?" Friedrich holds out his hand, shaking. Pulls at his lower lids so I can see his sclera, bloodless. "I almost died last night."

"You're the only one having these symptoms. I had my episode, but now I'm fine. Ned looks ready to run a marathon, and Tony is prettier than me."

"It's progressive. Each iteration gets you sooner. All you have to do is look at Ali to know she's been around the hindsight block more than is good for her."

"Ali does drugs. She's an alcoholic."

Friedrich sniffs at my coffee. He pulls out his flask and adds a measure until the liquid reaches the brim. Then he takes a swig himself. "Listen. The Assignments Committee have *me* in their sights, not you. It's *my* name on that Facebook page, *my* name all over the forms for this support group."

"I signed them."

"Nobody can read the scrawl." He rubs at his neck, stretching it in an exaggerated arc. "I can't keep doing this. Couple more go-arounds, I'll be living in Fairmount Park. Talking to squirrels. Picking lint out of my beard."

The newsstand guy. Greasy hair. Nicotine-stained fingers. Pathetic little clay saints. I take a big gulp, grateful for Friedrich's intervention. He only drinks the best.

Friedrich shoves his hands into his pockets. "You think we're a bunch of sorry individuals, don't you, doc? Freaks to be pitied, kept at arm's length." His indignation makes two bright spots on his cheeks, unnerving against his pallor. "You're not like us. You have a home. Family. People who care about you. You even have a man for when the loneliness gets too stark. Why should you make any special effort?"

"That man took care of me in Oberholt when you wouldn't. Stood by me when you refused. He was a good man. He *is* a good man. He's . . . he's . . ."

". . . an excellent pool player. He relieved me of a week's tips the other night."

I settle in my chair, wrap myself in the fuzzy blanket lowering with the Vicodin and booze and imagine Friedrich following me on my dates. Sitting at the bar while Stanley and I play. Watching us on the night we kissed. "He was betting?"

"What we call gentlemen bets. He more than made it up to me with the beer and I found most of my losses returned to my coat pocket when I got home. He even paid for my cab. Sunovabitch never would have done that in Oberholt."

Friedrich picks up his pack. "It gave me hope. If a guy like the Freiherr's cousin can reform himself, maybe my repeated bouts with hindsight means the universe hasn't given up on me yet. I'm not sure where I read it, but I've heard it said, Heaven's methods can be harsh, but they're never unkind."

38

In the seventeenth century Cardinal de Retz said, "There is nothing in this world without a decisive moment."

I find Friedrich's parting words a half hour after he leaves my office. *Totable Quotes and Pithy Proverbs.* Page 214.

Forget it. I'm not deciding the truth of hindsight based on wisdom by somebody calling himself Author Unknown.

I call Stanley and tell him Ma got the dates wrong for Uncle Nic's memorial mass. Even if hindsight's a crock. Even if Stanley's Oberholt version is a figment of my imagination. Stanley has enough ethics to return a struggling student's losses and enough compassion to load him into a cab and pay for his ride home. I can trust a guy like that to keep his hands off my 403(b).

"As long as you're okay with The Dinner," Stanley tells me the following Saturday evening at a pool hall near the waterfront.

"You been talking to Luigi."

"He's old-fashioned. Traditional. He's also scared to death of you."

"That's ridiculous."

Stanley rounds the table, yanking balls from pockets. "When he calls your house, Angela's never available. When he stops by, Angela's never home. Somebody's always blocking his number on her cell and when we came over for Chinese after you were sick, you ordered him shrimp fried rice."

"I didn't know he was allergic."

"Why are you against him?"

"I'm not. He's a nice guy. You wouldn't lie about that. There's nothing you haven't told me." I point to where the skin puckers at his temple. "Nothing about bar brawls with bad outcomes."

Stanley deflates. "So Joey told you. That's fine. I figured he would. And I was going to tell you myself. Eventually."

"So tell me now."

"Not a lot to tell. Best not to mix bets with beer. Luigi got the worst of it. And he won't get his foot fixed. Personal penance, I guess."

"He said he fell down the stairs."

"Shoved is more like it. But never named the bastard who did it. Claimed he was too drunk to remember."

Luigi. Drunk. Brandy and bratwurst. Acid and sweat. The Vicodin calls me, its voice sweet, like chocolate after sex, promising just one won't hurt, give sobriety another chance tomorrow. "Betting. Beer. Fight. Joey gets the scar under his eye, Luigi, the limp, and you, a permanent hearing loss. No wonder Joey hates gambling."

I cross my arms, certain I've figured it out. *Really, what's the big freaking deal?*

Stanley fishes the lemon wedge from his ginger ale. He squeezes a little into his drink and sticks the rest between his teeth and cheek. "I wasn't betting. All I did was play pool."

Oh. "Then how come—"

Stanley cuts me off. "Listen, I didn't accept your mother's invitation so Luigi and Angela can get married. I accepted for myself, because it makes me happy. But if you don't want this relationship, tell me. Because none of this matters if you're not happy."

"Don't shift this to me. You wanted to break up."

"And you didn't tell anybody about it."

"How the hell could I?"

"Five words, 'Stanley and I broke up.'"

"If it's so easy, you should've said it."

"I didn't think it was my place to do the informing. Just didn't seem, I don't know—"

"Chivalrous?"

"Gentlemanly," he corrects me, his voice cold. "I figured you could tell them you did the breaking up. I know that kind of thing is important to women."

"What's important to women is not having to listen to an hour or more of everybody moaning and groaning about how could I break up with you, you're such a nice guy."

"You're thirty-three years old. You don't have to explain anything."

"Sure I do. I have to explain everything and I have to explain it to everybody. That's how it is for us women. And it's all complicated because, guess what? They all like you. They think you're the bee's knees and I couldn't think of a way to tell my mother you broke up with me because we hadn't slept together."

Stanley stops looking huffy. "That is not why we broke up."

"Pray tell, noble Knight, what was?"

"Because of this." Stanley rounds his index finger to indicate he's encompassing the conversation. "Because there isn't enough of this."

"Hollering and hand waving?"

"Communicating. Back and forth. Like normal couples."

"We talk all the time."

"I talk. I talk and talk. You don't talk back."

"I talk plenty."

"About the weather. Your family. Maybe about what you did today. But never about your feelings, your thoughts. What makes you angry, makes you sad, makes you feel alive."

My cell rings. *Somewhere Over the Rainbow*. Friedrich's tune. Little shit. I click it over.

Stanley waves his hand. He points his finger, arcing it in the air between us. "In books, people are always out to find happiness. Like they're on a treasure hunt. They figure once they find it, they'll enjoy it. Thing is, happiness is always there, in every breath, in any situation." He stops waving and takes my hands, holds them tight. "You have to stop thinking maybe there's just one more thing around the corner. Or at the next bus stop. Take the time to see what's here. In front of you."

There it is. And always the same. I want what I want and always there's some man, somewhere, telling me I should want something else. "You don't know me, Stanley. You think you do, but you don't." *Somewhere Over the Rainbow* lilts out of my cell again. I click it over again. "You have no right to tell me what to think, what to do, tell me to stop looking."

"But you won't give me a chance to know you. Every time I try to get close. Every time I—"

Somewhere Over the Rainbow. Third time. Stanley seizes my cell.

"Because of shit like this. You're out with me, but you always got this guy calling." He shows me the faceplate. "Number three in your speed dial." He pulls out his cell, hits a number, and waits for the connection. "Did you drop me anywhere on that list? Assign me a ringtone?"

Oh, no. Please, no. Sweet Mary on My Keychain . . . no.

I go for my phone. It flies out of my hand, skitters under the table. And slides, far and fast along the polished wood. I dive after it. Stanley dives after me. He grabs my leg. Then my waist. His grip strong, sure. And achingly intimate.

I give up, collapsing beside a bottle cap and a button, chest heaving, tears threatening, the memory of candied orange peel too strong.

"Anybody lose a phone?" A guy at the bar holds my cell high, so all can hear Stanley's ringtone.

Ring My Bell.

Clear and funky and suggestive. And loud. So. Damned. Loud.

My cheeks catch fire, embarrassment burning clear to my toes.

Stanley hoists me up. He pulls a dust bunny off my shoulder and another out of my hair. "You wanna get outta here?"

Hell yeah I want to get out of here. I want to get so far out of here I'm coming in the back door. I push past, grab my phone from the idiot at the bar, and exit onto the street. Stanley chases after. I let him catch up, then poke his chest. "You're number two, okay?"

"Not okay. I want to be number one. Tell me how to do that."

"You can give birth to me." I point to the top listing in my speed dial—Ma.

Stanley waits until I turn off the display. He watches while I shove the stupid phone into its stupid pocket on the side of my stupid purse. Right next to stupid Mary.

He squares off. "Let's go to my place. We need to talk. Just you and me. No family. No crowds. No loud music. No pressure."

"It is time, liebchen, I'll protect you, but you must come. Now." The other voice, the other time, rolls in so strong, I smell the saddle soap Oberholt Stanley used to keep his rigging clean.

This man is nothing like Friedrich. He's mature. He's responsible. He thinks about people other than himself.

I want to go home with him, nuzzle his neck, feel his breath on my hair, his hands traveling down my back. I want to crawl on top of him, encourage his caresses, lose myself in the promise of safety, of security, of a life without worry, without fear.

He reaches for me. I step closer. His hand in my hair, my mouth over his. Whatever my course, in this moment, it's fixed exactly where it should.

"Well look at you two, all nice and cozy."

Joey.

And Carlotta. Crossing the street to join us. She flicks her head behind them. "They just let out at the film festival."

"Shoulda let out sooner." Joey puts out a hand and shakes Stanley's. "Some ancient B-movie about the French resistance in World War Two. Subtitled and symbolic. Carlotta likes that stuff."

She play-punches his arm. "It had meaning."

Joey puts on his best Rocky and goes into a boxing feint. "Yo. Carlotta. Whipped cream on 'sparagus stalks all cut in with Nazis crashin' into a French resistance cell. Too smart for a schmoe like me." He knocks off the fancy footwork. "Lead actress was a mouse. Hair falling in eyes. Tiny voice. Unassuming. Turns out she's the Vichy collaborator. She points to everybody, accuses them of being Nazis. The last frames, she points to the audience, 'And you're all Nazis, too.'" Joey points a finger at me to imitate, then rubs his hands together. "Come with. For coffee and dessert. Carlotta wants to check out that new place on South."

Carlotta digs her fingernails into Joey's arm. "Maybe they have plans, honey."

"What plans could they have at this hour?" He indicates the hall. "Stanley been telling you his pool stories?"

Stanley's grip tightens. And I know.

Whatever battle he and Joey are fighting, he just lost. And whatever the real story between them, he's already lied about it.

Joey puts up a hand to call a cab. We pile in.

"Front and South," Joey says.

●●●

Front and South. Where professionals in Prada meet college kids in snapbacks. It's all here. Bellhops and chop shops. Salsa and Sinatra. Meatballs and catcalls. Punk. Funk. Fab. Plaid. Shawarma. Dharma. Gypsy. Glitzy. Flippant. Fervent. Authentic. Synthetic.

And everything in between. Whatever your kink, South Street provides it, in any color of the rainbow.

Joey turns up his collar against a sudden breeze. "Look at that line. The cheese must come from virgin goats."

Carlotta buttons her sweater. It's new and has the generous proportions she's lately adopted for her wardrobe. "Cheesecake is made from cream cheese."

Joey draws her close, nibbles a lobe. "Like what we buy at the store? Or is it special virgin goat cream cheese?"

Stanley does his best to bridge our growing distance by pointing out flyers. People for the Ethical Treatment of Animals. National Rifle Association. John Birch Society. American Civil Liberties Union. Sierra Club. Young Republicans. Planned Parenthood. Crisis Pregnancy Centers. Hydronics. Hydroponics. And colonics. He squints at one faded bit of cardboard and gives conversation one last valiant go. "Is the National Organization for the Reform of Marijuana Laws still around?"

I don't answer. I can't. Loneliness for my ballsy Lutheran soldier puts my heart on lockdown. He never ever lied to me. Never made me feel like he was giving me half a story. Not once. So he killed the Greek. Any member of the militia would have. Actions don't always speak to a person's soul. Sometimes circumstances have to be taken into account.

Something buzzes at the back of my mind, like a mosquito in a darkened room.

A sign that screams REDUCE YOUR PAPERWORK! quashes the mosquito and reminds me I still have to do my paperwork for the paramedics. "Just a minute," I tell Stanley, then pull out my phone, and call my work voice mail to remind myself.

Joey nudges us. He points to the hubbub milling about the entrance to the hallowed dessert restaurant. "Let's go. Must be a Tastykake or two hanging about our place. I'll even make the coffee."

Joey. Makes coffee. By himself.

The cell makes the connection, but a mechanical voice tells me my mailbox is full.

Why? A student had an asthma attack, fer chrissakes. I didn't bomb Portugal.

Stanley swings me around to face him. "Let's salvage the evening. I'll take you home. Mine. Yours. I don't care. I don't want the night to end like this. Not with us on a sour note. And I sure as hell don't want to end it eating Tastykakes with your brother."

The rest of what Stanley says is lost. Lost in the shop window behind him. Because displayed in the glass, beside an eclectic collection of beaded safety pins, ear dangles, and pot pipes is a chartreuse poster:

HINDSIGHT: THE UNSPOKEN BURDEN
SUPPORT GROUP MEETS EVERY MONDAY AT 7:30 P.M.

The e-mail address for the Facebook page is listed below, preceded by the words "For information contact" and, Holy Mother of God, the college switchboard. And my extension.

I look at the shop's sign. BUTTONS, BANGLES, AND BONGS. Kyra's shop. Long closed up for the night.

A second flyer graces the side of a *City Paper* dispenser. A third, tacked to the lamppost beside. There's one a half-block down. Another a half-block up. Across the street. Tough to read. But there. Probably block after block. On the one street in Philadelphia certain to attract them from all corners of the asylum.

No wonder my voice mail is full.

39

Delete. Delete. Delete. Text messages, voice mails, e-mails.
Are you dealing with childhood abuse?

Do you help people who make bad life decisions?

Are you selling tickets for that new emo band? Do you need back-stage help? Are you looking for venues?

And most disturbing of all: Have you cleared this with the Assignments Committee?

After Tony called my home that time, I set my university voice mail to forward to my cell when its limit was reached. I'd empty the box now, arrange to have the overflow forwarded to the headquarters of the American Psychiatric Association, except I have this stupid, freaking—

Donna points to my khakis and loafers. "You're wearing those?"

—Dinner. *Delete. Delete. Delete.* The fact of which, apparently, makes me incapable of dressing myself.

Donna goes through my closet, debating, rejecting. Angela hunts in my drawers. She holds up a red cotton-knit sweater. "Wear this."

"It's two sizes too small."

"It's way baggy on me. It'll cling just right on you."

"I'll need pliers to take it off." Seriously, Angela. Shut up. My cell phone pulses the theme from *Jaws* again. I click Maurizio to voice mail and keep scanning the spam.

Your continued failure to respond is worrisome. Please expect
a field worker.
Anders Dripzin
Assignments Committee.

Must be an Elysian Field Worker.

My head pounds. I drank too much at Joey's. I need a nap. And some privacy. "I'm moving out of here. I'm cleaning the crap out of Joey's room and redecorating."

Angela stops sorting. "But, Ma—"

"Joey didn't die. He got married. You don't set up shrines to people who get married and people don't die because people redecorate. People die because they don't watch when they cross the street and get hit by a bus." I point to Angela's cigarette. "Or they smoke and get cancer. Or they drink too much wine and go racing down dark highways with bad brakes and no seatbelts. Or react badly to feathers. Or eat a bad peanut."

I slam my laptop closed. "They die because they have rotten luck. Because the universe has it in for them. Because it's their time. Not because I paint the freaking walls white."

Angela tosses the red sweater onto her bed. "If you don't want to wear it, say so. No need to shout."

•••

Stanley hands Ma a tin of real nougat candy from Italy, tied up in a gold ribbon. "So nice of you to invite me, Mrs. Panisporchi."

Ma beams. Stanley pecks her on the cheek, then sniffs the air. "Whatever you're cooking smells delicious."

Ma points him to the armchair of honor, denuded of its plastic slipcover for this occasion. My place is next to Ma, on the far side away from Stanley, so nobody will suspect this meal is what it is, a chance for the family to size Stanley up before he's shipped out the door, the expectation he's not to wait too long to make his move.

This is just dinner. Like we have every Sunday. Everybody in church clothes. Three pastas, three meats, three vegetables, and a basket of Cacia's rolls spread on the hand-crocheted tablecloth Nonna's mother brought all the way from Italy. Set with silverware buffed to blinding brightness. Beside china washed a second time before placement.

Ma places the tin of nougat on the coffee table. "So expensive, Stanley. You shouldn't have. A young man should save his money." Ma looks at me. "For the future."

Stanley catches my eye. He winks.

I cross my legs. The loveseat's brown velvet fights the movement, hitching at the bright cotton skirt Donna and Angela assured me would bring out my eyes.

Unfortunately, it also brings out my thighs. I tug the material back down, the velvet clutches me about the hips. I go to stand, the sofa won't let go. Stanley springs to his feet, puts out a hand and hauls me off the cushion. "Upsy Daisy."

The couch releases me. With a sucking sound. I shake out the skirt, yank it back into position, decide if I ever have my own house, all my furniture will be leather, then drag Stanley into the foyer and halfway up the stairs. "I'll be nice, if you'll be nice."

"I'm being nice." He runs a palm up my arm, nuzzles behind my ear. "Mmmm . . . new perfume?"

"Stop it. I was drunk last night, out of sorts. We're just not right for a long-term relationship. Not for anything serious. I'm here for Ma."

"And I'm here because your mother invited me. Then she uninvited me. Then you called with some cockamamie story about crossed signals and mixed-up memorial masses and invited me again, and by the time you uninvited me again, it was too late to uninvite myself. And why are you presuming what sort of relationship we'd be good for? Or anything about the size of my penis?"

Memory of our conversation after the Tastykakes returns.

The sudden drop-off from the living room reminds me in a house as small as ours, no distance is distant enough. I back down a few steps, my plan to check the calamari.

Donna hops up, the sofa uninterested in her parakeet green belted sheath. "I'll take care of it. You stay with Stanley. Get to know him better."

We pull a cork on a fresh bottle and fill more glasses.

"I understand you're an actuary," Aunt Theresa says to Stanley when everybody settles again. "How exciting."

"I like to think so."

"Busy job, though. Must be hard on your own."

"Hard. And long. The more I work at it, the harder it gets." Stanley looks straight at me. "Kind of a lonely way to live."

And Donna steps in again. "Can somebody pass the antipasti?"

Dinner is an efficient affair, each course passed down opposite sides of the table full, and the serving bowls returned empty. Each time a lady stands to get something from the kitchen, Stanley half rises. Every time a lady brings something back, he does it again. Carlotta nudges Joey. Angela nudges Luigi. Carlotta's mom nudges Carlotta's dad and my aunts nudge my uncles. Soon all the men are rising along with Stanley—up, down, up, down, bob, bob, bob—until the spectacle resembles an orthodox synagogue on Saturday morning.

All the while Stanley utters benedictions:

"Wonderful soup, Mrs. Panisporchi."

"Delicious manicotti, Mrs. Panisporchi."

"The gnocchi are so light!"

And my favorite: "How do you keep the lamb from getting greasy?"

"Eugenia could tell you," Ma goes. "She did most of the cooking."

I stuffed three cannelloni.

Angela brings out the salad. Fruit and cheese appears. The women . . . gather plates.

It's the birthday party all over again, except this time Stanley is going to stand their ground. He's going to let them wear me down with their disapproving stares just to teach me a lesson about presuming anything about anything about him.

He doesn't. He reaches for his plate like he's going to take it into the kitchen himself, but Joey gets it first. He holds it out to me. "Here ya go, Eugenia. Man shouldn't have to raise it on his own."

Halfway returned from the kitchen, espresso cups in hand, Ma waits.

And waits.

And waits.

Please. Blessed Mary on the Windowsill. *Do something.*

The doorbell rings.

And the ladies cross themselves.

Somebody's dead. Somebody *has* to be dead. Why else would somebody ring? On a Sunday afternoon. Uninvited and unexpected.

Carlotta goes to answer. We hear a mumbled exchange and Carlotta returns, looking gobsmacked. "Eugenia?"

Behind her trails Kyra. In Goth garb. And Tony. Dressed exactly like Jackie Kennedy on that fateful day in Dallas. Right down to the watermelon pink pillbox hat.

Tony holds up a matching shopping bag. High enough so all can read the half-foot-tall black flourish emblazoned diagonally across its side:

FOOT FETISH, GLAMS FOR YOUR GAMS

Then beneath it, in a half-size script:

SPECIALIZING IN THE HARD TO FIT OF ANY GENDER

"Hello, Eugenia. Look how *nice* you look. I don't mean to interrupt, but . . . your shoes arrived."

40

Chaucer's Wife of Bath was loud and crude. She was also well-read and insightful, a student of life as well as love, versed in marriage, but also in herself. Some scholars believe Chaucer wrote the Wife of Bath as a feminized version of himself. Those scholars are wrong. Because the Wife of Bath knew the one thing no man will ever know. She knew what women want.

Just like Tony.

Friedrich shoots a rubber band at an Independence Hall snow globe somebody left on a windowsill of the lecture room two terms ago. The band bounces. And lands atop my latest issue of *National Geographic*. "You shouldn't have told Tony where you live."

"He must have looked me up online."

"Did he do anything strange?"

"He took orders. Carlotta bought fifteen pairs. My mother asked where he buys his clothes. And you should have seen Donna. Sat there porking out on pizzelles and pumping him for information."

That information jostles Friedrich's juice. He takes his feet off the back of the desk in front of him. "The little blonde from your brother's wedding. The Freiherr's cousin."

"Tony recognized her. Recognized everybody. Kept looking at me funny. Right before he left, he said, 'Oh honey, somebody really set you up with this one.'"

I stop. "How come nobody from Oberholt hangs around you?"

"What do you call the denizens of the support group?"

"I don't mean them. I mean in your family, your life."

"I have no life. And I have no family. None of us at the support group do. Except you."

But his sweaters. The scarves. The strange color combinations. I point to his cardigan. "I presumed you had a grandmother someplace making these for you."

"I did. Until last Christmas. When she died. Breast cancer. That's why I skipped out of class early."

"But you never . . ."

"Told you? What for?" Friedrich crumples the flyer I ripped off the lamppost on South Street. The one I've been railing about since class ended. He mashes it into a wad he holds so tight, his wrist tendons pop. "You don't care about me or my problems. You don't care about any of us." He waves an arm. "All you care about is THIS."

THIS is a lecture room. It contains a lectern, a trash can, a whiteboard, a digital clock, and a collection of right-handed student desks arranged more or less in rows. Left-handed students, like Friedrich, have to twist to make notes. Three times a semester, I e-mail administration about it. Three times a semester, they ignore me. I bring my own markers for the board.

My office is worse, a graveyard housing my career in a desk, filing cabinet, and bookcase crammed among a library of literature nobody cares about anymore. And there's my phone. Which, since spotting Friedrich's hindsight posters on South Street, blinkety-blinks enough to send an epileptic into a seizure. Because my voice mailbox is full. My voice mailbox is full. My voice mailbox is full.

I gather my papers, pick up my briefcase, stuff the markers into a side pocket, clip it shut. "What do you want from me, Friedrich?"

"Your forgiveness."

I look up, ready to flunk him all over again, but his face is sober and there's no derision in his eye. "Forgive you?"

"But you have to mean it and you have to forgive me for everything."

I won't ask what everything means. "I forgive you and all this goes away? The support group, the flyers, the phone calls, the repeated signing up for my classes."

"Well, we're already into the support group, kinda hard to dump that. And the phone calls. I mean, it's going to take a while for those to taper off, but definitely I'll stop taking your classes. And I'll stop hounding you."

I wave my cell at him. "The college switchboard thinks I'm using my extension for commercial purposes. I told them there must be a misprint somewhere."

"I'll go to South Street, pull down what posters I find."

"It's not enough."

Friedrich thumps the whiteboard. "Something has to be enough. 'Cause I'm not doing this again. Whatever my fate, I'm out to meet it head on, full throttle."

Somebody *rap-a-tap-taps* on the jamb. "Be sure to wear your seatbelt."

●●●

Joey makes scooping motions to the street vendor, then turns to me. "You sure you don't want any?"

Sauerkraut is gross. Tastes like horse sweat. Or how I imagine horse sweat would taste. Even the smell of it makes me want to shower.

Joey hands off my hotdog and joins me on the bench. "I take it Speed Racer back there is Friedrich. Kinda young to be number three on your speed dial."

"You're a jerk. Number four is the guy in the dress. Stanley feel threatened by him?"

"I think Carlotta did. He looked pretty good. Interesting company you're keeping lately."

"Not near as interesting as the company you used to keep over at Ignacio's."

"Pool's like poker. Sometimes the games stay friendly. Sometimes they don't. When they don't stay friendly and you got a bunch of guys drinking, guaranteed somebody's going to end up with a bloody nose. Or, in our case, a broken ankle, a broken head, and a broken cheekbone."

Joey points to the scar running under his eye. "Good thing I lived on campus. Made it easy to hide. Ma woulda had a fit."

"People were betting."

"Some were."

"You?"

"I never gamble. You know that. But I'll give you fifty-to-one if you can answer a question." Joey pulls out a handkerchief and lays his hotdog on it. A blob of mustard lands on the starched whiteness. He curls fingers around imaginary handlebars and makes torqueing motions like he's revving a motorcycle. "What do Speed Racer, Jackie Kennedy, Elvira, and a Chaucer prof have in common?"

"Nothing. Student project that got out of hand. It's over when term ends."

"Maybe you should end it sooner. I don't like the idea of you hanging out with drug addicts. Friedrich's too thin and his nose was running."

"He's allergic to everything. That doesn't make him a drug addict."

Joey points to his cheek, where his own scar is. "Just wondered if maybe he does drugs because somewhere, deep down, he doesn't want to face himself. We all have something we'd rather hide."

"Like your pool playing."

"Yeah. I guess the secret is figuring out who to share all those some-things with." Joey wipes at the mustard blob with a paper napkin. He folds the cloth, encapsulating the mustard within, until all that can be seen from the outside is the white.

Who's doing all that starching?

Joey blinks. He looks at his shirt. "Worried you'll have to iron Stanley's?" he says like I asked that question out loud. "Relax. I send them to the cleaners. My wife has better things to do and I've better things to do with her. We don't even own an ironing board. Traditions are great. So is culture. But not if they stymie your soul. You and Stanley make what way you want for yourselves. Don't worry what Ma says and don't worry about Luigi and Angela. I'm going to talk to all of them." He reaches a finger to lift my chin. "And if nobody listens, I'll have Father DiLullo do the talking."

I shrug him off. "Jesus. Joey. I'm not six years old." I think about the day I found the boys fishing on the beach. How Joey and Stanley talked to each other. The subtle animosity. "I thought you didn't like Stanley."

"This is about you. About you doing what you want, and not pushing yourself into something because Ma's worried the *mal'occhio* will curse Angela and Luigi and make their children ugly."

Alone with my Facebook page, the world wavy under the Vicodin, convinced the universe was handing me a cosmic kick in the ass by making my sister fall in love with Der Weasel, the notion didn't sound silly. When Stanley mentioned it, my confidence shaken by Friedrich's contact with him, it still didn't sound silly. Sitting on a park bench alongside Founder's Garden, the centerpiece of Temple's campus, under a blue sky and listening to my brother explain it . . . *Christ! I'm such an idiot.*

My cell phone again thumps out the theme from *Jaws*. I click it over.

"And that's another thing." Joey taps my phone. "You gotta get rid of Maurizio."

Like I gotta stop hanging out with drug addicts. Or not care Angela's marrying somebody who attacked me four hundred years ago. Or carry a man's plate into the kitchen for him.

Be nice to Ali. Understanding with Friedrich. Compliant with Futz.

Day after day. Examine my attitudes. Take a moral inventory. Forgive those who trespass. Confess my culpabilities. Admit my shortcomings. Provide for the common good. Don't eat meat on Fridays. Brush after every meal. And trust a brave heart and courteous tongue to carry me through this jungle.

So one day. In some far-flung future life. I'll finally get the chance to live it just the way I want.

Fuck that.

"What's with you, Joey? You gotta tell everybody what to do. Defy tradition. Tell Ma she's wrong. Luigi, he's old-fashioned. When are *you* planning to tell *us*? On the baby's third birthday?"

Every expression I've ever seen on Joey's face falls away, replaced by something happy. And hopeful. And full of bubbles. "Baby?"

I think of Carlotta's thickening waist, her ever bulkier sweaters, and proceed.

With unwarrantable and impertinent boldness. "She hasn't told you?"

He runs hands through his hair, collapses elbows to knees like a wave caught him by surprise, then sits back, chest so puffed, I half expect him to take flight. He whips out his cell, hits a speed dial. "Hon? Are you pregnant?"

Yammering exits the other end of the line. It doesn't sound like happy excitement. Joey's smile flattens, his expression sobers. "Then why's Eugenia saying you are?"

Uh-oh.

Joey hands me the phone. "She wants to talk to you."

41

Carlotta's not pregnant. She's fat.

"They been trying. Been seeing a doctor." Ma sorts. Whites, colors, mixed. She untwists another set of panties. "She gets shots. Takes drugs. They mess with her appetite. You made her feel bad. Joey, too."

Joey confident. Joey angry. Joey in love with Carlotta. But . . . feeling bad? "I'm sorry, Ma."

Ma presses her lips together, no doubt working hard to keep all the hair she can on her tongue. She hands me a basket of laundry. "I'm not the one who needs the apology."

I head into the yard. And find him out there. The source of all my misery, the real start to my story.

Der Weasel. Disguised as Luigi. Kneeling in front of Blessed Backyard Mary, the picture of piety. "What're you doing here?"

Luigi crosses himself and kisses his rosary before rising.

"Alley lock is sticking. I tried to adjust it." He pulls a screwdriver from his back pocket and holds it up like he needs evidence. He shakes the door, then points to a wad of duct tape. "Best I can do for now. But the tape won't hold. I'll find a replacement."

"The ironwork's too old. Modern locks won't fit."

"I know. What I meant is, I got a friend. He does ironwork. I'll bet he could refit this one."

Yeah. I'll bet you got a friend. "No need. I'll stop by Home Depot. Pick up a lock and chain." I pull a tablecloth from the basket, snap it at Luigi, toss it over the line, figuring he'll take the hint and go.

He doesn't. Instead, Luigi shoves the screwdriver back into his pocket. "I owe you an apology. I had no business asking you to go through with The Dinner, to pretend with Stanley because of my father's *maledizione*." He lowers his gaze. "I was wrong. Dead wrong."

I stop hanging, breath caught in my chest.

And watch the justice roll down like water. The righteousness as a mighty stream.

Der Weasel just apologized.

To me.

Luigi shakes his head. "Four years of seminary. If it taught me anything, it should've taught me not to put credence in curses of convenience."

Stanley's comment from our long-ago lunch date, the one I went to only to find out why Luigi went to seminary, why he left, wells in my memory.

If I want to know, I'll have to ask.

So I do.

The question that seemed to confuse everybody doesn't even make Luigi blink. "I needed a place to think, to reflect."

I point to his ankle. "About that?"

Luigi nods. "I was in the wrong place at the wrong time and too drunk to care about it. Water under the bridge."

"That water flowed a dozen years ago. What took you so long to find a place to think?"

Luigi laughs, the sound pure and true and rising on wings. "Some of us need a little more grace to get through our time on this Earth. That's me. I needed respite to think carefully."

"*The Parliament of Fowls*." I guess Stanley's talked to Luigi, too.

"More like fools. Goethe said when one commits, Providence moves, too. I went to seminary thinking I'd find here." Luigi points to his head. "What I had to find here."

He lays a palm on his chest.

What's he got to find? A little regret, a little excess, a little maybe-he-coulda-been-nicer. He's not atoning for anything big. Not for life as a weasel. Or a guy who did a crappy brake job.

Apologize away, Bratwurst Butt. But what you do now can't fix what you did then. Not if you don't know about it. And never will.

I grab a T-shirt and hang it, jabbing the pins over the lines. If Luigi's mood were a balloon, I'd pop it.

The Very Blessed Fussbudget gives me a nudge. *Doesn't he have the right to be judged for who he is now?*

I pin up another tee, willing the tears to settle. *Don't I?*

Luigi returns to Mary. He lays a hand on Her head. "She's a beauty. It's a shame about the damage."

Fear, full and foul, smacks the air from my lungs. I clasp the clothesline, wanting to rush to Her, to shove him away. "Joey dinged Her with a baseball."

"I don't mean the chip off Her nose." Luigi taps along the divots in Mary's cheeks. "See the edges? There's a century or more of wear on them. Looks like somebody splattered Her with a strong acid. An interesting effect. Like tears. The kind of thing zealots would make pilgrimages to see. She's a Wooden Mary, you know."

The world goes wavy. I drop my clothespin. A napkin flutters after.

Luigi picks them up. He drops them in the basket. "She was cast in a wooden mold. That's why Her robe flows so naturally. Her makers were able to add details at a more reasonable expense than had they been carving from stone. They sometimes call them Roman Marys, because of the cement they used."

"Who used?"

"The Ignacios. They were a small order of monks in the hills of Sardinia. They used *pozzolano* in their casting. It's a volcanic rock mixture, sometimes called Roman Cement. It's very strong." Luigi indicates Mary's ears, and the tips of Her toes. "It's the reason these haven't worn too badly with the weather. Although, baseballs. Not much Mary could do about those."

The world levels up. This is bullshit. Roman Marys and *pozzolano.* He's a plumber. He talks like a scholar.

Luigi tips Mary on Her base. "Look on the underside. The cross and stein."

Like beer stein? Despite myself, I drift over. There it is. A cross superimposed on what I can only call a beer stein. There's even foam running down its side.

"I know it sounds ridiculous, but the Ignacios were originally a Bavarian order, known for their ale." Luigi steadies Mary back on Her feet. "They only exported these pieces for a short period in the 1800s. Because of their weight, shipping costs made them expensive on this side of the Atlantic. How'd your family find Her?"

I gaze at Mary with new respect. No wonder She looked so natural in makeup. "My father got Her. For Ma. Probably from one of his worksites. Lots of times he got salvage for cheap."

"She's some salvage. There aren't many Marys like Her left in Europe. The Ignacios died out decades ago. Nazis used their monastery as a base during World War II. Allied bombers destroyed it. Nothing left of their cement works but a few holes in the ground."

Nazis. "You know so much."

"Marian history. I did some papers in seminary. Iconic representations. Raised funds to restore pieces like this. I hate to see them decline."

Der Weasel wants to work out his karma. He broke Mary and now he wants to fix Her. A pilgrimage he set on to fix himself. He doesn't know why he does it, but does it with all his heart. To smooth over the hurt places. Lighten his burden. And fix his course in a new direction.

Maybe it's enough. "What were Bavarian monks doing in Sardinia?"

"They relocated during the Thirty Years' War. The Lutherans turned them out of their monastery, removed their icons, whitewashed the walls. Some converted and became teachers. The others left." He rearranges the flowers at Mary's feet. "If we follow Her thread far enough, this Mary links us back to that time."

Luigi pinches the dead leaves from a pot of purple pansies. "It's an obscure bit of history. I happened on it by chance. A fortuitous Googlewhack. Two words in one Google that yields one result. Some people attach mystical significance to it." He dusts potting soil from his hands. "Synchronicity, I suppose. Considering my ignominious history at the pool hall of the same name, what are the odds I'd find an authentic Ignacio in my fiancé's backyard?"

••

I can tell you the odds. Somebody who hates math as much as me shouldn't have a decimal dogging her every turn.

What two words? We don't get to be who we are until we deal with who we were. Baker, bookbinder, bell ringer only get me random references.

False Memory and self-induced schizophrenia. Futz and Ali. Alcoholics Anonymous and Anorexia. My fingers flow across the keyboard like drunken sorority girls over a Ouija planchette. *When one commits, Providence moves, also.*

I pull out *Totable Quotes and Pithy Proverbs*. The quote is there. The quotes are always there—wisdom on demand, in sound bites short enough for even the least enlightened to grasp.

Perhaps specificity will help. I add quotes. "Josef and Weasel." "Brewer's daughter and Baker." "Fireman and Bell Ringer." "Shakespeare and Chaucer." "Goethe and Jung."

Nada nada nada. Zip. Zilch. Niente and . . . Hooooooly cannoli.

Right there. Dioptrical synchronicity. Refracting causality.

I click the link.

"'When one commits, Providence moves also'—half a philosophy from Goethe, completed by Carl Jung, with delineation of the doctrine of synchronicity. For certain individuals, a very small percentage, the universe proactively bends synchronous events to help the individual along the continuum. An act of *extremis*, in a condition rife with recidivism, dioptrical synchronicity is a gift from Heaven, an extra boost to help the individual recognize a destructive pattern and break it before it becomes irretrievable.— From the writings of T. N. Mann.'"

I check further on the site. Link after link returns "Error 404, the file you seek is no longer on this server." Images of little clay figures make me wonder. YouTube videos are dead, but a last link leads me to a blog titled *Gray Theory* owned by a certain Play-Doh Man. The following quote subtitles the space:

A USELESS LIFE IS AN EARLY DEATH.

The cosmic Spirograph creaks out of its recess to start another circuit. Memory of cookies at the kitchen table with Donna circuits with it, dragging me along a course I do not want to go. I read:

"'The bell ringer and the charwoman screwed each other and anybody else willing to pay their fees, for and against, without loyalty, compunction, or recourse. So did the baker and the bookbinder. Each made a deal with the Freiherr, but they got taken same as the rest. The monk knew. He must have. That's why his people left.

"'I should have gone when I had the chance, killed myself when I didn't, cut out my tongue when they questioned me, broken my fingers so I couldn't write. I need to say so. Until somebody listens, somebody forgives. Except the bookbinder. I think he sold us. I think that was his deal. I think the baker helped.'"

The world shifts, the light bends my way. Josef didn't sell them. He was just trying to make his connection with a man he didn't know was already dead.

Because I didn't tell him.

42

*C*haucer wrote in allegory. Living in perilous and political times, allegory let him speak his truth and keep his head. His characters weathered the centuries because of the unvarnished honesty with which they were portrayed. Portrayed with such honesty because they, Chaucer confided to me over a pint at the Society, represented persons known from his own life. "In order not did I them tell, but in such a way as fitted the circumstance. For that which is written well, some useful truth may therein dwell."

Until scholars get hold of it. Then the Wife of Bath ceases to be a woman full wise of experience, with a string of dead husbands and an earthy lust for living, and elevates to a feminist ideal, so confident in her womanhood she wears it proudly. Even when she's a guy named Tony in a classic Chanel suit gazing with incredulous calm upon Futz, who puts forth the question, "What is history, but fable agreed upon?"

The *Temple News* guy pulls out a red highlighter. "Napoleon asked it first."

Totable Quotes and Pithy Proverbs, page 272.

Beside me, Friedrich hunches in his seat. "I can't believe you're letting Futz take over like this."

"He can take over the whole support group for all I care. Do you know how many people showed up on Monday looking for a meeting we'd rescheduled? Those stupid posters. I hope you got them all."

Friedrich's expression goes all pinched, like the ice cream shop ran out of his favorite flavor. "Some of them may have been real."

The *Temple News* guy highlights something on his page. "Listen, I'm only a reporter, but I gotta ask, Dr. Panisporchi. All these meetings. What do you hope to accomplish?"

"To learn the truth. Or prove this a delusion."

"You coulda learned the truth in Meeting One. All you're doing now is denying it." He goes back to his highlighting. "'What you resist, persists.' Page thirty-three."

I whip out *Totable Quotes and Pithy Proverbs*. The *Temple News* guy is right. It's there. It's—

"Jung." Futz draws another circle on the whiteboard. "Odd how we keep coming back to him. If we take his theories on synchronicity and combine them with Goethe's observations regarding—"

Ali groans and pushes at a self-inflicted haircut. "Don't explain again. Take a panoramic of your whiteboard and turn it into a PDF. Bring it next week. We'll read it."

"I'm almost done." Futz moves to another part of the board. "In delusion, it is typical to deny the one true thing. If we could agree this group suffers from a collective psychosis induced on the extreme end of False Memory Syndrome, we could work backward. Find the origin." He takes a breath. "Do any of you belong to a seventeenth-century reenactment group?"

The *Temple News* guy glances at his watch. "'You can educate a fool, but you cannot make him think.' Page forty-two. The shortest path from A to C crosses B. Why won't anybody take it?"

"Very well." Futz marks a great big *A*, *B*, and *C* on the board. He circles *A*. "The prevalent memory occurred four centuries ago. How come nobody remembers any other life?"

Ali raises her hand. "I was an actress two lifetimes ago. In France. My best movie plays at the Riverview every year. I go and watch myself."

Kyra plucks a crystal from the collection she's arranging by the door. "Love that movie. Sublime. Nazis. Nazis. We're all Nazis."

"Ha." Ned takes a long noisy slurp on his water bottle, then tips it at Ali. "Don't try to fool us, girlie. I remember you. You seduced Mr.

Chaucer's assistant." He snaps his fingers at Friedrich. "What was your name, again?"

Nicholas. A poor, young astrology student. With a lot to answer for. "Wait a minute." My turn to finger snap. At Ali. "Is your full name *Alisoun*?" The landlord's wife. Object of Nicholas' desire.

Ali stops picking at her pfeffernüsse. "Who wants to know?"

I knock a hand to Ned's shoulder. "And you knew them?"

"Sure did. I ground the grain for the estate. Used to bring it over in big barrels."

Every synapse in my brain fires. In glorious Technicolor. Ned's 80-proof water bottle is how *he* hides. "You're more than Oberholt's bell ringer. You're also Mr. Chaucer's Miller."

The guy who told the *Tale*.

"Omigod." I dash to the whiteboard and pull the marker out of Futz's hand. "It makes so much sense." I point the marker at Friedrich. "The subtle tension between you and Ned." And wave a hand at Ali. "And why *you* complain Ned talks too much. You're an adulterer. He told the *Tale*. And you don't like it."

Ned sways to his feet. He throws his arm about his midsection and bows.

Tony applauds. "Now we understand why our sweet pea cuts herself. To let out the sin. Saw it on Discovery Channel. Very medieval."

I return to the drawing, erase the circle from around the A and place it around the B. We've got this wrong. We've got this all wrong. Oberholt is the prevalent memory, but everything really started with Chaucer.

The approach of that great big wave Friedrich warned me about the first time he showed up in my office roars in my ears. If we could all shift the tiniest bit right, Providence might come along, push us out of its path.

And fix us on a new course.

". . . she sees a movie, decides the star is herself, and accuses everybody of being Nazis."

Futz has a new marker and is explaining again.

". . . false memory instilled by an innate sense of guilt, no doubt precipitated by some childhood trauma, unrecognized abuse, perhaps the death of a parent . . ."

Like when Dad got hit by the bus and Joey smacked Backyard Mary with the baseball.

". . . creates a fugue state not unlike that experienced in the mildest cases of multiple personality disorder, bolstered by additional revelation from a fireman, a person many consider reliable and trustworthy, coupled with the presence of a scholar in that groundbreaking work, convinces all they are characters from *The Canterbury Tales*." Futz smiles in what I think he wants to come off in a kindly way, but on him is kind of creepy. "Which is a work of fiction, is it not?"

Tony rubs at his temple. "Enough, doctor. No wonder we were scared to death of you. Has any portion of the DSM-V escaped your due diligence? You don't find it interesting, in either the Oberholt or the Canterbury construct, which personalities we've assumed?"

I sure as hell do. "Friedrich, um, might not have liked Ned recounting how he slept with another man's wife, *but* . . ." I point to Ned and Tony. "There's no contact between the Miller and the Wife of Bath in the *Tales*, beyond their presence on the pilgrimage."

Tony takes my marker from me. "The *Tales* are far from complete, dear heart." He draws five stick figures on the board. Then x's each out. He draws a sixth, draws a woman beside him, holding his hand, borrows the *Temple News* guy's highlighter and draws a big red heart around the couple. "The Miller was the Wife of Bath's sixth and final husband. Final because he outlived her. A happy union, because the dear man couldn't read. He left all the thinking to me."

Tony casts a mournful look at Ned. "You treated me badly in Oberholt because you thought me low. Ugly. *You*, a bell ringer with a harelip. Your confusion now isn't because I'm a man, it's because I'm a man who makes a beautiful woman, but this is a shell, a place my soul inhabits, but only for a time."

He sweeps an arm. "And this is another shell, a cocoon the Assignments Committee allows us so we can set our wrong ways right.

You made a deal with the devil. We all did. And the only way it gets unmade is if you decide to unmake it. So tell me, Cowboy. Exactly WHAT are *you* sorry for?"

"I'm sorry I slept with you to get information on him." Ned hooks a thumb at Futz. "I'm sorry I sold that information to the wrong guy. I'm sorry the Freiherr punished you for telling me, and"—Ned hangs his head—"I'm sorry I couldn't be there for the baby."

A single tear courses through Tony's pancake makeup.

The *Temple News* guy scribbles like crazy. "This is about time. This is about damned time." He nods to me—"You're cousin to the bookbinder . . ."—and bobbles his head around the room, like he's counting. "This is unprecedented. If you could finger Der Weasel, you'd have a quorum."

A quorum. For what? "Der Weasel's, um . . . engaged to my sister."

Tony's misery melts away. "That nice young man I met the other night? Oh my. What gave you the idea he's Der Weasel?"

Uhhhh . . .

"Friedrich drew me this sketch of Oberholt." *Blah-blah-blah.* "That got me thinking about Der Weasel . . ." *Blah-blah-blahdy-blah-blah.* My voice goes lower and lower, my explanation sillier and sillier. *What in hell must Futz be thinking?* "Then I went home and weelllll . . . I recognized his butt crack."

Silence. Deep. And complete.

If the clock weren't digital, I'd hear it tick.

Tony wriggles his fingers under the fluorescents, like Friedrich did the day he tried to explain how he wasn't reading my mind, he was reading my aura. "I employ a surer method. Your sister's fiancé is shiny. He's new. He's full of light. He can't be Der Weasel. He's the monk."

Luigi's politeness, his unassuming manner, his helpful attitude, love of roses, religious devotion. "But . . . he's a plumber."

"Habit doesn't make the monk, sweetheart. And gilded spurs don't make the knight. Now who could quote that better than you?"

Mr. Chaucer. From a corner table in the Dead Poet's Society.

Futz goes back to his whiteboard. "That's my point. Tony sees this man you presume to be Der Weasel and tells you he is not, he's somebody called 'The Monk,' a heretofore unknown entity . . ."

"He's not unknown. He made beer." Ali claps a hand over her mouth.

And the great big wave rolls in, clearing my misconception faster than a cockroach caught in a flashlight beam. It takes my last bit of professional discretion with it. I grab Friedrich by the collar. "You said we had to be careful, be understanding, be kind. You made me be all nicey-nice to her. She doesn't know you, you told me, doesn't remember, you said." I tighten my grip. "But she did."

I shake him. "And. You. Knew. All. A. Long."

Ned catches my wrist. "Take it down a notch, doc." He pries me off Friedrich, voice sober, eye clear.

Ned's not plastered. He never has been. The Drunken Fool is just the role he adopts for these meetings. We're all actors on a stage. Like Friedrich said.

I release my hold, tap my imaginary top hat, and face the others with a flourish. "Ladies and gentlemen of the Assignments Committee. I'm pleased to present for your consideration, *A Parliament of Fools*, a folly in multiple acts. Playing in tonight's performance are myself as The Sponsor. Friedrich as Facilitator. Tony as Truth-Teller. Ali as Innocent. And Kyra, as the Higher Self."

Kyra nudges Virgule and giggles. "Don't forget Dr. Futz. The Voice of Reason."

I resist the urge to giggle back, instead standing so tall, it feels like I've grown six inches. "Here we are, actors on a stage. Brought together for one reason. And one reason only. For Friedrich. By Friedrich. And because of Friedrich. So he could be with *her*."

Our gazes advance on Ali like she's a Blue Light special at Kmart. Friedrich steps in front of her. He points to the door. "Who ordered the pizza?"

Delivered by none other than the newsstand guy.

Making a special appearance as Vogt. The Instigator.

Tony pulls a compact from his alligator clutch and powders his nose. "Oh. This is rich."

The newsstand guy holds up the big red case. "It's anchovy and pineapple. And it's twenty bucks."

"I've got it." Kyra digs in her purse.

Tony looks around the group. "We're missing the Freiherr's cousin. The one who was always trying to matchy-matchy-poo-poo everybody."

In bustles a lady wearing a business suit and Nikes. She mouths "sorry, I'm late" to the group, takes a seat, opens her briefcase, pulls out a tablet, clicks it on, waits for the screen to light up, looks to the *Temple News* guy, and asks, "What have I missed?"

He tosses her his notebook, casts us a big freckled grin, and departs.

I tilt my head. "Donna?"

Donna smiles at me in a professional way. She flips through the notebook. "Yes?"

"What are you doing here?"

She turns a newly coifed and precisely cut multilayered style to look at this week's sign:

HINDSIGHT SUPPORT GROUP
No Open Flames or Smoke
No Photography
No Feathers

"The home office sent me. You were notified."

Friedrich pales beneath his rash. Donna turns to me. "You didn't tell him."

Uh . . .

"Oh, Eugenia! No wonder everything's such a mess." She addresses Friedrich. "I'm here to oversee things. It's standard. Everything has to be filed. Angelic Permits and whatnot." She waggles the notebook, then taps on her tablet. "It's all right here."

43

Donna holds up a last slice of pineapple and anchovy. "Kyra's so sweet. It's my favorite."

The waiter returns with cinnamon and shaved chocolate. Four latte grandes and Donna hasn't even needed a bathroom break.

I should have known. Nobody, but *nobody* can eat like she does and remain a size two. I gaze at the alternating dangles of copper circles and squiggles twinkling from each ear. So like the items on display at Buttons, Bangles, and Bongs. "*You* sent Kyra to the group. Not Tony."

She hovers over her tablet. "Tony told you he sent her?"

Never mind.

"Fine. Explain about the Facebook page."

"I used Friedrich's name from Oberholt because I didn't want anybody to know who I was."

Donna types. "In this life, or the Oberholt life?"

"This life. That one. What's it matter?"

She taps the back of my hand. "Everything matters."

My cell phone rings. "I'll be home soon, Ma."

"Are you all right? Cause if you're not, just say you forgot to get the bread. I'll call the police."

"I'm fine. Don't wait up for me."

"Are they listening in? Do they know what I'm saying?"

"Who?"

"The kidnappers."

"I'm not kidnapped, Ma. I'm in Center City. Having a cup of coffee with someone."

"Stanley?" Ma's voice lights with hope.

"No. Somebody else. A student and Don . . . um . . . somebody from administration."

"At this hour?" Ma's disappointment I'm not having wild make-up coitus with Stanley is evident in the sudden flatness in her tone. "They're not paying you enough, pumpkin."

I turn off the phone. "This is stupid, Donna. You already know about all this. You knew about it before you walked into tonight's meeting."

Donna pulls the notice from tonight's meeting out of her briefcase and hands it to me. "Mr. Dripzin wants to know why Mr. Palmon wouldn't file the paperwork."

"I was trying to maximize my contacts." Friedrich holds up his hand to the coffee shop's fluorescents. "My time's running short. I want to spend it working off my karmic load. I thought you'd refuse me."

I squint at Friedrich's hand, undecided if the faint purple tinge is a figment of tonight's dose of Vicodin and caffeine or if Futz is right—the expectation I'll see something is enough to make me see something.

Donna glances at his hand, too, then leans an elbow on the table and her chin in her palm. "Times change, Mr. Palmon. We're not used to dealing with a generation who can contact each other through a Google search. I commend you on the Facebook page."

"The Facebook page is mine."

Donna turns her cool green eyes to me. "Where did you get the idea?"

I turn on Friedrich. "It never occurred to you I'd use your name. You wanted me to take the heat." I crumple the chartreuse notice, twisting it until, I swear, I hear it scream. "Well, feel the burn, baby."

Donna puts the kibosh on that line of conversation. "He should have set up the Facebook page himself. You should have put your own name on it. Stop blaming each other. 'The perfection of man requires he discover his own imperfections.'"

She slips my copy of *Totable Quotes and Pithy Proverbs* from my purse. "It's right here, on page fifty-four. Saint Augustine. It belongs on page one. In big red type. Surrounded by gold stars." She tosses the book on the table. "Had T. N. done so, perhaps we wouldn't be having this conversation. But he doesn't always listen to me."

"You know T. N. Mann."

Donna flips to the dedication. "'For D.—Man's wisdom is an Angel's folly, but it will do for a while.'" She snaps the book closed. "I'm D."

"But that reporter guy knew the book also."

"Of course he did. He edited it."

"I thought he was from the *Temple News*. I—"

I stop. "Temple News guy. Temple News man. T. N. Mann." I drop my head into my arms. And groan.

Donna roots through my purse again. She shakes a couple of Tylenol into my palm and pushes my water glass closer. "It's time you give the Vicodin a rest. Give it all a rest. Both of you. You can't see your way clear if your spirit is fogged. This is very serious. Redemption is a solitary business. The Committee feels your use of the Facebook page, the support group, is cheating."

Friedrich smacks the table. "Redemption is anything but solitary. We create whole religions to ensure it is not. Gather in groups every day at churches and synagogues, mosques and temples, in clearings and glades. How is our group any different, except we chose to gather in Library Lounge C?"

"In the final summation, the only actions for which you will be called to account are your own. Consider your intent with starting your group. And your motivations. Both were primarily selfish, both intended to promote your own interests."

"Religions start for those reasons all the time," Friedrich fires back. "What about snake handlers, psychic surgery, those guys in the gold lamé chairs who beg for money on GOD-TV?"

Donna clicks open her briefcase, her knuckles whitening around its edges. "Are you under the illusion the Committee deals kindly with them once they make their exits?"

"Hey, I don't have anybody selling roses at intersections."

"You have them throwing punches in support group meetings, cutting themselves on park benches, taking wild risks in burning buildings, and abusing mood adjusters."

Donna drops the tablet into her briefcase, then pulls two sheets of paper from a front pocket. She slams the briefcase shut.

"Our largest concern is that the essential nature of the gift is not bastardized. Our underlying philosophy remains the same. First, do no harm."

Donna looks to the ceiling, like Ma does when she has to get hold of her temper. "Have you forgotten the primary directives? Impart no knowledge without assurance its landing will be soft. Provide no guidance without knowledge the path pointed out is proper. Seek no compassion, make no confession unless either benefits the other more than yourself. Fuck it up, you hang your backside in a cosmic wedgie." She takes hold of her briefcase. "Can you honestly say your motives were altruistic? That you expected the others to gain more than you did yourself?"

Friedrich hangs his head.

"Good. 'The confession of evil works is the first beginning of good works.'"

Donna points to *Totable Quotes and Pithy Proverbs*. "Also by Saint Augustine and also in there. You dug your own hole, Mr. Palmon, and dragged Dr. Panisporchi in after you."

Well, see there? This is Friedrich's fault. Donna's gonna give him a dressing down, we all make up and shake hands. And I head home never to think about this again.

I stand and gather my purse. Donna stops me, her expression compassionate. "I'm very sorry, but I don't make these decisions."

My brief relief evaporates. "What decision?"

She hands us each one of the papers, then picks up the computerized slip left by our waiter an hour ago. "Your Angelic Privilege has been revoked."

44

My stomach does the two-step tango. Bongos pound between my ears.

Vicodin. Filing Cabinet.

Donna. No.

I pull my hand back.

I dial her cell, get a bakery. Call the English Department at University of Pennsylvania, they've never heard of her. Ask Ma if she has Donna's home phone. "Donna who?"

I check the Facebook page, but can't get it to load. I check its e-mail, but the ISP doesn't recognize the username. I notify administration the support group is finished. They e-mail back they have no idea what I'm talking about. And has that phone problem worked itself out yet?

Maurizio calls. Stanley doesn't. Even Blessed Mary goes quiet.

My new reality flashes neon in my mind. Redemption *is* a solitary business.

The walls of my office close in. I imagine my life closing in with them. Angela and Luigi off and married. Joey and Carlotta moved out to the 'burbs. Ma finally passed, gone to be with Dad.

And me. Alone and aging. With only my *Riverside Chaucer* to keep me company.

I grab my briefcase, grab my purse, and get out. Out the building, down the path. Anywhere. Just not here.

And about trip over Friedrich. Pale and rashy and wheezing. He pats the space beside him on the park bench. "I wanted to talk to you about the group."

"There is no group. There never was. It was a delusion, a fantasy, a . . . a . . ." I punch up my college e-mail on my phone. "See, administration doesn't even know about it."

"Is this a joke? You wave your magic e-mail and poof! None of this ever happened?"

"It's in the fine print." I pull out the paper Donna handed us on Wednesday night. "'Revocation of Angelic Privilege is without recourse. Unused Privilege is voided as of revocation and may not be redeemed for future rewards. Certain restrictions apply. Not applicable for blackout dates.'" I look up. "What's that mean?"

Friedrich takes my paper and tears it into little pieces. "It means we can still do this. No more Internet. No more Facebook pages. We'll call the others, arrange to meet, figure out what to do next. Everybody except Futz."

"Why not Futz? We may just be crazy. Anywhere in that pea brain of yours is that even a possibility? That we're suffering from some kind of group delusion. Like he said."

And just like that, Futz calls. He talks about the last meeting, how he filed the progress report, how he made no mention of my physical outburst toward Mr. Palmon, but next meeting perhaps Robert's Rules should apply, and—

Friedrich ends the call. "Futz is full of shit. There's no progress report. Nothing to file. I faked it. Faked all of it. That's why administration doesn't know anything about it."

"But administration sent me papers to fill out."

"I faked those, too. Faked the phone messages. Paid acquaintances and actors to play the roles. I told you, people see what they want to see. You didn't want to be involved."

Friedrich waves his arms, looking a lot like Ned the Fireman. "I'm a liar. You have to believe me. This has been a setup from the get-go. Futz is a liar, too. He's always been a liar. And not just in Oberholt. He lied when he sent us to the showers in Buchenwald.

Lied when he said he didn't know Ali. That's cause people like him lie. He's a Nazi."

He stops waving. "We worked for the Vichy, Ali and me. It was just business. People do horrible things in war."

The little bit of resolve in which I've wrapped myself for the last five minutes cracks. "You lost your angelic privilege long ago. That's why you didn't approach Ali on your own. Why you were so hepped up for this group. You hoped to use mine. Or Tony's. Or Ned's. Anybody's. To find safety under our protection."

Friedrich slumps, head in hands. "First life I had hindsight, it was a curiosity, one I kept to myself because I didn't want to get hanged for witchcraft. Next life, I stuffed it into the back of my mind because survival took up most of my time."

Noisy lives. Disorganized lives. Other-lives-popping-in-at-the-worst-moments lives.

"I got angry. For all the ignoring, it kept happening. Like a record set to skip. Like, like . . ."

A crazy cosmic Spirograph etching an endless circular pattern.

Friedrich scratches at his jaw. "I got this idea. I could do more than survive. I could use my present life to set up for my next."

My scrapbook. The research on Tajikistan. My plan for convincing the Assignments Committee to let *me* choose.

"There was always a problem, always a reason things didn't work out. Then Ali and I hooked up again and she'd had the same idea." His voice becomes animated. "There's a jolt, an excitement at first, to know we pulled it off. But that faded, faster with each life, and the price we paid to do it grew steeper. The Vichy . . . that blew us apart. Maybe because it felt so much like Oberholt. And it hit me on the way to the showers. I'm talking a single note of clarity: 'I don't want to do this again.'"

The Spirograph ceases its crazy circling, delivering a note of clarity all my own. "Nothing changes when nothing changes. And when nothing changes, our course is fixed."

Friedrich puts his inhaler back in his pocket, hefts his backpack onto his shoulder. And goes.

I give it five minutes. Then ten. "I forgive you," I whisper. "Now go to hell."

Somewhere Over the Rainbow sings at my waist. I answer. "What?"

"It doesn't work unless you mean it, Dr. Panisporchi."

45

Two days after my run-in with Friedrich, registration sends his drop slip with the attached query: PASSING or FAILING?

If I say he was passing, administration will question my decision to flag him from taking my courses. He could show up again for summer term, rash cleared, asthma meds adjusted. Full of new schemes, waving new sketches, bent on sucking me right back to where we were. I mark the slip "failing" and send it back. I need answers, not more problems. I need somebody who won't notice if I keep pressing.

Somebody more absorbed in her own issues than in any of mine.

"Have you seen Donna?"

Angela shakes out a cigarette and lights it. "Who's Donna?"

"The gal with the red Miata. You remember. The one you came with to get me at the hospital."

Angela looks at me funny. "How could I bring somebody? There's no backseat."

"Then whose car was it?"

"Luigi's. He lets me use it lots of times. He's got the truck." Angela goes back to perusing the real estate listings, now freed to consider them in the open since The Dinner. "You don't look so good. Maybe you should see Dr. Frangipane. Get yourself checked out."

Yes, I'll see Dr. Frangipane. Talk to him about muscle aches and eye problems, dead web links and dead poets, Lutherans and Catholics, Vichy and Nazi, then wait for his pronouncement that I'm—

"—just fine, Eugenia. I've got the report from the specialist." Dr. Frangipane shows it to me when I go to see him. "No evidence of macular degeneration, myopia, presbyopia, retinopathy, vasculopathy, or Best's Disease. No evidence of visual disturbance at all."

"It's intermittent."

Dr. Frangipane looks at me even funnier than Angela. He writes something on his prescription pad. "I'm giving you the name of a colleague. Very good at what he does. A psychologist. After a trauma like yours, it helps to talk things out. He specializes in visual disturbances. Very small practice, but he sometimes takes on new clients. I can get the office staff to make an appointment for you, if you like."

I read the name on the paper. Virgule Futz.

Now where do I go?

●●●

Ignacio's. Scratched floor. Watermarked bar. Banged-up pool tables. A world away from Villanova's well-manicured and well-mannered environs. A place I could have reached on my own had I taken the bus, then the train, then a cab, but Stanley drives me the day after my appointment with Dr. Frangipane.

Stanley scribbles a few numbers, then sketches, lines and circles. The tendons of his hand move, lifting and lowering the light sprinkling of hair across its back. He points to a collection of equations. "Pool is about angles. I always knew what the ball would do. The odds were always with me."

He glances around the hall, shoulders tensed. If he were a terrier, his ears would be at attention.

I follow his gaze. A couple of students playing at a table in the corner. A single barfly nursing his brunch on the opposite end from us. "What are you doing?"

"What I did then. Looking for marks. Somebody who can afford to lose. We had young guys take the bets, somebody like the newsstand guy. He'd let me know if I was to win or lose. Split the take. I didn't do any actual betting, so it never looked like I was throwing the game.

Sometimes, with smaller bets, the newsstand guy lost on purpose, so it didn't look like a setup." Stanley puts down the pen.

"Joey's photo's hanging over the sticks. From what you tell me, it should be yours."

"Joey's a straight shooter. He always played to win. People appreciated that."

"You said you didn't know his name."

"Nicknames. It's not like we were keeping records."

Stanley didn't have to take the day from work and ask me to come. He could have written me off. Found himself a nice girl. A girl who'd appreciate his attentive manner, his wit. And his pecker, no matter what its size. "Your student loans were tapped out. You found an ingenious way to cover the shortfall making best use of your talents. You ended up in a fight, got your head knocked. Now you feel bad about what you did. People gamble all the time."

"If you can't lose, it's not gambling. It's stealing, as sure as if I'd put my hand into their pockets and lifted their wallets." Stanley points to the long-healed skin pucker on his temple. "I'm not the only one who thought so. I lied to the cops. Dazed as I was, I knew enough to lie. I was already mailing résumés. I sure as hell didn't want any of it to get out. 'It's easier to cope with a bad conscience than a bad—"

"—reputation.'" *Totable Quotes*, page 78.

Stanley pulls out his wallet. He rummages in the plastic flip folds, then shoves a photograph toward me. "Here."

Stanley. With a full head of hair, wearing a graduation gown and holding his diploma and cap. Another man, a few years younger, and looking enough like him that I can guess he's Stanley's brother, stands opposite the lady between them. She has a sweet countenance. Not pretty, not ugly. Not tall, not short. Not thin, not fat. She's like Stanley. Ordinary.

"My mother." He runs a finger along her hairline. "She never finished high school. Her father died. She went to work to help support the younger kids. It was important to her that I finish school, that I finish well. She wanted me to get my PhD." Stanley taps a finger. "Doctor of Actuarial Science. Can you imagine how dull I'd be?"

I smile. Stanley smiles also. It's nice to see, but it's fleeting. "I used my brother as one of the guys who took the bets."

"Was he hurt?"

"No. Thank God. Not a scratch, but he never forgave me. For Mom. I was in the hospital a long time. All those tubes. I think it was more than she could bear. At least, that's how my brother sees it." Stanley takes the photo back. "After she died, we sold the house, split the proceeds. Went our separate ways."

Stanley moves a wisp of hair off my cheek. "Let's get out of here."

••

And here it is, the long-awaited coupling, slick and sweaty and oh so good. A tangle of arms and legs. Whispered entreaties. Down the length of my back. Up my thigh. Along my stomach. His hand on my butt. My mouth on his neck. The pushing and pulling. The groans and sighs. To end. Finally. In that glorious place where wonder meets bliss.

I am satisfied. I am content.

I am hungry.

Stanley tugs on a pair of pajama bottoms, stripes and oh so adorable. "I'll make eggs." He heads for the doorway. "Poached all right?"

I follow him to the kitchen, in bare feet and his bathrobe, dodging stacks of actuarial magazines that seem to double as furniture.

Stanley scoots a pile to the other end of the counter, then indicates a large cardboard mailing tube leaning against a wall. "I'm planning a renovation. Have a look."

I pop the top off the tube, withdraw what turns out to be blueprints, and lay them on the pool table.

"A snail shower goes here, double sinks, copper bowls, the works." Stanley reaches across the counter with a cue stick, to point me to where he means. "There's room for a jetted tub, also. Luigi says that's good for resale. Not that I'm planning on selling." He rushes to the next sentence. "Not after doing all the work. Just not everybody likes loft living. The association fees get high. Some people want more than a balcony. They like a yard, a garden."

Stanley waves the stick over the table's felt. "I thought it'd be nice to have a dining area here instead. For entertaining. I thought I'd move the pool table over where the TV is and the TV closer to the fireplace. What do you think?"

"Sounds really nice."

"Luigi's bugging me about the kitchen. I know it's dated, but about the only thing I do in here is microwave." He holds up the eggs, each in the middle of a toasted slice of whole wheat. "And make poached eggs."

I come around the counter and wrap my arms around Stanley's midsection and give a squeeze. I'm ready for more nookie. Endearments. Fingers touching me in places I can't reach.

Not an hour with HGTV.

Stanley puts down the eggs. I'm hoping he'll turn, kiss me so-very-very deeply, lift me up to the counter, do it right here.

"I'm hoping you'll help with the design. Luigi said you'd like that."

Luigi's name, mentioned in the first moments of my imagined foreplay, has the effect of a spider down my blouse. I push Stanley away and reknot the bathrobe.

The setup, the use of shills to shake cash out of the unsuspecting. It's the summoner and pardoner. Der Weasel and the Freiherr. Despite Tony's assertion, I wonder if he got it wrong. "What *is* it with you and Luigi?"

Stanley blinks. "Luigi understands. His father. He's a big help to me. He . . . gets it."

"Gets what?"

"Gambling is like a drug. Combined with my knowledge of probabilities, the possibility for abuse is great. I didn't just hit on patsies at Ignacio's. I used other venues, darts, poker, blackjack, hit on anybody stupid enough to take the bet. I had tuition. Books. Groceries. And Mom. She worked so hard. I wanted her to have some nice things. So I told her I was waiting tables. Claimed I had an assistantship. Even faked paperwork that made it look like I'd snagged a scholarship."

Joey. The grant. Grading papers. Failing the newsstand guy.

Bullshit. "And Joey did the same."

"You have to speak with him. I can only tell about myself." He rubs at his forehead. "This gnaws at me. Imagine trying to raise kids, trying to teach them to play fair, give the other guy a chance. And all the while you know you bilked classmates out of their textbook money to pay the bar tab."

He moves toward me, draws me close. His breath, warm and citrus, puffs at the hair behind my ear. "I learned my lesson. I don't do it anymore."

I stiffen. He confesses his deep dark secret, makes love to me, goes on and on about how torn up about it all he is, then *lies* to me. "You did it a few weeks ago. Took a student for his tips. Got him drunk, then handed it back."

Stanley tenses. "How did you know?"

"He told me." I pull out my cell, show him the faceplate. "Good old number three."

I back to the bedroom, navigating around the counter, past the pool table, through the actuarial magazines, Stanley close on my trail. I grab my clothes and duck into the bathroom, shoving legs into Levis, feet into loafers.

All the while Stanley pounds on the door. "I can explain."

"Sure. You can explain. Guys always have an explanation for everything. Well, guess what?" I fling open the door. "I'm not stupid."

Then I'm out of his loft, down the hall and into the stairwell. One, two, three, four flights. With tears blurring the angles and Stanley clattering after. For once, Fortune smiles and there's a cab to be had on Penn's Landing.

Stanley hops across the sidewalk, barefooted, closing the space between us. "Euglissia. Wait."

I pull *Totable Quotes* from the side pocket of my purse and fling it out the window, hitting Stanley square in the chest. "And my name is Eugenia."

46

Ma stands on the top step leading into our cement yard, hand covering the phone's mouthpiece. "Eugenia."

"I won't talk to him, Ma. Tell him what you want, but if you give me that phone, I'll tell him to go to hell."

Can't have that. We're still eating the nougat candy. She retreats to the kitchen.

Backyard Mary sighs. Joey takes a moment to flick bird shit off one of Her pots, then sits beside me on the bench. "If you wanna hang Stanley from a cross, I got some lumber in my basement you can use."

"You should have told me what happened at Ignacio's."

"Why? We were a bunch of tapped-out guys making the best of a bad situation. Christ! Villanova. You know how that looks to a kid from Twelfth and Shunk. Ma wanted me to go. Wanted me to use Dad's life insurance. She said you could delay college. Go back later. That maybe you'd get married and wouldn't need to go at all."

Outrage gathers behind my lips. A firecracker in a closed container.

Joey puts out his hands, like Blessed Mary on the Windowsill. "I told Ma I had a scholarship. Told her we could use the insurance money for you. If you want to hang me on a cross next to Stanley, I'll stop by Home Depot, get you some nails."

Clarity clutches at my heart. The firecracker defuses.

Joey as Josef in Oberholt. In the hours before Der Weasel showed up. Palm smack to table. *You can't eat my promises.*

Joey, hollering into his cell the night the guy opened fire on my usual bus. "Why the *hell* didn't you answer your cell?"

Joey, making sure Stanley didn't disrespect me. Coming all the way to Temple to smooth things over after The Dinner.

And Joey, making deliveries for Mr. Olivieri. So Ma could buy groceries.

Heat rushes across my cheeks. "I thought you worked all those odd jobs to earn movie money."

Joey drapes an arm over the bench. "Dad worked hard. But three kids. A house. There just wasn't much. He didn't mean to leave. Didn't expect it . . . I'm sure."

Somewhere, a gear clicks into place. "You worry you'll do the same to Carlotta."

Joey tilts his head at me. "Maybe. My point is, don't let the past rob the future."

Or the future will be poor and barren. "Stanley says you used nicknames."

If the topic change catches Joey off guard, he doesn't show it.

"I was Bookie. I kept the percentages straight and I kept it all up here." He taps his temple. "Luigi was Father Flanagan. He always worried about the marks. Wanted to make sure we only hit on the rich. And the obnoxious. Made sure they had cab fare home so they wouldn't be driving drunk. Vogt was Play-Doh Man. He was young. And fell in and out of personalities at will. None of us realized it was because he really *was* all those people. We thought he was acting."

The theme from *Jaws* plays at my waist. I click it over. "What about Maurizio?"

"One of our marks. Wore a Rolex and designer polos. He figured out the action. Threatened to squeal unless he got a cut. Never did anything. Didn't help. Just showed up."

Joey digs a pebble out of one of Mary's pots. He wings it across the yard. "We had a special name for him. Special name for a special piece of shit. We called him Weasel."

An hour later, I press my office phone's receiver against one ear, my hand against the other, like that will somehow keep my anxiety from spilling onto my desk. "You see, Constantine, Maurizio was there when I took the tumble. He got affidavits, came to the hospital. I—"

"Maurizio Bracaconi?" Constantine's rich tenor undulates across the landline, giving Maurizio's name an ominous cadence.

"Yes."

Constantine answers with silence. Five seconds. Ten. "Your brother didn't mention him. Just wanted to know his own exposure in the case."

"You know Maurizio?" Stupid question. Of course you do. They probably called you Perry Mason and got you to post everybody's bail.

More silence, longer than the first. Then . . . "You want me to take this case, I'll need everything he's done for you, files, affidavits, notes on negotiations, everything."

"I don't have anything, I—"

"I'll courier over a letter you can sign. It'll instruct him to release your records to me."

"He's very concerned about his contingency. He's already done so much work, I—"

"We'll allow him a reasonable percentage for the work he's done so far. Either that, or a lump sum. I'll send something along detailing that also."

"But, I—"

"Didn't Joey warn you about him?"

Uh . . . yes.

"It's Friday. Let me get this going, or it'll be hanging over your head all weekend. Whatever you do, avoid conversation with him. Let me handle it."

"Sure, I—" but Constantine clicks off.

I dangle the handset, let the cord unwind. It twists in a slow revolution, gaining momentum until it rewinds on itself and slows before it starts its reverse journey. Wind. Rewind. Wind. Rewind. The dial tone is replaced by an officious female voice. "If you'd like to make a call, please hang up and try again. If you need help, hang up and dial your operator."

That message repeats until it's replaced by a staccato, acid beep. Warning. Warning. Danger, Will Robinson. Chemical leak! Hull breach! Nuclear missile launch!

"Dr. Panisporchi?"

Ali.

Hair limper, fingernails more chewed, face thinner than last I saw her. She picks at a scab on her wrist, the movement spasmodic. "That monk stood atop a table in my father's tavern. Face flushed. Hair wild. Arm outstretched. And poured our brew onto the floor. He declared it demon-spawned. No better than goat piss."

I remember.

"You laughed. So did your cousin. The tanner, the cooper—"

Both disappeared.

"—the bell ringer. The charwoman. That loud-mouthed pamphleteer—"

Ned. Tony. The newsstand guy.

"—even that damned parsnip farmer."

Mr. Olivieri. Despair rises. He didn't get away.

"About the only person who didn't laugh was Friedrich. So I married him." She pushes the hair out of her eye. "That monk broke Der Weasel's foot. Your days were numbered. I married Friedrich to save him. And all his lovely grains. I didn't think about you at all."

Beep. Beep. Beep.

Animosity goes hot and liquid in my chest.

Beep. Icebergs ahead.

I reach over, depress the plunger, retrieve the handset. And plunk it back into place. "You thought about me. Thought about all of us. Then you ran to tell the Freiherr."

"Your monk wasn't brewing beer. He was brewing sedition. Him and all his order. You had a printing press. Where did you think the Freiherr would think those pamphlets came from?"

The image springs forth. Josef and Ruprecht Vogt arguing in that alley the night before Hallowmas. Ruprecht Vogt didn't want the money he'd paid for his order returned. He wanted the pamphlets. Josef wouldn't give them to him. He said he didn't have them. They'd disappeared.

I didn't believe Josef. But maybe somebody else found them and took them. Somebody who had reason to see Josef brought down, his influence among the Catholics smashed. And his cousin's connection to the Freiherr, the lieutenant in the city militia, severed. Because she didn't just want Friedrich, she wanted what Friedrich was supposed to have, the printmaking shop. And the press. Because she wanted to leave me with nothing.

And all because we laughed at her beer. "You tacked the Papist shit to the door of the church."

Which got Vogt and Josef arguing, which brought Der Weasel around. The runner along Der Weasel's cheek the morning he interrupted my dancing on the morning after Hallowmas strobes with new significance, flashing point to point to point.

He and Josef got into a knife fight. Josef had to sell all he could and quickly to mollify him. But Josef's contact was dead, and Josef ended up arrested for being outside the perimeter. Which got him hung for . . . what? Sedition? Spying? "You're the one who started it all."

Ali shoves the hair out of her eyes. "Marrying Friedrich wasn't enough. He was a convert, but not a believer. His association with Josef, with you, made him suspect. I wanted to distract attention. I didn't understand how far it would go."

My phone rings again. Another judgment from the great beyond warning me my voice mail is full. I push a button.

Now my voice mail is empty.

"Write it down." I shove at my hair, imitating Ali's bulimic, mock-victimized, self-mutilating performance at the last meeting. "I'll read it. And then I'll send it to Loverboy. Because he thinks I've been unfair to you. I don't know why. You got a lot of people killed. For a load of barley."

"You got them killed for even less, a packet of bratwurst. What did you promise the Freiherr in return? To kill Der Weasel? Kick him into the root cellar?" Ali leans so close I see every dry patch around her lips and every hair in her nostrils. She clamps a hand over the Blessed Beer Stein. "You're so stupid. You played right into the Freiherr's hands. Your soldier sets Der Weasel up in the church and the Freiherr has his excuse to proclaim the start of an uprising. And I got my licks in. I pointed the finger at the bell ringer. Because that bastard had no business telling people about my business with Nicholas and that idiot old man I married. The story Mr. Chaucer put in his book. The one people still read and you teach. Over and over. All these centuries later."

Ali pulls the Blessed Letter Opener from the Blessed Beer Stein. She flips it over her head, catches it, then rams it into my desktop. "So there, you over-educated vindictive bitch. *That* is my confession."

She flips her hair out of her eyes, her stance suddenly perky. "Hmmm. Friedrich's right. I *do* feel better."

47

Friedrich answers the door dressed in pajama bottoms and T-shirt. He ruffles hair cut in a new and shorter style and yawns. I push past him. "Do I look like a Father Confessor? If she ever shows up in my office again, I'll rip her heart out through her cocaine-damaged nose—"

And stop.

I don't know what I expected in Friedrich's digs. Maybe a beer bottle collection on the radiator. Underwear hanging from lampshades. Dirty tees crumpled into corners. Not this very clean, very austere—

"Sanctuary," Friedrich offers.

A brown leather chair reclines by one window, a modern teak desk waits beneath the other. Laptop centered on its surface, artist's portfolio leaning against its leg. In the galley-style kitchen, a wooden bowl filled with bright red apples presides over a maple dinette.

"Crate and Barrel. Their Casual Contemporaries Collection." Friedrich closes the door. "Coffee? I got Kona."

He pulls a bag of beans from a cabinet colored spring green, grinds them in a Braun, dumps it into the top of a Krups, adds a measure of water, and hits a button. He yawns again. "Been working security at Temple Hospital. I'm pulling a double tonight. Have to be there at five. Hoped to get a couple more hours sleep."

He indicates the full-sized bed in the corner, rumpled under a fluffy comforter an even brighter white than the walls.

"You're allergic to feathers."

"Goose down's all right. That Scandinavian stuff."

Scandinavian. Of course. "Your rash is gone."

"Haven't needed my inhaler in a while, either." He pulls his shirt over his head, exposing well-defined abs, and a pair of nipples spaced perfectly across a hairless set of well-developed pecs. He ducks into the bathroom and pees.

I turn away. "Jesus, Friedrich. Close the door."

Running water answers my request. He exits, toothpaste foaming at his mouth. "You're joking, right? We were engaged. We've already seen each other naked."

This was a mistake.

"I have to shower." He plucks a bakery bag off the marble counter and tosses it at me. "Here. Toast bagels."

A great big stupid mistake.

"What did you tell her?" Friedrich shouts over the sound of the spray.

"To go to hell."

"Tell?"

"NO. HELL. GO. TO. HELL."

"TELL WHAT?"

I march into the room, sleek and stylish and straight outta *Dwell*. "G-O-T-O—"

He turns off the faucet and steps from behind the frosted glass.

"—h-e-l-l."

"Ohhhh." He wraps a towel around his waist. "How'd she take that?"

Coffee must be done.

Friedrich follows me out. "I warned you about Ali, told you we had to be careful with her."

I whirl around. "She blew the whistle on the support group."

"No, the Facebook page." Friedrich snaps off his towel, dons boxer briefs, slides into khaki green chinos, nicely-tailored and new, then holds up a button-down the color of raisins. "Does this coordinate?"

I step close enough to feel the warmth rising from his skin, and point out a tan pullover that will go better. He reaches around me, keeping enough distance that I don't feel trapped between him and the closet door, but not enough distance to keep the nipple tingle at bay.

I retreat to the kitchen. Open cabinets. Root through drawers. Dig around in the half-sized fridge. Pulling out mugs and plates, sugar and cream, butter and jelly so we can sit at Friedrich's pleasant little table. Eat bagels. Drink coffee. And pretend we don't want to go at it like overstoked pistons.

"Nice place," I say.

Friedrich joins me. "Thanks. I pay for it out of a box under the bed. Ali and I buried it back when we worked for the Vichy. We insisted on being paid in gold."

The furniture. The tile work. The appliances. The down. "You have a box of Nazi gold under your bed. From World War Two."

"God, no. I changed it out during my next life. Brought it over during my life after that. My portion, anyway. I don't know what Ali did with hers."

Probably shot it up her veins. Jesus, and here I thought Friedrich was living on Tastykakes and government cheese. "What's with all the jobs?"

He grabs half a bagel from the toaster. "Gets me out. Keeps me in the game. It mostly goes to charity."

Friedrich. Hustler. Manipulator. Fast-talker.

Philanthropist. "'Any man, learned or lewd, who loves the common good, shall unto a blissful place wend, there where joy lasts without end.'" Thank you, Mr. Chaucer.

Friedrich eyes me. "Yeah, a little karmic debt reduction, I suppose." He puts down his bagel. "I didn't send Ali to you. She did that on her own. Although, for thee, some grace, I hope, in her you find."

Chaucer again. *Troilus and Cryseyde*.

Friedrich extends his forearm, points out the birthmark he showed me before, situated in the same place as was his concentration camp tattoo. "Ali's got one, also. That's why she cuts herself, to get rid of the reminder."

"She told me what happened in Oberholt. Are you all right with it?"

He spits a clump of bagel onto his plate. "What kind of question is that? Of course I'm not all right with it. I'm not all right with any of it."

"But you're so nice to her."

"She drinks. She does drugs. She starves herself. She slices at her own flesh. What would you have me do? Flay her with a cat-o'-nine-tails?"

"But you're such a sunovabitch to me." I pull Friedrich's rewrite of my dissertation out of my briefcase, slam it on the table between us. "The monk didn't get killed. He went to Italy to brew his beer and make Mary statues. I know because he told me, even if he doesn't understand he told me. You acted like I had some fault in what happened to him."

Disbelief. Surprise. Anger . . . Hope. Friedrich's face flickers like one of those flip card movies kids used to make before YouTube. It settles on somber, his attitude on heartfelt. "I apologize for making you feel bad. I thought you left the monk out of the record on purpose."

"And why would I do that?"

"I . . . I dunno. I wasn't thinking, I guess." Friedrich spreads a layer of cream cheese across his bagel. "I didn't drop the group. I invited them for dinner. I made them fresh bread and German sausages. We met on Wednesday."

"But Donna—"

"—made it clear the problem wasn't so much the group as my motivations. So, I changed my motivations. I decided to be their friend, instead of their facilitator. You're welcome to join us next week. Ned's making pierogies."

I go back to buttering my bagel. "I don't like pierogies."

"Like you don't like my pfeffernüsse?"

"They're gross."

"Because that's how you remember them. Maybe they're not gross now. Maybe they were never gross as you thought. Maybe you never gave them a chance."

Me. Hanging over a bucket. Wanting to die. "I gave them a chance."

"How about you give them another?" Friedrich pulls a familiar plastic container from the fridge and pries off the lid. "We can accept we're already dead, ghosts at the window. Or we can take a leap of faith." He holds the container before me. "Please. One bite. And I'll never bother you again."

Like I haven't heard that before.

But . . . second chances. Not letting the past rob the future. Figuring out if what I got now is what I wanted all along.

You can do it, Eugenia. Take a breath. Take a pfeffernüsse. Take a bite.

Now.

Happiness explodes on my tongue. I take another. And a third, my hand reaching reflexively for a second cookie. "Did you take out the pepper?"

"Nope. Just as much as there ever was, or I couldn't call it pfeffernüsse." Friedrich takes a cookie, too, pops it into his mouth, his expression earnest and eager and shiny enough to slip on. "'In each estate do little hurts rest—God leaves for us to take from it the best.' People can change, doc. Just like my pfeffernüsse. That's why I brought them to you, class after class, semester after semester. So you would understand. I been workin' on them. Life after life. Just like I been workin' on me."

He smooths a crumb from my lip, covers my hand with his. "They're not perfect, but even you gotta admit, they're a whole lot easier to swallow."

48

According to Marlene Dietrich, once a woman has forgiven her man, she must not reheat his sins for breakfast. Chinese takeout at three in the afternoon cannot be considered breakfast.

"Don't let this deter you, Dr. Panisporchi," Friedrich shouts from his third-floor window before I get very far down the street. "Remember what Havelock Ellis said, 'It is on our failures that we base a new and different and better success.'"

Who in hell is Havelock Ellis?

Stanley has my copy of *Totable Quotes and Pithy Proverbs*, so Google provides the answer. The optimistic Dr. Ellis is a British social reformer and sexual psychologist who straddled the turn of the last century.

Thank goodness Friedrich used a condom. Most of the time.

●●●

Monday morning, after breakfast, after coffee, after catching hell from Ma because Stanley called ten times and Maurizio eleven, I head to Constantine's office. So I can watch him make notations on a legal pad.

I point to a listing two-thirds down the page. "You're still going for pain and suffering."

"You missed work, were stiff and sore through the Christmas holidays, and several months after. Doctor Frangipane sent me a report detailing an ongoing list of complaints. Nausea. Headache. Neck pain." He flips the page. "And visual disturbance."

Most of that has more to do with the hindsight than the accident.

"All you did was back away from a fight. Perhaps you should have watched where you were backing to, but given the emotion of the moment, Mr. Olivieri's and the funeral director's claims of contributory negligence seem specious. They are obvious defensive moves by their insurance companies prompted by Mr. Bracaconi's original complaint."

I think of how I reached for Luigi, how I overbalanced.

"I recommend you offer the pain and suffering monies to Mr. Bracaconi to get him off your back."

I do as much of the math as I can manage. "That's twice the percentage he agreed to."

"It's a fraction of what he's expecting. I slashed most of his preposterous demands." Constantine shoves a pile of paper my way. "Mr. Bracaconi's timesheets."

He even counted the times I didn't pick up the phone.

Constantine slides a pencil through his fingers and taps it to the desk. He flips it and slides it through again. Familiarity nips at my heels. Constantine clatters the pencil to his desktop. "Mr. Bracaconi can be very . . . persuasive, but all he really cares about is his cut. Pay him off. Settle with everybody else and get on with your life. Mr. Olivieri's insurance company will cover your medical bills and other incidentals, including revision of your scar and loss of your Geiger jacket, which is where you would have been had you left the lawyers out of it."

Heat creeps up my neck, and I know I'm blushing like a turnip. And feeling about as smart as one, too.

Constantine gathers the pages and puts them back in their folder. "Don't beat yourself up. You got caught in arguments and rivalries that go back years. Mr. Bracaconi tapped into that. He has…a special talent. I'll send these papers around, have everybody sign them, be back to you in a few days."

••

In lawyerspeak that means a few days to prepare the papers, a few more days to send them to the other lawyers, a few more days for those lawyers to talk to their clients, for the clients to come back with questions, for counteroffers to be made that have to be discussed with me before new papers are sent around—

Maurizio calls me while I'm sitting in the sunroom of Aunt Rose and Uncle Lou's seashore house, enjoying a last quiet weekend before the Memorial Day rush.

"These things are never quick." His voice takes on that nasal quality I always associated with bad sinuses, but which now sounds like whining. "Constantine's looking to make an easy buck."

"He's getting paid by the hour."

"So there's no incentive to do his best by you. He knows you can't afford much."

"I appreciate your concerns, Mr. Bracaconi. Direct further ones to Mr. DiPiero." I click off. Little turd got around my block by using a different phone.

Carlotta wraps her sweater tighter around her. "You should tell Constantine."

I take her advice without argument. Carlotta is pretty. She's kind. And she's forgiving. I'm not wasting one more minute berating myself for my misapprehension of her identity and direct that energy toward appreciating her for who she is: an overly chatty young woman who fell head over heels in love with my brother. After I hang up, I hold out a plate of antipasti so she can have first pick of the contents.

My offering turns out to be a mistake. The mortadella's nutmeg and cilantro notes combined with the smell of surf appear to be too much.

"Excuse me." Carlotta charges up the steps.

"Morning sickness." Ma turns her crocheting project inside out.

Booties. In yellow.

Nice of somebody to tell me. Really freaking nice.

I go through voice mails. The hindsight-related ones are gone. Friedrich doesn't bother me anymore except to text every couple of days how the group is working out its differences and won't I please consider joining them. Futz stopped calling once I let him know my part in the group was finished, and no, I'm very sorry, but Friedrich's cell number doesn't work anymore, as far as I know he's withdrawn from school, but perhaps Futz could get his address from administration. Except for the occasional nudge from Maurizio, I'm down to one stalker.

"It's Stanley . . ."

Delete.

"Eugenia, I . . ."

Delete.

"I was stupid . . ."

Delete.

"Please pick up . . ."

Delete.

"I should have told you from the get-go . . ."

Delete.

"I'm in counseling . . ."

Delete.

"Look, I love you . . ."

Delete.

Wait a minute. He loves me. Oh my God. He really loves me. He just said it. I got it on digital. Well. I did.

Hope rises. The corners of my mouth rise with it.

"I really do. I'm an idiot. I never should have lied to you. I never will again. Please call."

Luigi hands me another beer. "He's making it nice over at his loft. Keeps asking Angela what your favorite colors are, if you like shades or curtains. He's not doing that for his brother's annual visit."

I gaze at Luigi, the warmth in his eyes. Not a trace of Der Weasel in them. There never was.

Aunt Rose draws me into the tomato-scented kitchen and shoves a bowl of ground meat across the table, bulked up with bread crumbs and fragrant with oregano and basil. "Roll the meatballs."

She goes to work, too, slathering gravy into a thick layer on the bottom of a Pyrex baking dish. "I used to tell your mother life is like a lasagna, told her take time to parboil the pasta, simmer the gravy until it's thick because what results is rich and nourishing and satisfying."

She layers on a first level of strips. "*L'americani* make their gravy watery." She leaves off the trailing vowel and makes the *r* sound more like a *d*, so it sounds like *l'medigan*. "They toss the lasagna into the pan dry, not caring if they end up with something half-baked, too crispy on the edges."

I wait, wondering if Aunt Rose's lasagna analogy is going anywhere.

"I went looking for those photos. The ones of Emmy I told you about. The one who died in the car accident. Your namesake."

Scent of marsh and pine. Citrus and surf. A touch. A smile.

"I can't find them. Uncle Lou thinks maybe I took them back to Philadelphia in anticipation of Hurricane Sandy." I guess I look confused because she adds, "They used to be here. Emmy and her fiancé, they used this place all the time. Hard to get privacy while they were waiting to get married. He had his career and she was still finishing school."

A quiet breeze, the merest waft. "But they eloped."

"In those days, people weren't so understanding. It was easier to elope than wait for banns to be posted and hear the whispers later."

The ground beef goes cold in my hands, numbing where the mixture squishes between the knuckles. "Whispers."

"Counting on their fingers. Back in those days, you had a baby too soon, people could be pretty mean."

My breathing stops. My heart, too. The deepest regret I can imagine barrels out of its dark recess, squashes it to a pancake, then wells up. And spills over my cheeks.

A dress, a tux. Talk of booties and tiny knit hats. A place of our own. And a name. Something luminous. Like fireflies.

We could have had it all. A family, a future.

I dump the mixture back to the bowl, grab a towel, and hold it to my eyes. "Sorry. Got a load of garlic."

"Don't feel bad, sweetie." Aunt Rose runs her hand across her own eyes. "Now look at me, fussing about something that happened over fifty years ago. Thing is, you never know where life will lead. Your young man behaved badly, but he's trying to make it right. That's what matters. You do your best and if that doesn't work, you try something else. Eventually, something clicks and you end up traveling the course you were supposed to all along." She goes back to layering her lasagna. "I said the same to your brother. Back when he refused to set a date."

"You knew about Carlotta."

Aunt Rose flicks her forehead with a thumb and forefinger. "There I go, letting the cat out of the bag. Don't tell your mother. He didn't want to introduce her to the family in case it didn't work out. He was scared, afraid something would happen, like admitting his love for Carlotta would somehow jinx it."

Josef rummaging among the barrels and crates. Smack to the table, then to my cheek. Not angry. More than worried.

I raise a palm to where he connected, all those centuries ago, then reach to take Aunt Rose's. "I never thought of Joey as scared."

"Oh honey, everybody is scared of something." She gives my hand a squeeze. "He cried."

Joey. Crying. He didn't even cry at Dad's funeral.

Roll the meatballs, Eugenia. Roll, roll, roll. Give that revelation time to settle.

"Maybe he needed someone to give him permission." Aunt Rose throws a little marjoram into the mix. "He knows things. Born with the caul. Just like you."

Okay. Stop rolling.

"That's why your mother doesn't drink. She had two children so special. You modern girls, you don't know, but there's so many stories about children born with cauls. You can see the future, travel in your dreams to other places, other lives. You know right from wrong and truth from lie and if you deny your gift, refuse to use it for good, God will judge you harshly. People call it an old wives' tale, but your mother believes. She gave up alcohol as a sacrifice to the Mother of us all, asked Her guidance, begged Her to make everything work out for you two."

Aunt Rose pours a little olive oil into a pan, starts the first batch of meatballs browning. "Hard to tell how gifts will manifest. Look at Joey. New baby. New hope. He looks to the future. Important thing is to be open to possibilities, willing to change course. Otherwise you hang your heinie in a cosmic wedgie."

49

Summer term. Long classes, hot classrooms, and Ali's developed an interest in Chaucer.

"Friedrich said I should do it." She shoves up a sleeve, shows how the cuts on her forearm are healing. "Says the only way to break the cycle is to find my place in it."

He stops by my office an hour later. "This was Ali's idea. She wants to keep an eye on you, help if she can. We each seek expiation in our own way. This is hers." He leans against my filing cabinet. "We're still meeting. Everybody asks for you."

"Tell them I'm busy."

"Ah. You're still clinging to the possibility Futz was right. Figure if you dissect the whole into small enough components you can convince it to disintegrate into a pile of rationalized mush."

"Are you done?"

"No. You had hindsight before I was born. You can't blame me for that. I thought you were going to India, for chrissakes. All I did was contact you."

India. He knows about India. "You were stalking me at the Dead Poet's Society."

"Your karma's tied up with mine. It complicates my process."

"You're the great big karma guru now, are you? Your rashes go away, you stop wheezing and that makes you the go-to guy for conscience clearing." I glance at the calendar tacked to the side of my bookcase. "I'm late."

Friedrich follows my gaze. "Late for what?"

"You know. Late."

"Like . . . you're having a baby late."

I go back to grading my papers.

He pops his head into the hallway, then closes the door. "We should do this by conference call. Go ahead. Number two on your speed dial. Mr. Ring My Bell."

Anger gathers beneath my breastbone. "Why are you talking to him?"

"It was just pool. No bets. He refused. He's at Gamblers Anonymous, Alcoholics Anonymous, in counseling, working out. He may even have become a Boy Scout leader. And it's all for you. He told me so over a pitcher of cranberry juice." Friedrich flops his backside onto my desk. Right beside me. "He was more fun when he was executing Catholics."

"You . . . you . . ."

Friedrich grabs my hand before it does something I can't take back. "No. You. Why do you fight so hard? Third world countries are always looking for teachers. Statisticians are welcome additions to archeology teams. Get your paperwork in order, marry Stanley, and go to Tajikistan."

"Oh. My. God. And how do you know about Tajikistan?"

Friedrich releases me and backs to the bookcase. He scoops a pile of information from the middle shelf, pages and pages on grants, positions, trusts, government-funded opportunities, even a couple of Church-related documents on missions work. "Heh. I'm nosy."

"This is none of your business."

"How is this not my business? You just accused me of fathering your child. You need to find fault. You always need to find fault. And you always blame me."

"What do you mean *always*? What the hell are you talking about? Two lives, Friedrich. Two. This one. Oberholt. That's it. And believe me, it was enough."

He scratches at the underside of his jaw so hard he raises welts, so hard, I think if he doesn't stop, he'll scratch right through to the bone. "You see what you want, remember how you please. Two lives is *nothing*, doc. Nothing. We been around the block together so many times, we've worn a groove in the sidewalk."

And he talks. He talks and talks and talks, running through a litany of lives we've shared and sins committed, until my ears can't hear anymore, my brain can't think. The lives scamper past, most so fuzzy, I have to squint to get any sense of what they were about before Friedrich is off on the next, his crazy cosmic Spirograph on full throttle, until it circles back to Oberholt. "You left Der Weasel's body propped in the choir loft. With a Catholic missal in his hand. You *must* have known retaliation would follow."

Friedrich's last and most damning denunciation.

Stanislaus told me he would take care of it. He hid Der Weasel in a wagon, hefted him into the church. "I thought he'd toss Der Weasel down a flight of stairs. Dump a little beer on him. Drop . . . I dunno, drop an oil lamp beside. Make it look like he'd tripped while in a drunken stupor. Maybe burned himself on the flame."

My aura must let Friedrich know I'm sincere because the accusation on his face eases. "They hung me."

The revelation speeds in from left field . . .

"But they tortured me first."

. . . a fastball with a spin on it.

"For days."

Hits me in the chest.

"They tortured Josef even longer."

Sends me reeling.

"He was first in line at the gallows so we all got to see."

Enough.

"The bell ringer went down fighting, right in the middle of the square."

Stop.

"And the monk held his tongue, tried to protect us. You were so sure he made his escape, but they had him the whole time. They hung him from the town gate, then left him there, corpse rotting, the stench wafting through our cells. The guards told us they hung a sign." Friedrich cups his hands in front of his neck. "'Thus ends the heretic.'"

No. No. Palms pressed into my eyes. Block the image. Block the words. Don't see it. Don't think about it.

Luigi. In the monk's place.

The sobs start. Deep and full, the well never-ending.

None of it should have happened. Friedrich should have married me. Josef would have been safe. The Freiherr would have stopped focusing on the monk.

There would have been no fight with Der Weasel. I wouldn't have clocked him with Wooden Mary. Josef wouldn't have gone to see the Greek. The Greek wouldn't have been sneaking around.

Because there would have been no pamphlets. No reason for Herr Vogt to get into a ruckus with Josef about them in that alley two streets over from the square.

And what happened the next morning wouldn't have happened.

The question rises with my anguish. "*Why* did you marry her? Why wasn't I enough?"

"She told me she was pregnant." Friedrich punches the bookcase. "She wasn't. But she told me she was and would be showing soon." He slams the bookcase again. "You had your soldier. I thought he'd marry you."

My breathing calms. My tears stop. My anger dissolves.

We're done. No more accusations. No more argument. Just this growing distance, filled with the thousands of words we'll never speak.

And a pile of snot-filled Kleenex in the trash. "I hate you."

"You're in good company, because I hate myself. And I don't know how to stop hating myself. Remember what the Merchant said in his Tale. 'The wedded man repents his decisions often, and sooner than the single one.' I have been wedded to Ali, in body or thought, for more lives than seems possible. Truly, she has become my purgatory."

I glance to the Blessed Beer Stein, yearning for a little guidance, a whit of wisdom. Something to carry me through the next minutes and hours, days and weeks and years.

But Mary ain't talking.

I'm on my own. "So in all that mess, the brewer's daughter came through just fine. Did she at least attend your hanging?"

"She died like the rest of us. I made sure of it." Friedrich picks up his book bag, stance defiant, expression hopeless. "I was foolish to trust a woman with anything that might hazard life or limb. Don't look so shocked, doc. No man knows what he will do if the stakes are high enough. Murder will out. At least, Mr. Chaucer thought so."

Am I shocked? Am I surprised? Horrified? Intrigued? Mad? Sad? Glad? Or am I inwardly laughing my ass off at my million presumptions? Holy Mother of God . . . what's *wrong* with me?

That crazy cosmic Spirograph starts in again, circling the full array of our lives together, my lives alone, hearkening back and back and back, until it touches on me and Mr. Chaucer sitting at a table in the Dead Poet's Society. Me, sobbing into a hanky. He, offering advice and ale.

Where do I fit in that grand constellation?

Friedrich throws his hands in the air. "You stand at that lectern, semester after semester, devoted the better part of your life to its study and you still can't figure your part in the pilgrimage. You pegged me for one of the hostages in the Knight's tale, one of the guys willing to fight his cousin to the death for the love of a woman neither had ever met and who knew nothing of them. I'll bet you think the other cousin was Chaucer."

Based on his time as a hostage in the Hundred Years' War.

"And the girl we were fighting over?"

"Some version of Ali." So seemingly innocent, yet so willing to stand on the sidelines and watch the blood flow. I gather my papers. The schedule for summer semester is merciless and I'm not wasting one more minute of it thinking about that psycho brat.

"All your degrees and you're so damned stupid, Dr. Panisporchi. The girl wasn't Ali. The girl was you. You're Emily."

And the Spirograph is off and running again, but in jerky motions, fits and stops, like it's grounding on shoals, then lifting with the next wave, only to ground again.

Not the Emily of the Tale, a noblewoman fought over by two knights. But Emily, a simple French girl, daughter of a local magistrate, fought over by a couple of wandering mercenaries.

The Spirograph bears down, grinding exceedingly slow. "You didn't fight because you loved me. You fought because you thought my father could grant you your freedom."

"Bingo. And it worked. He freed both me and my cousin. Then we killed each other in the town square."

"If you killed each other, Mr. Chaucer wouldn't have survived to write the story."

"The other cousin wasn't Mr. Chaucer. It was Stanley. And that's why Mr. Chaucer also cast him as the teller of the tale."

The Perfect Knight. A man of war. But also of breeding. At times shortsighted, but loyal and true, with a heart as big as a cannoli. He told his *Tale*, so he could speak his truth. And perhaps, just maybe, hoped someday I would understand.

My heart swells. The fluttery feeling takes hold. Somewhere beyond the ceiling I know blue skies preside and the Spirograph flies clear of its confines.

But Friedrich's still talking. "So I hollered at him after our Oberholt life and every life after. Every single time I could get back to the Society. I told him to get off that damned barstool and give the Wheel of Fortune another go. That he could hide behind a language fewer and fewer understood, or come back, write his truths again, except more and better truths, print them, copyright them, and distribute them in a language we could all comprehend."

"Who are you talking about? The knight?"

"Mr. Chaucer. He finally put in his paperwork. And the moment he got back, declared he'd never leave again." Friedrich moves in closer. "He came back as Mr. Kipling. Couldn't you guess? No disrespect intended, but why else would somebody as well-known as he spend so much time drinking with a girl who, in so many of her lives, didn't learn to read?"

The Spirograph swings back around to crash through the last of my misapprehensions.

The wit, more subtle than it was, better suited to the age. The way he sometimes wrote in Middle English, mimicked Chaucer's style. The facility with verse, his dead-on capture of character voice, highborn or low-, well-educated or not, his penchant to let animals do the speaking for him, to write at a child's level words rife with deeper meaning for the adult. And the changes that came with his own growth. The jagged edges. The deep emotion he poured forth the times his own heart got too full—

"He felt bad." Friedrich looks like he feels bad, too. "Felt responsible. The Wife of Bath let him know what women want, and he wanted you to have your chance."

—Rudyard's story about two men in mortal combat over the love of a woman who had no interest in either, and destroyed by a forgery of a previously unknown Chaucer manuscript.

Not synchronicity. Karmic wishful thinking. One more story never copied or recopied and Mr. Chaucer wanted out there, even if only in his Kipling subconscious. But . . . my GOD . . . while we were at the Society . . . "Why didn't he just *tell* me?"

"He did tell you. As Mr. Kipling. He put it in the story about the forgery. 'All evil thing returneth at the end, Or elseway walketh in our blood unseen.' You didn't understand." Friedrich takes my hands, holds them tight. "You weren't always what you became. There was a time before. And for every action, every word, intended and unintended I made that turned you into the kind of person who would make a deal with the Freiherr, then bludgeon a man after he was down, I am most heartfeltly and forever, sorry."

He's sorry. He's *sorry*? That's it. And now we get back to eating bagels?

Friedrich eases his grip. "If we can't forgive each other, how will we ever be able to forgive ourselves?"

His entreaty flies across the emotional distance, brutal, honest, and bearing an olive branch. For me, the doubting Noah. I had only to accept, to believe, to hear with my heart. And I'd make landfall.

I fling him off, then fling myself as far away from him as I can within the confines of this modified janitor's closet I call my office. "I don't want to forgive you, Friedrich."

"Well you have to do something. Anything. Because things can't continue as they are. Look what happened to Kyra."

"What happened to Kyra?"

"Nobody knows."

50

I nab the next bus south to stand in front of Kyra's shop, examine the beads and buttons, ear dangles and charm bracelets, bongs and rolling papers. There are no chartreuse posters advertising the support group in the window, or the lampposts outside. A middle-aged lady in tweed and sensible shoes identifies herself as the owner. She has no idea about a woman in Goth gear who favors white high-top sneakers. And lots of her customers are blonde, green-eyed, and size two with multiple ear piercings. To which did I refer?

I text Friedrich. "Maybe Kyra was lying."

He texts back. "Was Ned lying, too? Because his battalion chief has no idea who he is."

Two days later, Virgule Futz drops a report on my desk—*False Memory Syndrome, Applications in Past Life Regression.* "Preliminary findings. No real conclusions yet. Mostly based on my practice, though your group added an interesting anecdotal level."

I leaf through. "You left out Ned. The fireman."

Futz scrunches his forehead. "I don't remember a fireman."

The newsstand guy latches onto me on my way home from the bus stop. "Ruprecht's sorry for what he did to you. He wants you to forgive him."

"What'd he do?"

"Ruprecht told the baker how Josef wanted your father's business. He'd never let you inherit. He'd already worked it out with the Freiherr. Whether you married or not, the business would stay with him."

Josef made a deal with the Freiherr. Against me.

Then the pamphleteer said the baker boy wouldn't marry me, slapped my butt, and brought Mr. Olivieri, the florist, then a parsnip farmer, into the fray long enough to pull me out. He took me home. And everything more that happened, happened.

Because everything matters. A careless word here, ill-considered act there. Pebble by pebble, stone on stone. Give it a kick, you got a landslide.

And *now* the newsstand guy is sorry.

No wonder Mr. Olivieri and the newsstand guy don't care for each other. Something so small, from so long ago, snowballed into an unplowed sidewalk that landed me on my ass. And set everybody on this course.

The newsstand guy unsnaps a bundle of *National Geographic*. "Ruprecht was bitter, angry over those pamphlets. He's sorry. He can't tell you himself. That would be breaking the rules. But I can tell you about me, about your lawyer, and about what he paid me to sue your brother back when my customer slipped so he could get an extra cut from your brother's insurance company. How he tried to pay me to do it this time." He rubs at the gap in his teeth. "I didn't. I won't. I learned my lesson. I'm done."

I turn and walk. Quickly.

"*Confiteor Deo Omnipotenti*." the newsstand guy shouts after me. "I confess."

The next morning, a yellow police tape marks the boundaries. Neighbors and local news are abuzz with the story of how the space heater set the newsstand afire in the wee hours, how the stand collapsed, how it crushed the windpipe of the newsstand guy.

Angela crosses herself. "Why was he using a space heater? It was like ninety degrees out last night."

He confessed. He was done. That's why. Did Ned confess? Did Kyra?

Will I?

Stanley calls. I send him to voice mail. He sends flowers. I refuse them. He sends letters. I mark them Addressee Deceased and put them back in the box. Constantine sends the final settlement papers with little yellow stickies marking where I need to sign. Friedrich asks if I'll have coffee with him. Ali asks that I don't. I come home early one afternoon to find Mr. Olivieri in our kitchen.

In his bathrobe.

Poaching eggs.

It's like being caught in a Fellini film. Without the credits rolling in the end.

Carlotta stops puking. I start. My breasts fill out, everything smells funny to me. Angela asks me point-blank. So does Ma. I break down and buy a home pregnancy kit. Then another. Then I run to Dr. Frangipane. He gives me a referral, tells me to stay calm because there are lots of reasons for missed periods, but his blood test is accurate. I'm not pregnant.

So why am I crying?

Tony goes missing. A call to Foot Fetish corporate informs me I must be confused. Foot Fetish has no representatives. Their business is strictly mail order, but if there's any problem with my purchase, they'll be happy to make it right.

"Man. It's weird," Ali tells me one day after class. "It's like being one of those unpeople that guy who wrote that book talks about."

"George Orwell."

"Right, but not the one with the pigs. The other one."

I teach classes, I mark papers. Every uncovered manhole becomes suspect, every crowded subway station treacherous. I stop crossing against the light, stop stepping on cracks in the sidewalk, avoid black cats, and give up eating fatty foods. Death, once anticipated, becomes a bogie man, a wraith, a quagmire of the unknown I fear to navigate.

My next-life scrapbook mocks me. Photos of Tajikistan, its people and culture, food and history. Girls with skinny butts and manageable hair and boobs that don't need extra support. I tear the photos into strips, then burn it all, page by page, along with my *National*

Geographics, in the backyard barbecue. The last page whooshes. It singes my eyebrows.

Okay. Okay. I get it.

I call Constantine. "I'm dropping the suit."

"Which one?"

"All of them. Send me a bill for your services, another for Mr. Bracaconi's, and let everybody know we're square."

"Are you certain? You deserve the medical expenses, the scar revision. Your requests are reasonable."

I think of my reaching to hurt Luigi, how he put out his hand to right me. Mr. Olivieri letting Joey make deliveries. Dr. Rossi's dead wife's coffin lying in a snowdrift.

Nothing was reasonable. "I'm certain."

"All right. I'll send notice around, but don't worry about my fees, or your settlement with Mr. Bracaconi. That's already taken care of."

He won't tell me by whom.

Friedrich calls. "Check Futz's page on the Temple site."

I input Futz's name in the search box, then check the staff listings. "Send me the link."

"There is no link." The line goes staticky, his voice patchy. "There's no listing . . . called the school . . . never heard of him. I checked the course catalog. None . . . there. I checked last semester's and the semester before." Friedrich stops.

Oh God. He's winking out.

I dash to my stoop, looking to boost the signal, but it doesn't help. I run to the yard, hold the cell by Mary's head, screeching, "Listen. I should have told you. I'm not pregnant. I'm fine. I was angry. I'm sorry. You've been good. You tried. I forgive you. For everything. I swear. Go in peace. Can you hear? Friedrich. Friedrich?"

He pops back, the signal strong, his voice assured. "Shit. Stop shouting. I was walking through a tunnel."

"You're not gone?"

"Still forgive me?"

I hang up and turn off my phone, unsure who I mean to punish by my avoidance. The kitchen phone rings. Ma picks it up, stretches the cord into the yard and all the way to the bench. "For you."

Little jerk. I told him about calling on the family line. I snatch the handset. "STOP. CALLING. ME."

"I can't. I love you. Now and forever."

Stanley.

Embarrassment rushes up my neck, across my cheeks, over my forehead, and out the top of my head. "What do you want?"

"Will you marry me?"

51

The Overlooks Lady is who you see when you don't know who to see. It's not witchcraft. It's intercession. And she doesn't need an appointment. She needs a fifth of Aunt Gracie's Special Blend. Because she doesn't take payment for her services.

I bring her two, so I can be assured of her discretion until the next time she and Ma share a seat on the bus to Atlantic City. When I see what's sitting atop her television, preserved in a silver-plated frame beside the Overlooks Lady's Blessed Mother on a Doily, I vow to bring her a third, maybe even a fourth. "Who's that?"

"My brother." She runs a finger along the frame's edge. "Stefano."

I take the moment to let the name settle, to appreciate its beauty with a human breath behind it. "You're from Atlantic City."

"Easy for you to know, you were born with the caul."

I shouldn't be surprised, I'm sure Ma told her.

"I can see it." She points to my eyes, then traces along the top of my head. "Here. And here. So sad." She pours olive oil from a cruet and anoints my brow. "Crushed garlic gives the oil power, and lemon clears unhappy thoughts. There's a dark place." She points to a spot just left of my breastbone. "Here."

I look down. All I see is the coffee I spilled on my shirt this morning. I pull the Mass card from the frame's corner and check the date of death.

I put a hand to my heart. Joey could still be him. "So young."

The Overlooks Lady takes the photo back. "His death certificate says alcohol poisoning. Doctors." She spits over her shoulder. "What do they know? He died of a broken heart. He had a wife. She was a wild one. But I won't speak ill of the dead."

I search the Overlooks Lady's face, seeking the young girl I remember, a tomboy in pigtails. Next, I think of the photos I commandeered from Joey, the fuzzy ones I'd presumed he'd taken of himself and an old girlfriend in Aunt Rose's house. Last, I think of Trailer Park Mouse, whose husband was her brother.

My insides turn to stone. "I have to go. I'm so sorry for your loss."

"Here. For protection." She presses a Miraculous Medal into my hand. "The Holy Mother never fails us. Even when we fail ourselves."

The medal pulsates in my palm and Blessed Mary glows. I wrap my fingers around Her wondering if the Overlooks Lady noticed, if her benediction means Mary's silence is over. I don't wonder what protection she thinks I need. I have a bad feeling I already know.

•••

Nature abhors a vacuum. In Joey's bedroom, nature has a field day, sucking the detritus of thirty-seven years into an ever more compacted bundle under Joey's bed.

"Why in hell would he keep all this stuff?" I sweep an arm to encompass the posters and GI Joes, Matchbox cars and seashell collections. "He should sell this on eBay. People pay a lot for old Stretch Armstrong dolls."

Ma stops date-ordering Joey's *Mad* Magazines. "Maybe he thought he'd need it someday."

Back into the abyss. The next box lands me pay dirt. "Hey, Ma. Photo albums."

Ma snatches one from my outstretched hand. She flips its pages. "Look. You and Joey on Christmas morning. And here, down the shore."

The photos are washed out with that awful yellow Plasticine look of three decades ago. Ma traces along Joey's graduation photo. She places it beside a photo of Dad, smiling at us from a moment twenty-five years in the past. "They're the same age now."

She means the same age as when Dad died. I give her knee a squeeze. "Ma. Joey's fine. Nothing's gonna happen to him."

She closes the album. "I have to get dinner going."

I wait until I hear her step on the stair, glad to have her gone because the last album, pushed aside, is older than the others, covered in real leather, with pictures secured by old-fashioned corner tabs. I open it.

Stefano. And myself. As Emmy. Perky boobs, slimmer hips, my complexion darker than in this life, my eyes brighter. On the beach, playing volleyball, eating pizza. I squint, mentally imprinting Joey over Stefano's face, pushing down the tears when I'm unable, uncertain if they well in frustration. Or in relief. Or in mourning for the life depicted.

It doesn't matter. If Stefano was Joey, Joey doesn't remember. He loves Carlotta, has a baby on the way. His future is set. It will be happy.

Please, Blessed Mary, let it be happy.

I swallow hard, sad to think Joey might have died of alcohol poisoning, wondering if it was painful. Then I stop wondering because in some of the photos another man appears, tall in olive drab. And a gal with him, adorable in what has to be his army cap.

Big hair, big boobs, big heart.

Carlotta.

And that means, it must mean, the man I saw in my vision on the beach, the man wearing a uniform and handing off the bottle of wine wasn't Stefano. It was this man. And, put a gun to my head and make me commit, this man was Joey.

Stefano's very good friend. No, not his friend. His cousin.

Relief trips a happy tune across my apprehension. So happy I hug the photo album to my chest. So happy I toss it into the air. Whatever commonalities I might share with Ozark Lady, Miss Breasts, and Trailer Park Mouse, whatever heinous sins I might have ever committed, whatever course I'm fixed on, whatever path I'm not, at least I never fucked my brother.

A piece of foolscap tumbles from the back of the album, written over in black, three-quarter-inch-high calligraphy. "Dear Mr. Panisporchi, We have reviewed your request, but based on your history we regret to inform it has been denied. Sincerely, Anders Dripzin, Assignments Committee."

The universe takes a collective breath. And the wave rolls in.

Joey knows. That's why he took this album from Aunt Rose. Why he seemed concerned I'd found those previous photos. Of myself and Stefano from our Atlantic City life. Photos that seemed a sexy idea from the depths of drunkenness but which Stefano planned to find and destroy once we got to my Cousin Rose's on our wedding night. Except we never got there.

He knows. That's why Joey's so strange with Stanley, so friendly with Luigi, and hates Maurizio so much. It has nothing to do with pool and payoffs, lawsuits and scams. Joey's riding a wave four hundred years in the making, carrying the culpabilities and compunctions of four hundred years past. The wave roars forward. And finally crests. Over a tiny bedroom on the second floor of a row house near Shunk Street in South Philadelphia.

Friedrich was right. People see what they want and mostly they don't want to see even when the truth's been sleeping down the hall for thirty-three years.

Joey's one in three hundred. Or three thousand.

Blessed Mary on Joey's Bureau reaches down and smacks me upside the head.

He knows I am, too.

And he never told me.

52

Joey shoves a stack of multicolored storage containers to the side. "I wanted those Matchbox cars for my kid."

I sit on the basement steps and point. "Try the red one."

Joey grabs a container.

"No. I said the *red* one."

Joey's gaze darts, one to the next. He scratches his head.

"You don't know which is red, do you? You're colorblind. That's why your socks are always black and your shirts white. So you don't have to figure out what coordinates."

He goes back to looking. "So I messed up a color. It's dark down here."

"You could've cleared out your room long ago. You wanted me to go looking. Wanted me to find those photos, the letters from Mr. Dripzin."

Joey stops sorting. "Aren't we chatty? We're not supposed to be talking about this."

"You weren't supposed to send Der Weasel on the morning after Hallowmas to take care of your unmarried pregnant cousin, either. You were my guardian. You were supposed to protect me. It wasn't enough you had my father's love. You wanted the printing press. And you wanted to make damned sure I wasn't there to make a claim on it."

Joey snaps to. Every one of his angles takes on an angle. Arms, legs, shoulders, spine. Head to toe. Side to side. Sparkling with precision. With purpose. "I wanted a life of my own. You were supposed to have a husband. You didn't need a trade. Then you get pregnant, the baker ups and marries somebody else, and the only person willing to take you off my hands was the Freiherr's cousin. You can guess how long my agreement with the Freiherr would've lasted. He'd have handed the shop off to your soldier and I'd be scrabbling in the dirt for a living."

"I was trying to help you, Joey. I told the Freiherr about Der Weasel. Told him he was double-skimming."

"Why the hell would you do that?"

"To get us food. Protection. Dammit, Joey. I was hungry. I wanted to eat."

Joey swipes the bottom of his T-shirt across his forehead and goes back to opening containers. "You should have talked to me."

I stand, my back to the kitchen door, Mary on My Keychain between my knuckles. "You stole my dowry."

"I didn't steal your dowry. I paid it to the baker. Fair value for the bookbinding business. He took my money, told me you were pregnant, told the Freiherr you were pregnant, said the baby wasn't his, the contract was broken, and he deserved the dowry as compensation."

Joey shoves another container out of the way. It lands hard, the sound of breaking glass inevitable. "I am so tired of this. You can't imagine how tired. You're tied to me. We're tied to each other. I've been trying to work within the rules. All our little talks. Even nailed Bracaconi as Weasel. Figured once you met with Constantine, you'd give up the game, but no, you ran to your little boyfriend, you—"

"Constantine."

"Jesus! Eugenia." Joey runs his hands through his hair. "He was the Greek, the guy I sold to in Oberholt."

The complexion. Shape of the nose, slouch of the shoulder. The resemblance uncanny, even that end-over-end with the pencil, like the dowel the Greek used to make sure the barrel was filled with flour all the way to the bottom, or prove the spice box was full.

No wonder he and Stanley are on the outs. Stanley killed him. That has to rankle. Even on an unconscious level.

"—since he's your nephew. I figured at some point—"

Hold it.

"From your last life. Your sister's child.

The Greek mother.

My bones turn to overcooked spaghetti, sliding me pulls a bottle of Aunt Gracie's Special Blend from behind paint cans, pulls the stopper, and hands it to me. "Last of last y stock. Don't tell Ma I know where she stashed it."

The liquid burns on the way down. My nephew. Jeepers. And here I thought he was kind of sexy. Ozark Lady, Miss Breasts, and Trailer Park Mouse would feel so vindicated. "What the hell is all this about? How do you know you're tied to me? How do you know you're not tied to somebody else and I'm just along for the ride?"

"Do you have any idea how many times I escaped death in Oberholt? Then you get trampled in the panic and they hang me three weeks later. In Atlantic City, you get wrapped around a tree. Next thing, I'm shipped out to Vietnam so I can get a bullet in my brain. I've seen you die of plague, get trampled by water buffalo, overdose on drugs. Hell, I once even saw you eaten by crocodiles. And I'm always out the door shortly after. If I could, I'd pack you in Styrofoam peanuts and keep you away from open flames. We've been on this circuit so many times I get dizzy. When you flipped over Mr. Olivieri's van, all I could do was thank God my life insurance was paid up."

"So this is my fault. You think I chose this. Chose you."

"Grow up. Nobody chooses their life. They make the best of what they're given, each minute, each moment, because next time around"—Joey makes a clicky noise and draws a thumb along his throat—"they're likely to get more of the same."

I reseal the bottle. "You could have been honest with me in Oberholt, explained what was going on. I wanted to share the business with you. But you wanted it all to yourself. And that's why Mr. Dripzin denied your request. Whatever you're asking for, you haven't yet earned."

"Alls I'm asking is to be left alone." Joey kicks at the last box. "And find those freaking cars."

"They're gone. Courtesy of the Philadelphia Department of Sanitation."

, bright red, and, Blessed Mary

s. "It's always about you. There's

you, or give to you, or give up for

, we're fixing it. So I can be shed of

ae stairs. I turn and scramble, into the

nd. I put the table between us. Joey leans

to the Overlooks Lady. You smell like salad

oto next to her Blessed Virgin Mary."

`1c

left the supp

his hand."

Der Weasel to fix Stefano's brakes. When we

drunk and stupid, you shoved a last bottle into

Joey rounds toward me. "I didn't recommend that mechanic. I warned Stefano off. I didn't give him that bottle, I tried to take it away. And I didn't send Der Weasel to find you at the shop. I tried my damndest to get back before he did. Don't you get it? I want you to be happy. I want you to be delirious. Because until you are, I won't be free."

I grab the handset on the phone and round further, cord stretching with me, then reach under my collar, hold out the Miraculous Medal. "Stay back. I'm warning you."

"Are you insane? I'm not a vampire." Joey grabs the table with both hands, and shoves it against the counter so I can't move around it anymore. "You have this all wrong. I have to pay my own penance. You have to pay yours. Redemption is a solitary business, but we don't have to keep doing it alone." He steps closer. "Now give me that phone."

I'll give it to you.

Joey grabs at his eye. "Ow! Sunovab—Eugenia. Wait."

53

dial Friedrich from the C bus. "I started the Facebook page because I was curious about other people like me, maybe talk to them. I just didn't want to talk to you."

"Where are you?"

"Heading toward Center City."

"I'm at work. At the hospital. I get off in half an hour. Are you willing to talk to me then?"

"Where?"

"My apartment. I'll be good."

I hesitate. It's about redemption, rebalancing the scales, making points. And, as Stanley mentioned that day at Ignacio's, giving the other guy opportunity to do the same. "Did you pay my attorney fees?"

"Fees? Attorney?" Friedrich sounds confused, rushed. "Listen, there's a coupla things I need to tell you."

A whirring noise in the background obscures his words. I smack my phone, check the volume level, but it continues, getting louder. "I'm listening."

"First off, about Ali," Friedrich says, his voice tense, but still quiet. Whatever I'm hearing, he's not hearing it on his end. "Who Ali is, how she is, that's her responsibility, but here's what's mine, the one thing I never did, the one thing she needed more than anything—love her for who she was, instead of for what she could do for me." The whirring noise increases, rising to an intolerable pitch, then drops dead. "And I did the same to you."

In the heartbeats that follow, booming in the sudden silence, it comes clear what the sound was: Friedrich's own crazy cosmic Spirograph circling around to its stop.

"Friedrich, I—"

—want to talk to you. To clear the air. Make my wrongs right and fix my course in a new direction. And I'd have finished that thought, except Friedrich interrupts.

"Here's the other thing." The whirring picks up again, this time broken by the sound of static. "It's about your Lutheran soldier. And the monk (*squish, squawk*) wasn't quite fair, no, not at all. (*squelch, errrr, click*) I was angry at you, too. Jealous. I'm so (*shush, plink, plunk*) about it. I had no right, no right at all (*squeal*) to burden (*crackle, hiss*) and make you think (*hzzz, climp*) so wrong of me (*zizz, fizz, pop*) And sorry (*pfft, umph, eek*) really (*kaboom*) okay?"

I wait for Friedrich to clear the tunnel. Or the transformer. Or the unshielded radiation source at the hospital. So I can ask him to repeat what he's saying. I wait until the whirring gets so loud I have to hang up and call back. It rings and rings and rings. Then, it says, "We're sorry, but this number is not in service."

Please. Mary. Don't.

Friedrich's apartment door is opened by a collection of frat rejects in baggy jeans. Behind them, Friedrich's homey little efficiency has transformed to the usual collection of mattresses, unmatched sheets, empty beer bottles, rolling papers, and condoms.

There's Ali. But her number makes no connection, her latest quiz is not in my "To Be Marked" folder, she's not listed on my roster, and registration hasn't the foggiest whom I'm talking about.

I make a detour on the way home, getting off the C bus at Morris and walking the blocks toward St. Nicholas. I glance to the colored glass by the entrance and push through the heavy wooden door, seeking refuge—a neighborhood bar east of Passyunk and west of the church.

Angela collects me two hours later when, in a drunken need for companionship, I call her.

"Lucky for you Ma's at bingo. Joey's got a lump on his forehead the size of a meatball and babbling he's an idiot." She looks me up and down. "Guess it takes one to know one."

She hands me my house keys. "Joey says you dropped them. You coming or not? I don't have time for this. Luigi's taking me bowling."

•••

Mea culpa. Mea culpa. Mea maxima culpa. Quia peccavi nimis cogitatione, verbo opere et omissione. I have sinned through my own fault, in my thoughts and in my words.

Betcha Father DiLullo doesn't hear it in Latin much anymore. I try to explain, prattling on for ten minutes, then another five.

Defende me contra nequitiam et insidias diaboli. Defend me against the devil's wickedness.

My cell trips out the theme from *Jaws.*

Never was it known that any who fled to Thy protection, implored Thy help, or sought Thy intercession, was left unaided.

Another five minutes, another plea for help, and Father DiLullo interrupts. He suggests I be kinder to myself and those around me. And admonishes me to lay off the sauce.

I drop a twenty in the box for Catholic Overseas Missions and exit the side door, determined to give Joey a wide berth, put in applications for teaching positions in Montana, and keep a vigilant eye for city buses and falling pianos. But first, I have to eat. And brush my teeth. And bathe.

I stop at Cacia's to pick up brisket and peppers, a ten-dollar spray of roses to brighten the table, and fresh rosemary to flavor the meat, help me sober up, and ward off evil spirits. And sea salt. Because I'm starting to wonder if maybe all this craziness is because my electrolytes are out of balance.

Thunk. Thunk. Thunk. The meat flattens out, butterfly thin. *Chop. Chop. Chop.* Blade on wood, the scent of sweet pepper and balsamic vinegar fills the kitchen. A consoling rhythm, the heartbeat of life, one that assures my place in this world, this minute, this moment, because Joey was right: How much more can anybody claim?

Oregano. Nutmeg. I get out the Pine-Sol to cleanse the surfaces of any bad juju left from my altercation with Joey, and find the last bottle of Aunt Gracie's Special Blend. I bring it out, set it on the counter. Joey must have brought it up when he retrieved my keys.

The calm satisfaction I took in my cooking evaporates.

Somebody rattles the alley gate. Maybe a neighbor who miscounted the entrances. Or a stray in the trash can. I peer through the window, then step outside, aware the gate's lock doesn't work so good. Aware I never got to Home Depot to buy a chain to secure it. Aware I should have let Luigi get it fixed.

"Hello?" Call 911, dummy. Maybe get one of the neighbor boys to check for me. Instead, I say it again, "Hello?"

Nobody answers.

Back inside. Lock the door. Back to chopping. But it's not consoling anymore. It's lonely.

And again with the gate rattling.

Out the door, to the yard, past the pots, past Blessed Backyard Mary. Fling open the gate.

Nothing.

Look out. Look up. Look down.

Still nothing.

To the end and check the crossing street.

Clear.

Back down the alley, back through the gate, back up the steps, back into the kitchen. Ma's still at bingo, Angela's still with Luigi, and Joey's probably still in the emergency room, waiting for stitches, and explaining to Carlotta how come his sister tanked him with a telephone.

The door slams shut behind, my body catapults into the table. Roses scatter. Salt tumbles. A sneeze, a snuffle, my heart in my throat, nasal rasp in my ear. "I earned that contingency. You shoulda talked to me."

Maurizio.

He's been drinking, I smell it. His words slur. His knuckles bear down, catching the sensitive place below my voice box. I cough. He twines my hair in his fist and shoves my face into the laminate.

"Like Constantine, do you?" Maurizio presses close, knee between my legs. "Must be giving you his extra special service."

A pulse pounds behind my lids. Maurizio forces me up, then down to my knees. The jostling rolls Aunt Gracie's Special Blend after, the heavy glass making a gentle thud as it lands. "You and me have to come to an arrangement about that payment. I got expenses, people counting on me."

My fingers claw, just like in Oberholt. They close on the sea salt, fling it backward. Maurizio makes a gaggy kind of spitty sound. "That shit won't work this time, slut."

He drags me back up. I take the Blend with me, use my teeth to pull the stopper, and shake the contents over my shoulder. *Christ. Is there anybody in my life who doesn't have hindsight?*

Maurizio yelps. He twists my arm, up and behind, holding tight. He wipes a sleeve across his eyes. "It burns. Bitch. What is that?"

"Something special, you sniveling shyster. Compliments of my Aunt Gracie."

He kicks the bottle away, smacks me back to the floor, gets in close. "Playtime's over. You're gonna keep this cool. Gonna tell everybody you slipped in the alley, banged your face on the cobbles. Then you're gonna tell Constantine you won't be needing his services. You're gonna let me refile all the motions. When the check comes in, you're gonna sign it over to me."

"The hell I will. I took you down once. I'll take you down again."

Maurizio punches my side. "I got friends. People who owe me. People who don't mind seeing old ladies bleed or messing with pretty little things like your sister."

I go limp.

"We'll go for an expedited hearing. Given Constantine's inept handling of your case, shouldn't be hard to secure. We'll sue him, too."

His fingers again tighten about my throat. My tongue cleaves to the roof of my mouth, unable to form the intercessory prayer. Refrigerator Mary towers from Her perch, head glowing in the overhead fixture's fluorescence, and looking like the Assumption.

I give the refrigerator a kick. *Do something.*

The front door squeaks.

Maurizio drags me up again. He turns me face out, his breath hot on my neck, knife close at my throat, so I can see Joey, standing in the doorway to the kitchen, looking panicked under a bruise of Kodachrome intensity.

"Back, Panisporchi." Maurizio presses the blade closer. "I mean it."

Joey goes still, the weight of emotion draining under a veil of calm so palpable, it reaches forward to comfort me, then moves over my head. And takes on my assailant. "Catch."

Something whizzes past my ear to land with a meaty *thwap*. Maurizio releases me. I fall, twirling to the tinkle of broken glass.

Freeze frame.

Joey jerks Maurizio away.

Freeze frame.

Pulls back a fist.

Freeze. Knuckle to nose.

Freeze. *Crack.*

Maurizio flies backward. Hard against the refrigerator. He's up, arms windmilling.

And. He's. Down.

In a puddle of Aunt Gracie's Special Blend.

Refrigerator Mary topples after.

Joey sits astride Maurizio, pummeling him. One fist, then the other. He grabs Refrigerator Mary, cinches up, raises Her high, chest heaving, eyes wild.

"No." I tackle Joey, drag him off, take Refrigerator Mary with shaking hands. "Enough. I don't want to do this anymore."

Joey rolls over. He plucks a handkerchief from a pocket and hands it to me.

I feel the blood running, out my nose and over my lips, taste it on my tongue, see it dripping onto my new white tee.

Joey points to his eye, to the stitches crawling along the worst of the bruise. "Small mercies. We'll tell Carlotta I got this here." He pushes himself up. "Tell me one thing. Then I won't bother you about any of it again."

"Okay."

"Back in Oberholt. Why did you print those damned pamphlets? The ones that ended up tacked to the church door. You must have known they'd cause trouble."

There it is. The question nobody asked, demanding an answer only I can give. "You took my birthright and my father's time when you came to live with us, and even got control of my person later. It wasn't fair. I wanted to do just one thing, make one decision, for myself."

Joey looks like he's going to say something, but I put up a hand. "It was immature. It was shortsighted. It was stupid. What did you expect? Maybe I had lifetime after lifetime of experience upon which to draw, but up until then, I'd never gotten past seventeen."

I put Refrigerator Mary back in her place. The still-lit burner catches fire, fueled by olive oil spilled in the ruckus. The stove catches and there's another frenzied few seconds while Joey and I smother the flames, hose it all down with the sprayer from the sink, and knock the smoke alarm off the ceiling with the broom handle.

"Think Ma will let us redo the kitchen?" I crawl forward, pull myself up, and pluck Joey's baseball from a pile of broken window glass, its final resting place after it ricocheted off Maurizio's temple. I hold it out. "Here."

Joey waves it off. "Dad told me it was special. Said when it was time to pass it on, I'd know. It's time. Keep it safe. And if the timing seems right, give it back to me on my seventieth birthday."

Maurizio moans. Joey hits him again, then dials 911, reports an interrupted home invasion, and asks for an ambulance. He turns off the phone's display.

"Joey?"

"Yeah?"

"What condition does Carlotta think I have?"

54

Donna dumps out the purse, spilling the contents onto the coffeehouse's counter. Notebooks and datebooks. Jujubes and mints. Midol and Vicodin and Tylenol and Advil and Soma. And a joint. "Yours?"

"Friedrich's. That's the time he forgot to wear the condom."

Donna dumps three more packets of raw sugar into her frappe magnum and goes back to the purse. Nail polish and tooth whitener, toothbrushes and floss, a deck of cards, gum wrappers, paper clips, hair pins, three combs, hair gel, a can of mousse, feminine hygiene products, even my prescription for birth control pills.

"Forgot that was there." Not that it matters anymore.

A pair of socks, a pair of pantyhose, bra and panties, each encased in its own Ziploc bag. Eyeglass cleaner, nail file, callus buffer. Can of mace, can of pepper spray, and one of those whistles I'm supposed to wear around my neck and blow in case of trouble.

"Should have taken the whistle out to the alley with me."

A volume of Chaucer, another of Donne, Danielle Steele's latest, a copy of *Fight Club,* and the Tug McGraw baseball. Donna holds that up. "A last bit of the puzzle. Joey whacked Stanley on the head during the bar brawl. He meant to hit Maurizio."

"And Maurizio sent Luigi down the stairs."

"These things have a way of coming full circle."

"I didn't recognize Maurizio for who he was."

"Because you'd already assigned Der Weasel to Luigi. You didn't leave room to see him as anybody else. You knew you had it wrong. Deep down."

A breeze, cool and refreshing, tickles under my collar. I check the shop door. Closed. Check the air vents. Quiet. "That's always what it comes down to. What we know deep down."

Donna smiles.

"And you sent Mary to watch over me."

"She sent Herself, to be what you needed: God's whip or God's tool, a place to lay blame or seek comfort."

I glance at Mary on My Keychain, so patient amid the jumble, shamed at my reckless treatment of Her.

"Don't feel so bad." Donna hands Her off to me. "Mary's a mother. She's tough. Besides, She likes hanging with you. You should have heard Her going on about what a good time She had joyriding through the moonroof."

Fine. I'm glad. But I'm still never wrestling Her out to Joey's red mustang again. "Joey gave Maurizio that runner along his cheek."

"And Maurizio, the scar under Joey's eye. What sins we don't expiate, sometimes repeat. But not for Joey. Not anymore. He's done."

My joints seize up. So does my tongue. Please. Blessed Mary. No. Please don't.

Donna seizes my hand. "Not that kind of done. He tried. Hard as he could. The Committee has reconsidered his request. They're giving him a chance to rise or fall on his own. He'll continue, but without memory of this. No hindsight. Nothing. Just him and his wife, his new little baby, and all the babies to come. And I gave him back the Matchbox cars. Heaven can be harsh, but—"

"—it's never unkind." I lower my gaze, feeling sullen.

"This is what you wanted. You prayed for this."

"I prayed for Joey to be happy. Just, he's plenty happy, already. And if he doesn't have hindsight anymore . . ."

"You're alone."

Petty. Yes. Immature. Yes. But still . . . geez. Y'know?

"You didn't know he had hindsight when you made that prayer. You didn't put any conditions on it. Do you want to now?" Donna's expression takes a harder edge, not frightening, but not pleasant, either.

I think about Joey. Free to work out his life the way he wants. Lucky bastard. "No. It's fine."

Donna brightens. "Now why so uncharitable? Life is good. Have a cannoli. The calories are on me."

Seriously? Wonder if she'll take the hit for one of those full fat magnum thingies. A chocolate one.

Donna laughs. Her copper and nickel ear strands tinkle an accompaniment.

No doubt somebody, somewhere, just got their wings.

Donna lifts a finger, asks the kid for two cannolis, the coffee, and a trash can. She points to the stuff littering the table. "It's all crap. You don't need it anymore."

"Everything?"

She picks out the cards, the Chaucer, the Donne, my wallet, the baseball. And my copy of *Fight Club*. The rest she sweeps into the big metal bin. She smacks me on the shoulder. "You could have saved yourself a lot of heartache if you'd only listened to Rudyard. 'We have forty million reasons for failure, but not a single excuse.' Stop giving excuses. Start giving reasons. That's the start of enlightenment."

"You could have just told me."

"'You cannot teach a man anything; you can only help him to discover it in himself.'"

"You have a quote for everything."

"The quotes endure because they are true and if you'd taken just five minutes to consider them, you might have avoided your run-in with Maurizio, your fight with Joey, the disappearance of your friends, and sex with Friedrich."

Can't say I much minded that last bit.

"He's very charming. Might be best if you two don't cross paths for a while."

Please don't send him to another concentration camp.

"We don't 'send' anybody anywhere. We put them in a life, and the life happens around them. Don't worry. With his unique . . . temperament, Mr. Palmon's likely to land on his feet. Which reminds me." She reaches into her briefcase. "For you. From Friedrich."

A sketch. Of me and Stanley in a sea of grass, holding a baby. A family portrait that can never be. I've been to the specialist. I had my chances. And I blew them. "There will never be any children."

"Never is a long, long time."

"Not that much time. The others…" Ned, Tony, Ali. "They're all gone. I'm next."

"They're not gone. They're just not here. Wherever they are, they're like you. Reevaluating. Rethinking. Reimagining."

Futz?

"'Some people end by resembling their shadows.' Another good one from Rudyard." Donna leans forward, her expression serious. "You were pilgrims, passing to and fro, Mr. Chaucer your point of contact. An ordained grouping, a unique constellation, finally, returned to your proper places. It's over. Take what good you may and leave the rest."

Take the good. "Do you see the good in everything?"

"I've seen it in this assignment. Your family is fun and the food was great. I'm going to miss both."

"You won't be back for the next round?"

"Nope. I'm being kicked upstairs. This is my last tour earthside. That's what Kyra was about. Been training her. She's my replacement."

Buttons, bangles, dangles, fringe. Fun.

Donna pops a straw into the frappe. "You have questions. Ask."

"Why were you helping the Freiherr? You purchased the items Der Weasel stole. You were his best customer."

"Oh, Eugenia, I wasn't helping the Freiherr, I was trying to help all of you, to save you by marrying you to the people in power, to keep as many as I could from falling under suspicion. I wanted to match you with Stanislaus. Josef refused. Friedrich seemed your safest choice. When that fell through, I again tried with Stanislaus, but Josef was adamant. As for the trinkets, I held them against a better day, my hope to restore them to their rightful owners." All of Donna's bright places go dark. "Oberholt was not one of my shining moments. I failed you all on so many fronts."

I give that revelation a few heartbeats. "Friedrich told me he killed the brewer's daughter."

"This is the first lifetime he's admitted it to anyone other than himself."

My eyes fill. Omigod. How? Why?

Donna hands me a hanky, then lays a hand over mine. "What Friedrich did in Oberholt was wrong, a monstrous act. I don't want you to ever think there's excuse for his action, but it was not predicated for wholly selfish reasons. He worried what Ali would say if she were called to testify. She would not be reasoned with, she would not run away, she would not be quieted. He feared the havoc Ali would wreak in her efforts to protect him. Friedrich was desperate. He did not think through his options. He will be paying for that act, and many others, for a long time to come."

Options. What options? We were trapped. So. Damned. Trapped. "Why did Stanislaus do what he did with Der Weasel? Why did he leave him in the choir loft like that, propped on his knees with a missal?"

"Friedrich told you. Or your brother."

"Friedrich. But then, just before he . . . winked out, he said he had something else to tell me about Stanislaus, and the monk. That he'd been unfair to them."

Donna whips a notebook out of her purse and scribbles something. I can't see from where I am sitting, but I think Friedrich just earned a few points. She puts the notebook away. "First the bitter. Stanislaus despised Der Weasel. It was the most profane thing he could think to do with his body. He regretted it immediately, but the bell ringer had already entered the church to ring the noon hour, and people were gathering outside."

"Why did he leave? Why did he let the bell ringer take the blame?"

"He didn't let the bell ringer take the blame. He wasn't thinking about the bell ringer at all. He was thinking about you."

Stanislaus's voice swells in my memory. "It is time, *liebchen*. But you must come. Now."

The rest rises with it, suffocating, so real I fight the urge to jump to my feet, get out now. "We were running. He was holding my hand, pushing people away from me. But soldiers came. They ran between us. Then . . . then . . ." Boot in my back. Knock to the chin. And it was gone. All of it. What small happiness I'd found in that time, in that place, was . . . gone.

I wanted to wail. I wanted to shove my full chocolate double double caramel mocha onto the floor, let it join all the other useless baggage Donna had shoved into the big metal bin. "What did I do? What could I have done?" And how do I go on living with the knowledge?

Donna snatches the cup away. "Here's what you have to understand. From any of it, any situation, any eventuality. You may not have a hand in starting evil, but you can have a hand in stopping it. Or, at least, stopping your part of it. In Oberholt, none of you did. Be wise. Remember. Learn this at a soul level. And. You. Will. Have. Peace."

Peace. Not happiness.

Donna straightens, her manner suddenly brisk. "Now, I promised you the sweet. About Stanislaus and the monk. Ali betrayed the Ignatians and the Freiherr ordered them executed, not exiled. Your Lutheran soldier received the order and went straight away to the monk, to help them to safety. Stanislaus had friends among the militia, a fifth column, and they played along. They spent three days wandering in the woods, then returned to claim the monks slipped away just before they caught up with them."

Oberholt. A Bavarian town little known and long forgotten, filled with tragedy and cowardice and sometimes great heroism, its history hidden, but yearning to be told. "The monk died. Friedrich told me they hung him from the city gate."

"Not through any fault of Stanislaus. The monk stayed behind, determined to save the monastery's sacred treasures. He dropped them with your cousin and followed after, but the Freiherr's guard caught him, and when the panic was over, the Freiherr chose to make an example."

"Why did Stanislaus help the monks and kill the Greek?"

"No, Eugenia. No. Stanislaus made that claim for show. He found the Greek outside the town walls. He took his goods and sent him away, then said he'd left the body for the wolves. He brought back the Greek's wares as proof. He meant to tell Josef, but Josef was off with Ruprecht Vogt, and . . ."

"Circumstances got away from him."

Donna nods. "Stanislaus was brave. So was the monk."

So was Josef.

I mattered to him. He wanted to protect me. I should have known. Should have noticed. Should have told him. Should have cared. The tears spill again. "All this trouble over a few pamphlets."

"There was plenty else going on besides those pamphlets. You were one snowflake in the avalanche."

I grab another napkin from the holder, blow my nose. "If Stanley and Luigi and Josef were so valiant in Oberholt, how come they had so much trouble in this life? The whole Villanova pool hustle scandal."

"They were brave, not perfect. Any other questions?"

Brave. Not perfect.

Then it's clear as clear can be: nobody is.

I know what I have to do.

"Yeah." I put down the napkin and pour an extra dribble of real cream into my latte. "What was that whole getting me eaten by crocodiles when we crossed the Nile thing about?"

Donna hunches her shoulders. "Another of my less than shining moments."

●●●

"*You* paid my attorney fees."

Stanley stands in his doorway, in sweatpants and tee. "Constantine wasn't supposed to tell you."

"He didn't."

Stanley clears laundry from the couch and papers from the counter, dumping them behind the pool table. "Sorry. I was just cleaning up. Why are you here?"

"Came to collect my book. The one I threw at you." I put out my hand. "I want it back."

He pulls something from a pile of what looks like actuarial tables. An illuminated volume of Chaucer, obviously a custom order, at least two centuries old.

I step past him. "The loft looks great."

Walls the color of wheatgrass set off the bamboo floor. Lemon-polished wood. Leather scrubbed in saddle soap. Amazing in mid-century modern. Potted blooms line the windowsills and set off a fireplace which would have felt at home in a French country house. White flowers. And red.

To make a garland for my head.

Framed on the mantle is a photo of me in a yellow ochre bridesmaid dress standing beside Stanley, in bow tie and tux.

He picks it up and runs a finger along its nickel-plated frame. "I got this from Carlotta."

"It's very nice."

"I'm not always good with words. Not when they matter."

"Try me."

"At the wedding, you were so pretty. I couldn't think what to say, so I started quoting decimals. Got so nervous, my hands shook. Then I dumped my vodka tonic on your dress. You must have thought I was such a *boombatz*. Then, the way I groped you. I'm amazed you went out with me." Color fills his face. "I was drunk. I always meant to apologize. So . . . I apologize."

"So do I."

And this is how it starts. Back. And forth. In kindness and respect. Forever.

Stanley puts down the photo. "Can I get you something? I was just making tea. I, um, don't drink anymore. I don't know if Luigi told you."

"He did."

"And gambling," Stanley makes that sideways motion, a gesture I always associated with my Lutheran soldier, but a good one, one that meant he would do as he promised. "Never again. Not even gentlemen bets."

"That's good."

"So. Tea. Or coffee. And soft drinks. I have plenty of those." He heads to the kitchen. "We could talk. That is, if you'd like to stay."

I would. For a while. And maybe for longer than that.

I go back to the photo. A light permeates the edges, its source uncertain. It gives Stanley and me an ethereal air, makes both of us better looking than we are. I walk it into the kitchen. "Donna's supposed to be in this picture."

Stanley pours steaming water into cups, shows me where he's arranged cookies on a plate. Italian cookies. Not pfeffernüsse. *Unchained Melody* pours out of his iPod, the Perry Como version. The sweet, slow rhythm draws me back to a less-complicated time, one I squandered. And I never want to squander again.

Stanley puts out a hand, palm up, but he's not asking me to dance, he's getting ready to respond to my statement about Donna, but I already know what he's going to say. Just as I've always known. Because I've known him so well elsewhere, and though I have yet to know him so well here, at this time, in this place, I still already know him enough to be able to finish his thought.

"Who's Donna?" we ask in unison.

•••

Friend. Guardian. Teacher. I miss her. Miss them all. I especially miss Friedrich.

Stanley and I decide on a Christmas wedding to take advantage of my school break. We plan our honeymoon in Tajikistan. Angela and Luigi go ahead and tie their knot. Whatever they weren't much doing before, they learn to do more later. So they trade the Miata for a Prius and start shopping for cribs.

Constantine tells me Maurizio's likely to get three to five. When

DNA evidence is discovered under the newsstand guy's fingernails linking Maurizio to his death, Constantine tells me he probably won't be bothering us for a long time to come. Mr. Olivieri and Ma spend a weekend in Atlantic City. Ma stops wearing support hose.

Summer passes. So does fall. Carlotta presents Ma her first grandson, four weeks early and named for Dad. She and Joey ask Stanley and me to be godparents. Ma stops worrying painting Joey's room means one of us is going to die. I teach my classes, give my quizzes, spend lazy Saturdays with Stanley, and impassioned nights in his loft. Yet always, somewhere at the edge of my contentment, lurks the sense that this life will never be what it could, encumbered as it is by the ghosts of all that was.

Sometimes I see Donna. Around a corner, down the street, sitting on a park bench. When I get close, it's always somebody else.

Same with Friedrich. I call his cell number until it's reassigned. Always, after I hang up, I tell him I forgive him, to be at peace. I thank him for his sketch, for the vision I wish I could build for myself, then stand in full sunshine, hold my hand high and squint, wondering if I can bend Play-Doh Man's light in my direction. Transform my almost happy to real happy. Like Joey now enjoys, free of the past's constraints.

One morning, I hold my nephew while my brother makes coffee and wonder about the mystery of his curious letter from Mr. Dripzin. Stupid of me to ask about the Nile and forget about this.

"Joey? If you could have anything in this life, without boundary by heaven or earth, what would it be?"

He points to his son, then out the window to his yard where Carlotta is hanging Christmas lights from *their* Backyard Mary. "I have it now."

He pries the lid off a small metal tin, then pushes it toward me, like he means to emphasize his statement with its contents. "We don't know how long we'll be here, so it's good to be here while we are."

I peek inside. And the memory surfaces.

Ma counting, Joey counting with her.

So Joey could buy the taffeta ribbon candies like Dad used to get us at Wanamaker's when he took us to see their annual Christmas display.

I pick one out, all soft pink and blue and buttercup yellow. Folded back and forth, one layer over the other. Recalling a time when Dad and me and Joey and Ma and Angela were complete, when our lives were certain. And all our stars moved in their proper courses.

One of Play-Doh Man's light beams slants through Joey's kitchen window.

Joey wanted exactly what he has, a life without hindsight and the freedom to choose his own course. That's why he married Carlotta so fast, why he didn't tell us about her. He defied the Committee and he worried they'd get him for it.

I listen, waiting for the whir of the crazy cosmic Spirograph to swing past and confirm this revelation. A little feathery feeling trips across my soul, instead. Something resembling hope takes up residence, sends out pulses, a new life waiting to take form. I wrap myself in that welcoming goodness, letting it gestate, uncertain what it will develop into, but dedicated to its nurture.

Stanley notices.

"You're glowing," he tells me a few days later while Christmas shopping on South Street, catty-corner from Buttons, Bangles, and Bongs.

I stop in there on occasion. The middle-aged lady in the tweed and sensible shoes doesn't wait for me to ask. She lets me know right away nobody fitting Kyra's description works there or ever has, neither has anybody like her stopped by or asked for me. She'll show me a pair of earrings, or a safety-pinned wrist bangle. I usually buy it, more because they remind me of Kyra than because they're my style. So when I glance across the street, and see Kyra, bright and shining and standing in front of the store beside a Salvation Army Santa Claus, I take the vision as a sign, one of Play-Doh Man's slanted bits of light casting sprinkles of approval on the reality I'm trying to create.

I think that when she waves me over, certain it can't be her. I don't care, I drag Stanley to check anyway, certain it's not her right up until I hear the brakes squeal over the Santa Claus's bell-ringing, feel Stanley's hand tighten around mine, and turn to see the flat square front of the big blue and white SEPTA bu—

Amor Vincit Omnia.
Bactria-Margiana Archaeological Complex, Tajikistan
32 years later

The vid always rings during breakfast and always I'm in the middle of lesson plans. I let Steve get the call. I tell Ma, but we're nine hours ahead, living in a world a millennium behind. And she likes to get to bed on time.

"Hello, Mama Angela. Fine. Everything's good. Eugenia's with the baby. The dig's going great. How's Papa Luigi?" Steve adjusts the earpiece. He makes open and closing movements outside the vid's view with his fingers to tell me Ma won't shut up. His eyes crinkle at the corners, enjoying the joke. "Uh-huh. Uh-huh. The baby's wonderful. Looks more like Uncle Joey every day. He loves the Tug McGraw baseball. Developing a good pitching arm. Naw. They're never too young to learn."

Steve nods some more, tilting his head on occasion and pressing the earpiece closer. He's a little deaf. Got beat up in a pool hall brawl when he was in college. Won't get an implant to fix it because he doesn't want to forget. He never got drunk again.

I know what this call is about. We have to go home for Christmas. We didn't go home last year and Uncle Joey died, a month shy of his seventieth birthday. Aunt Carlotta tells me Ma did novenas for months. Doesn't matter I was pregnant as a house at the time. Doesn't matter we brought the baby to visit for Easter. Doesn't matter Steve and I are working twelve-hour days to complete this part of the dig so the board of the Friedrich Palmon Trust doesn't think we're wasting their money.

The Trust aren't people you want to upset, as manic about archeology as they are about every one of their educational or charitable endeavors, and endowed with apparently limitless funds, the source of which nobody will reveal. They plucked Steve and I from our positions at Penn with promises of adventure and more money than either of us ever hoped to earn in our lifetimes. So the paperwork has to be done. The artifacts have to be mapped. And we have to get them all catalogued on time. So we can get home for Christmas. So nobody dies. And Dad can get Ma out of church.

Steve puts a thumb over the vid, looks to the heavens, and shakes his head. That means if Ma keeps on, I'm gonna have to call him, pretend like I need help with the baby. Because once Ma gets going she doesn't stop. She's so proud of what we do. Spends half her time saying so when she calls. "Your aunt had a scrapbook filled with pictures of Tajikistan. She wanted to go there. Wanted to bring your uncle with her."

That would be Uncle Stanley. He's not really my uncle, 'cause they didn't get married before they died, but I call him that out of respect. He left all he had to my aunt, or her heirs, so it didn't matter who predeceased whom. That meant it went to Nonna and Nonna put it away for our college, me and my brothers and sisters and cousins. My uncle was a protector and a provider, Dad tells me, like a knight in shining armor, the kind of guy who did his best by those he loved. Maybe that's why, when Nonna first met Steve, first thing she said was, "He's so like your Uncle Stanley."

Because, she didn't mean in looks. I've seen the photos. Then again, Nonna doesn't see so good, despite the laser adjustments. And she's past a hundred. It's easier to pat her elbow and nod than disagree. She'll put her hand to my cheek, rub at it with a knuckle, and say, "You're like her. When things don't go your way, you're always willing to try again."

That's how I got my name, because I'm so like my Aunt Eugenia.

Lucky me. I got a man's name. With an *a*.

Steve makes a rolling motion with his finger to indicate he's wrapping up. "Okay. Okay. Yes. Love you, too. Say hello to Papa Luigi. Kiss Nonna for me. Here's Eugenia." He hands me the earpiece.

Little Joey lets out a wake-up wail.

Steve brushes his lips across mine, then scoops our son from the basket, humming a tune, a remix, lately popular on the nets, called *Unchained Melody*. It's sprightly. Upbeat. Massive def, as my students would say. Nothing like an early version Steve played for me so I could make the comparison, all scratchy and quaint and sung by a guy named Perry Como, yet very like it at the same time. Steve tells me that's because times don't change, they just change form.

I don't know what he's doing in anthropology. He's a philosopher at heart.

"I'll take him, Jenny," he tells me once I have the earpiece adjusted. "You and your mother have a nice talk."

He carries Joey in the crook of his elbow and walks him across the compound. He waves an arm and I know he is explaining how far the grasslands go and how beautiful the mountains are.

Acknowledgments

The path to publication is pitted with plot holes. I want to thank the people who prevented this story from becoming a fifty-car pileup.

First, my glorious Bunions, whose laughter and love kept the lights on. Second, critique partners who bugged me to write better. Third, editors who made me "Think different." Fourth, beta readers who provided thoughtful commentary. And, of course, Mr. Chaucer and Mr. Kipling.

Sharon Anderson, Jenn Windrow, Dana Lin, Liz Bardawill, Margie Lawson, Kelly Crawley, Lisa Sergienko, Stephen Parrish, Sandra Ruttan, Angie Johnson-Schmit, Jen Pooley, Lois Berkowitz, Lesley Lustgarten, Linda Hodges-Powell. And Anna Sanchez, for providing plenty of encouragement along the way.

Last, saved for best, my husband and kids, who watch me stare at a computer screen and occasionally check my pulse to make sure I'm still alive. Ian, Avi, and Rosie, I love you.

Book Club Questions:

A. Why, as readers, are we drawn to stories about second chances? How does the possibility of an opportunity for a do-over resonate with our own lives?

B. Why does Eugenia's relationship with The Blessed Virgin Mary persist and remain so strong through the centuries? Do you think Mary chose her, or she chose Mary? And why?

C. How does the setting affect this book? Could the author have told this story, this way, in another setting? How does Eugenia's cultural upbringing affect her choices and reactions in this story? Consider her relationship to her mother, her sister, and her brother, as well as Friedrich and Stanley.

D. How does Eugenia's references to her father resonate with *Hindsight*'s underlying themes of loss and abandonment?

E. How do you feel about the way the story ends?

About the Author

© Ian Cassell

R aised by traditional people in a modern world, Mindy Tarquini is a second-generation Italian American who grew up believing dreams are prophecy, the devil steals lost objects, and an awkward glance can invite the evil eye. She is an assistant editor with the *Lascaux Review* and a member of the Perley Station Writers' Colony. A native Philadelphian, Ms. Tarquini resides in Phoenix with her husband, where she divides her time between writing and wrestling with her bread machine. She does not have hindsight.

Ms. Tarquini loves the internet. Connect with her at:

http://www.mindytarquini.com
https://www.facebook.com/MindyTarquiniAuthor/

SELECTED TITLES FROM SPARKPRESS

SparkPress is an independent boutique publisher delivering high-quality, entertaining, and engaging content that enhances readers' lives, with a special focus on female-driven work. Visit us at www.gosparkpress.com

Tracing the Bones, by Elise A. Miller
$17, 978-1-940716-48-0

Eve Myer becomes consumed with the world of healing arts—and conflicted emotions—when new neighbors/instructors Anna and Billy move in. Shortly after sessions for her chronic back pain begin with Billy, Anna and her small son drown in the bathtub. As Eve's life unravels, her sessions with Billy culminate in an experimental trip into the freezing woods, threatening the remaining bonds of Eve's marriage and finally uncovering the reason for Anna's death.

The House of Bradbury, by Nicole Meier
$17, 978-1-940716-38-1

After Mia Gladwell's debut novel bombs and her fiancé jumps ship, she purchases the estate of iconic author Ray Bradbury, hoping it will inspire her best work yet. But between her disapproving sister, mysterious sketches that show up on her door, and taking in a pill-popping starlet as a tenant—a favor to her needy ex—life in the Bradbury house is not what she imagined.

Found, by Emily Brett
$16.95, 978-1940716800

ICU nurse Natalie Ulster has a desire to see the world and a need to heal, which is compensation for her own damaged heart. Natalie grabs life by the globe and accepts successive assignments in Belize, Australia, and Arizona. When Natalie meets Dr. Joel Lansfield she's not sure she's ready to make room in her heart for love. However, too many near-death coincidences force her to ask herself a frightening question: Is someone trying to kill her

About SparkPress

SparkPress is an independent, hybrid imprint focused on merging the best of the traditional publishing model with new and innovative strategies. We deliver high-quality, entertaining, and engaging content that enhances readers' lives. We are proud to bring to market a list of *New York Times* best-selling, award-winning, and debut authors who represent a wide array of genres, as well as our established, industry-wide reputation for creative, results-driven success in working with authors. SparkPress, a BookSparks imprint, is a division of SparkPoint Studio LLC.

Learn more at GoSparkPress.com